W9-BGB-099

UNTOLD MILLIONS

NOVELS BY LAURA Z. HOBSON

The Trespassers
Gentleman's Agreement
The Other Father
The Celebrity
First Papers
The Tenth Month
Consenting Adult
Over and Above

BOOKS FOR CHILDREN

A Dog of His Own
"I'm Going to Have a Baby"

UNTOLD MILLIONS

a novel by

LAURA Z. HOBSON

1817

HARPER & ROW, PUBLISHERS, New York
Cambridge, Philadelphia, San Francisco,
London, Mexico City, São Paulo, Sydney

 For information address Harper & Row, Publishers, Inc., 10 East 53rd Street, New York, N.Y. 10022. Published simultaneously in Canada by Fitzhenry & Whiteside Limited, Toronto.

FIRST EDITION

Designed by Ruth Bornschlegel

Library of Congress Cataloging in Publication Data

Hobson, Laura Keane Zametkin.
Untold millions.
I. Title.
PS3515.01515U5 1982 813′.52 81-47587
ISBN 0-06-014924-8 AACR2

82 83 84 85 86 10 9 8 7 6 5 4 3 2 1

To Irving Robbins

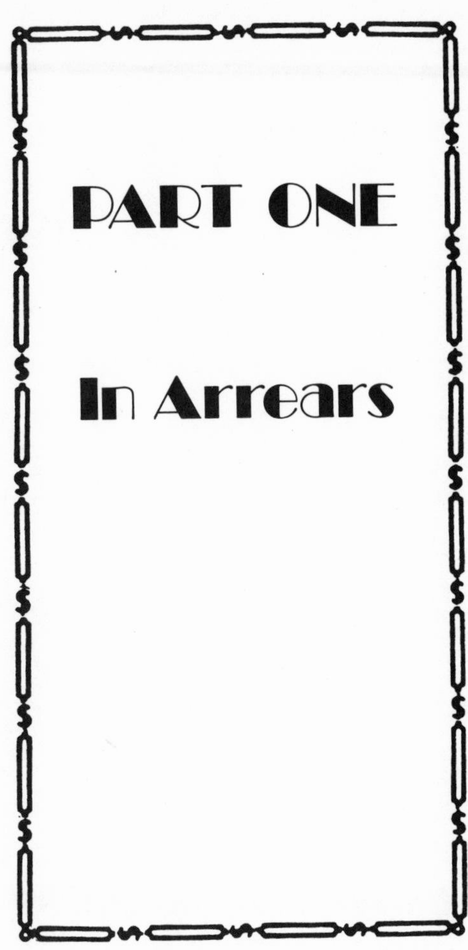

PART ONE

In Arrears

One

"What is it, Rick? What's wrong?"

"Nothing."

"I can always tell. That paper—is that it?"

He made an involuntary gesture, as if to hide it. He looked at her with the same leap of surprise he still felt whenever he saw those dark intent eyes, and for an instant he considered telling her some lie rather than have her know this about him. But from the beginning they had promised each other never to lie or dissemble or cover over.

"It's something you shouldn't have to worry about, Jossie."

"I do worry. You have that look you get when you're miserable about something. Darling, what's happened?" She reached for the single sheet he held. It was a document of some sort; she could see printing on it, and spaces filled in, and the round Braille of a notary public's stamp.

"It's a dispossess notice," he said. "I owe them three hundred dollars."

"For what?"

"Three months' rent."

"A dispossess notice? To evict you?"

"My furniture right on the sidewalk."

"They'd never—"

"That's what dispossess means. I just paid this month's rent, but not those three. If I'm still here by the fifteenth, and still owing them—"He made a wide sweeping gesture over the room. "Out."

"There must be something we can do, some way we can stop them."

"Not 'we' can," he said gently. "I told you at the start that my life and my problems must never do anything to hurt you or make problems for you that you wouldn't have if you didn't have me."

"But I do have you." She gazed around his apartment, which she had come to love in the three months since they had begun. It was the kind of place she had never lived in herself, a living room with a fireplace, with books and a Victrola and a shelf of record albums, with matching red armchairs and good prints of famous paintings, each so well framed it looked like a treasured original. Beyond it was his bedroom, with another fireplace, and, through the windows, the trees and vines and bushes of a back garden, now bare with winter.

To have your own apartment, to have it to yourself, with its own entrance, up three stone steps from the street in an old house of red brick, right in New York, right here at the northern fringe of Greenwich Village on West Tenth—this had once been her dream for after college, a dream that was still unrealized except for the hours she spent here with Rick before catching the last train home from Grand Central at ten-thirty.

She hated that last train to New Rochelle, dreaded the moment when they had to start for the station. She had begun to long for a car of her own, at least, so she could have some leeway about the moment of separation, but a new 1923 Ford runabout cost $265, and even a used one about $40 or $50. And though she was still on schedule about paying back her college loan, a car or a place of her own lay outside all the possibles.

Now she opened the document Rick was holding out to her. "September, October, November," she read aloud. "Why, Rick, that's all the time we've been together."

"There's no connection on earth between our being together and this." He took back the paper and threw it at the table. He put his index finger under her chin, tilting her head upward so she would look at him. "It's been unexpected things, the ones you never figure on: Jean's impacted wisdom tooth, that blaze in the fireplace chimney, Kenny's broken finger last summer, dentists, doctors, fire extinguishers—everything."

Jean was his wife, and Kenny one of her two small children, the other, Kathy, being a year older. They were hers by her first marriage, to a member of the faculty at Princeton, a man much older than she. He was a reserve officer in the army, and the day America entered the war, he had returned to active service, only to be killed in an accident at camp a month later.

When Rick and Jean had married five years ago, the children were babies, one and two years old, and he had wanted to adopt them. But the professor's grieving parents had been opposed to it—"They'll grow up thinking he's their real father"—so bitterly opposed that Jean had suggested delaying it until the period of keenest mourning had ended. That time had kept putting itself off, and off again, and the children had come to know him as Uncle Rick. That's the way it had remained.

He had told her all about Jean and the children before they had finished their first lunch together. "I ought to tell you straight off that I'm married," he'd said. "I always make that part of my first five minutes with a girl." Later he told her that he so abhorred scenes in books or plays where the heroine says, "But you never told me you were married!" that he had made it a required phrase in any encounter, no matter how casual, no matter if he were in no way attracted to the girl to whom he said the words. "A kind of precautionary tactic, I guess," he added. "Sometimes I think it's a bit cheap of me, but it is a kind of traffic sign. Go slow. Danger."

"I don't want to get married for five years at least," she had answered. "Maybe when I'm twenty-eight and starting to worry about thirty—but that's so far ahead I don't need any traffic signs. Anyway, it's not cheap, it's decent."

She had liked it that he had told her on their very first date, and wondered whether it stood up there for him, in his path, blocking the beginning of anything new until he told it, just as there was a boulder standing in her own path, waiting to be cleared before she could take the first step toward any new friendship for herself.

"There's something I want to tell you straight off too," she had said, the day he told her about Jean and the kids. She hated the moment as she always did, but she went ahead as she always did, just to get it done and over with and avoid the conflict there would otherwise be, about when to bring it up, whether to bring it up at all. "To tell you that the name I use at work isn't my real name; it's my mother's maiden name."

"Jossie isn't?"

"Jossie is. That's for Joselyn and it's mine, all right. My last name, Stone. That's Anglicized for Stein, and that's my mother's maiden name. My real name is Yavnowitsky, my father's name—he's Polish and Jewish, and you know I'd never get a job at any ad agency on earth with that name, or on any newspaper either."

He was surprised and showed it so easily that she knew it was going to be really nothing, instead of a pretended nothing. He was pronouncing the syllables of Yav-no-wit-sky; she could read his lips because he made no effort to conceal what he was doing. Then he smiled.

"It's nicer than Stone. Not as hard as rocks."

She laughed, with a spurt of relief. Other people always said that foreign names and being Jewish didn't matter, but with Rick Baird they actually did not.

"I'm supposed to be an Episcopalian," he said then. "What I really am is Southern, and that blots out everything else."

"But you haven't any Southern accent."

"I put my mind to it, to drop that badge of shame before I ever got to Princeton. A Southern gentleman—" This he said with a marked drawl of melodious voice. "Shabby genteel after the War Between the States, but a Southern gentlemen still—No suh, ma'am, you can keep it."

The spurt of relief came again, this time mixed with pleasure. He wasn't rich, he didn't maintain that set-apart stance that rich people always had, openly or covertly. His dismissal of status, family background, social position was real; she could tell. She had never known anybody before who had all three and ignored all three. The girls she had known at college who did have them were always conscious of the fact, as if they were precious jewels that embellished them, lent them quality, set them off, like beauties at a ball. Until college she had never thought about status and social position except to know that she was bereft of both. In her family of teachers the use of those words, even, would have been laughed at. There were no such things, they would have insisted, except as the results of exploitation and economic injustice.

Of course she disagreed; she always disagreed; half the fights she ever had with her father were because she disagreed. When she announced that she couldn't afford the newspaper job she had always wanted because of her college loan, that she was going to try for a copywriting job instead, at an advertising agency, he had gone red with fury and scorn and rage, as at a betrayal. But if she had given in to him, she would never have met Cedric Baird.

Now she reached again for the document Rick had put on the table. "Within ten days, it says. If you paid part of it in ten days, wouldn't that stop them?"

"A big chunk of it, maybe. But I just sent off Jean's December money. There's no big chunk left."

"Could you borrow from Andy Bellock or John Slade?"

He put up his hand, palm showing, fingers stretched taut. "I can't. I've had to, before this, and I can't ask again, either one of them."

"How about—?"

"This isn't anything for you, Jossie. I'll find someplace else to live, and that's it."

She looked around the room again. "You can't move out," she cried. "We love it so."

"I should never have moved in. I told you I'm a jack about price tags and budgets when I want something enough."

"Wait, Rick, wait a minute." She could see her savings book tucked away in her purse. December was when she made her yearly payment to the Student Loan; she saved two dollars a week, and there was a hundred dollars there. She had planned to send a money order next week. "My college money," she said slowly. "That would be a big chunk, a whole third. Wouldn't they extend—?"

He waved the idea aside. "Not a chance." He sounded embarrassed, even vexed.

"They'd take it as a sign of good faith; they'd have to."

"I meant, not a chance I'd take money from you."

"Not 'take.' It would be a loan."

A darkness fled from his face. He looked his old self, confident, loving her, wanting her as he had their first night together. She read his changed expression: her offer touched him; he was grateful to her and loving her for it. Nothing else mattered to her so much, nothing could match the importance of that sense that he approved of something she had said or done.

Once he had said suddenly, "You always *listen;* most people never really listen." The phrase kept coming back in her memory for days afterward. They had been walking downtown from the office, and he had glanced sideways at her and found her turning toward him as if she were a lip-reader. Ten times during the next few days those words came forth in her mind, leaving everything of the moment in the background. *You always listen; most people never really listen.*

Now he went over to an empty bookshelf that served as a bar, sloshed some gin into a glass, tossed in an ice cube and then a few drops of vermouth. He stirred the drink with his finger and said, "I can't borrow a hundred dollars from you, Jossie. Owing money is something I don't give a damn about, but not money from my own girl."

"Why not me? Why not somebody who wants so awfully to help you?"

"I don't know. I can't explain it, but I can't."

The Southern gentleman, she thought. Maybe he wasn't as free of convention as he believed, maybe he did care about things he avowedly had outgrown. She couldn't put the thought into words; it would sound like a challenge. She never had questions about Rick, never weighed anything he told her, testing for validity. He was always open about what he said, never left you confused about where he stood on anything. Right now he was miserable again, and withdrawn, needing silence.

He looked even handsomer than usual, almost a caricature of handsomeness, like an Arrow collar ad. She had always distrusted very handsome men, or been ill at ease and on the defensive with them, and when she first saw him at the office, she had thought *Arrow collar* and had a private snicker at the analogy. He wasn't tall, true enough, and he once made a joke about how he had hated the six-footers at college, as though he had long since stopped any such boyish envy. But for their first evening date, she had left her only dressy pumps, with their high heels, at home and had spent $8 for new low-heeled shoes that were not quite right with the silk dress she wore. Dancing that night in the place they went to on West Eighth, her cheekbone exactly fitted to his, she resolved never to wear even medium-high heels, fashion or no fashion.

She no longer even thought about his height, but again and again she found herself gazing, almost in surprise, at his handsome face. So regular were his features, so perfect the adjustment of bone to bone, line to line, under gray eyes and thick brown hair, that she felt herself almost vulgar in her admiration, like a silly showgirl looking in Tiffany's window, oozing admiration for a diamond bracelet displayed there.

Rick kept telling her she was beautiful, but she was not even pretty in the ordinary meaning of the word, and she knew it. "Striking" was a better word for her; her wide Slavic brow made her face look round and her nose stubby, even thick. Her brown eyes were her best feature, and her body: "clothes horse" was what the girls called her at college, and it was true that whenever she did wear something new, people always noticed and said things she pooh-poohed but secretly liked. "You ought to be a mannequin for a fashion photographer," a saleswoman had said the last time she had tried something on in a department store, and that had been only a sweater and skirt and scarf. "You have a way with clothes—most people just put them on."

"Do you want a drink, Jossie?" Rick asked suddenly, and before she could answer, he added, "Thanks for offering to lend it, though."

"What will you do?"

"What counts more is what they'll do." He fingered the dispossess notice and then thrust it away from him. "Ten days from now."

"What can they do?"

"Garnishee my salary, for one thing. Even after I've moved out."

"But the whole office would find out."

"Things like that do get on the grapevine pretty fast."

"You mustn't. No, honestly not. You might even be fired."

"Ashley and Company do prefer copywriters who are above such mundane things as garnishees. Let them fire ahead—I'd get another job."

Her eyes filled with tears and she turned away, huddling down into the red armchair so he would not see her face. She looked like a gargoyle when she cried. Her older sister, Nell, had told her that once when she was in a ten-year-old's crying fit, and ever since then she would hear the taunt again, the moment tears came.

Rick sat on the arm of the chair, one arm encircling her shoulders, drawing her to him, not urging her to stop crying, just waiting. As she grew quiet he said, "You're *good,* Jossie," and began to kiss her hair, her forehead, the nape of her neck. Everything changed when he caressed her. His silence lent its own meaning; she turned toward him, and as they found each other, problems vanished, and the only pressure left was their equal need to make love.

○ ○ ○

Until her last year at Cornell, Jossie had never lent anybody more than a nickel for an urgent telephone call, nor borrowed more than a nickel for an ice-cream cone when she was passing the Sweet Shop and was stricken by an uncontrollable urgency of her own.

She had never thought about lending or borrowing at all. She had thought about money and debt, yes; her father had raised scenes of unforgettable fury during her early childhood when they were building their house in New Rochelle, scenes caused by her mother's suggestions about this or that change in the blueprints: an extra closet, another cupboard, or, most horrendous of all, her passionate desire to install the two washtubs in the basement not on a side wall but right next to the cellar door and its exit to the back yard and the clotheslines.

"You think nothing of running up the costs with your new ideas," her father had yelled during one such scene. "You think nothing of adding twenty feet of water pipe, know nothing of drainage systems, of extra charges for altering the architect's plans, nothing, except 'it would be nicer, it would save steps.'"

Jossie could still remember her mother bursting into tears and running from the kitchen, routed and in disgrace. "Extra charges" and "running up costs" became phrases imbued with vice and sin.

But at the end of her junior year, just before summer vacation, she had been summoned one day to the office of her faculty adviser, Professor Archibald Smithson.

"I have recently learned," he greeted her, "that you are working your way through and have been doing so ever since you came to Ithaca."

"Yes, sir. It's easy."

"And you plan to go on working next year, your senior year."

"Yes, sir. I won't be waiting tables, though. I never have."

"That's not the point. I know what you do, and that's not the point either. Spending hours doing it—that *is* the point."

"But my state scholarship is only a hundred a year, and tuition's two hundred. My family can't send more than twenty-five a month, so there's nothing else I can do to stay in college."

"Would Andrew Carnegie have done that?" He glared at her.

"Done what?"

"Wasted time in college to earn a few dollars a week? Of course not. He believed in credit."

"You mean borrow? Go into debt?"

"Debt is a moralist's word, a poor man's word. Andrew Carnegie would have arranged a loan and paid it back after he'd had full use of the money for his purposes."

"But Andrew Carnegie had—he had—"

"Collateral. You have collateral. You have character, and you are an exceptional student. I'll write a letter to the University Loan Office today."

He had written and the loan was granted, payable in ten years at an annual interest of three percent. For the first time in her twenty years, she had come face to face with debt, not as an abstraction, not as something in her parents' lives, but as a personal possession. And though this was surely what might be called an honorable debt, as opposed to frivolous ones for pretty clothes or vacations, it had a solidity in her mind she had never known before, a bulk sitting there, looking at her.

It was larger than she had thought it would be. Naively she had envisioned it only as money for tuition, but in casting up an estimate with her of what sum she should apply for to have one year of complete freedom, Professor Smithson had also ridiculed the idea of her living for another year in her $8-a-month boardinghouse off campus, sharing a room with another girl.

"You should have at least one year's experience of dormitory life—inestimable training for getting along with people in the future."

She had enjoyed being like everybody else at Prudence Risley Hall, room and board and laundry all paid for, had enjoyed having meals with other girls, had caught on quickly to lots of minor matters she had never known before, the small pleasant commerce between friends of lending sweaters, swapping scarves or hats, conspiring to dress somebody up for a dance when her own clothes were all wrong—she had never seen this aspect of college life at all.

But what with $450 for the dorm, what with lab fees and books and that treacherous category Miscellaneous, which included silver fillings as well as loose-leaf notebooks, the total loan had managed to achieve the alpine peak of $800.

Her senior year, it was true, had turned out to be her best year scholastically, way ahead of her good grades of the first three years. Freed of the never-ending need to write little items to *Women's Wear* about what coeds were wearing to football games or regattas, to send in news about college theatricals, student elections, girls' crews, and field hockey teams to the school pages of the *Evening Mail*, no longer having to run down the hill to the railroad station every other night, to entrust her copy to the porter on the train for mailing right in New York—rid of all this by the small miracle of borrowed money in a savings bank, she worked harder than ever and topped all her preceding grades. She also had entered the competition for the Stratford-on-Avon Prize, with a fifty-page essay that undertook no less a task than a comparison of Shakespeare's tragedies with those of Aeschylus. She called it "The Tragic Flaw." There was a first prize of $50. She had won it.

In his inimitable way, Professor Smithson had congratulated her on her success. "Remember Andrew Carnegie."

Yet what she came to call "my Andrew Carnegie loan" achieved an unexpected weight in every plan she made for after college. The idea of trying for a newspaper job was out. Twenty-five a week was the going pay for any starting job in anything, but on a paper it would stay there or thereabouts for years, while in an advertising agency, everybody said, there could be fast raises. A girl she knew, at Batten, made $100 a week.

But getting into an advertising agency wasn't the speedy little procedure she had hoped for. At every interview when they asked about experience, asked to see her proof book, she would say she had no experience and therefore no proof book. The personnel manager would invariably look remote, taking on a glazed patience as she said "Leave your name and phone number."

All summer and fall she had taken "fill-in jobs," hating them, first as a salesgirl at Wanamaker's, then as a comparison-shopper at Gimbel's, and in the winter as a private tutor for a backward child in Kew Gardens, Queens. But when the spring semester of 1923 was starting, bringing with it the usual longing for Cornell, the thought of college courses hit hard. Why hadn't she thought of that before?

She enrolled in an evening course in copywriting at the Columbia School of Journalism, and her very first assignment was a breeze. The students were to write a piece of "house copy," not for some manufacturer but for the advertising agency itself, selling its own services in a "prestige campaign" addressed to possible advertisers seeking to introduce some new trademark or brand name to the public.

She had thought about it for a day or two and then somehow, from somewhere, the idea had come to her: whole, certain, not tentative at all.

A silver dollar and a piece of ore

> Suppose you had a piece of silver ore worth one dollar, and offered it at a subway booth for fare, or at the box office of a movie house.
>
> You couldn't get in. They'd laugh at you.
>
> But suppose you had a silver dollar, worth no more than that same piece of ore.
>
> It would be accepted instantly at both places. That's because it bears a trademark everybody knows.
>
> When you, a manufacturer, have a product you want everybody to accept on the instant, you have to make its brand name as familiar as that trademark on the silver dollar.
>
> We at the John Jones Agency are pretty good at doing that for you. A phone call to us costs only a twentieth part of that silver dollar.
>
> • JOHN JONES ADVERTISING, INC. •

The teacher read it aloud to the class. "Here's a piece of copy," he said, "that shows the writer has a natural bent for the eye-catching headline, the bright idea. This is what copy chiefs look for—flair."

The ad became her lucky piece. When she began to have interviews at agencies again, a few weeks later, and the glazed patience had duly appeared, Jossie quickly said, "But I do have a few things I wrote for a college course in copywriting."

The first glance at the first headline would crack the glaze. In the end the silver dollar and the piece of ore had got her the job at Ashley & Company. And there was Rick Baird.

He had been there for years. He was a senior copywriter, with three major accounts he wrote himself, one on an automobile, one on tires, and the last on a razor and blades. But he also was copy chief on other accounts, in charge of other copywriters. To her that meant he was a star.

"Welcome to this idiot place," he had greeted her, and she laughed at the joke. But as she got to know him, he let her see that it was not merely a joke. Yes, he liked Ashley, yes, he knew it was one of the best firms in the field, yet on the whole—but on the other hand—

"I don't want to give you any false impression," he said. "You find out what *you* think as you go along."

On their second or third luncheon date she began to talk about a book she was reading, the latest volume in Mencken's series of *Prejudices.*

"Good old Mencken," Rick said. "He's giving up *The Smart Set,* I think, and starting a new magazine."

"Do you know him?"

"No, not in a personal sense, but I had a letter and a check from him once."

At Princeton he and one of his friends, Scott Fitzgerald, he told her, had each sent in a short story to *The Smart Set*—"this must have been in 'sixteen or 'seventeen, because Scott didn't stick it out for his degree"—and Mencken had taken both stories, paying each of them twenty-five dollars.

"And he wrote each of us a letter, Jossie, saying the same thing, in almost the same words: 'You're a writer.' "

"How wonderful that must have been."

"So look what happened," Rick said, lightly enough.

She didn't say anything. She hadn't read *The Beautiful and the Damned* yet, but she was still at college when *This Side of Paradise* appeared, and like everybody else she had been dazzled by it.

So that's it, she thought, that has to be it. What *it* was, she did not put into words for herself, but that there was some buried, hidden, not-to-be-talked-about substance affecting Rick's life, of this she had no doubt. For the first time she felt awkward about saying anything to show Rick how much she liked her job; at times she was a little ashamed that she did enjoy it. That morning when she had handed in a piece of copy to her own supervisor, Mr. Jerton, and he had read it and said, "We'll run it, try another," a jump of pleasure had gone through her, but when next she had seen Rick, she had said nothing about it at all.

In a way it was the same thing when she was at home with her own family. If her father was around, she never even mentioned advertising, much less the fact that it felt good to be good at it, to be considered a bright young thing, "Mr. Jerton's white-haired girl," with a big future in advertising. When he wasn't at home, she did tell her mother about the office, seeing her mother's eyes light up as if it were her own triumph as well as Jossie's. But that was the big difference in life—your mother versus your father. Nearly everybody Jossie knew had something of the sort, one parent who was fine, the other who was unbearable. If not unbearable, then at least unfair, over-positive, too demanding. Because Nell was a teacher too, they had assumed that their other child would follow in their footsteps and become a teacher in the city's high schools, but though her mother proved tractable and understanding when Jossie first said she did not want to be a teacher, the immediate resistance of her father was the first major shock of her life.

"What will you be? A secretary? A bookkeeper? A saleswoman in a store?"

It wasn't just a question; it was a taunt, an accusation, a fling of ridicule.

"I'm going to work on a newspaper."

"How many girls get jobs on newspapers?"

"Harry," her mother put in. "Jossie will be the one who does."

That had placated her father for a time, but when the reality arrived, of getting a job in advertising instead, the house had rocked in the hurricane of his wrath.

"Prostituting yourself," he had finally shouted. "A whore in the world of big business! Doing it for money—"

"Harry, that's too far—you're going too far."

"Her college loan! A subterfuge, an excuse, an alibi." He had flung the phrases at her mother as if they were bursts of furious air. "The college gives her ten years to pay it off, but she must sell herself to pay it off faster."

"You always pay things off the first moment you can."

Jossie could stand it no longer. "If a man owned a button factory," she flung at her father, "and wanted his son to go into buttons, you'd say a father had no right to dictate what his son's career should be—"

"S-s-s-sh, Jossie, s-s-s-sh," her mother said, as surprised as Jossie herself that she had stood up to her father in one of his rages.

"Teaching is a profession, that's what Pa means. We only wanted you to have a real profession. Not just a job."

From her first day at Ashley, Jossie remained silent about the office in her father's presence. He taught mathematics at DeWitt Clinton High, and his travel time elongated his working days so that he left early and came home late, depleted and tired. Her mother taught English at New Rochelle High and never seemed worn out and spent, though she too was already past fifty.

But a similar silence with her mother would have been impossible, as well as needless. Her mother seemed to remember what it was like to be young, to look ahead, to want things hard if you wanted them at all, not mildly, not reasonably, but insistently, immediately, not off in some future where security and solidity mattered, but right this minute when you were young. It was so easy to tell her mother that Mr. Jerton at the office had praised some special piece of work, it was so pleasant to see her mother's face turn pink with sudden pleasure, that Jossie almost was prompted to tell her other things as well.

Not about Rick exactly, but yes, about Rick in a vague way. "Sometimes when I stay overnight in town with Nell," she had recently confided, when they were alone, "I'm not there the whole evening, just later, to sleep."

"Does that mean"—she was all eagerness—"there's somebody you like whom you go out with first?"

"It's a man at the office, and his family lives in Paris right now, and sometimes we have dinner or go dancing, and then if I miss the last train, I stay at Nell's."

"His mother and father live in Paris? Is he French?"

"Oh, no. His mother's dead and his father lives in Richmond, Virginia. It's his own family. He's not a kid, he's twenty-eight." She stressed the *own*.

"You mean he's married, but they're not living together."

"For a while, yes. She's studying art for a year, maybe two. But she knows he goes out with other people, and he knows that she does too; living over there by herself, she'd have to have friends." She paused, studying her mother's expression.

Her mother had nodded several times, as if to offer agreement multiplied, that she understood, that these were modern times, that an amount of freedom in marriage was completely within the circumferences of a liberal's values.

"Yes, darling, of course, they both need friends." She reached over and squeezed Jossie's shoulder. "I want you to be happy, you know I do. It would be bad if you let yourself be hurt."

"Oh, never, Mama."

"Soon you'll be wanting to move out to a place of your own."

"Not for a long time."

"It would be a place in New York, not here in a small town."

"Just imagine living right in New York. I would love it." She hesitated. "As a matter of fact, one day last summer, during that awful heat wave, I answered a room-for-rent ad, just out of curiosity."

"That means it's already begun, this next step in your life. Where was it? What kind of room?"

"Studio apartment is what they call it—one big long room with a tiny kitchenette and a bath."

"Where was it?"

"On West Fifty-third, in a row of brownstones. Imagine just walking to the office every day, no train, no commutation ticket—"

"Why didn't you take it?"

"It was $25 a month." She looked off beyond her mother into some vision space of her own. She saw herself standing just inside the threshold of the large rectangular room, taking one last look before closing the door upon it, feeling how it would be to go there after work every afternoon, lighting the lamps one by one, flinging herself down on the sofa, being in her own house. She could change the sleazy curtains at the two long windows, make slipcovers for the worn-looking sofa, and throw a few bright pillows about. But twenty-five a month. And three for a party-line phone, fifteen or so for food, two more for electricity!

That was before she had met Rick, but she had told him about it, and once they had even walked by the place, just to have him see it. "I might live there one of these days," she had said.

"And the hell with Grand Central forever?" Now her mother, seeing the faraway look of speculation and memory, only said, "Don't hurry too much, Jossie."

○ ○ ○

Don't hurry too much, don't let yourself be hurt. Even her mother would never understand, Jossie thought, the morning after the dispossess notice. If you loved a person, your one thought was to keep him from being hurt, from feeling trapped. Until they had left for Grand Central the evening before, Rick had put on his jocular mien, as if he were trying to convince her that landlords and evictions were part of the absurdity of the commercial world he looked down upon. But as they turned off Fifth Avenue at Forty-second Street, the jocularity dropped and the real Rick was revealed. He was helpless and he was angry.

"We'll find a way out," she said as they neared the vast lighted square of the station. "There must be one, and there's ten days to find it."

"Not 'we,'" he repeated. "This isn't your doing, and I'm not going to let it be your undoing."

"My undoing!"

The exaggeration made them both laugh, but on the train and through most of the night, it was as if her mind had a strength of its own, an energy, a willfulness, like a rearing horse they had seen in a movie recently, bucking, prancing, charging, wheeling, defying every effort to gentle it or rein it in.

But when she awoke the next morning, everything stood clear; she had found the solution, could almost see it before her like a palpable thing, smooth and shining. Would Andrew Carnegie move out because of a dispossess notice? Would he risk having his salary garnisheed, risk losing his job?

Rick couldn't borrow at the office, but she never had and she could. Not from Andy Bellock or John Slade—she didn't know either of them well enough to approach them—but Mrs. Dunwoodie? Mary Watts? They both were older women, one a widow without children, lonely, rather sad, who had taken a sort of gossipy and affectionate interest in Jossie from the minute she arrived at Ashley, and Mary Watts, Mr. Jerton's secretary, who looked on Jossie as a kind of office pet, to be cuddled on behalf of her boss, as if he had charged Mary with the specific job of training her in the right direction, with the right amount of encouragement and promise, so she would feel that a job at any other agency was too wrenching an idea, tempered by a certain judicious caution about being fooled by early success into expecting too many raises too soon.

Mary would say yes, and Mrs. Dunwoodie would too. Fifty dollars from each. That would be two hundred, together with her own hundred. And her own sister, Nell, would let her have the other hundred.

"A big chunk" wasn't what Rick needed. Leeway wasn't what he needed. He needed to be free and clear again, to have time to find a smaller place at less money, to devise a tighter budget, so this would never happen again. They could give up going dancing, going to restaurants; he might write a story, or even free-lance an ad or two—relieved of this awful three-hundred-dollar incubus, he would be free again.

She could see his face when she told him. It would be gorgeous to see the worry vanish. All night through, his dear face had come to her, the changing moods she had seen in it, the separate meanings. Never as long as she lived would she forget that day, the third or fourth time they had gone out together, when she saw the special Rick look she had never seen before. It was different from all his usual expressions of amusement or affection or irony; it was different from the way college boys looked at girls, or even the few older men she had gone out with after college. Suddenly Rick's was a look that offered, asked, promised; any girl would know what it asked and offered and promised, and all her own hesitancies rose up to meet it, rose up demandingly, rose up without quibbling. This was the time, this was at last the time to say yes, to let it happen, to give up that eternal *But I never have.*

And now this was just as demanding, this need to help Rick, to set his mind at rest, to give to him, to show him what it meant to her that he be happy. She telephoned Nell before she was dressed, but Nell had already left for school. She called the school, Washington Irving High, but she had not yet arrived. "Could I leave a message? It's an emergency," she said, keeping her voice low, urgent. "I'm her sister, and I know she has an empty period after her first class. Please, would you tell her I'll be there then to see her? Tell her it's not anything like an accident or sickness, so she won't worry. Oh, thank you."

But Nell did worry, and as her first class drew to a close she rushed to the faculty room where Jossie was waiting. Jossie had stopped at Grand Central to phone the office, to say she would not be in for part of the morning. She had a toothache and was rushing to her dentist, who was going to work her in ahead of his first patient. What excuse she would offer Nell she did not know, but she was inventive, she liked spur-of-the-moment necessities.

She had gone next to her bank with her savings book, emerging with a bank check and a lordly feeling she could not explain. It unexpectedly fortified her in the slight nervousness about facing Nell. Nell was four years older and could still manage phrases as vengeful as the old gargoyle, but now it was politics that brought them out, not big-sister nastiness. Nell was married to a man Jossie couldn't stand, Ed Resnick, who was forever praising the marvels of the Russian Revolution, to end all oppression, all poverty, but who worked for his father to squeeze every last dime of rent from the shopkeepers in his four tenements on Delancey Street on the Lower East Side. Nell had only her teacher's salary, which couldn't cover the munificence of hundred-dollar loans, but Eddy was rich, and Nell could talk him into things.

"Joss," Nell cried as she met her sister. "Any accident? Mama? Pa?"

"I told them to tell you *not*, no accident, nobody sick."

"Then it's you. Something's happened to you."

"Wait, Nell, calm down a sec. It's about me, yes, and it's—" She looked away. "It's pretty serious. It's—I hate this, but I just have to have a hundred dollars, secretly, I mean. Nobody must know about it." She looked away again. "Not even Eddy. And of course not Mama or Pa."

Comprehension flooded Nell's face, and with it a kindness, a sympathy. "You poor kid. Are you sure?"

"It's not what you're thinking," Jossie said emphatically. "It's nothing like that at all." She could see that Nell did not believe her, and she thought, So be it. In her mind a small chuckle formed;

maybe Rick was right, that there *was* something you had to look down on in the world, something a little cheap, defensible perhaps and natural, but a little cheap.

"You don't have to tell me," Nell said. "Are you sure?"

"I'll tell you all about it some other time, but not right now. Is that all right?"

"You poor kid," Nell repeated. "Of course it's all right. I'll tell Eddy it's for—I don't know what, but I'll think of something. He's not like Pa about money. Is tomorrow okay, or the day after? Do you want me to go with you?"

"You don't have to—I already—do I have to tell you who, or anything like that?"

"Not until you feel like it. I think I know, anyway."

"Thank you, Nell, *honestly,* thank you." Again she turned away but a moment later turned back and threw her arms about her sister, silent and tense.

"Come on, Joss," Nell said. "It's going to be all right. I'll meet you after school tomorrow, and I can have it in cash."

○ ○ ○

Two days later Jossie dropped a sealed note on Rick's desk. He started to open it in her presence but she said, "It's private, or I wouldn't have licked the envelope so hard."

She could hear him tearing it open as she left his office, and an elation raced through her. Mrs. Dunwoodie and Mary Watts had also agreed quickly to lend her the money, apparently each believing implicitly in the story she told, about falling behind on her college loan—it isn't even a lie, she thought, I *am* falling behind. She had told the same story to each, and had openly told each of them that she was also asking the other for a $50 loan, so there would be no surprised discovery later on.

Her note to Rick was brief. She had torn up eight longer versions. "Could you meet a girl at five-thirty tonight in the Fountain Room or whatever they call it at the Prince George? Something's come up. Something rather nice."

He was there before she arrived. They never left the office together, never were stupid enough to meet at the nearest corner. Tonight she had planned to be a little late, wanting him to keep on wondering. How she had kept it all to herself for the past two days she would never know; at times she felt herself sputtering with it. Once she had thought, Maybe he'll jump to conclusions the way Nell did, but writing the note dispelled all fear of that. He knew her too well. She would never be light and flirtatious about anything serious, would never write that sort of note if it were.

In the dimly lighted room, she could see him sitting there, watching the door, expectancy etched into every line of his face. He rose as she came near the table, held out his hand in welcome.

"You sure know how to keep a man guessing all day."

"Darling, look." She sat down next him on the banquette, opened her purse, drew out her bank check and laid it out flat on the table before him, put two $50 checks, made out to her, on top of it, and then counted out ten new $10 bills.

"Three hundred," she said. "You just have to."

He stared at the assorted pile before him. He stared at her and then back down at the checks and bills. He said nothing at all. But she heard the deep inhaling of his breath.

Two

Cedric Urquhart Baird had grown up, he sometimes thought, amused by his parents and ashamed of his grandparents. One of his earliest memories was of whistling through the air on a swing under a blue-white hot sky and hearing his mother say, as she gave him his starting pushes, "If it can't be real silk, then I'll not even try it on"—(push)—"No second-best, never as long as"—(push)—"I live. My Aunt Emmeline, she was my great-aunt Marylou's first cousin on my father's side"—(push)—"Aunt Emmeline always said, 'If it's not the most perfect, nobody in this family would even consider it.'"

By this time he was swinging freely, doubling his own body up and then straightening sharply, his body his own motor power, widening the arc he was cutting through the flower-laden air, and he could only catch wisps of the ensuing talk beneath him. He could no longer recall what the non-silken object was, whether dress, petticoat, handkerchief, or other miscreant, but he could remember the rhythmic bursts of speech, remember his mother's agitated firmness in dismissing anything second-best, as he slipped in great half-circles through the scorching air of summer, knowing that if it were not the absolute best, it had no place in his family.

It was a large family back then when he was a child in Virginia. Even at his tenth birthday, in 1905, his grandparents were still alive, all four of them, all well into their seventies and all still prefacing a large portion of their remarks with "before the war" or "just after the war." With a fierce unanimity, they all lived *in* the past, *with* the past, indeed, *on* the past, drawing nourishment not from its old splendors, for there had in fact been very few splendors in any of their lives, but from its old premises, from its old assumptions that they were of the elite and thus entitled to pattern themselves on the life of the elite, the courtliness, the good food and perfect wine, the entertaining of guests, the fascination of travel.

That there had seldom been enough money to underwrite any of these felicities never annihilated the value they set on the felicities themselves. The Baird and Urquhart ancestors, as far back as they could be traced, had never known the glories of plantation life or of splendid inheritance; they were nearly all lawyers or teachers of modest means, living in various small communities in Georgia and Virginia, in modest houses, unlike the porticoed and be-columned mansions of legend.

Rick's own mother and father were unsympathetic to the long-lived grandparents and their memories of the South of their own youth. Rick's mother, Mary Urquhart, a beautiful girl of twenty when she married Cedric Davis Baird, had already begun to disown and disavow all the remembering and backward-looking, dubbing it a kind of daydreaming in reverse; she could not see, however, how much of it she was capable of doing herself. So imbued had she been in her earliest childhood with the sense of superiority of "our kind of family" that she never questioned it for her first fifteen years. This did not mean superiority over blacks—that had never even come up for consideration. It did mean superiority over people who bought and sold goods, over shopkeepers and artisans, over anybody in trade, as the British might put it. Her own people had all been professionals, with pedigree and status, and thus of the Southern aristocracy. Only in late adolescence did Mary Urquhart even wonder why they never had large houses and pretty furniture and shining silverware and handsome carriages, the way some of her friends had. And not until she married Davis Baird, son of another shabby-genteel Southern family, did she finally come upon the answers she could accept as real answers.

The truth was that her charming and handsome husband was not much of a lawyer, scarcely more of a lawyer than her own father had been and, like him, a man who drank far more than he should and worked far less. His clients were the very people he looked down upon, the tradesmen of the town, occasionally the farmers of outlying districts. Sometimes they were professional people too, doctors, ministers, teachers, and thus gentlemen and their ladies, most of them equally given to frequent mention of family trees and family connections and how it had been for their own parents before they had "lost everything in the war."

By the time Mary Urquhart Baird had a child of her own, she had begun to quarrel with her parents and her husband's parents about all the talk of the past; she was testy and bored as well with their unceasing talk of reconstruction and the New South, whether it was to be treated as conquered territory or as an integral part of the nation, never secessionist, never separated, certainly never brought to surrender on the field of battle.

To Rick as a little boy, many of the places he kept hearing about might have been countries or foreign kingdoms—Chickamauga, The Wilderness, Antietam, Vicksburg—and very early he learned that he could never understand what the grown-ups were talking about; their endless malignment of current life flowed by like a faintly murmuring stream that was somehow unpleasant, though he knew that flowing streams were supposed to murmur in gentleness and delight. His only defense was to shut out the sound and escape the unpleasantness, which his parents interpreted as sullenness, and later in life he was to admit cheerily that he knew less about American history than anybody in any of his classes.

He was sent to a military school in Richmond, which he promptly hated as a choice enforced by the traditions of bringing up a Southern gentleman, and by the time he was sixteen he vowed that he would never go to Duke or the University of Virginia or any other college or university in the South, only to Yale, Harvard, or Princeton, where nobody would ever haul in all those dangling explanations about first cousins on whose side, about uncles and aunts and great-uncles and great-aunts.

The family shock at this rebel son soon had to yield to successive bouts of deep mourning, as one after another of the four grandparents, all now in their eighties, died within one year, and when at last the string of funerals ended, there was an official *finis* to that almost tangible chunk of time called "before the war."

That was at the close of the first decade of the new century, and Rick had already begun to outlaw the cadences and pronunciations of his native speech. At school he was promptly named "Cub," because of a going-away present, his first suitcase, of heavy leather marked with his initials. He rather liked being called not Rick but Cub, until one of the school wits in his class loudly asked, "Would that be lion cub or bear cub or cubbyhole?" This was a boy a head taller than Rick, a rich boy and a bully whose every *mot* elicited loud approval of smaller boys, and this time a salacious laugh as well, over the accent on the word "hole."

Thus Rick became Hole for the rest of his days at the academy and had his most emphatic lesson in how a Southerner and a gentleman is supposed to act under stress: with totally false dignity.

He was a fair student except in English Lit, where he excelled. He loved books, he loved to read, he wanted to write. By the time he was a freshman at Princeton, on a partial scholarship, he answered every question about what he was going to be when he got out of college with the simple statement: "I'm going to write books." The story bought by Mencken for his famous magazine shut down anybody's derisions or doubts, and he and his friend Scott were regarded by their peers as two of a kind.

That the very name of Scott Fitzgerald would all too soon become a source of ignoble pain never occurred to Rick, but for the next years, whenever he sent in a story to *The Smart Set* or the other "quality" magazines, *The Atlantic Monthly*, *Scribner's*, *Harper's*, and then received it back, rejected, he wondered whether he was ill-advised not to do what Scott was doing. But he could not, and felt a brief triumph that he could not. Never would he try his fortunes with second-best magazines, certainly not with those he called trash. If his friend Scott, a year younger than he, had already come to the point where he was willing to see his name in *The Saturday Eve-*

ning Post with short stories puffed up from formula dough, so be it, but that level was not for him.

In Rick's junior year, Scott left college, and writing somehow came more easily, far less troubled. But Rick's stories still kept coming back; it became a sore point with him to enclose the prescribed self-addressed and stamped manila envelope when he sent off a manuscript, as if he were making a concession in advance. A resentment, like some subtle drug he had small tolerance for, began to seep through his nervous system, and he found himself facing his desk more and more reluctantly.

At the beginning of his junior year he had gone to a faculty-student party at the house of Professor Arthur Kimble, who gave several courses in art: medieval art, Renaissance art, and modern art, including the Impressionists and Cubists. Kimble, a devoted spare-time painter, was young for a professor, and his wife Jean even younger, for she had been a student of his in a summer course he gave at the Art Students League in New York. Campus gossip had it that the real talent for painting in the Kimble household was hers, not the Professor's, and privately Jean agreed. Despite marriage and early motherhood, Jean had every intention of protecting that talent from the easy atrophy of domesticity.

They lived in a small house about four miles off campus, and three times a week she took the morning train to New York to spend most of the day at the League on West Fifty-seventh Street. Whenever there was an exhibition of students' work, Jean Kimble's canvases were among those hung, and on two separate occasions Jean managed to let Rick know the date of the next showing. Each time, he went to the city and saw not only her paintings but Jean herself.

He had never known any girl like her. She had never been South, not even on a visit; she had been born in the town of Princeton in the same house where she now lived, her own house, left her by her parents, who were both in their forties and childless until she was born, and who died while she was still in her teens.

She made it clear to Rick very quickly that she found him attractive, and made it clear, too, that perhaps any marriage was ill-fated where the man was nearly twice the age of his wife. She was twenty-four then, three years older than Rick, and they both talked learnedly about seeking father images, though Jean laughed off "this new Freudian stuff," and the prime literary heroes Rick paid homage to were Bernard Shaw and Havelock Ellis.

In the spring, with America at last part of the Great War, Jean's husband, though never having reached the front, became one of the first Princeton war heroes, and Rick was one of the first students to offer his condolences to the new widow.

They were married on the day Rick himself enlisted in the Air

Corps, that June day in 1918 when he received his degree.

° ° °

Jossie knew all about Rick's life with Jean; she knew what Jean looked like, and at first she often found herself staring at the large framed photograph of her that he kept on the desk in the bedroom. Jean was one of those pure blondes, so fair that her eyebrows hardly showed up in the picture. She did have the small regular features that made a pretty girl. The picture had been taken a few years ago, and at that time, certainly, she didn't look as if she were older than Rick; she was laughing and looked like a girl at college.

It surprised Jossie to find herself wishing the photograph wasn't there in the bedroom. Maybe if it were in the living room, she would soon have become unaware of it, but right there on his desk, even though its back was all you could see from their bed, it seemed at times a presence that should not have been there while they were making love.

But she said nothing of this to Rick; it would seem childish, as if symbols mattered more than the reality she had so thoroughly accepted.

He had told her enough about his marriage to Jean to give her a true insight into it, more than the mere recitation of dates and facts. He had said that he had regarded it from the first as high adventure to find himself suddenly loved by two small children and adored by a talented girl like Jean. After their marriage she went on signing her paintings Kimble, "because I'm getting to be a bit known as Kimble and I'd have to start all over if I signed them Baird." And Rick was modern man enough to wish only that she had begun by signing her work *Ganther*, which was her maiden name.

"At the easel you're *you*," he said, "not somebody's wife."

"Not even Mrs. Baird?"

"Off the canvas but not on."

They lived in Jean's house, and when Rick returned from the army, jobless, it was Jean herself who urged him not to go rushing about looking for any old job, just because that was the expected thing for a returning veteran to do. Apart from his demobilization pay, there was, after all, the death benefits from poor Arthur's army insurance and his regular life insurance, not to speak of her own small inheritance from her parents; the mortgage was only thirty a month, due to her father's ambition to have his house "free and clear."

"We had only one month together before you went off to camp," Jean had said, "and now, if you're in an office all day every day—first a funeral, then an absentee husband."

He had agreed not to rush things. But her fees for art lessons, wages to the maid, the rising cost of everything—rather quickly Rick had found that a family meant earning a living.

"That's where Andy Bellock's introducing me to Ashley comes in," Rick ended. "You know all about me since then."

"All about you and Ashley, but not about you and what really counts."

"About me and Jean."

He always knew what you meant; you never never had to spell things out so you felt prodding and cheap. "Rick, if you don't want to go into that . . ."

"No secrets, remember?" He became thoughtful, getting the past few years in order. "After a while, maybe three years or so, things did begin to go pretty much the way Jean had predicted—a kind of absentee deal, with me in New York five and a half days every week—and when the kids started school, it emptied out a lot more. That was when she began to talk of studying in Paris. She could manage most of it on her own, she said, sell the house for eight or ten thousand, and then I would take care of emergencies or not have to send any money at all." Again he looked thoughtful, even sad. "I said I'd send money for the wine and escargots anyway, and we settled on a hundred a month—a fourth of my salary, it came to then."

Wine and escargots, Jossie had thought. They're separated for good. But this thought she kept to herself, and by the time she met Rick at the Prince George Hotel, she had reached a point where she thought of Jean only rarely, and when she did, it was like thinking of a long-gone acquaintance, an old college roommate, whose life had veered off in a new direction, away from the continuing reality of day-to-day existence.

This was reality for her now, this rush of pleasure at helping Rick. They went together the next morning to Rick's landlord; it was Rick's suggestion that she go along with him. He made a rite of it, as if there was in him the need to make public acknowledgment that she had helped him and that he had at last accepted her help.

"Better go to your bank first," Rick said. "If you endorse those two checks over to the Mason Realty Company, either Mrs. Dunwoodie or Mary will sure wonder why you didn't endorse them over to the Cornell Student Loan."

"I never thought of that."

"And then some day they'd find out that *my* landlord is Mason Realty, and about sixty cats would be let out of sixty bags. You know that office. Any large office."

At the small reception room of Mason Realty, they were kept waiting and Rick grew impatient. He picked up a new magazine that had recently come into being, called *Time*, and was riffling through its pages. Jossie sat there, not wanting to read, wanting simply to wait for this nervous feeling to be over, this worry that for some reason they would refuse to rescind the dispossess notice. Too late, they might say, the deadline is past.

At the receptionist's desk, a buzzer sounded, and the girl there looked up and caught Jossie's eye.

"You can go in now, Mrs. Baird," she said.

A tremor went wavering through Jossie, a small earthquake barely large enough to register on any seismograph, but for an instant her world seemed to falter and shift. "Rick, you can go in now," she said, and as she sat waiting for him to return, she kept hearing the strange syllables, *You can go in now, Mrs. Baird,* hearing them reiterating themselves, like a receding afterimage, not an echo but an image, receding but reappearing again and again, fainter and fainter, yet still perfectly formed on the screen of her mind.

An ineluctable sensation arose within her, a longing that it be true, not merely an error of assumption, but the truth, the fact. How deceptive one's inner convictions could be; from the start she had told Rick, believing her own words thoroughly, never questioning them, that she was nowhere near the notion of marriage, that knowing marriage was impossible mattered not a whit, certainly not for the next five years, which was to say forever. Yet here this accident, this verbal gaffe, threw open a vast pit of longing. It shocked her that it should be so, that there should be in her any unknown pit of longing, any aching of desire, and a premonition of distant pain invaded her.

Just then Rick came out of the office, in his hand the torn halves of the offensive document. His look of triumph aroused in Jossie a glee that banished premonition and everything else negative.

"Let's go apartment hunting at lunch," he said.

"I'm so happy it's over, Rick. Here, let me have that." She seized the torn sheets and began to shred them further, then to roll them up, pushing them, pummeling them into a pulpy mass. This she finally put into her pocket.

"What do you plan to do with that?" he asked.

"I don't know. Just look at it maybe."

"You could have it cast in bronze."

They met at the Automat for lunch, but their nickels were wasted for they barely ate their sandwiches or drank their coffee. Rick had set a limit of $50 a month for his next rent, and though they had both clipped many fine-sounding ads from the papers, they soon found that every one they inspected sent their hopes plummeting.

"They're fit for their resident roaches," Rick said at last, "but who else?"

"We'll find something," Jossie said, but the ring of conviction was so faint that she dismissed her words herself.

For the next four days they went searching during every free minute; the very smells in the hallways began to be familiar, the wretchedness of everything at or near $50 a month appalled them, the cracked and peeling walls, the unshaded lights, the torn carpet underfoot. Each time they went back to Rick's apartment after a bout of househunting, the contrast only added to their discouragement.

"Maybe you could raise the ante to sixty a month," Jossie said one day. She regretted it the moment she said it; it was like reopening the whole question of how he could manage. She felt a bit mystified that the question should exist at all, since Rick's salary by now was $6,000 a year, but she did know that he "was more responsible for more things than you'd imagine," including, perhaps, some monthly support for his father in Richmond. He didn't like to be too specific about his burdens, and she respected his right to privacy wherever he wished it.

"Raise the ante?" Rick asked, all at once cheerful. "What do you know about poker?"

"We played for lima beans at school."

He laughed aloud, but soon he was despondent once more, and their determined forays into the city's empty apartments stopped being lighthearted or optimistic. He tried not to show his changing mood to Jossie, but there was no concealment from the intuitive and caring girl beside him. In a mood unusual for him he began to foresee the next rent bill, this one marked January 1924. God, here he had paid it all up just a few days ago, and bang, another $100 was about to land on him.

"Darling," he asked Jossie abruptly one evening, "how much do you contribute at home?" They had been out for hours, this time after work on Saturday afternoon, and they were weary. They had finally gone for spaghetti and a carafe of cheap chianti to a small restaurant on Minetta Street and come back without even one address to consider. Rick had lighted the two logs in the fireplace and they faced each other, slumped in chairs in exhausted silence, watching the leaping energy of the flames. Rick was to think later that his question had leaped alive spontaneously, of its own will, like a bright spark above the andirons.

"Ten a week," she answered. "Five for my share of the food bill, and five for general expenses, phone, light, everything. Why?" Her mother had agreed to cut this in half for twenty weeks, so she could pay off Mrs. Dunwoodie and Mary Watts, but she hadn't gone into that with Rick, and it hadn't occurred to him to ask how she meant to repay them both within the six months she had promised.

"And your commutation ticket?" he went on.

"Twelve a month. Oh, Rick, why?" But she knew why, and her heart began to race. Had she thought of this herself, suppressing it so firmly that it now seemed to spring up as her own idea? Or had the receptionist at Mason Realty implanted the first seed of this suddenly burgeoning great tree of desire?

"Well, darling," he said carefully. "I was just thinking. If you wanted—"

"If I wanted—"

"To live with me, to come live with me, right here where we are."

"Just move in for good?"

"For good. You must have thought of it."

"Fifty-fifty on the rent and not have to move out at all?" She waited for his nod. "But what would we—how could we—the office—"

"Nobody has to know at the office, not right away. We'd think up some plan later on."

"But my mother, my sister—if they wanted to phone me?"

"You said your mother's been expecting you to have a place of your own one of these days."

"Oh, she really does. But it would be someplace where she could drop in on me; anyway, phone me—"

He made no answer. Perhaps this was too much for Jossie, premature. She was so young in terms of real life, so vulnerable. Yet she had become vital to him by now, so needed in every private moment of all his days and nights. Perhaps it was wrong of him even to speak of his idea; giving it voice had made it momentous to a degree he hadn't foreseen.

"I could manage it somehow," Jossie said. "If the phone rang, I could be the one to answer it."

"Suppose you were in the bathroom?"

"Then you'd say you were the butler." She laughed, but added reflectively, "I'm not much good at a lot of little lies. I'd rather go in for one big one."

Again he remained silent. He too had heard the receptionist at Mason Realty; a swift bullet of fantasy had pierced him, that he was free again, free to ask this delicious Jossie to marry him, this necessary Jossie, to remind him how it had been when he was himself in his early twenties, unattached, without burden, with responsibility.

"One great big one," he repeated. "Like saying we're married? Like *being* married? Is that what you meant?"

"I don't know what I meant."

○ ○ ○

A week later she moved in. At home she told her mother that she was taking a place in New York after all. "Not that one-room studio

I told you about—it's rented anyway. This is a stunning place on West Tenth Street, with a fireplace and everything, and I could never afford it by myself, but I'm sharing it with another girl—I mean, if it's all right with you that I won't be chipping in on expenses here."

"Of course it's all right. I told Pa already, that you'd be living on your own sooner or later, to prepare him."

"Will he mind? Will he raise the roof?"

"Now, Jossie."

"The phone's out in the hall," she went on rapidly. "A pay phone, and the janitor answers it and calls people, so don't be surprised if you have to wait a bit." She went on to describe the apartment, and its furniture and its framed prints, an excitement rushing along her phrases.

"It's lovely to see you so happy," her mother said. "I've sometimes wondered of late if you were a little strained or too tired."

"Only busy and—" She flung her arms wide, curving them, embracing the air. "Oh, *everything*, Mama." Impulsively she went over and hugged her mother. "I used to think that once I was out of college I'd never be so happy again. Everybody's forever telling you college is the best time of your life, but boy, can they be wrong!"

She's in love, her mother thought. It isn't a girl she's moving in with; it's the man she stays in town for. They're having an affair, and now they're going to live together.

Aloud she said, "It's like young people thinking life is over when they see the first gray hair. They find out soon enough that the real joy of life comes later, when you have children."

"So *you*, at least, aren't upset that I'm moving out." To her astonishment, her mother's eyes suddenly filled.

"The only thing that could really upset me, dear, is if you never wanted to move out at all."

Jossie understood. She was twenty-three; her parents had always preached the need for independence, for "leaving the nest," for making one's own life. But her mother was ready to prove it; God knows what her father would put her through before showing that he meant it too. Probably accuse her of whoring around—he pronounced it, for some obscure reason, *hooring*, the way his own father had pronounced it, though he had been as uneasy about his father's other foreignisms as the most cringing son of immigrants ever could have been. *Hoor* and *hooring*, however, remained in his vocabulary, unchanged, unchallenged, as if the very sound of their long *o's* spelled out the disgust he felt implicit in the words. And he a great liberal, defending the underdog, defending unions and antimilitarism and the League of Nations and decrying injustice in any form.

"Except where his own daughters are concerned," she said, and, at the immediate question in her mother's face, realized that she had spoken the words aloud. "Just a train of thought about Pa," she said lightly, "and how different the two of you are." She put her arms around her mother's shoulders once again. "I love you so, Mama. I'll go start packing."

○ ○ ○

It was remarkable, how natural and easy it was. From the instant Jossie saw the changed strip of lettering in the small brass letterbox in the entry to the house, Mr. and Mrs. C. U. Baird, replacing the sliver Rick had previously cut from his business card, she felt transformed, felt that she *was* Mrs. Baird.

When she went to the corner grocery around on Greenwich Avenue and ordered food, charging it, she said, "Baird," and gave the address without a flicker of hesitation. It felt right. It felt real. One morning in the first week of living with Rick, he stopped the janitor at the front door as they were leaving. "Joe, this is Mrs. Baird, back from Europe at last. Darling, this is Joe Marvin, the best superintendent anybody ever had. He's in charge of our house and the two next to ours."

"How do, Mrs. Baird, ma'am." If there was skepticism on Joe's face along with his surprise, it was fleeting. His Adam's apple rose and fell twice, and then he retreated toward the door leading to the basement, an odor of brass polish in his wake.

At the office only one person knew about it, Rick's closest friend, Andy Bellock, and that was only after Rick had asked Jossie whether it would be all right to tell him, and ask him home. Again it was remarkable, how glad she was, to have another human being know about Mr. and Mrs. Baird, and the first time Andy came to dinner, she spent $4 on a great thick steak, twice the size of their usual ones. She herself had already confided in Nell, but having Rick want to tell Andy Bellock made it an official announcement, gave it an existence of its own, not just a sisterly secret but an open declaration.

"I bet I could tell my mother about us," she once said, "and in a way I'd love to, right this minute. But she might feel duty-bound to let my father in on it, and then good night."

"When the time's right, you'll tell her, and if you want, I'll go and meet her. I'd like that."

Would the time ever be right for him to tell Jean? Jossie suddenly wondered. Was he thinking the same thing? She never thought of Jean, or hardly ever; now she could understand a Mormon wife or a Rajah's wife knowing her husband had other wives, being able to stand apart from them, as if they did not exist in the same way she did. It was an ability to wipe out certain facts so perfectly, so superbly, that they existed only as dreams exist, on some plane other than one's own.

"Will the time ever be right for my telling Jean?" Rick asked. "Is that what you're wondering?"

"I—well, not really. I suppose so, yes."

"It will be, and she'll be marvelous about it. She always takes things the way they are, about me. I do too, about her, if the truth be told. She's had an affair in Paris—it's over by now, but she wrote me about it. That's the deal we made long ago."

She knew of their pledge, never to go in for cheap little accusations of betrayal and infidelity, never to hide, never to lie.

"And Jean knows I haven't been celibate over here," he added. "No friar, no monk, not me. I did tell her there was a girl, sometime last fall, October, maybe."

"But if you told her you weren't just having an affair but really *living* with someone—"

"When I do tell her, my dearest little love, I'll make her see how this all came about, and she would see it. One way or another, Jean and I will come out all right, and you all right too."

° ° °

The shock came on the tenth day into the new year. It was at the grocery store, where she had ordered supplies for nearly an entire week. "Please deliver it," she said, giving the address, though they knew it as well as she did.

"Nine fifty-three," the owner said, looking over the cash register at her. "But I can't charge it."

"You what?"

"I could send it C.O.D. Or maybe you have the cash with you."

"But we have a charge account."

"Sure, Mrs. Baird, but I was totting up—right after the new year I always go over the accounts—and it's been four months since a payment."

"That can't be. There must be some mistake." Rick paid all the bills, most of them at the office. Her forehead felt a charge of sudden heat, as if she were sunburned. Rick had flourished the check for the January rent, grinning, saying, "You're half of it, don't forget," and had elaborately licked the two-cent stamp before slapping it down on the envelope. It had been a happy Christmas; Jossie had had a small bonus and a $5 raise, and Rick a bonus and a $10 raise. They had had a tree—she had never had a Christmas tree before—and Rick gave her a chiffon nightgown and her first silken dressing gown. "Now you can junk that old flannel bathrobe from dear old Cornell," he had said as she tried it on in delight.

The grocer was spreading out a ledger he had drawn up from beneath the counter. Two customers behind her made noises indicating impatience, and she flushed once again.

"Never mind," she said hurriedly. "I have enough money for this, and I'll ask my husband to check—to see—there must be some error." She took out a $10 bill. "But please do deliver it; there's so much canned stuff and fruit, it's far too heavy—"

She could hear her own flurried tone, and on the sidewalk she halted, breathing as if she had been running for a train. Most of the monthly bills went straight to Rick at the office; he had told her that they fell like confetti around the first of the month, but that it was always simpler to open charge accounts when you gave your business address, especially when it was a firm they recognized, like Ashley.

What did Rick do with all the confetti he spoke of so airily? Were there other bills he hadn't paid for four months? Many others? And for longer than four months?

She didn't want to ask him. She would have to, but she wished she didn't. It was the first not-wanting she had ever had about Rick.

° ° °

Never could she have predicted his reaction. "Remember that new market opening on Ninth?" he asked jauntily. "It's twice as big and modern and twice as good. We'll open an account there." Before she could speak, he added, "Hey, wait a minute."

He went over to his bookshelves and unerringly put his hand to a volume—he knew where every one of his thousand books was to be found, on which shelf, to the right or left, down below or up above, as if some divining rod were leading him to the precise spot.

The volume was an old one, its spine and corners bound in tan calfskin, framing panels of a blue and red marbled parchment. He had comforted her for her embarrassment at the store but had then swiftly changed moods. She waited as he began searching the table of contents for the chapter he wanted, half muttering the words, "How to live on nothing a year." In a parenthesis of pause, he said more clearly, "I laughed my head off in school when I first read it." He thrust the volume toward her so she could read the title, *Vanity Fair*.

"I left the key word out," he said triumphantly as he turned to the proper page. "The old boy called it 'How to Live Well on Nothing a Year.' Live *well,* not just live, not just exist, not just keep alive, but live *well.*"

"Don't. You're making a joke out of it."

"Living well in this damnable world is no joke."

"The grocer doesn't think so either."

"The grocer. I bet he's socking away his little weekly sum in the stock market like every other jackass in the city."

"Please don't get off on jackasses and stock markets and the grocer's weekly little sum. Are there other unpaid bills at your office?"

Suddenly he was serious. "Plenty. They pile up, but I'll get at them—I always have."

"Pile up? You mean there's lots of them? Not just one or two but piles of them?" Her voice sounded gritty. "I'm not butting in, but—"

"Then drop it, Joss."

"Okay." There was command in his tone. She had never heard it before. She concentrated on her fingernails. "But if you do worry, more than you let on, if maybe one big reason you can't write in your spare time is because deep down you are all taken up with bills—"

He was studying her expression, as if he were reappraising, questioning her motives. Nor had she seen this skeptical look before.

"Maybe if we could clear the decks," she added hastily, "you *could* write at night or weekends."

"I'm just not that noble. Write shit all day and then write something worth writing?" He shook his head. "Maybe someday I'll have the willpower or whatever, but for now—"

"But it *is* now." Suddenly she remembered her father yelling about the twenty feet of water pipe, suddenly saw again the stricken face of her mother running from the kitchen while he shouted about "running up costs" and "extra charges." Her own voice had risen, grown emphatic as she said, "But it *is* now." She could hear it. There was something awful about money, about costs and charges and paying bills, something hateful and degrading, with a terrible power to make trouble and give pain.

Three

"I wish I had begun this," Jossie wrote, "when the first period of my life ended (school, college, virgin) and the present one began—this one of beauty and love and unafraidness with Rick."

She turned back to the preceding page and wrote at the top, "March 20, 1924," and reread what she had written there in her legible, squarish calligraphy on the lined sheets of a narrow loose-leaf notebook.

> Again I keep a diary, after seven years of not, only this time I call it a Journal—why the formality, I don't know. This I do know—the impulse to begin again came after I read my early diary to Rick. He was curiously touched by it—not by the personal, so much, the seeing of what I was at 17, but at seeing the strange way the ego in a growing person reaches out—any person, not just me—groping for experience, for sensations, the many things which give it its crystalized form. Its crystalizing form.
>
> Here I was at 16 and 17, eager for everything I deemed good and alluring, writing my adolescent ego into a book—showing how I was confident and powerful about some things, uncertain about others—it's interesting to have it now to look at and understand. I wished that I had kept on with it through Cornell and later. The first time I got the thrilling gorgeousness of just "thinking" abstractly, the first time I knew that the love of physical beauty—not people but trees, rivers, gorges, lakes—that this was to be a great force in me, the struggle to arrive at a moral code for myself while I was being naughty.

She crossed out "unafraidness with Rick," ended the paragraph, "and all my emotions about sex and passion—the beauty of the very first exploration into these astoundingly lovely things," and continued writing.

> Well, I didn't, but now the Journal begins again. It will be as complete and honest as I can make it. Maybe it's just ego, but it will be interesting to me since it's about me. That's all I'll write for today—simply the "few appropriate remarks that an auspicious occasion demands."

She closed the black leather notebook, only about half as wide as the loose-leafs she used to have in college, and put it away under her underwear and sweaters. She gave it a little pat of fond approval.

This was not one of the things to share with Rick, despite all of Havelock Ellis's injunctions about complete sharing with the beloved, disdaining secrets and subterfuge. They were reading Ellis's book *Impressions and Comments,* a collection of his little essays written during the war, and Rick had said it would be a sort of introduction, "to get you ready" for his new book *The Dance of Life*.

How lucky she was to have Rick to guide her in what she read, what music she heard, what pictures she saw. Never before had she been to a concert or an opera—there had been only her mother endlessly playing Caruso records of Italian arias, marvelous but so familiar there was no discovery about listening. With Rick it became real—last week they had gone to the Metropolitan uptown on Broadway, climbing fifty thousand stairs to sit under the rafters, like two birds perched on a high branch under a sweet sky, hearing the music pour forth from human throats way down below, lifting up to them above the other sounds of strings and reeds and brasses. It was *Die Meistersinger,* her first opera, the first great music she had ever heard coming not from a metal horn on a box but from living men and women, and her own throat grew so tight it was hard to swallow, but she had to gulp back any words even during the bursts of applause, for if she had tried to tell Rick what she was feeling, it would have sounded all mushy and young.

It was like the opening of a new perception, like seeing for the first time if you had been blind from birth and then suddenly given sight. Rick made everything like that—books, ideas, poetry—opening it all to her, expanding her vision and all her senses, so that everything in the world seemed changed. A lovely morning was lovelier than any other she had ever known, brighter, sweeter, a love song more piercing, a poem more poignant.

How could an unpaid grocery bill measure against that? Anyway, Rick was being punctilious now; he was bringing the monthly bills home from the office, checks made out and signed, letting her seal the envelopes and mail them, so she could know for herself that they were really done with. Or, on the ones that were not paid in full, that at least they were being reduced by a regular payment each month.

They had cut out going out for dinner and dancing because an evening would come to $6.00 or $8.00, but Carnegie Hall was 75 cents each and the Met and most theaters $1.00, so they spaced out these indulgences and enjoyed them all the more for the anticipation in between.

Anticipation heightened so many things, she thought, as she turned away from the bureau and her new journal. It was good to know that in a day or so, she would be writing in it again, and that in a week, she would be going into Mrs. Dunwoodie's office with her own check for $50 precisely three months from that wintry day last December when she had borrowed it. Each week when she had put aside that "Dunwoodie fiver" there was a small thrill, almost like the swift little stir of sex at the first touch, and now that the moment was so near it was almost like climbing up for that final tumble into climax.

That's awfully young and mushy too, she thought ruefully, but when she finally tapped at Amantha Dunwoodie's door, she actually was excited.

"Guess what I've got, Mrs. Dunwoodie," she said, holding out the folded check as she stood in the doorway. "I don't know how to thank you for helping me out."

"You already have." She reached for the check, dropped it on her desk without looking at it, and said, "Do you want any coffee? They've fixed the machine."

"I'd love some." This had never happened before; there was a certain formality about Mrs. Dunwoodie that put up walls and fences and markers to keep you away. She was copy chief of half the women's accounts in the office and had been there since Ashley started twelve years before. Some of the copywriters called her by her first name, but they were all as old as she was and had been there from the start too.

Amantha Dunwoodie was past forty, and to Jossie this vast spread of years between them was not only a fence and a marker but also a book of etiquette that told you what you could or couldn't do. First names with your bosses was one of the *nots*. People said that the looseness of manners and morals born of wartime was now laxer than ever, that morality was disappearing, and there were a million jokes about the wickedness of flappers and their boyfriends in the wildness of the Jazz Age. But nobody young would dream of calling Mrs. Dunwoodie Amantha, and now as Jossie watched her pour coffee into a large china mug, sudden bands of shyness tightened about her. She didn't know what on earth to talk about.

"It's probably gone cold by now," Mrs. Dunwoodie said. "Joan filled my carafe over an hour ago." Joan Sidings was her secretary.

Jossie sipped. "It's just fine."

"Cream, sugar?"

"I like it this way. It's just fine."

Mrs. Dunwoodie pointed a pencil to the top page of her office calendar. "Look what it says." She slid it across the desk so that Jossie could read it.

The foreign-looking handwriting Mrs. Dunwoodie used said, "J.S. 50,3/7." Through the final number there ran a slanting crossbar, bisecting its stem.

Maybe that's why her writing looks so funny, Jossie thought, but aloud she said, "Not even a question mark about March seventh?"

"Never for a minute. Usually I don't approve of loans inside the office, but—"

"Oh, I'm sorry—I didn't know that."

"I never hesitated over yours, did I? But if your college loan bothers you again, there are things you can do about more money outside the office. Did you know that?"

"One of those borrowing plans?"

"No. Free-lance here and there."

"Isn't that against the rules?"

"Not if you stay off conflicting accounts. A couple of people here do it. What's wrong with it?"

"Nothing. I never knew—I never even thought of it." She sat forward. "You mean I could write copy for some extra money, and it would be perfectly all right?"

"You'd be discreet about it, not tell everybody on earth about it, so the whole office could think they could manage it too. Most people can't, but you're a girl who could."

"Oh, Mrs. Dunwoodie, thanks. I might need—I don't right now—I still have three more months for Mary Watts—"

She felt she was burbling out sentences between excited little gasps, childlike and immature, but under her rapid phrases she was hearing again her father's scornful question, "How many girls get jobs on newspapers?" and her mother's quick reply, "Jossie will be the one who does." Here was Mrs. Dunwoodie doing the same thing her mother had done. It was even more wonderful coming from somebody in your office.

Amantha Dunwoodie saw that Jossie was flustered and decided to change the subject.

"You're not commuting any more," she said. "That must make life easier."

"Oh, it does. Except in rotten weather, I can walk to the office."

"I know. I see you every once in a while."

"See me?"

"I live just off Fifth, on West Tenth. You start out about half an hour earlier than I do and go right past my house." She waved her hand. "I'm past walking it, I grab a cab."

"It's only eighteen blocks up Fifth and then one over to Madison and I do love it, past Madison Square and—" She broke off, more flustered than before. Did Mrs. Dunwoodie mean *I see you every once in a while*, or *I see you and Rick?* Most of the time they followed their rule, even in the mornings, and went their separate ways, he up Sixth under the growling el, along all those dinky little stores and houses, and she up Fifth, meeting only after they reached the office and said good morning to each other like everybody else. But of late, it was true, it had become harder and harder to stick to their old rules about separating; it was so delicious to leave home together, walk together, never split off at any arbitrary fork in the road and go off alone.

"It was about a month ago," she said, as casually as she could, "that I moved in with this girl I know. We went to school together; she's in real estate, and I'd asked her if she knew anywhere I could find—"

"How lucky. Sharing apartments can be pretty dismal."

"It's way over west, past Greenwich Avenue. Do you know that row of little red brick houses?"

"I'm not a walker, as I said." She laughed a little. "I never get that far west."

The telephone rang and Jossie jumped up, made a gesture of farewell, and left. In a glassed-in space just outside Mrs. Dunwoodie's office, her secretary, Joan, was answering the phone, and Jossie darted by as if she were rushing to an appointment. A weaving discomfort shuttled through the frame of her feeling, back and forth, threading itself in and out of the tight strands of a new agitation. Mrs. Dunwoodie knew about Rick, knew about them living together, had seen them morning after morning, or enough mornings to know it was no accidental meeting on the way to work.

Was it awful that she knew, or didn't it matter? Had she told anybody else in the office? Did everybody know? For the rest of the morning Jossie was conscious of every look she received from anybody, no matter how casual. Was there a message behind it? Did it go "shame, shame," one index finger stroking the other index finger in the pantomime of childhood? Nobody but Andy Bellock was supposed to know, and he would die rather than give away their secret.

But he had given his word to Rick, and Mrs. Dunwoodie had never been asked to; if she had found them out by herself, would she feel honor-bound to reveal it to nobody else, the way Andy did?

I see you every once in a while. That was all she had said, after all; it wasn't Mrs. Dunwoodie who was going shame-shame at her, it was her own self, imagining that there was more to the phrase than the simple words. Maybe she *had* been alone the "once in a while" when Amantha Dunwoodie happened to look out of her window around the corner from Fifth. Probably she never had seen them together.

But a moment later Jossie knew she was simply trying to fool herself. Rick would accept this little episode for what it was and not try to hide behind the thin screen of maybe-she-didn't-mean-it. He was at a client's office this morning and would be there through most of the day. The afternoon went inching by, and she left at the dot of five-thirty, though she had never been one of the office clock-watchers.

It was seven before Rick got home, and as soon as she had told him what had happened, he ruled out any possibility that Amantha Dunwoodie didn't mean it. "She wouldn't have brought it up if you'd been alone," he said promptly. "What she meant was, 'I saw you and Rick on your way to the office after you had spent the night together.' The poisonous old bitch."

"Did she want to scare me, or warn me, or what?"

"She's like all women her age—jealous of anybody young, anybody attractive, anybody in love."

"I don't think 'jealous'; look at the way she lent me that money, look at the way she let me know I could free-lance and not get into trouble. She's been so kind—" She cut her sentence sharply. "I'm always thinking everybody is so kind! I know she'd never have mentioned it if she'd just seen me walking by myself."

"Whatever she's got in mind, just let her try it on. We'll figure out what she's up to and beat her at it."

"But we'd better never go by her house again."

"I'm not so sure about that. We might just take to going by there every damn morning from now on."

o o o

His dismissal of Amantha Dunwoodie cheered Jossie. There was a strong independence in it that gave her a new strength of her own. You didn't live life scared, once you were grown up; every time it threw a new problem at you, you had to take hold of it until it stopped being a problem at all. Out of this nettle, danger—something something. The rest of it would come to her any minute.

The next morning they did go right past Mrs. Dunwoodie's corner, though they did not know which specific house was hers, not even on which side of the street it was. They walked briskly as they neared Fifth Avenue, neither one looking up to check any of the windows.

It was one of those mild mornings that come in early March, promising warmth and brightness in the days ahead, though the trees and bushes in Washington Square Park and in the surrounding streets were still stripped tight with winter.

Jossie had come to love the entire neighborhood, so different from the busy, garish area known as Greenwich Village that was physically so near, and yet so far removed. She particularly loved West Tenth Street. It was a quiet street, untouched by modern times, looking the way it must have looked in the nineteenth century. There were rumors that a college was to be built there, or perhaps on West Eleventh or Twelfth, between Fifth and Sixth Avenues, not an undergraduate college, complete with leafy quads and football fields, but a college that would look like an office building, a college for adults, for advanced studies and special lectures in many fields.

There was no sign of it yet, nor of the apartment house, twenty stories high, that was to go up at the corner of Tenth Street and Sixth Avenue, but she wished that neither building would ever materialize.

She loved West Tenth Street just as it was. Two streets north of Washington Square with its noble arch and lovely park, its houses were all of a kind, red-brick and low, usually four stories above the basement floor. They had old fanlights over their front doors and long slender windows on their parlor floors. Many of them retained a flight of steps from the sidewalk to the level of the parlor floor, though many others had been modernized by having the flight removed, putting the entrance at street level, with a narrow well running the width of the house along the two windows that invariably belonged to the kitchen.

Rick's house was kin to all of them, though it had neither a long flight of steps nor the door at street level. It had instead three flat steps of white marble, like pictures she had seen of old houses in Philadelphia and Baltimore. The smaller rectangular well inside the low steps was outlined by an iron railing, painted a green so dark it looked black, its three supporting posts topped by small pineapple-shaped ornaments of brass, polished by Joe Marvin, the superintendent, so they gleamed and twinkled in the sun.

She would hate to give up walking on West Tenth, Jossie thought, just because of Amantha Dunwoodie. In the office, she felt an excitement because of their act of defiance that morning; there was a symbolism in it she could not name, and an exhilaration. Rules were made to be followed only by the rule-followers of the world.

Toward noon she was passing Rick's office, carrying two large layouts on crackly drawing paper and several sheets of copy. Through the frosted glass panel in his door, she could see that he was alone, and on impulse she tapped at the glass and went in.

He was pushed well back from his desk, back from the opened top drawer in it, the large shallow drawer revealing a litter of monthly bills from department stores: Lord & Taylor, Macy's, Altman's, McCreery's, twenty bills, perhaps thirty, as well as unfamiliar ones from Brooks Brothers, Knox, Dobbs—

She had never been inside expensive places like Knox and Dobbs and Brooks Brothers, but their names were familiar, and their reputations: luxury stores for men's clothing, suits, hats, shirts, ties, often called cravats. Even their bills set them apart from all the others, being smaller, more discreet; somehow their very choice of typeface, their quality of crisp paper, announced that they were not for ordinary people, and that they were perfectly content to reveal their snobbishness.

More discreet even than these was a bill from a firm called Drew, Tailors to Gentlemen. She had never even heard of it, had never seen any advertisement about it, and instantly she hated it, for it told her she was an outsider, laughed at her for thinking she could ever inhabit Rick's world, belong in it, be of it instead of merely visiting it.

"Why, Rick," she said. "You meant it when you said they pile up." She dropped the layouts and copy on his desk, looking only at the opened drawer.

"Sure," he said cheerfully. "Like a pile of shit in a stable."

"But I thought you were bringing them home."

"I do, but the ones I can't manage for the moment stay up here."

"You mean you owe money on all these?"

He slapped the drawer shut and stood up. His color deepened, but just then Betty Reed, the secretary he shared with Andy Bellock, came back, so he said composedly to Jossie, "The layouts are great, and the copy too. Jerton will okay it, you'll see." He smiled as he spoke, his usual smile, handsome, charming, but she took it for the dismissal she knew it was and left with a vague wave of her hand at Rick and Betty and the room in general.

But she kept seeing the spread of bills, a recurrent scene, like a movie projector gone crazy and repeating one scene again and again. Each time a blare of rage raced through her, roared through her, tonal as if it were shouting.

Head over heels in debt and he doesn't care. Head over heels in debt and he doesn't care.

Then I mustn't care either, she thought. I mustn't get to be like Papa, yelling about prices and running up costs and keeping out of debt. If Rick doesn't give a damn about all those bills, then I mustn't either. If he thinks it's funny to live well on nothing a year, he has every right to feel easy about the ones he keeps waiting. He'll get around to them when he's good and ready; he told me so, and he will.

When he came home that night, she was cooking dinner. She had become a reliable if not wondrous cook; gone were the early days when she had flipped open the oven door on lamb chops that had caught fire, only to singe her eyebrows and the hair above her forehead. She thought now of that night almost with fondness—Rick had been terrified for her, had cared so much, had babied her, tended the flaming skin of her forehead, first with butter, then with some ointment he had in his army kit, had brushed away the burnt wisps of hair, made her lie down, brought her a drink, though she never needed a drink for any crisis.

Why was she dwelling now on that small happiness? She heard his key and ran to the door and at once saw something new in his glance, a tightness there, a coldness. She should have said nothing at the office, whatever it was she had said. She couldn't remember exactly, but she wished now that she had never said it at all. She certainly wouldn't mention the bills again.

"Rick, you always say we're not to keep secrets from each other."

"About real things, not about unpaid bills."

"Unpaid bills are real things."

"I also always say that my problems aren't to become your problems, and those bills in my desk *are* my problems." His voice was hard. "They're just none of your business."

Fear coiled through her, coated in an unnamed misery, like a metal wire inside a thick insulating tubing. He had never talked to her that way, never looked at her that way. If she ever lost Rick she couldn't bear it.

"I didn't mean to butt in." Her voice faltered, like a boy's voice when it was changing during adolescence, and her eyes suddenly stung. She could think of nothing at all except that she must not cry; people hated it when you cried. But the tears came, hot and intractable.

There was no sympathy in Rick's face, only disapproval, perhaps disgust.

"I'm sorry," she said. "I'm honestly so sorry." He said nothing and suddenly she thought, All of a sudden it's turned around, and I'm the one apologizing. It's always that way; whenever I have a fight with anybody, with Nell or Papa, it always gets twisted around to where I'm the one who's wrong. I shouldn't have said this; I shouldn't have felt that; it's all my fault.

She turned toward the kitchenette. "I guess we have to have dinner."

"Not me," Rick said abruptly. "I'm going out."

The door closed behind him softly, and she stared at its blind surface. Then she turned off all the burners on the range and went to their bedroom. There was no way to stand this surge of pain, the fine metal wire now white hot, its tubing grown large, gummy, a viscous stream flowing into the tiniest cells throughout her mind and body.

○ ○ ○

At ten he returned, rushing to her, half lifting her from the bed into his arms. "It's all my damn fault, darling. Something got into me, I don't know what." He brushed her hair with his fingers, feeling the dampness at the nape of her neck; he kissed her eyes and lips and cheeks, tasting the salt on her skin.

"Oh, Rick, I couldn't bear it," she said.

"I couldn't either, my darling girl." He was opening her blouse, opening his shirt. There was a new energy in every gesture, as if he were still angry; gone was the gentleness, gone the quiet of his usual approach to sex with her. Again and again he came to her; each time he would be more powerful in his thrust; each time, after a brief rest, he would turn back to her and make love to her again.

Not love, Jossie thought. This wasn't like making love; she didn't know what it was, but it was new. She ought to hold back from it, maybe, resent it, feel somehow shamed by it, but none of that was true. It was marvelous.

At last he said, "I'll never do that again, darling, rush out on you like that. Never. Something went haywire, I suddenly couldn't take it. If you're angry at me—"

"I'm not anything except happy." She thought, I *am* happy.

○ ○ ○

A week passed before they spoke of the unpaid bills, and it was Rick who brought up the subject. This time he was himself again, open, considerate. "Jossie, it *is* a problem that affects you as well as me, and I know it. I can't just partition off one part of my life and say, 'Keep Off the Grass.' It's just that when I'm low, I get this impulse to go to Brentano's, say, and buy a couple of decent books; there's a sort of push inside, like Dostoevski's gambler who couldn't make himself stop."

"Low about what? Me? Us?" She paused. "Jean?"

"Mostly about the day-to-day work I do, writing lousy commercial stuff instead of what I want to write."

"Oh, Rick, if only you could write at night, here at home, even a little bit—"

"If only! A hundred times I've told myself I was going to start that same evening, give it a try, get something started. But by the end of the day at Ashley, nothing; it just doesn't happen." He ran his fingers through his thick hair, turning a strand of it round and round on his index finger. It was a habit, a trick of personality, but she had come to know it as a signal: of deliberation, of perplexity, of distress.

"Maybe it's not only the day-to-day work," she said tentatively. "Maybe there are other things on your mind that you don't even think *are* on your mind."

"Like money?"

"You wouldn't be the only one in the world. Oh, darling, can't we work this out together? We could save a lot on daily household bills and—"

"Save a lot? On what?"

"We could cut out some of the things we just take for granted, and never miss them after a while."

Again he said, "Like what?"

"Well, if I read your copy of the *World* every morning, instead of letting them deliver two separate copies—"

"That would save six cents a week." He laughed openly. "Maybe for a while we ought to get two copies on Sunday too, so you could cut out yours and save another five cents."

"We could save a dime if we read *Time* magazine at the office instead of buying it, and a nickel more if you did that with *The Saturday Evening Post*."

Again he laughed, this time indulgently. "So far we've saved twenty-six cents a week, my darling, and not a damn thing in the house to read."

"There must be other stuff, if we tried to think," she persisted. "Oh, Rick, it would make me so happy to get some of your money worries off your mind, and you started writing."

"With you sitting around every night, just watching me write?"

"I wouldn't care. If you could feel happy, sort of free enough to work at what you want to do—there must be some way we could change things so you could get started."

Suddenly he kissed her. "You're good, Joss," he whispered. "What they call good goods. I love you. Maybe we *could* change. We'll try." He glanced over to their bedroom, where the small desk he used stood up against the tall window that looked out at the garden plot, still rigid with winter. He went over to it, brought forth a small sheaf of empty pages, picked up a pen, and sat down. "Voilà," he said.

But that night he began to work. He asked if she'd mind his not talking about what he was doing, if she'd mind his not letting her read any of it until it was done.

"It's something I've had in mind quite a while," he said, "even though it won't run to more than thirty, forty pages."

"Of course I don't mind."

She looked at the bedroom door closing after him and was buoyed up on a fresh tide of trust and hope. This was a new beginning for them; he was trying a story, a serious story it would be, not about golden debs and ritzy parties but something for Mencken's new magazine, *The American Mercury*, or some other fine literary publication. All he needed was to see his work in print once again, and that would be influence enough to keep him at it. He had been so young the other time, a college boy, and then had come marriage and war and a hundred responsibilities; here was the second act beginning. And this time she was part of it.

° ° °

He kept it up evening after evening. He would leave the table, taking his coffee with him, and close the door of their room. He wrote in longhand, so there was no tapping of a typewriter to hear, but it was almost as though she could feel his pen gliding over the yellow paper he used, and until he emerged two hours later, she never shook free of the sense of participation in this new phase of his life. Work well, darling Rick, be happy.

"God, I feel good," he said one evening as he came back to the living room where she was playing the Victrola softly. "You know what a helpmeet is? You're my helpmeet."

"Is it—do you like it?"

"I think yes. It's going along." The phone rang and he spoke into it in the parody Southern accent he could summon at will when he was in high spirits. "Yes, suh, Mr. Baird's residence, suh." Then he laughed. "Hey there, Andy. No, I just finished tonight's installment, and if you don't get off that comedy line, I'll shove your teeth back a couple yards." A moment later he turned to Jossie and said, "How'd you like a weekend in a log cabin by a lake that's still frozen? He says I rate a reward for diligence."

"At Andy's? I'd just love it. Which weekend?"

"Saturday morning. He and Edie are driving up to list it with real estate agents up there, and said would we like to, despite the rotten weather."

"And you said, 'we'd love to.'"

"We'll have to sleep on army cots in the living room," he said as he hung up.

"I'd sleep on the floor. If only tomorrow were Saturday."

He laughed. There was the eternal child in Jossie; she was never tepid about anything. She *wanted,* she couldn't wait, she never was calm and judicious about life. It gave her a ceaseless spring of energy he envied; long ago he had known it himself, within himself, but somehow it had quieted down and seeped away without his even knowing of the loss. Had it begun to return, these past nights of work?

"They might not be using it much this year," he added. "Their third kid must make it impossible. My guess is that if they don't sell it right away, they might lend it to us now and then."

o o o

They set out in a sleety rain under low skies, trees whipped by raffish winds all the way up to Peekskill. The countryside was bleak; it was easy to visualize Sing Sing Prison a short distance from them on the Hudson. But as they arrived at the Bellocks' cottage, set close to the edge of Peekskill's Lake Mohegan, Jossie's mind eradicated the drabness and deadness of the woods, the expanse of water glassy with ice, a world muted and inert, and felt instead how it would be in another few weeks, the trees and bushes coming into their first frail greening, flowers appearing everywhere, the air alive with the singing of birds.

"Oh, I love it," she cried as they left the car. The cottage was an elongated low cabin, its logs horizontal, made longer by a surrounding porch that seemed to wrap itself around all four sides. She could imagine herself and Rick up there alone over some hot summer weekend, if the Bellocks did indeed ever lend them the place, could imagine them swimming and paddling and fishing during the day, then in bed together, the night dark and sweet and silent, except for the sounds of the woods around them.

Before the day was gone, she found herself hoping the Bellocks wouldn't find any takers for a month or two at least. They were asking $3,000, half in cash, and it was a good enough buy, but other families with children, like Andy and Edie with their three, also had to have more than one bedroom and might be forced to reject it despite its appeal and charm.

"If we had fifteen hundred in cash," Rick joked at supper, "you'd be writing a bill of sale tonight." He looked across the table. "Wouldn't he, Jossie?"

"I've never been in a summer place half as nice," she said. "My father always thought living in New Rochelle was 'enough summer place for anybody.'" She laughed ruefully. "'What's so wrong with a trolley ride to the beach?' he used to say."

Instantly she was back there with Nell, begging their mother to make their father see why it was so awful to be the only ones they knew who didn't go away to the shore or to the mountains, for the whole summer or maybe even for a month, just so they could tell all their friends later on where they had been and not have to listen in a private anguish of envy while their friends described all their own summer delights.

"Everybody I know," she had cried out one night at supper, "is getting packed to go somewhere the day school is out."

"Everybody," her father had mocked. "We always have to hear about this everybody. Does everybody's parents teach summer school every year? Or you want to go off alone?"

"You needn't be sarcastic—"

"S-s-sh, Jossie," her mother put in. "The beach is lovely. You always say so yourself."

"But lugging wet bathing suits, and taking sandwiches along, it's so rotten. If we were *poor*, that would be one thing, but we're not poor—"

"Rich, poor," her father said, rising from his chair and leaving the table. "If you had to pay mortgages and water taxes and everything else, *then* you could talk about rich or poor."

"So it won't be a quick sale," Edie was saying, bringing Jossie back to the present. "We might have to rent it out for a summer or two, at that."

They had already found another house, on the far side of the lake, with the required extra rooms, and put down a deposit on it. They had all gone to see it, and it was delightful in its own way, more spacious certainly, far more formal. Jossie had murmured all the appropriate remarks, meaning them on the surface of her mind and rescinding them in her interior scale of measurement. The new house was for family life; the cabin was for youth and new love.

o o o

On Monday morning there was a letter from Paris. As always Jossie felt a faint tug of unwillingness at the sight of the handsome French stamps, as if they were code for "Don't forget me; I'm still here." She never knew when Rick wrote Jean, for he did all his mail at the office, but Jean's letters always came to the apartment, and no matter what else was in the morning post, there was a high visibility about the ones from Paris.

Usually Rick read parts of her letters aloud as he went along, bits about the children, about Jean's lessons, certainly anything about her work being considered for an art show or actually shown to a dealer. But this time he read from beginning to end in silence. He was distressed, and as yet unready to reveal the reason.

What if, thought Jossie, Jean were saying that she had decided to come back home to live? What if, after all this time, she was suddenly protesting what she knew of Rick and herself here on West Tenth Street? Being civilized, being modern, accepting the needs of others under given circumstances of separation—all this was very well in theory; had she not herself, Jossie, been more than able to absorb the knowledge that there was another part of life for Rick that she did not share?

It was so easy to forget that other part of Rick's life, she thought now, until one of the letters from Paris came in its pale blue envelope with the beautiful foreign stamps that were so much more intriguing than ordinary American stamps. It had been a month or so since the last letter from Jean; try as she would, Jossie could not think of any of Jean's letters as "just mail," and now, as Rick sat on silently while she cleared the breakfast dishes, the uneasy sense of occasion deepened.

"That was bad news in Jean's letter," he said suddenly as they left for work. "She's never seriously sick, but this might mean an operation."

"What kind of operation? Oh, Rick, I'm sorry."

"A hysterectomy."

"Oh, no." An instant later she said, "I'm not sure what that is."

"It's removing the uterus."

"How terrible."

"It's not certain yet. They're doing tests."

"What tests? What makes them think of operating?"

"She's often been irregular about her periods, but for a few weeks she's been staining between periods, and finally she went to a specialist. That's what they're doing tests about. It might be just polyps or something else minor, but—"

"When will they know?"

"They can't even tell her that. She sounds pretty frightened."

They walked on in silence. Then Jossie asked, "Are you thinking of going over there, in case—I mean, if it is going to be an operation?"

"I don't know what I'm thinking." It was truer than he could let himself say aloud. Mixed with his fears for Jean, mixed with his caring for what she must be going through in this time of waiting, was a resistance that he could not admit even to himself. Specialists cost money, hospital bills could not be ignored as tailors' bills and department store charges could be. It was shameful even to think of such mundane matters now, but there it was.

"I've got to earn more money," he said abruptly. "Emergencies come up, and there's not a dime's leeway."

"Ask for another raise?"

"No, they never give interim raises. I might look for a better job."

"At another agency?"

"Ashley isn't the only place in town. By now I could put together a proof book that would land me a spot at one of the younger shops, where they're paying top dough to get staffed."

"Of course you could."

But looking for a job was one of the most nerve-wracking things in the world. Maybe Rick had forgotten, because he'd been at Ashley so long. But it was still vivid to her. And then when you found one, there was the whole new-broom period of proving yourself to the new copy chief, the new account executive, the clients themselves.

They stopped at a Western Union office, and Rick went in to send a cable to Jean. "I told her not to worry," he said when he rejoined Jossie. "That if it had to be the hysterectomy I'd be there, and that whatever it was, I'd manage the money end of it somehow."

"I know you will."

That evening as she brought their coffee to the table, Rick stayed seated, glancing toward the desk in the bedroom and then away.

"Let's get out of this high grass," he said at last. "Let's go to

Gypsy's for a drink." Gypsy's was a speakeasy on Sheridan Square. "Or even to Henri's." Henri's was a famous French restaurant, too expensive to go to often. He had taken her to Henri's the first night they'd slept together. "I'm too restless to write anything worth a damn tonight."

They went out.

Four

"Spring—and my heart full of it," she wrote in her journal three weeks later. "A good deal of sadness at the idea of spring in the city—visions of Ithaca in April and May, with beauty everywhere, the gorges full of feathery trees, serene and tranquil over the crazily rushing waterfalls, the hills across Cayuga changing into a patchwork of the lushest softest greens, the lake itself, the lilacs, the firm sweet grass underfoot."

> Spring in New York, with all the noise and clang of trolleys and els and trucks and cars, the hot fetid smells, is a peculiar twisting of this time that should be so quiet and shimmery and young. But it doesn't *get* me as it would if I were here alone. I don't mean that my being so happy with Rick gives city streets any sham loveliness, but they don't make me miserable as they would if it weren't Rick and me together.
>
> We read in Walt Whitman's *Specimen Days* last night—his love of trees and birds and bees and flowers goes through his life untouched by any pain or loss. I sometimes feel humbly grateful at this good accident that put this deep susceptibility about these lovelinesses into me. I might have simply not had it—might have lived without this, one of the deepest happinesses I know.
>
> We read for an hour and then talked—about the way reading something really moving can help you understand more about other emotions. It made me feel better about being able to be so happy while poor Jean still doesn't know what the outcome is to be.
>
> This is the first really unhappy time I've had about Jean, and in a way it's terribly selfish, thinking what might be ahead for me, instead of only what might be for her. I've had half hours of jealousy of Jean before, her being Rick's wife, bearing his name before the world—really bearing it—but they were easily shipped out by my bigger feelings of unafraidness and serenity. But this time of continued waiting—they've done a curettage (sp?) on her and still remain unsure if that's all she needs, still can't decide whether she'll have to have the operation that would cut out the living vital elements in her, rob her of this beautiful energy and spirit that has its roots in sex, leaving her feeling different, useless. Not that she'd ever want any more children, but just the inner knowledge that she's still *complete*.

> I've been feeling that if it did happen to her, it would be some sort of end for me too. Because then I could never let Rick tell her more fully about our life together, our love, as he has been planning to do, not let him add to her feeling of *finished*, sort of flaunting my youth and health and sex.
>
> I've come to share Rick and Jean's perfect sureness about honesty with each other, the way H. Ellis felt about a sort of purity of honesty between him and Olive Schreiner, and then with his wife, Edith, even when they each went off with other lovers and went through the temporary pain or jealousy of letting the *true* love know, the abiding love, so there was never any cheap deception, never the nasty lies and secrets. Just as Rick told me from the first about Jean and then told her about me.
>
> Please, no surgery. Please. Then the day can come when Rick will be talking to Jean not only about the two of them but also me as a new part fitted into them.

She reread the last page and set the journal aside, wondering why she suddenly felt a little sad. Maybe seeing it written out that way, all that about not letting Rick ever talk to Jean *if*—maybe putting it down in her own words, as if it were a sort of equation—something in those words she had herself set down all at once seemed to contain a warning. Of what she did not know, but there was an uneasiness in it, nearly a hurt, but a hurt she could not locate or define.

She closed her fountain pen and stretched the fingers of her right hand, surprised to find them tight with cramp. She must have been writing for a long time. She rose from the sofa, went to the closed door of their bedroom, and stood still. Rick had asked her once not to come in while he was writing, and she was punctilious about it; she never minded being interrupted when she was working, but most people did and she could understand that.

Behind the closed door lay a total silence. There was no crunch of a sheet of paper being rolled into an impatient ball and thrown at the wastebasket, no sound of a match being lit, no sound of Rick's pacing back and forth while he thought out some sentence or idea.

Tonight was the night when he had suddenly said at dinner, "Enough of this—back to the factory," rising and taking his coffee and leaving the table. She had said, "Good," clapping back into her vocal cords a dozen other words clamoring to be said: "I thought you'd never" or "I was so worried that you'd keep on making excuses"—anything like that would have been inexcusable. But the words had said themselves in her own mind in the last days, as there continued to be no definite word from Paris, not for a second week, or a third. Night after night they had gone out the minute dinner was over, sometimes only to walk the streets of Washington Square and on into the Village itself, with Rick saying, "I just can't get back to it until I know one way or the other."

"Nobody could."

But even after the curettage, when the French gynecologist had said, "We'll now wait until the next period, to see if all is again normal," even then Rick had been unable to get back to his desk in the evening.

Trollope's mother. She suddenly drew back, as if she had said the words out loud, a cruel stab at him, a goad not to be borne. But though the words rang in her own mind so vividly that they seemed to have taken shape and voice, she could not have uttered them aloud, for Rick had not stirred.

In English Lit at college she had had to read *Barchester Towers* and been bored stiff with it, but later, on her own, she had come across *Phineas Finn* and lost her heart to it in three nights of "reading my eyes out," as she put it when she talked about the experience of a book that completely enthralled her. The phrase was one her mother often quoted, her mother the English teacher who was constantly frustrated and rebuffed by high-school students who thought of books mainly as "assignments."

"Here, Jossie," her mother had once said, "Trollope's autobiography—you'll like it. What a family."

She loved talking about books with her mother. They liked the same things, often fell over each other's sentences in their enthusiasm for something they had read and were discussing. Her mother never sounded like a teacher when they talked, never grew pontifical or authoritative about what was good in a book or what was not. And on the rare occasions when her mother said, "Here's a book—you'll like it," she tore into it at once, like a child on Christmas morning opening a bright package.

And she had stayed up for hours that very night reading chapter after chapter, fascinated by it all but stunned by the young Trollope's own view of his mother, who had been fifty before she wrote page one of chapter one of her first book, and who had then gone on to write over a hundred books until her death—travel books, novels, everything. In thirty years she had never found a reason for not writing. She had written because she had to, to earn money for her family, had written no matter what, no matter how tired, how weary, how heartbroken. There was a period, Jossie suddenly remembered now, when she had been the sole nurse of a dying son and a dying husband, giving them their medicines, tending them, bathing them, and sitting by their deathbeds writing half the night away, because she was bound by the need to "keep a decent roof over them to die under."

The phrase rushed back into Jossie's mind, swift and clear, an arrow. It was taking on a piercing meaning now, and she drew sharply back. It was futile to compare writers or painters or composers, even more than to compare ordinary people. No two teachers taught alike; surely her mother was a teacher more equable, more patient with her pupils than her father with his; even at Ashley, some copywriters could dash off a piece of copy and never rewrite it, while others, herself for one, could dash it off just as quickly, but then look at it with distrust and go at it word for word, cutting, transposing, rewriting, erasing, discarding in favor of some other approach, often building up such confusion and uncertainty in her own mind that she finally came back to the first draft as to an island in a storming sea.

But she was the stubborn type. One of the family stories was about her mother's sending her out one afternoon when she was six years old, to get a loaf of bread and a bottle of milk at the grocery store. It was Good Friday or the start of Passover or something, but her mother had forgotten about the holiday. Their own grocery store was closed, so Jossie had gone a few blocks to another, and then to another and yet another, until she came to one run by some Protestants or atheists or somebody who didn't close early for either of those holidays, and bought her loaf of bread and bottle of milk.

When she finally got home, it was almost dark and her mother was in hysterics, on the verge of calling the police for her child, missing or kidnapped or murdered as she had to be, to account for her three-hour absence.

"Jossie sticks to things." That became the slogan, the shibboleth, which she cherished for a while as a compliment and then began to regard as a criticism. They could make it sound either way, meaning either that she was strong, admirable, or that she was fanatic, obsessed. "'Jossie sticks to things?'" her sister, Nell, would mock her after some tug-of-war. "You mean she can be a pest."

It was one of life's little tricks, that the same words could lift your pride or hurt your feelings. Why was she suddenly remembering that childhood story now, facing Rick's closed door and the silence beyond it? From Trollope's mother to that six-year-old's grocery hegira—there was a train of thought for you. She retreated in embarrassment at the notion; she detested holier-than-thou attitudes in anybody. Yet it was true that if she had been Rick, she would probably have been back at that desk long before tonight, worry about Jean or not.

If you had work to do, you did it, no matter what. You could put it off for a day, two days, three, when you were sick or distracted about something, but then you went back to it despite the sickness or distraction. But Rick was Rick; he had his own ways, his own rhythms. And he had finally gone "back to the factory."

She moved closer to the door, her ear touching the wood. Still nothing. She started to call out, but instead put her hand to the knob, turning it so gently there was no sound. The door opened on a sliver of light; in that single perpendicular bar of illumination was their bed, and Rick on it, sound asleep.

She withdrew as if she had seen something illicit, as if she had spied upon a helpless victim of her own greed to know.

° ° °

The next morning four letters came from Paris, but not in Jean's pale blue envelopes. These were business letters, bearing doctors' names, and before Rick tore them open, she knew they would be bills. He glanced at them one by one and then read each one a second time before tossing them over to her.

"How can any man stay the hell free enough to—?"

She finished his sentence for herself as she went through the four bills. One was from Jean's gynecologist, one from an anesthesiologist, another from a laboratory, and the last from the hospital. They were in francs, thoughtfully translated into dollars. The largest was from M. Leclerq, for five visits: $25. The smaller ones were for $10, $4, and, for Jean's three nights in a private room in the hospital, $21. She totaled them quickly but said nothing.

Rick said nothing either. They walked to the office slowly, for the weather had suddenly turned hot enough for June. "Days like this," Rick said, "I regress to the ole South. Shady side of the street and just amble."

"What shade?" She pointed to the tentative leaves of a newly planted maple, its slender trunk encircled by padded bands of burlap at the lower branches, from which retaining wires ran down to stout pegs in the ground.

"It's the principle of the thing."

"We're ahead of New Rochelle, anyway. Our trees up there are always two weeks behind city trees. Behind our house we have three fat old dogwoods—they'll be starting any day now."

At the office she telephoned her mother. Just as with Nell, she knew her mother's teaching schedule by heart, knew when she would be teaching and when she would have an empty period to spend in the faculty room. In a family full of teachers, the only one she never called during school hours was her father.

"Happy springtime, Mom. It's me."

"Is it lovely in the city too?"

"Today is. I just realized we hadn't talked in a while."

"Haven't we?"

"Why don't you nag at me to phone more often, the way you're supposed to?"

"I know the limitations, that's why. How are you?"

"Fine, mostly. This sudden heat wave reminds me of Ithaca."

"New Rochelle can't compete with Ithaca, but would you like to see the season in, up here, maybe this weekend? The forsythia's a marvel."

"Gosh, Mom, I can't. Aren't you ever coming to New York?"

"Actually I am, on Saturday. I've an appointment with Dr. Herbst. That inlay is coming loose again."

"Good. I don't mean good about the inlay, but good about you coming in. Why don't we have lunch?"

"Fine, Jossie." There was a pause. "Are you all right? You sound a little—"

"A little what?"

"High-strung, I guess. A bit nervous. And you're calling me Mom instead of Mama or Ma."

Jossie laughed, but now it was she who paused. "Oh, Mom, I wish I knew the answers to various things."

"You know more answers than most people your age. Anyway, if you want to talk about whatever it is, we can on Saturday."

It was late that afternoon that Jossie got the idea. She was idling through the uninspiring pages of a periodical, *Glass World*, one of the dozen or so business magazines that were regularly routed through the office as they appeared. Most of them were trade papers she had never heard of before she came to Ashley: dental magazines, dairymen's journals, ironmongers' monthlies, others dealing with the automotive industry, with lumber, farming, tool and die manufacturing, even this dull one about making and selling all kinds of glass. She paused at an ad by the Empire State Plate Glass Company of New York.

A piece of glass, she thought, and a plate-glass window. Suppose you looked through any old pane of glass—but then looked through a sheet of pure plate glass.

She heard a small sound issue from her throat. She was chortling. Chortles were something she knew only in books; she had never ever heard anybody in real life chortle. Laugh, yes; guffaw, yes; chuckle, maybe. But chortle? She finished the ad. Dull, dead.

Then it was that she thought, I'll write them and see.

She began to read the articles and other ads about the world of glass. There were uncountable kinds of glass, window glass, mirrors, glass pendants for chandeliers, glass vases, glass ashtrays, special glass for windshields on cars, lenses for spectacles, for microscopes, telescopes. . . .

She was dumbfounded. Not only by the profusion of objects made from glass, but by the profusion of species in that single area of human endeavor, all of the above and a hundred more: crystal for wineglasses, Venetian glass, stained glass, spun glass, engraved glass, combustion tubing, and now this newly developing laminated glass that was the subject of the stuffy ad by the Empire State Plate Glass Company of New York.

She read the ad once more. Their factory was somewhere in Pennsylvania, but their executive office and salesroom was right in New York City. Right on Fourth Avenue, a few blocks from Ashley. A salesroom? Did they have panels of glass hanging there, and were they all as dull, as opaque, as the copy in their ad?

The word *opaque* made her chortle again. It's first cousin to a chuckle, she thought; that's what a chortle is, only deeper and more secret.

She hadn't thought of Mrs. Dunwoodie's little speech about free-lancing since the morning she'd heard it, but suddenly it was sitting there looking at her from the pages of *Glass World*.

She reached for a sheet of office stationery but immediately set it aside. It would be unethical, perhaps, to use Ashley stationery, and certainly inadvisable. She had none of her own, but she slipped out and went straight to Lord & Taylor and bought a box of white vellum with envelopes to match. She chose the long narrow kind, mannish-looking or businesslike, instinct telling her to avoid anything fluttery or feminine.

Already she was making up the letter in her mind. It would go to the Advertising Director of the firm, and it would have to catch his eye in the first sentence or he would never go on to the next. How would it go? *Dear Sir,* to start with, and then what?

> Opaque or translucent? Dull or clear? So many ads in the April issue of *Glass World* struck me as being dull that I'd like to try a little window-washing with a different kind of copy.
>
> I'm a copywriter at Ashley & Company, just getting past the cub copywriter role, and I've been told there's no objection to doing a little free-lance copy outside the office, provided there's no conflict with any account here.
>
> And I have an idea that, I think, might add a bit of sparkle to somebody's campaign about this new laminated plate glass. Perhaps even yours.
>
> My telephone number at the office is Murray Hill 4211, and I do not need to keep it a secret if you should call. Which is what I hope you will want to do.
>
> Thank you in advance.

She mailed the letter the same afternoon; the next morning she was barely seated at her desk before the bell rang. Mr. Grover Cleveland Albright, Advertising Director of Empire State Plate Glass Company, would indeed like to see her. There were no further ads on this year's schedule, but would she be interested in writing one or two direct-by-mail letters until they began planning next year's campaign?

She would indeed. At noon the next day she went to the office of the Empire State Plate Glass Company, taking with her proofs of all the ads she had ever done for Ashley and, for luck, her dear old silver dollar and piece of ore.

° ° °

"Rick, I'm so happy I could die," she said, holding out the check. It was a large gray check, and her name was punched out in small raised letters.

Rick whistled. They had just came in from the office on Saturday, and the afternoon mail had just come.

"Twenty bucks," she said, "for two short letters. It was so easy. Oh, darling, isn't it wonderful?"

"You're what's wonderful." He hugged her and then held the check high above his head. "Let's frame it—a bright red mat around it and one of those modern new box frames."

"And they want more. They really do. Maybe real copy for real ads in the fall."

"They'd have to spring for more than ten dollars for a real piece of copy. My smart intelligent gifted girl."

"I couldn't have done it without you."

"Flattery will—"

"No, honestly. All your help? Reading every new version, making edit suggestions, being *with* me all the way—I can tell in a second if you think anything's wrong in anything I show you."

"So you found out I'm a good copy chief. Good! But the star is the one who writes it, and that's you."

He seized her, and then fixed drinks to celebrate, and later took her to bed. This, Jossie thought, is where everything becomes so wonderful you can't bear it. Here is where you really discover what you mean to another human being. This is why you're born and grow up and wait and look and hope that some day you'll find out for yourself—

God, did this happen to other girls in love, was there any other kind of joy that could compare with this, this gorgeous something sweeping through your whole body, your whole heart? This then was the perfect full meaning of what it meant to be in love. Why didn't anybody tell you while you were growing up toward it? They never did tell you, not your parents, not those lying classes at college, where they talked in diagrams and organs and cells and cycles and never once dared to speak out about beauty and this marvelous pleasure, starting at a touch and then turning into this golden molten crystal bursting like all the stars in the universe.

They fell asleep, and when Jossie awoke it was early evening. She tiptoed to her purse, took out her copies of the two letters, and read them again, pretending that she was not herself but Mr. Grover Cleveland Albright, reading them for the first time, reading them as if he had just opened the envelope bearing them in the office mail, seeing those sentences and phrases for the first time and not knowing yet whether he would like what he read or not, whether he would want to use those letters for his company or discard them.

She glanced at Rick, hoping he would remain asleep. There was something surreptitious in what she was doing, but she was amused at it. A mutual admiration society, she thought, me admiring me.

They were *good,* the two letters. Rick had indeed helped her, had kept her from being flip—"cute won't do"—but he hadn't even questioned her main idea or edited out her own turn of phrase.

The first letter began with a square inch of glass pasted to the top like a postage stamp, just under the letterhead of The Empire State Plate Glass Company, Inc. If she were Mr. Grover Cleveland Albright, who had been okaying the insipid flat boring old stuff appearing in the trade papers—if she were he opening this letter for the first time, that square inch of glass up there would have been like a nice fresh gust of air in a spell of steaming humidity.

"Enclosed you will find a small square of glass," the letter began.

> It isn't broken, isn't splintered, wasn't shattered by the stamping device at the post office.
>
> It is a sample of the new unbreakable glass we have recently introduced to our customers.
>
> There are other unbreakables in the world of glass, but we believe there is nowhere anything as perfect or reliable.
>
> It costs more than ordinary glass and it should.
>
> If you are one who looks constantly for new achievements in the world of industry, you will want one of our top salesmen to call.
>
> We think you are; thus this letter.

She had got the idea of the square inch of glass right there in her session at Mr. Albright's office. It had been like a cram course in the intricacies and mysteries of glass manufacture, and for a while she had gone groggy with his talk about synthetic resins and autoclaves, and lehrs, anti-actinic glass, anti-caloric glass, and the whole developing story of the search for glass that would never shatter. The only part she really took in was the story of the early years of the search, how a French chemist working on some sort of cellulose nitrate dropped a bottle of it and noticed that though the bottle broke, the mess still kept its bottle shape, the tiny splinters and shards apparently clinging to the evaporated cellulose nitrate film.

"That was before the war," Mr. Albright had said, but she scarcely listened as he went on to the British experiments in the same sort of "resistance glass" and its first use for gas masks as protection against the Germans' mustard gas.

Paste a piece of it on the letter, she was thinking. Why can't we stick a small square of it right at the top? Even if it did go wrong in the mail, it would keep its squareness.

She had gone into the meeting not yet sure of what she would say if he reminded her that she had introduced herself by saying she had "an idea that might add a little to somebody's campaign." It's only half developed, she would have told him, and still needs working out. But he hadn't asked anything as direct as that, and she had rather fobbed off any difficult questions by her own eagerness to learn more about this still-to-be-perfected laminated glass that was already used for the windshields of the most expensive and superior cars.

But even as he answered her own questions, even as she jotted down hasty notes of all the technicalities she knew she would never use in actual copy, she kept on thinking, We could paste a piece right under their letterhead, like a shiny little flag.

Now she opened the second of her two letters. On this, too, a small square perched atop the lines of typing, but this one was of shattered glass, glued carefully so its tiny fragments would not, could not fall apart.

> We sent you last week the dead opposite of this sorry mess—a sample of our new improved unshatterable glass that showed you a new generation of plate glass.
>
> That sample showed up this flawed and broken one as the obsolete thing it is fast becoming in many industries.
>
> We told you that our new unbreakable glass costs more than the old vulnerable kind, and we are already making further cost analyses of how great an increase there may have to be in the 1925 manufacturing price.
>
> Thus it would be to your advantage, as well as to our own interest, if we could have a discussion of possible sales to your company, and have it quickly.
>
> One of our top salesmen could be in your office within a day of a phone call.

Behind her there was a stir and a mutter of speech. "What are you doing?" Rick asked. "Standing there stark naked, reading mail from your beloved?"

There was laughter in his voice, and approval. He knew perfectly well what she was doing; they had both talked about the special satisfaction there was in reading something they had written *after* it had been officially accepted, after it had changed from the tentative to the positive, after it had stopped being a "maybe" and had become a "yes."

"I was wondering if I ought to show them to Mr. Jerton at the office," she said.

"Sure if you want to. There's no 'ought to' about it."

"Maybe Mrs. Dunwoodie instead. She's the one who said it was okay to do it."

"You're not obligated to say a word to her either."

"But I'd feel sort of sneaky if I kept it to myself."

He grinned. "You're itching to show off. And who can blame you?"

"Then you do think I should. I wouldn't want her to think I'm conceited."

"Look, Jossie, everybody who ever writes anything good wants it to be read by somebody else." He gave her a conspiratorial grin. "It sure couldn't hurt to have Madam Amantha know you pulled it off, first try."

"I'll think about it."

By ten after nine on Monday morning she called Mrs. Dunwoodie's secretary, Joan Sidings.

"It's Jossie Stone. Is Mrs. Dunwoodie all tied up for the day?"

"Not yet. She has her first appointment at half past. Why?"

"Could you work me in for five minutes, Joan?"

"You mean right now?"

"If you could, it would be great."

"Emergency? Sure."

"Nothing like that. Just, I'm sort of excited about something."

"Well, come on, then. She's having coffee."

Unexpectedly, the sight of a carafe on Mrs. Dunwoodie's desk, and the feel of the smooth china mug in her hands, sent a twinge of memory to life. *I see you every once in a while going past my house.*

"Well, Jossie, something good's happened, by the look of you."

The memory fled. "Oh, yes, and I just had to tell you, because if you hadn't said I could, I never would have. . . ." She drew out the two letters but turned them face down and began a rapid recital of the past week, beginning with *Glass World* and ending by handing over the letters, still folded in threes.

She tried not to watch Mrs. Dunwoodie as she read them, but so dignified a pose was beyond her, and she saw the older woman's eyes light as they saw the first square of glass, watched her expression as she began to read, kept on watching all through the second letter.

"You really have it," Mrs. Dunwoodie said. "And they'll get results. This Mr. Albright will be after you again."

"He said he would. Oh, that means *you* like them too."

"Very much, but—" She looked thoughtful.

"But what? Are there any buts I should know about?"

"But don't stretch it too far. Don't take on too much outside work—that could mean trouble."

"I wouldn't dream of it." A certain heaviness pulled at her. "What would be 'stretching it too far'?"

"I can't say. Just that you musn't make your work suffer here at Ashley. We think you have a big future here, if you want it."

"Oh, I do."

"In the meantime, congratulations. I hope they paid you what these deserve." She handed back the letters.

"They did! Twenty for the two."

"Fair enough. Now don't use it all for that college loan of yours. Treat yourself to something you don't need."

Or to something *nobody* needs, Jossie thought, as she picked up the letters and left the office, like those damn doctors' bills from Paris.

○ ○ ○

"It's *your* money and *my* doctors' bill. Are you trying to show me up as incompetent or something?"

"What a thing to say!"

"So you went and earned some extra money, you're clever, you're disciplined—I'm not disciplined, I can't even make myself write things I *want* to write. Is that it?"

She turned away, her eyes stinging. There was no way to stand it when he was this angry at her. If love could bring with it such pain, maybe there was no way to stand being in love. Not the way she was in love. Rick didn't love her that way or he couldn't lash out in this sudden temper.

It was early evening, and she had just finished telling him about Mrs. Dunwoodie and the things she'd warned her about, as well as the praise and the lovely hint about the future. He had been as pleased, hearing it, as she was telling it, had nodded in agreement at the final suggestion of treating herself to something she didn't need.

But she had gone on for just one more sentence, had trusted him to understand that one more sentence, that wanton thought which had filtered into her mind as she was leaving the office, and even though she had made it perfectly clear that it was merely a notion, a fleeting idea, the very phrase, "one of those doctors' bills," had touched off the explosion of his rage.

At the beginning, she hadn't guessed that Rick had a temper, buried there under his gentle usual self, but every once in a while it came roaring out at her and seemed to burn her to ashes in an instant. She knew people could have a fight and still keep on loving each other; she knew that passion in one part of your life couldn't possibly go along with any namby-pamby passivity in the other parts. And passion was part of Rick, part of his total self, indispensable in keeping him the wonderful man she loved so much. But when he turned against her, there was nothing to help her stand it.

"My darling girl," he was saying a moment later. "I shouldn't have said that, not any of it." He came to her, cradling her shaking shoulders, holding her, running his hand lightly over her wet cheeks, brushing away tears with his fingers as if she were a weeping child. She wanted to resist this sudden remorse of his, wanted to remember that it was he who had thrust this pain at her, still racing through her, but she could not do either. The pain fell away, thinned down, evaporated, giving way to a wave of gratitude that he knew so quickly he had hurt her, knew he was wrong to do it, wished he had not.

"I only thought—I only meant—" she began.

"I know, Jossie. Some sort of masculine rage got loose in me because you're the one pulled it off, when *I'm* the one should be earning extra money."

How honest he was, admitting it, seeing it so surely and admitting it so openly. He had more insight into what made people behave one way or another than anybody she had ever known. He could see what made for jealousy or pride, not only in other people but in himself, and he was strong enough to look at all these human foibles straight, strong enough not to make up thin excuses, and especially not for himself.

"Oh, Rick, I love you so," she said. "When you get angry at me like that, I feel as if I were all crumpled and shattered like—"

"Like the glass in the second letter."

She suddenly laughed. "Shattered and scattered, and all the king's horses and all the king's men—"

"I'll put you together again, my lovely bright girl. I love you more every day, did you know?"

Five

It was Andy Bellock's wife, Edie, who made the suggestion about the cabin, and it was not to Rick that she made it but to Jossie. It was the long Memorial Day weekend, and the log cabin still remained unsold. Andy would not come down in his asking price, and they had already moved into their new house across the lake. After inviting first his own parents to spend a weekend in the cabin, and then Edie's parents, Andy had announced to Rick, "It's your turn again. How about this one?"

Edie was a hard person to know, Jossie had decided, but worth the trying. There was an edge of reserve in her voice when she and Jossie were alone, as if something changed between them when their husbands went off without them, sailing on the Hudson or fishing. *Husbands* was the word Edie used, though she knew all about Jean in Paris and all about West Tenth Street. "Up here at the lake, it's better to get the habit of saying husbands," she had said to Jossie, "so I won't make any gaffes with the neighbors."

"Sort of a pseudonym for the summer," Jossie had said, and they both laughed, Edie with unexpected fondness, as if she were all at once Jossie's closest friend. That time the reserve was missing, replaced by a willingness, a kindness, as if Edie wanted to make it clear that she had no disapproval of two people who lived together like married people when they were in fact not married.

"Edie will take it the way Andy did," Rick had assured Jossie months ago, when Andy had asked if he was supposed to keep it a secret from his own wife. "They're the sort of people we are."

Edie was nine years older than Jossie, and when they were together, all four, for an evening in town or this delectable three-day weekend in Peekskill, Jossie was more conscious of her age than she was anywhere else. At the office she never thought about being young any more; by now there was a man in the art department who was a year younger, and in Rick's copy group another who was two years younger, just out of Yale and still very much the college boy in his V-neck sweaters and saddle shoes on Saturday mornings. But with Andy and Edie both in their thirties and Rick now twenty-nine, and all of them teasing her about being the baby, she did think about being younger and found that she rather liked it. Imagine how it would be if she were ever the oldest in any group!

"You *sound* like a kid sometimes," Andy said to her suddenly on the last afternoon of the weekend. They were on the sundeck built out low over the water, the Bellocks' dark green canoe drifting in the breeze at the end of their small dock. Jossie had been paddling in it all alone and had just come in, saying, "I could live in it forever."

"You can't," Lisa Bellock cried out. "It's mine," Lisa was six, the middle child and only girl.

"You can't live in a canoe, stupid," her brother Tony said, his two years of superiority sounding. "She just means she likes it."

"Go have another swim, you two," their father said. "We're having drinks in a minute, and you know kids and drinks don't mix in this family."

"I've this uncle coming from England," Edie said without transition, as the children ran off. "He's a don at Cambridge."

"Interesting social note," Andy said. "Why bring that up now?"

"Don of what?" Rick asked. "I like English dons."

"Sinology," Andy said. "Interesting cuss for a don."

"Sinology," Edie repeated, looking up at Rick, standing within the few inches of shade cast by a window awning. "It means he's an expert in the history and literature and everything else of China, past, present, and future."

"Thanks, ma'am," Rick said. "You're a mighty fine tutor, ma'am."

"You," she said, giving him the back of her hand. "So he's on a transfer professorship at Columbia for a year, and they're getting here next week." She looked at Jossie with a special intensity, as if this were a coded message only another woman would immediately understand. "He and his wife, Midge."

"Ouch, Christ in a bucket," Rick exclaimed. He had just stretched out on an aluminum deck chair and was clutching the backs of his knees, both his legs raised high in the air.

"Your poor legs," Jossie said. "Here, use some more of this." She handed him a jar of cream that was supposedly good for sunburn.

"Never believe ads," Rick said, grimacing. He stood up carefully and started for the kitchen door. "I'll try the hot vinegar compresses again."

"Not too hot, now," Edie warned. "Want any help?"

He shook his head and they watched his retreat, the flaming burn behind his legs making Jossie wince. He had warned her against too much sun, and she had heeded him, but his nonchalance toward his own amount of exposure had been complete, and he would be paying the price for several more days. Last night had been the first time in their life together that they hadn't made love.

"The dumb jerk," Andy said. "I'd better go in and feed him some cold gin while he's at the hot vinegar."

"For a fact," Edie said to Jossie, her voice bare of sympathy, "Rick can be a dumb jerk. He burns as if he were a golden blond, and each summer he comes up here and dares the sun to do its worst." Then, again without transition, she went on, "They're going to want a furnished apartment in town for the summer months, my uncle and his wife."

"I thought you said a whole year."

"He'll be teaching at Columbia for the full year, but after Labor Day, the professor who's going to England is swapping his apartment for their house in Cambridge."

Jossie looked at her expectantly. There was something in Edie's manner, some slight suggestion of conspiracy, a smiling conspiracy, in the tone she was using.

"And you and Andy are lending them your place in town until Labor Day?"

"I thought you knew—we've sublet ours for the summer."

"I didn't know."

"That Andy. He either talks too much or never says a word. I thought he'd told Rick."

Jossie shook her head, beginning to smile too, not knowing exactly why. Edie was enjoying something and she wanted to enjoy it too. "What's up, Edie? You've got a sort of look—"

"They're as rich as Midas. They could easily pay one fifty a month for a furnished apartment as attractive as yours and Rick's."

"For ours? Where would we live?"

"Just guess." She looked across the lake at the log cabin.

"Up here? For the whole summer while we sublet—oh, Edie, you angel."

"Andy wouldn't rent the cabin to anybody else for fifty a month," Edie said. "But he would to you and Rick. And if you get a hundred fifty for your apartment and pay us fifty for the cabin, you'd be living rent free for June, July, and August."

"In the cabin, while your uncle—oh, I can't take this in yet."

"His name is Bruce Winfellen, and she's Mignon, called Midge. They're nearly sixty, so no bathtub gin parties to wreck everything you own."

Jossie jumped up as if a spring had suddenly been released. "I can't *stand* it, it would be so wonderful. Let me go ask Rick."

"Hold it, wait a sec, let's think about it a minute."

"What about—you mean commuting? He used to, when he lived in Princeton." She sat down again. Edie meant something, a possible obstacle. Her tone showed it, and the brief aversion of her gaze. "Think about it how?"

"Anything about money, and Rick goes so Cedric Urquhart Baird you want to punch him. That's how."

Jossie laughed a little. "You mean because he owes Andy some money. He told me about that."

"So if he takes it into his head that this is some scheme of mine to let him save three months' rent to pay us off with, he'd be spitting fire."

"Oh." Did Rick still owe them money, after all this time since the dispossess notice when he'd said he couldn't borrow at the office, either from Andy or John Slade? Had he been paying it off or just letting it sit there month after month? And was it so much that it would take all the sublet savings to pay it off? Money again, debt, something that ought to be paid and wasn't. Was there nothing any more that wasn't somehow linked to money?

Suddenly she was seeing Mrs. Dunwoodie's desk calendar that morning back in March with the funny-looking foreign 7 on it, J. S. 50, 3/7, when she had gone in with her $50 check, and as if in a double image, was also seeing Mary Watts's cheery smile three months later, when she'd repaid the $50 she owed her. "Any time, cookie," Mary had volunteered. "You're a fast payer. On the button."

With his friends, did Rick have that "on the button" feeling, or was he as carefree with them as he was with stores and tailors and hatmakers and landlords? She'd probably never know; she couldn't just up and ask him, nor could she ask Edie or hint that she didn't know.

"So let me and Andy," Edie went on, "offer Rick the cabin to save money for *us,* instead of having it empty all summer. That's where my big idea comes in, of Uncle Bruce and Midge being *your* tenants while you become ours."

"You clever thing."

"We kind of like you, Jossie." She said it shyly, with the faint air of reserve coming back, and Jossie was touched.

° ° °

The cable came on the second morning after the weekend. It was delivered to Rick's office, and he tore it open with such haste that he ripped the sheet bearing the printed ribbons of the message in half.

DECISION POSTPONED UNTIL OCTOBER

one part read, and relief leaped high. He read the other half in a euphoria so sunny that he was for an instant blind to the tentative quality of the whole message.

WITH FURTHER TESTS SEPTEMBER WRITING LOVE

We can take the cabin, he thought. Last night he had jumped at Edie's idea as eagerly as Jossie had, had gone further, asking about commuter trains and the cost of a used car, which was essential, since the lake was five miles from the railroad station and the town of Peekskill itself. But later, when he and Jossie were alone again, he'd said, "What if Jean—what if I *do* have to go to Paris to see her through it?"

"I forgot about Jean."

There had been the sound of guilt in her tone—he could still hear its minor chord—a guilt he had at once forgiven. Of course she must see Jean's illness as a stumbling block; probably she unconsciously resented it right now, not being an angel of purity and goodness.

"I can't see you managing all alone up here," he'd said, "if I did suddenly have to go. The commuting, that woodstove, the hot-water heater, cranking up an old car—it's not like living in town."

"I couldn't stand it in the apartment with you not there. I'd just go home to the family while you were gone." She shook her head sharply. "And go mad."

"Let's go send a wire and see how it looks now. There must be some town near here, Ossining or wherever, with a cable office open on a holiday night."

They had commandeered Andy's car. The night was starlit and the air flower-scented and balmy. Locust trees were in blossom, and honeysuckle and wisteria and early roses. They drove in silence along the narrow roads of black asphalt, losing their way twice under the deep summer foliage of old trees, the drive turning into an unexpected treat, for they had never had a car to themselves to go driving in before.

"At least up here," Jossie had said at one point, "weekends would be full of tennis and swimming and the canoe—I could bear it better up here if you do have to go. Oh, Rick, is it rotten of me to pray you don't have to?"

"If it is, I'm rotten too."

Now he glued the two halves of the cablegram together. Here was respite. For one brief instant he remembered the way Jossie had sounded—"I forgot about Jean"—and discomfort invaded him. Then he phoned Jossie at her desk, said, "All's clear all summer," and made out a check to Andy Bellock for the June rent of the cabin.

o o o

In Paris, standing before a blank canvas on the easel in the large room that was her bedroom and studio, Jean thought about the cable she had received the night before from Rick, and about her reply. There was an insistence in Rick's, and a vagueness, that seemed to be rooted in something more immediate than concern for her health. The wording of cables, of course, was always a constricting band around anybody's mind; she had rewritten her answer a dozen times to get it all into ten words, and even his much longer wire—

good old Rick, not bothering to count—had that elliptical sort of phrasing that was at once evasive and strangling.

She went to the kitchen where she had left it and picked it up once more, her own ten-word reply written and rewritten all over the back of it. The kids had tried to read his wire, but neither Kathy at eight nor Kenny at seven were notable readers of anything beyond cat and dog, or *chien* and *chat*. They were bright enough at school and already spoke French with scarcely any American accent. Her own French had become fluent in this year and a half that they'd lived in Paris, but since everybody's idea of a fetching compliment was to tell her that she had the most enchanting accent, she knew that one's thirties were already too late for acquiring flawless Parisian French.

Both children knew the cable was from Uncle Rick, and each asked, "Is Uncle Rick coming to see us?" She had a ready reply. "No, he can't come every year. He works in New York, and mostly he has to stay there."

"Why can't he work here," Kathy had demanded, "like Pierre and Claudette's uncles?"

"Their uncles are French so they live right here and work right here."

"Do you have to live right where you work?"

"Yes, if you work in an office, like Uncle Rick, or on a farm, or in a factory."

"Or in a college, like Daddy?"

"That's right, Kathy. Your daddy taught art at Princeton, so we lived in Princeton. I'm lucky because I can work wherever there's a place for my brushes and paint."

"By a north window," Kenny observed, and she laughed. At seven he was always the one to surprise you with unexpected offerings of information. Trying to explain Rick's message was too complex a task. Their first Christmas in Paris, he had sailed on the *De Grasse* and spent a week with them, timing his vacation so he could. But last year he had written that he was "full of dispossess notices and other nuisances, and can't manage it this time." There had been nothing complex about explaining that; she had merely said, "Uncle Rick can't come for Christmas, but he's sending you lots of presents," and they had switched interest at once to "What kind of presents?" With this new cable, she had merely said, "It's about business," and their interest had promptly vanished.

HAVE CHANCE SUBLET APARTMENT AND LIVE RENT FREE PEEKSKILL COTTAGE THREE MONTHS BUT HESITATE WHILE OPERATION UNCERTAIN STOP IS THERE ANY CHANGE IN DIAGNOSIS OR SCHEDULE WRITING LOVE

A cottage in Peekskill for the summer? Where was Peekskill? She couldn't place it, though she had heard of it and thought it was near Poughkeepsie, where Vassar was. But that would be almost to Albany, too far for commuting six days a week to New York City; it had to be about the same distance Princeton was, except that it was north, along the Hudson.

Commute to and from the office every single day for three months, the whole summer? Rick hated commuting in hot weather, and here he was arranging for it again? Spend the night in his cottage, wake at six or so in the morning, commute for an hour or two to the city, and then turn around and do the whole thing at night. All summer long? That didn't sound very much like Rick.

Unless that girl he had written about, or some other girl, was going to live there too. No, he was still seeing Jossie; his last letter, a couple of weeks ago, had mentioned her again.

That must be part of this rent-free cottage plan; he couldn't fit all that into a cable, but he would tell her of it in his next letter, as he always did.

Rick still believed it, as he had when they had married: Honesty was everything in a marriage, truth, trust, without shabby posturing and lying and concealment. Part of her still believed it with him, and yet this wire, with its sudden picture of a girl in a cottage in the country for the summer, this carried with it some freight of unwillingness or distaste that ought not be there, if her own convictions hadn't begun to thin down or alter.

Away from Rick, she had perhaps regressed to her old ideas, stuffy and ordinary though they might seem to brilliant theorists like Havelock Ellis. You *had* to keep certain things secret, didn't you? Perhaps too much honesty had cruelty imbedded in it; perhaps a tactful silence at times was actually a kindness. She had written Rick very little about François, except at the beginning, before either she or François had seen that this was to be more for them than one of the little pleasantries of life, quickly begun and soon enough over. So technically she was still living up to their promise about honesty always, yet she well knew that the real sharing of a truth was a far cry from the technical recital. "I met this man, François Ciardeau," she had written. "He's with Morgan Trust on the Place Vendôme. He's the one handled my letter of credit; that's how we met, and now we've become involved, and it does help with all sorts of loneliness. Don't fret, Rick darling, it will change nothing for you and me later, when we're together again."

That had been a year ago, and he had written back in his strong clear way, "I do fret a little, and will from time to time, but we both have for a long time now taken leave of the mean little jealousies and watchfulnesses and possessivenesses of most marriages, and an occasional fret, or even a frequent fret, never tips the scale of values we live by for more than a swift small dip. Then it rights itself again and we're on a balance more level than ever."

He knew she was still seeing François—she mentioned him in her letters too—but most of the surrounding canvas was empty. If she and Rick still lived in Princeton, she would have filled in all the developing colors and shadings as they came along, but writing was so different. If telephones could reach across the Atlantic, she certainly would have offered Rick lots more; even your voice could create shadings and color. But cables and letters—unless you were a born writer like Rick, they stiffened you up, circumscribed what you could say, and narrowed you down to outlines and synopses.

So this girl in the office, this Jossie, would be living with him all summer. Rick was not a man to live in celibacy for any length of time; he never had been and never would be for the next twenty or thirty years. That was one of the electrifying things about him, his sweetness about sex, his incredible sustained power in it, and his equal sweetness about pleasing you along with himself, as if he could not, would not, achieve unless you were achieving too. It was like a goal, a horizon to be reached together; there was never any singleness of purpose in Rick's lovemaking. He was the only man she had ever loved of whom she could say that so truly.

But there were other things besides sex in the months and years of living, and she had begun to leave them out of her letters too, because even in practical, unemotional everyday matters, long detailed explanations had never come easily to her. When she had begun to see the small persistent inroads made into what remained of Arthur's army insurance, and into her own capital from the sale of her house in Princeton, she had asked François whether he might not find some safe investment for what she had in the way of capital, rather than let it dwindle down in her letter of credit at his bank. He had put her into some French municipals, and a pleasing little trickle of new income had begun to appear.

But she had kept all this to herself, finding it clumsy to explain in letters. Rick was never really interested in money matters anyway, or at his best about them; he had a sort of carefree expansiveness about such things, and it seemed only natural to her to skip all the details when she wrote him.

There was a rightness in this reticence which somehow led her along the path of other reticences. When she thought of herself, as she occasionally did, as "regressing" to old-fashioned ways, it didn't seem a deplorable possibility; rather, she found it pleasant and more instinctive—her parents had believed in the tact of little white lies in a marriage, and they had been happy people until they died.

Now, with Rick's cable whispering possibilities to her, and her answer summing up what she'd been meaning to write him for the past ten days, she drew out one of her blue sheets of stationery and began to write.

The cable had really summarized it, she wrote. There was still some staining between periods, but less frequently, and though her periods were sometimes irregular, they were far more moderate. Dr. Leclerq believed that the curetting had restored enough normality in her general condition to make it advisable to delay surgical action for three or four more periods. That meant after the summer.

She rose and prepared fresh coffee, the chicory-heavy French kind she had come to love. She drank it slowly and returned to her letter. She wanted to write about the cottage and her speculations about his summer there. But now she seemed tongue-tied, with the pen in her fingers halted in midair. She had easily enough sent Rick a postcard during the spring when she had gone with François for a week to a small inn near the salt flats at La Baule, saying perfectly honestly that she was there in Brittany "with François and two other friends," and Rick of course had known what she meant. But now nothing she started to write seemed easy or natural.

For sharing a life, perhaps, one needed to share the hours of each day and each night. Direct-by-mail might be very effective in the world of advertising and merchandising, but she was beginning to wonder whether, between two people parted by an ocean, it had enough life blood to keep it vital and alive.

○ ○ ○

"I'm writing this in the train," Jossie wrote in her journal, "and if it gets all smudged and sooty, it's because the windows are open and we're right behind the locomotive, being inundated with ashes and smoke every time the wind blows backward."

> I ought to hate these hot plush seats and the steamy heat that never lets up, but there's so much that's wonderful up at the lake, I don't care, and neither does Rick. He reads the *World* and the *Times* during the trips, but I—oh, joy of joys—have too much work for reading, and I do it right on the train.
>
> I have *two more free-lance accounts*, and in this month of June I've made $60 extra.
>
> I want to shout it out to everybody I see, but those sly little words of Dunwoodie's keep doing a fox-trot in my head: *Don't stretch it too far*. I haven't said one word about my two new accounts to a soul at the office except Rick and Andy B.
>
> One account is Houbigant Perfume, and the other is Lacq, a new little company making an enamel nail polish that you brush on instead of going crazy with pumice and a chamois

buffer. It's a new field and they're tiny compared to other people who got there first, and I just pray Ashley doesn't get near any rival product, because it's fun to write cosmetics. I never have.

Stop buffing—brush it on was my first headline, and they loved it. The copy started, "Put away your long oval buffer with the chamois that always looks a little dingy, and put away that jar of powdered pumice too. Now there's a new modern. . . ."

Brush the shine on was my second headline, and they liked that too. This isn't direct-by-mail; they're real ads, a quarter page in the *Ladies' Home Journal,* with artwork showing two fingers holding a tiny brush over an opened bottle.

So far they just have a clear pearly-looking polish, so it looks like your own nails buffed to a fare-thee-well, but they're planning on adding pink and even red color, in the new style, and then I suppose I'll be looking for headlines about blushing nails and all sorts of crazies. But it's fun.

I needn't take time away from Rick and me being together, because it's true I work only on the train—except for those stretches where the N.Y. Central tracks run right along the Hudson and I go off into a star-gazing trance. River-gazing, I mean. In the city it's like a different river, chockablock with piers and wharves and packing-houses, but up here it's pure glorious open river, with the Jersey Palisades on the far shore. Peekskill is ¾ of the way to Albany, in Bear Mountain country, north of a lot of beautiful villages like Croton and Mt. Kisco and Harmon, where—ugh—you change from the locomotive to the electric train that takes you into Grand Central.

But about 50 miles on a train means 1½ hours of commute each way, and you can get a lot of copy written in three hours a day, river-gaze and all.

And the happiest part of it all is that I'm adding so much to our household account that I'm starting to feel a bit more like Rick's equal. He still earns $6,000 a year to my $1,100 officially, but with his having to send $100 or more to Jean every month and another $100 to his father in Richmond, and with the better clothes and smarter restaurants expected of a copy chief, it seems a lot closer. Anyway, we share all our living expenses, rent, food, phone, commute, light, everything. If there weren't any unpaid bills left hanging around (for me *not* to worry about!) and not too many unexpecteds, we'd soon be on an even keel indeed.

Even keel reminds me of the lake. How I love it, love swimming, love canoeing, love sailing on the Hudson in the Bs' boat. They're wonderful about lending the canoe. There's something about being out under a hot summer sun, gliding along on glistening water under a high blue-white sky that just makes me happy I'm alive. In a funny way it's like night and being in bed and making love, the opposite of it, but all lovely and intense and beautiful.

I've never been so happy as this past month of June up here with Rick. I've become a much better driver—we did get an old two-seater Ford runabout for $40, and cranking it up is a bit hard if I'm alone, but the minute I put my foot on the running board and get in, a sort of excitement starts racing around inside like the wind blowing through my hair. (The canvas top is always down unless it pours.)

The only bad thing is my feeling more nervous about the office finding out where I'm living. Rick had to give them his Peekskill phone number where he could be reached nights and Sundays in case anything went wrong with some copy being set overnight or when they were plating the artwork of an ad, and since he's copy chief of four other writers, so much is going on all the time that it does happen.

But I just said around the office, and to Dunwoodie, that I was going to live with my family during the summer, and I meant to tell Mama right away how to manage any phone call that might come for me, but I keep putting it off—I don't know why—because then I'd have to tell her about everything.

I will anyway. Really, I want to. She'll be wonderful about it, but she'll be very emotional about her baby girl growing up, and I kind of run away from that, I suppose. Darling Moth.

How funny that looks when you write it, like the lepidopterous (?) insect that flies into the flame. When I say it, it's so right, just the first part of Mother, with the uncertainty left off. I'll call her today.

See how much you can write during just one trip on the way to N.Y.C.?

o o o

"Any more inlays for Dr. Herbst to fix up?" she said into the phone an hour later. She had canceled their other lunch date in the rush of Mr. Albright's two letters.

"Not a one. How was your weekend with the Bellocks?"

"Lovely. They're such fun." All month Andy and Edie had provided the alibi for her continuing Sunday absence from New Rochelle, even in the hottest weather.

"The Bellocks or whoever," her mother now added.

"You're too smart, Mama. I have something I want to talk to you about, *been* wanting to talk to you about. Are you going to be in town any time soon?"

"Any time you say, before summer session starts. I could bring your birthday present along, two weeks early."

"I forgot about my birthday. Thanks in advance."

They met in a small restaurant on Madison the next day, and in the first minutes of ordering, of being complimented on her deep bronzy tan, Jossie found herself, unexpectedly enough, floundering about what to say. She had thought little about it in advance, for she always relied on a last-minute instinct to come to her aid, like that time in blessed Mr. Albright's office, or the other time when she'd met Nell at school. Thinking too carefully beforehand leached out all spontaneity, either writing or speaking, formalized things, made what you did say sound like a rehearsed speech, rigid, even false. In business you sometimes gained by these artifices, but with anyone you loved?

"You've partly guessed what I want to talk about, Mama," she said as she put her menu down. "Haven't you?"

"Partly." She smiled. "How much is 'partly'?"

"Well, you guessed way back that I wasn't living with another girl, sharing the rent with her—"

"Are you happy, Jossie? You look happy. Don't you remember telling me about this man whose family is in Paris, *his own family*, not his parents?"

"And about his not being French, and being twenty-eight." She felt a little foolish. "I was probably dying to tell you lots more even then."

"I knew you would when the time came. Is this the time?"

"Only about where we are now and a few things—I sort of can't spill things out about—his name is Rick Baird, Cedric Baird."

"You don't need to spill anything out. It must be all right, by the look of you."

"It's a fib, about me weekending with the Bellocks up there in Peekskill. We've rented their log cabin, right on the water, and I can't tell the office, so I said I was living home for the summer."

"And if they ever phone you at home, you want me to say you're out for a few minutes, and then call you so you can get back to them right away. Let me get a pencil."

"Oh, Mama, you're so terrific." She squeezed her mother's fingers in her own. She gave the address and phone number of the cottage and added, "If you ever wrote, you'd have to address it Baird."

"B-a-i-r-d. Mrs. Cedric Baird?" At Jossie's silent nod, she added, "Does Nell know?"

"In a way, but I sort of can't start telling her out loud how wonderful it is. Or telling anybody."

The waiter brought their salads, and silence fell. She's fooled me, Jossie thought. Not a word about her baby growing up, nothing about married men or living in sin. Well, phrases like that would be the last thing you'd expect from either of her parents, even her cranky father. They were far too modern.

"Without any spillage," her mother said, "tell me a little about Rick."

"Well, he's going to be a writer. He sold his very first story to Mencken, and he writes with a sort of lucid, strong, sensitive—the things he's let me read just get to me. There's never anything ordinary about them, no *Saturday Evening Post* formula stuff, not ever." Her eyes shone and she talked on and on.

"One thing, Jossie," her mother said slowly at last. "People *do* get pregnant."

"Well, I won't."

"If it ever should happen, though, I hope you won't try to handle it all by yourself. Okay?"

"But Rick and I—of course I've wondered what I'd do if it ever did happen." Her mother said nothing. "If Rick weren't married—but he is, so there'd be only one thing *to* do." She waved her hand casually. "It's not going to happen."

Again a silence fell and Jossie found herself wishing the luncheon were over.

"You and Pa lived together before you were married," she said, to her own surprise. "Nell told me that once, when she was getting married."

Her mother nodded. "For nearly a year."

"It's an intelligent way of testing—"

"But neither one of us," her mother put in gently, "was married to anybody else, dear." A moment later she asked, "Is Rick planning to go and live in Paris later on with his family, do you think? Or have them come back here?"

Jossie shook her head positively and talked of Jean's painting and the reasons for her choice of where to study. "A few years," she ended, "is what they agreed on. It's been about one and a half."

"And then?"

"Who can think that far ahead? I'm going to be twenty-four, and you know I don't even want to get married for a million years."

"And in a million years, you'll only be a million twenty-four, and a knockout."

Six

"Prepare yourself for a surprise," Rick said as they left the train on the last Saturday afternoon of June. "A birthday present and a vacation present rolled into one."

"Eight whole days up here is present enough."

Because Rick had been at the agency for six years, he was entitled to three weeks of vacation with pay, whereas Jossie was still held to the single week that Ashley employees were allotted for their first three summers, a boon that was doubled in the next two, and which reached its most expansive only after one's fifth anniversary on the payroll. But Rick was taking only the same week allowed Jossie, holding two weeks in reserve in case the autumn should, after all, mean the trip to Paris.

Since Saturdays were only half-days, it was past three when they reached Peekskill, and nearly as hot as it had been at noon. Parked in a vacant lot across from the railroad station, their Ford runabout, its top down, was lined up in an orderly row with perhaps six other cars; the commuting population of Peekskill, as was true of other small towns in upper Westchester County, was never large, and less than half that number undertook daily travel to any place so distant as New York. Nearly eight hours had elapsed since they'd left it there to bake in the sun, and now it was hot to the touch, the metal, the leather seats, even the wood steering wheel defying immediate contact to bare hands and bodies encased in flimsy summer clothing.

"E-e-e-e," shrieked Jossie as she sat down, clutching the edges of the seat, stiffening her arms and raising herself as far above the leather as she could. "What kind of a present?"

"It's a surprise, idiot girl."

"Are you going to keep me guessing until tomorrow? Or just to one minute past midnight?"

"Just till we get home."

They stopped at various stores for their weekend supplies, and Jossie kept wondering what her present would be. For Rick's birthday in May, she had given him a new wallet, of fine black pinseal, with narrow curves of gold around the corners and his monogram on a tiny rectangle of gold. He had loved it, had instantly emptied out his old wallet, which was peeling apart at the long seams, and transferred everything into the new one.

"If ever a present was a ten strike—" he had said, and she had floated on success at his pleasure. Perhaps he would counter now by giving her a new leather purse; her old one was nearly as tattered as his wallet had been.

She wished they were going directly to the lake. But Saturday afternoon was the time for a dozen chores that had been building up all week, so in addition to their stops at the grocer's, the butcher's, and the vegetable and fruit market, they also had to stop at the dry cleaner's, the laundry, and the garage for gasoline. Jossie's impatience and curiosity about her present grew.

It was nearly five before they reached the lake and their cabin, and there was already that special afternoon sunlight slanting through the leaves of the trees. The lake itself lay there, a burnished disc—

Then she saw it: a red canoe, its enameled length gleaming new, rocking gently on the water directly in front of their cabin.

"Whose is it?" she asked.

"Yours, darling. Happy Birthday."

"It can't be, you didn't—I can't believe—*mine?*" She stood motionless, a girl of stone. Her face had flushed; under the deep tan, there appeared to be a new sunburn. Without saying anything, Rick lifted the bags and packages she was carrying and set them down on the narrow wood-plank walkway that ran from the front porch of the cabin to the edge of the water.

Freed of her parcels, Jossie ran forward to the canoe, pulling its bow ashore, kneeling down, running her right hand along its scarlet length, as far as she could. Just that contact was enough to set the rest of it swaying from side to side, and the two paddles lying on the twin cane seats inside shifted a little. A faint aroma of wood and canvas and new shellac arose toward her, and Jossie lifted one paddle, balancing it on the palms of her hands as if it were the flat of a sword.

"Go out in it," Rick said behind her. "By yourself the first time." He was untying the thin rope that ran from a metal loop in its bow to the lower branch of a rhododendron bush beside the walkway.

"Oh, Rick, I can't believe it's mine. Of all the things in the world that I thought of for my birthday, this is the most unbelievable—" She turned to him, embraced him, kissed him.

"Hey, that paddle's like a ramrod down my back."

They burst out laughing, the way children laugh, but Jossie spoke through the laughter. "Thank you, oh, a million times thank you, darling Rick. Is there anybody else on earth who can see *into* people the way you can?"

"Get your bathing suit on and try it—I want to see you actually using it. I've pictured it to myself long enough, God knows, when I should have been thinking about work."

"How *did* you think of it? My very own canoe, my absolute own."

"I didn't want you forever borrowing the Bellocks'—that's how. Go on now. Into your bathing suit."

She raced into the cottage. Three minutes later she was out once more, wearing the black alpaca bathing suit she loved because it had no waistline and no sleeves and ended several inches above her knees.

"You come too. I'd rather the first time was both of us."

He shook his head. "Let me watch you. I always love to watch you."

She was so deft, so agile that the canoe barely wavered as she ran it deeper into the water and seated herself in it, shoving out from the shore. As she slipped her paddle into the water, it shot forward in the long clean motion of a racing shell.

"It's like a feather," she called back to him. At Cornell she had been on the girls' crew, had won her '22 numerals—only men could earn the big red C; coeds could earn only their class numerals—but won them she had, and now for a swift moment she was back there in Ithaca on Lake Beebe, Cayuga's little sister, where the girls' crew practiced, back there seeing the girls' oars feathering, their backs straight, moving in perfect rhythm to the command: *Stroke, stroke, stroke.*

Her heart had soared with the joy of it then, but compared to what she was feeling now, her eyes half closed, the knowledge of Rick back there watching her body bend and straighten, of his loving her body—she held her paddle motionless, her arms suddenly limp.

At the far shore of the lake she turned and made for home as if she were again racing in a paper-thin shell. She could see Rick standing there, shielding his eyes from the descending sun, watching her, his face visibly pleased at her happiness. He didn't enjoy paddling as much as she did; he had done this only for her. After dinner, in the moonlight, she'd persuade him to go out in it with her. Could you make love in a canoe without capsizing? They'd made love in a hundred wild places, but in a canoe?

In a canoe she owned all by herself? The car, the apartment on West Tenth, even the log cabin that she was helping pay for, all were really Rick's, all had his name down on some lease or bill of sale, but the canoe was hers, only hers. She had never owned anything all by herself, except for her bike when she was small and her ice skates and tennis racket up at Cornell. They had been wonderful to have, but everybody in God's world owned a bike or skates or racket, while she must be one in a million girls to have her own canoe.

It was then that she suddenly thought, How much does a brand-new canoe cost anyway? Fifty dollars at least. It was an Old Town, made up in Maine and shipped down from there, the best canoes in the world.

Did Rick pay for it out of Uncle Bruce's July check, received this week? Last month they'd been forced to use a big part of the Mason Realty money that wasn't coming out of their own pockets this summer for the Ford and one new tire and their commutation tickets, and country things like flashlights and rakes. But now all the savings were supposed to go only for Rick's assorted bills, old ones or new ones like Jean's.

And suppose a canoe cost more than $50: $100? Suppose all the extra money from the rent-free summer would end up being spent on new things to make them happy instead of old things to make them even?

"You're a gorgeous thing to watch," Rick was saying as she neared the shore. "Does she handle easily?"

"*She's* what's gorgeous," she called back, and then a new thought hit her.

Suppose he hadn't paid for it at all? Supposed he had just found some way to charge it?

o o o

Rick was writing. He had told Jossie that during their week of freedom he would put in two hours every morning at his work, and now he was ensconced in a deep wicker chair on the porch, legs propped up on a canvas-covered stool, largely oblivious to everything but the sheet of paper on his clipboard and the fountain pen in his hand.

He wrote on yellow paper with a special smooth finish; it cost more than an ordinary scratch pad, but he drew an actual pleasure from the silky glide of his stub pen over its surface.

"I'm a hedonist, all right," he had told Jossie once, when she asked why only this particular paper would do. "Or a sensualist—whichever you like better."

Now he watched her briefly, as she launched the canoe, and warmed with the memory of her surprise and delight. Apart from a man's power in sex, there was nothing that could match his own sense of himself as much as the ability to make his beloved happy. She had been enchanting last night. They had gone out at nine, waiting for the moon to rise, and with both paddling they had circled the lake several times in an effortless sweep of motion that was in itself a kind of sexual excitation. It was a hot night, a midsummer night, filled with stars and the whisper of breezes that were indolent and elfin. On their return they had undressed on their unlit porch and crept out to the beached canoe.

He was trying to write it down now, as part of this piece he was doing on the unique quality of so-called forbidden love, and there was a positiveness within him about the way it was developing. Up here, a thousand miles from Ashley and the drudge, he could feel himself expanding into a larger personality, feel himself reaching for a brighter horizon. He reread the half page he had just written.

> To renounce a lasting love because it is, in the cold eyes of Calvinist morality, impermissible, is to renounce one's deepest selfhood, just as to abandon one's creed of doing a free creative work in lieu of paid writing is to bury one's self in unhallowed ground indeed.
>
> A man who obeys this inner clarity is, to that extent at least, kin to Havelock Ellis, who once wrote: "So, like the magnet that is held toward the north, I am fixed in continuous vital tension towards my Polar Star. '*As though the emerald should say: "Whatever happens I must be emerald.*"'"
>
> Ellis was quoting Marcus Aurelius, a footnote tells us, but the response to a noble quote from an earlier civilization is in itself a conferring of a new immortality.

Rick rose and began pacing up and down the narrow porch, keeping in from the strip of sunlight encroaching as the hour moved toward noon.

Some fool of an editor might tell him his work was unconsciously derivative, and perhaps in a way it was. When you admired a man's work as he had for years admired Ellis's, it was probable that your innermost psyche wished to attain some fraction of the loftiness and beauty already staked out by the one you revered, and that your own absorption of that other fecundity managed to make itself felt in your own work.

But careful rewriting would strip away anything derivative and leave the work purely his own. Worrying about that prematurely was merely to set up deliberate hurdles in one's path. As if there were not enough hurdles already in place, unexpected new hurdles as well as the old weatherbeaten ones. Like the sudden tiff with Andy yesterday at the office, about the canoe.

"Tell her it's a joint gift," Andy had said when he told him about it. "From you and me both."

"What's that crack for?" he had asked, but he knew. It was so out of character for Andy to remind him that he still owed him money, that he had skipped several monthly payments, ignoring the schedule he had himself set up the last time he had asked for and received a loan. These things got out of hand in some mysterious way of their own; he never could figure out the speed with which loans became debts, and debts became impossible.

"You're dead right, old man," he had conceded. "The thing is, you've said a dozen times, No hurry, don't worry—"

"Sure, but that doesn't include big expensive surprises and let-him-go-hang for another few months."

"Why, you tricky bastard," Rick exploded. "Springing one on me like that. If you want the money right off, say so right out." It was the first time he had ever lashed out at Andy. "The day vacation's over, I'll go to the Morris Plan and pay you every dollar, all of it."

That had been unpremeditated, but it suddenly seemed a great idea to him, and evidently to Andy also. They shook hands on it, and Andy apparently regained his usual good humor.

"But don't ask me to be one of your co-signers," he'd joked, and they'd both guffawed.

It didn't seem quite so funny in retrospect, nor as fair. Rick found a residue of resentment in his heart and thought that Andy most likely still felt angry, despite the surface good humor. Not only had Andy repeatedly assured him that there was no hurry, he had even seemed to enjoy this obvious superiority as to finances, what with the money he had inherited several years ago from his financier father. Rick had understood this feeling of status or power in Andy and had never held it against him; now, out of the blue, their first anger.

Rick again read the last paragraphs he had written and thought, Damn the hurdles; full speed ahead. He set his clipboard down and went indoors for a beer. The clock atop the icebox said 12:10. Good old yardarm, he thought. He put the beer back and mixed himself a hefty gin and tonic.

o o o

As Jossie came gliding toward the Bellocks' small dock in all her new splendor, Edie emerged from the house with her little girl, Lisa, each carrying a child-size paddle. Lisa was not allowed to go out in the canoe by herself, though her brother Tony was. The baby was of course too small.

"Happy birthday," Edie called.

"Isn't it glorious?" she answered, fanning her hand along the side of the canoe. "Did you know about it?"

"Not till yesterday when it came by truck. Rick asked me to sign for it and tell them which cabin to tie it up at." She was helping Lisa lower her small body into their own dark green canoe, and Jossie drifted around them idly, waiting for them to paddle away from the dock.

"Can I go with Aunt Jossie instead?" Lisa cried. "Hers is nicer than ours. Can I?"

"After you've had your lesson," Edie said. To Jossie, she added, "What a day I put in yesterday, keeping the two of them out of yours! Now they think ours is just an old wreck and want a brand-new red one for their own."

"We'll have a nice long trip right after lunch, Lisa," Jossie promised and watched them paddle away, their zigzagging process the inevitable result of the inequality in their strengths. Try as she would, Edie could not reduce her own motive power to match that of a little girl of six; the result was this constant left-right-left the canoe was taking, with Edie reassuring her daughter that it was she, Edie, who was at fault and that Lisa was doing everything right.

Jossie smiled. She and Edie had become good friends in the past month. There was still Edie's natural reserve to remember at times, when forgetting might make some cool remark of Edie's seem like a rebuff. There was never a rebuff to be inferred, she knew now; Edie did not deal in implications. If she wanted to rebuke you, she would rebuke you straight out, with no undertones to be interpreted or misread.

Edie's voice came clearly to her across the water. Lake Mohegan was no more than a mile long, rather crescent shaped, small even in comparison to Beebe, but it had a charm for Jossie disassociated from dear old college days. It had instilled in her a proprietary pride, as if it were *her* lake, a secret possession that other people could use and enjoy but which remained somehow hers.

"Come on in and get your birthday gift," Edie called out as Lisa's lesson ended.

"Save it till this afternoon when we have drinks."

Edie shook her head, beckoning her ashore, tilting her head at Lisa in the international signal of all parenthood, meaning, I can't explain while she's around.

"It's a bit touchy about our coming over for drinks today," Edie said when they were alone. "There was a sort of dustup yesterday between Andy and Rick. Let's skip a day or two."

"Dustup about what?"

"Money, but they came out of it after a bit. Even so, I'd think separation is indicated for a while, so let me give you my little gift right now." She started for the kitchen but Jossie stopped her.

"About money? How, about money?"

"Nothing new. Don't you get into it, now."

"He *has* been paying it off, hasn't he?" The moment the words were spoken, she was uneasy. Conducting an investigation behind Rick's back? "Never mind that, Edie," she said quickly. "I was being a Nosy Parker."

Edie eyed her thoughtfully. "Yes, he's been paying it back. Sporadically."

"How sporadic?"

"Now and then. When he gets around to it. Don't look like that, Jossie."

Jossie was staring at her red canoe. A constriction took her heart in unseen fingers and closed it in on itself, squeezing out the froth of joy that had been there since yesterday evening.

"How much does it come to, Edie?"

Edie looked reflective. Perhaps, under the guise of friendship, she had been doing that basest of all things, meddling, being a troublemaker. Yes, she had, and it was time somebody did. Jossie was not one to want the wool over her eyes; she was too direct a person, too reliable. Reliable—what an unexpected word to use about a new friend.

"It's about five hundred," Edie said at last. "But just yesterday Rick decided to go to the Morris Plan, he told Andy, and clean it all up."

"Five hundred dollars! I never dreamed—"

"Oh, he'll pay it all back. At his own pace, but every last dollar."

"But five hundred!" Jossie repeated. "It never once occurred to me it could be anywhere close to that. I'd thought maybe fifty, sixty—if I thought about it at all. Oh, Edie—"

"Don't look like that, Jossie," she said again. "Don't take it personally. I just didn't want to make any lame excuses about why we wouldn't be coming over for a bit. Now I wish I hadn't told you."

"So Andy hit the ceiling when he heard about Rick's spending God knows what on—I don't even know what a new Old Town costs."

"About eighty-five dollars. Plus shipping."

"Oh, no!" There was a silence. "I'd better get home and do lunch."

"Wait. Let me get your gift. It's not much."

She went inside and came back with a small flat box with a large green card saying, *Happy 24!* Jossie accepted it and said, "Whatever it is, thanks a million," started to undo its ribbons, then said, "I think I'd rather wait a little—is that all right?" At Edie's nod, she took it with her and returned to the canoe.

But alone on the water she thought, Sporadically. The one thing I mustn't do is get mad about it. She remembered the terrible night after she'd seen the litter of bills in the open drawer of Rick's desk.

She sat back, trailing her paddle. It had turned into a searingly hot day, brilliant, glowing. She drew her paddle into the canoe, bent forward and immersed both hands in the water. Coolness, like wisdom, washed over them. Her astonishment about the five hundred began to recede. Rick was Rick, and she loved him more than anybody on earth could love another human being. She wasn't going to make the mistake of trying to change him, the fool's errand of so many women's lives.

She slid the paddle back into the water and headed for home.

o o o

"Darling, what's the Morris Plan?" she asked easily while they had lunch. "Edie said you'd told Andy you'd go to the Morris Plan."

"So she told you about our run-in." He looked cheerful. "It would feel good, at that, to wipe it all out in one swell foop—I don't know why I never thought of it before."

"But what is it?"

"It's sort of a workingman's lifesaver when he needs a loan and can't go to a regular bank."

"Why can't he?"

"You can borrow from regular banks only when you've already got money or real estate, investments, dividends. If you're poor, drop dead."

"Or go to the Morris Plan? I've never heard of it."

"That's a bank too, but with a special setup for loans. You don't need collateral or tangible assets, only a steady job and steady pay. They interview you, to be sure you seem respectable and can get two other people with steady jobs and steady pay—what they call 'good earnings potential'—get them to co-sign your note with you."

"Co-sign meaning guarantee, I gather."

He nodded. "That if the borrower doesn't repay, one or both co-signers will do it for him."

"How does it work? Say you wanted to borrow a hundred dollars?"

"You'd sign a note for the hundred and they'd hand over ninety-two. That's minus a year's interest in advance, six dollars, and two more for a service fee. Then you pay back two bucks a week. In a year you're paid up."

"That's six-percent interest—twice what I pay at Cornell."

"They're not in this for the love of education." He grinned. "And if you borrowed five hundred, they'd hand over four-sixty and you'd pay ten a week for fifty weeks."

"How come you know all the details?"

"I phoned them yesterday, after I got sore at Andy. I have an appointment for the day we get back."

"Do you know who'll be your co-signers?"

"I already asked John Slade. I've been all squared away with John for months, and he said sure."

"Who for the other one?"

He looked at her, not answering. It was good to have this all on the table so soon; he had planned to put it off until their brief vacation came to a close, but he had never had a moment's doubt about what she would say when he asked her.

"Me, darling?" She jumped up in sudden excitement and went around the table to him. "You're thinking that it could be me. I'd seem respectable in an interview, and I have a steady job at steady pay with plenty of earning potential. Oh, Rick, let me help you."

"You dear girl." He drew her down into his lap. "I've never known there were people like you."

° ° °

Jossie was too excited to sleep. All this about Morris Plans and co-signers was so new, and having Rick want her to be co-signer was in some crazy way such a compliment! It was only a gesture; unless something happened to Rick, some accident or awful illness, it would remain no more than that. But if ever she did have to make good on her pledge, she knew she could manage it.

Ten a week to the Morris Plan? She could earn it doing extra free-lance work and pay that off week after week, and there'd be nobody like the Bursar at Cornell to write supercilious little letters about too-frequent payments.

Soon after the dispossess notice, something had prompted her to send in a $2.00 check every time she got her salary, so there would never again be an accumulation as large as $100 sitting around in her savings account for that annual payment to Ithaca, money she might impulsively use for something else.

But after the fourth weekly check, she had received a letter from the Bursar's office.

> Dear Miss Yavnowitsky,
>
> This is to acknowledge the receipt of your check for $2.00 as part payment on your University loan, the fourth such check this month.
>
> These small payments necessitate a continuous flow of secretarial and accounting work. Therefore, this is to request that you send no amount less than $50 to be applied to the balance of your loan. Perhaps you might make these weekly payments into a bank or postal service savings account until you wish to make the minimum $50 payment to the University.
>
> Yours very truly,

She had flushed with embarrassment as she read the letter, but not for long. The idiots, she had thought then, almost gaily. Can't they understand that the point is to get it sent *off* every week, so I can't get at it for anything else? They'd rather have me open to every temptation, just to save their additional secretarial and accounting work.

Actually, though, she could see the thing from their point of view, could envision the weekly entry of $2.00 on their ledgers or in their files, could see the weekly calculation of interest, the receipt to be returned to her, the weekly envelope to be addressed. They must have felt they were being drowned in $2.00 checks and hated her.

But the Morris Plan wouldn't hate her for being regular. She wondered whether you'd have a little book like a savings bank passbook or something more elaborate. She could imagine herself standing in line at some teller's window while other people with steady jobs and steady pay, good character, and earnings potential preceded her, paying off their tidy little sum each week.

In the dark she grinned. Beside her, Rick was asleep on his side, one knee raised halfway to his chin, his leg in a triangle, the other leg stretched down alongside her. She put her arm lightly across his inert body; he slept so deeply, nothing could disturb him. The feel of his shoulder sent a current of tenderness through her. Why was it so wonderful to be able to do a favor for the person you loved?

It was just a gesture, true enough; Rick never got sick and there'd be no awful accidents. But there was something new here between them, at least the possibility for something new.

The word *possibility* ticked off a tiny signal somewhere in her mind. She was growing sleepy, but the tiny signal drew her to full wakefulness again, the slumbrous vagueness of a moment before vanished.

Possible. Possible. There was something so different about having a student loan at Cornell and owing money to a bank. A college loan was personal, easy, with ten years to pay it off. Like borrowing money from your parents—from your mother, in any case. She had paid $100 on schedule the first year, skipped the second, and was now nibbling away at it each week without any sense of worry or pressure. In fact, Professor Smithson had hinted that they'd rather you did not pay it back too promptly—ten years' worth of interest was how the University Student Loan Fund grew.

But the Morris Plan had nothing easy and personal and leisurely about it. It would be $500 all in one year, and God knows what if you fell down on it—dunning reminders in every mail, loan collectors on your doorstep, finally garnishees at the office to disgrace you in public.

A shudder, like a small thrill, rippled across her mind. It would never happen.

But that word *possible* was not there for nothing. Something was changing in her life. Or could change. Up to now, she thought, it's been me worrying about Rick's unpaid bills, me the onlooker.

But if it ever did happen, I wouldn't be an onlooker. I'd be me with a brand-new $500 debt, all my own.

Seven

Mr. Jerton actually got up from his desk and came around to where she was sitting, the copy and rough layouts spread on the long low table before her.

It was early in August, a stifling day. Two weeks before, Jossie had been asked for two more letters by Mr. Albright, and a few days later he had told her he was now convinced that there was better work to be had than his firm had been getting from its old advertising agency. Thereupon he had offered Ashley & Company the advertising account of the Empire State Plate Glass Company, with the proviso that Miss Joselyn Stone be one of the copywriters on the account, perhaps the main copywriter.

The annual billings would be modest to start with, but for Jossie a small surge of fame in the office had followed, and that most unheard-of thing, an interim summer raise to $40 a week, with the promise of $50 at Christmas if all went well.

The copy on the long low table was her first in the office for Empire State, and Benjamin Jerton himself was to be in charge of the account until it was well launched. By now he was one of the vice-presidents of Ashley.

"You have a real future, Jossie," he said. "If you stay with us and keep on turning out work as good as this, you'll wake up one day to find yourself earning ten thousand a year." Ten thousand a year, she thought. Untold millions.

A burning shock went through her, blazing, golden. She had never even thought such words in connection with herself. Ten thousand dollars a year, $200 every week—it was limitless, like the sky, like a wild sea under sunshine. What couldn't she do with $200 every payday! Bills, debts, worries over payments would vanish; she and Rick never again would have that film of tension between them, unseen but always there, a wall of film, almost not there until you tried to traverse it, when suddenly it turned into bruising brick.

"You're making me feel awfully good, Mr. Jerton," she said. "It means you really *do* like it." She glanced down at the artwork and the three sheets of her copy.

"The client will like it—that counts even more."

Never as long as she lived would she forget the day in Mr. Albright's office when he told her of his plan, to offer his firm's advertising account to Ashley & Company.

"And tell them the one condition we make is that you write the copy."

"Oh, Mr. Albright."

"You told me there was no secret about your free-lancing. That was really so, wasn't it?"

"Oh, yes. I even went and showed the first two letters I did to Amantha Dunwoodie—she's supervisor of half the women's accounts there."

"That's all right, then. I had to consider whether you might have glided over things with me. At some firms you'd have been fired for doing outside work, so I would have had to do a little finessing to get you on the account without—ah—incriminating you." He smiled.

She pretended the shock of innocence, but the fact was that if it had been Houbigant or Lacq making this fantastic decision, much more than finesse would have been called for, since she had told nobody official at Ashley about doing work for either firm. As it was, there was no stratagem needed.

"Mr. Jerton," she had said, returning to the office in an elation she had never experienced before, "could I see you for a few minutes about something pretty important?"

He must have been astonished. It was the first time she had ever asked for an appointment, the first time she had ever initiated any meeting with him. His secretary, Mary Watts, had been astonished enough and had said, "Are you sure, cookie, that you can't tell me what it's about? That's the usual way."

"I'd never ask you to be unusual, but this is something so special, I have a feeling if I tell anybody else first, it would fall through."

"Superstitious?" Mary Watts laughed. She no longer looked on Jossie as a kind of office pet; Jossie had gone well beyond that cute-beginner status in Mary's astute scale of personnel values. "Oh, well, let me ask him."

Jossie had to wait for hours before he was able to see her. A dozen times she had the impulse to see Amantha Dunwoodie first, to ask if she had ever told Mr. Jerton about the two plate glass letters, and to remind her that it was she herself who had given Jossie permission to do a little work outside the office. But each time, something restrained her. She didn't want Mrs. Dunwoodie or Mary Watts to be the first one to tell Mr. Jerton about this; she wanted to do it herself.

Ben Jerton was about the same age as Amantha Dunwoodie and had been at Ashley for the same length of time. It was office gossip that the two disliked each other, despite the fact that they often worked together, as all copy supervisors did, when it came to matters of general policy, changes in procedure with clients, new methods of making presentations, new scales of billing for artwork, and the like. It was also office gossip that the reason for the strained relations was that years ago, when Ashley consisted of a four-room office down on Lafayette Street, near Wanamaker's, back there in

1912 or so, Ben Jerton and Amantha Whatever-her-maiden-name-was had had a very un-secret love affair and announced a wedding date, and that suddenly it was all over, with Ben Jerton marrying a girl he had just met, and Amantha rapidly becoming Mrs. James Dunwoodie, an old beau she had once discarded for Ben Jerton, and who was destined to have a bleak enough revenge three years later by dying and leaving her a widow. By now Ben Jerton had four charming children, whose pictures adorned his desk; she had never remarried and was childless.

"Offices are full of romances and broken romances," Rick had remarked when he had told all this to Jossie. "And of presumptions about romance and broken romance. You can never be sure how much is true and how much is sheer enjoyable malice."

It was hard to imagine these two in love, now that they were both in their forties, harder to imagine them making love, almost as hard as imagining one's own parents ever amorous or passionate in bed. As with parents, the only antidote to this distress was to ignore the entire possibility, which was what Jossie had managed, however precariously, to do.

Entering Mr. Jerton's office late that afternoon, she startled herself by asking, "Did Mrs. Dunwoodie tell you about me free-lancing?"

"No, have you been?"

"She said it was okay, if there was no conflict with one of our own products."

"That's been the general policy—we're thinking of changing it. Is there any specific reason you bring this up, Jossie? Did somebody offer you free-lance work?"

"Oh, Mr. Jerton, wait till you hear this." She proceeded to tell him the whole story, starting with the day she was leafing through *Glass World* in the office, going on to her first appointment at the office of the Empire State Plate Glass Company, going on to her first two letters, the two more recent letters, and ending with Mr. Albright's announcement that very morning.

"He's writing you formally about wanting Ashley for his agency," she ended. "You'll have that tomorrow first thing, but he said I could tell you today." She laid all four letters on his desk. He read them rapidly, his smile growing more definite with each one.

And now here she was with the first copy she had written for Empire State under the aegis of Ashley & Company. And Mr. Jerton was right there, sitting beside her near the long low table where clients usually sat during meetings, penciling in his small "OK to set, B.A.J." on the lower right-hand corner of each piece of copy, and uttering those incredible words about $10,000 a year.

° ° °

She forced herself to wait until they were on the Peekskill train that evening before telling Rick. Several times during the afternoon she had passed his office, seeing him alone at his desk through the frosted glass, but if she were to go in there, there would be no way she could keep an everyday face or a low controlled voice while she told him *this.*

They always entered the train separately at Grand Central and sat in different cars until it was clear that nobody else from the office, except for Andy, was on the train with them.

Today the waiting was nearly beyond her. The timing of this was in itself a miracle. Just last week she had had her first failure at Ashley, or what the client called a failure. More accurately, what the client called unacceptable, though the best minds at Ashley had assured them her campaign would not be a failure at all.

It was a testimonial campaign for Starlight Cream, a rival of Pond's Cold Cream. Mrs. Dunwoodie had asked Jossie if she would like to try her hand at a basic new idea for it. Starlight was one of Ashley's big cosmetic accounts.

"I'd just love it."

A testimonial was no longer rare—as when Pear's Soap in England long ago used the famous Lillie Langtry to endorse their product—but it was still a fresh approach to "authenticity" if the fee to the star were large enough. Jossie thought there must be some new way to go about it, and when she found it, she went to Amantha Dunwoodie with an odd sureness of success.

"If we can get her," she began, "I thought of using Marcia Malone for this. Great big picture and her signature—"

"The Ziegfeld Follies star? You do shoot high. Let's see the copy."

My friends think I'm 25
but I'm really 35—
I use Starlight Cream every night

"No actress on earth would admit she's thirty-five," Mrs. Dunwoodie protested.

"She would if she were really forty-five," Jossie retorted.

There was a burst of laughter from Amantha, but when the campaign was formally presented to Starlight Cream, Inc., there was no laughter.

"Never mind," Mrs. Dunwoodie told her. "It *was* clever; it would have been the talk of the town. Some day we'll get another client to use it and Starlight will go wild."

But rejection stings, and Jossie had felt it. Now, within days, Mr. Albright and Mr. Jerton had turned her world around. When Rick heard about it, he'd give her that look that sent her sky-high.

The train seemed to remain in the tunnel for an hour. She could wait only until they passed the stop at 125th Street, and then she went straight to him. The seat beside him was occupied.

"Come on out to the platform," she said. "I've got something to tell you, can't wait."

"It must be pretty terrific," Rick said as he followed her out. It was a dangerous place to stand, open to the elements, one side given over to the iron steps, the other a low picket fence of metal railing. In a moment the conductor would order them back inside the train.

She told him. Her voice rose, not only in battle with the screeching of the wheels on the rails but with her own excitement. Rick's excitement at once matched hers; his praise was instantaneous. What a coup this was, how proud of her he was. He kissed her; they clung together above the swaying of the car and the clanging of the wheels.

"Do you remember that thing about 'how to live well on nothing a year'?" she asked at last. "Imagine how well we could live with me earning ten thousand a year and you—"

There was a check in Rick's mood, as if her words were reins that pulled him up short.

"And you probably earning even more by that time," she added quickly. "Probably up to twelve or fifteen."

The postscript did no good. Something had been halted, and there was a faltering silence. The swaying of the train suddenly seemed more emphatic, the low railing inadequate, their being there too perilous.

"We'd better get back inside," Rick said.

They stopped just inside the door, in the narrow aisle between the lavatory door and the water cooler, before the seats began.

"Look, Jossie," he said, and paused. There was something stern in his face, a frown of intensity. "What you're going to earn in a few years has nothing to do with what I'm going to earn. We're not in competition with each other."

"Heavens, no, never."

"By that time I hope I'll be out of it altogether. Look at the way it went during that one vacation week."

"It was so wonderful to see you so happy. And so wonderful when you let me read some of it."

His expression softened. It had been a heady time for him, a sweep of sureness day after day, writing more easily than was usual to him, working on what was still amorphous in some ways, but developing under his pen and mind. He thought of it as if it already had a title, and each time he thought the title it moved him: "As Though the Emerald." Sometimes the phrase condensed itself and became a single word: "Emerald." That moved him too.

The train jolted them and they were thrown together. "This is wonderful too, darling," he said. "We'll talk more when we get home."

° ° °

Suddenly the summer was over. They were back on West Tenth Street, and soon there was a marked acceleration in the arrival of the pale blue envelopes with the beautiful French stamps.

They were indeed going to operate. The continuing tests during September had led to a consensus of opinion among three specialists that Jean was in the earliest stages of uterine cancer and that a hysterectomy was definitely indicated, not a partial one but complete.

Rick was sailing September 20. Surgery was scheduled for October 1.

Try as she would, Jossie could not dispel the sense of foreboding that invaded her. It seemed a part of her, a spirit residing in her, tenacious, a dybbuk. She wasn't clear about what a dybbuk was supposed to be, but it sounded right, threatening, menacing; once she said to Rick, "I'd better light a candle Friday night or whatever, and see if I can exorcise it."

"I'm nervy too."

Her foreboding arose not only from the dread of cancer, and the apprehension always attached to major surgery, but also from something Rick had said. "At last I'll be able to talk to Jean about you and me."

"Oh, Rick, not while she's facing an operation."

"Of course not. Later, when it's all over and she's fine again."

"Maybe she won't feel fine, knowing—"

"She's a pretty levelheaded woman, Jean is," he said. "She's not going to go into any mental spin at the idea of a hysterectomy, any more than she went into postpartum depression after Kathy and Kenny were born."

"Are you sure she didn't? That was before you'd ever met her."

"I'm sure. I'm always sure with Jeanie, as she is with me."

He had never said Jeanie before; there was a tenderness in it, a sympathy, that perhaps he didn't want to put into words. Jossie thought of what she had written in her journal, about that awful sense of being finished, and wondered if Rick now was thinking the same thing and if that "Jeanie" had welled up out of his compassion.

Or was she assuming that what she, Jossie, felt had to be what anybody would also feel? What Jean would feel, this unknown woman who was already so much a part of her life. Would they ever meet? Would they ever become friends? Friends as she was with Edie, or something closer than that, like another sister, another part of her family? Or was Rick all wrong, and would they be enemies?

"But Rick, what if she isn't levelheaded about you and me, after all?"

"We'd have to work that out, then. It might take time, but unless the unforeseen happens, some postoperative complication nobody expects, we *would* work it out."

She hesitated. "Darling, you've said that all along, but could we talk a little now, about *how* you think it might work out?"

He took her hands into his. He understood this rising anxiety, now that he would be seeing Jean so soon. "Do you mean, what am I going to say, how am I going to put it? I haven't come to specifics like that."

"I don't mean specific words. Just, how do you see it over all? Suppose she decided to come back to New York for good. This apartment isn't big enough for you and Jean and the kids, so you'd move, but then where—I mean who would live where—I get so mixed up."

"I never meant anything like all of us living together—no ménage à trois or anything as bohemian and modrun as that."

He always said *modrun* when he was ridiculing; she had never thought he meant a ménage à trois either.

"Look, Joss, Jean isn't going to leave Paris for at least another year—all that was her choice, remember. But suppose she was here, right this minute, and suppose I had a job where I had to be away every weekend, a traveling job of some sort, a salesman, say. Would that put up impossible problems for Jean?"

"If you were away every weekend?"

"If I lived at home with her and the kids Monday, Tuesday, Wednesday, Thursday, and then had to be off Friday and the weekend, would *that* be so terrible?"

"You mean a sort of split life, each of us knowing and accepting the way it was." She said it slowly, testing it word for word. Would she, Jossie, think it too terrible? Would Jean? It sounded so simple when Rick put it this way, so rational, so attainable, but could she or Jean accept such a shared existence?

If you loved Rick enough, she thought almost angrily, you could. If you understood his abiding need to feel free of too-tight bonds about anything—about work, about marriage, about so-called virtue or fidelity—you could. Rick was so different from most people, so variegated, so gifted. Recently he had read her more of his book; it was fine and strong and brilliant. What he had read was a sort of interlude, a digression, a short piece embedded in the whole, about "pathological coxcombery," and she had found it original and delightful.

"Not exactly a split life," he said now. "More like a contrapuntal life. At least for me."

"What a wonderful way to put it," she said. "With all the elements playing against each other to be fuller and richer. Oh, Rick, I do see how it would be."

o o o

"If only it weren't September," she wrote a week later in her journal. "This is our anniversary."

> It was just a year ago, on the 10th, that first night I slept with my dear love, and whatever is to happen now, it will always remain the sweetest year I've ever had, since that night, coming out of girlhood and virginity so gladly and gaily and freely, through the days and nights of reading gorgeous poetry or books, talking together, feeling deeper and deeper into our real selves, knowing more surely that we had made no mistake in finding each other.
>
> Now, in ten days, I'll be alone again, a month without Rick, a month of an empty bed, without his gorgeous physical thrillingness. I'd thought of going back home for the month, but I'd rather be alone to think of him and write him and get his letters without anybody watching to see how many or how often. Not Mama, I don't mean, but Pa, who probably knows by now, since I never asked her not to tell him.
>
> Anyway, I'm staying right here where all our lovely life has been. I haven't been going around sniveling; most of the time I'm finding myself calm, contained, and not very goddam boisterous. It's going to be a month of wondering—

She laid her head down on the narrow pages of her loose-leaf book, the three metal rings digging into her cheekbone. She knew her tears were running into the blue ink of the page and lifted her head, jerking the book aside as if to blame it for her crying.

Rick was asleep. He had been working intensely, getting ready to leave, doing Ashley copy that was coming due in the next weeks, not his own writing. That had to be set aside again in the crush of preparing for an extended absence from the office. He was furious at having to interrupt it, he said, but when you had no choice, you had no choice. It might even be a good thing for his writing, to let it lie fallow for a while.

Jossie returned to the paragraph she had left. The phrase *a month of wondering* stared up at her. She glanced at her watch; it was nearly three. They had finished their packing and gone to bed and fallen asleep together. But an hour later she was awake and had been unable to fall asleep again. She hadn't written in her journal for weeks; she had turned to it as to a good friend, but tonight that single page was all she could manage. Now she closed it, turned out the light, and went back to Rick.

o o o

The twentieth of September was hot and clear, a pure summer day with no hint of autumn's brisk winds and changing colors. As their taxi neared the pier of the French Line, they sat in silence, their hands interlocked, Rick's luggage at their feet.

"Suddenly I feel pretty frantic about leaving you," he said.

She couldn't answer, except through her tightened fingers. He had talked about "using the other two weeks of my vacation," as if that would be all the time he would need, but the *De Grasse* took eight days to get to France, and there went the two available weeks, just for getting there and back. Rick had already told the office that he would need a leave of absence without pay for another two weeks, perhaps for three. He hoped he would be back at Ashley by the end of October at the latest.

He had gone to the Morris Plan, telling them of major illness, and made another loan of $500, turning over $130 of it to her at once, for the four weekly payments he would be away, as well as his half of the October rent. His payments would now be $20 a week, but there was no other way to manage this emergency. The steamship fare, round trip, came to $195, and Dr. Leclerq and the hospital would doubtless take most of the rest.

"Don't worry about money now," Jossie had said.

"I can't worry about it now. But when I get back I might have to hit them for a fast raise or do what I said about another job somewhere else at more money."

"We'll see. You have enough on your mind right now."

"So have you. Don't ever think I can forget that."

He had bought a new suitcase to go with his old ones—the new one also marked C.U.B.—but he had refused to do any serious packing until just yesterday. She had done most of it for him. Rick could never pack properly; she had discovered that during their spring weekends at Peekskill before they had moved up to the cabin. How long ago those early weekends already seemed, how carefree and innocent.

The pier was crowded; the routine of embarking went slowly. They went up the gangplank together, to see the ship and his tiny cabin. She had never been on an ocean liner, and though this was a small one, one of the new single-cabin liners, she thought it handsome and romantic, the dining room and lounging rooms splendid and the very sense of being on an oceangoing steamship an excitement in itself. He had brought a Thermos with some martinis, and they tried to be gala, like the bon voyage parties in the cabins around them. But they were both relieved when the call came, "All visitors ashore."

From the dock she looked up at him, standing there at the rail. The warm September sun was pleasant on her face, the river sparkled as if it were that other river, up there near Harmon, miles away from the traffic and bustle of tugs and barges and ferryboats and great ships.

She saw only Rick, his hat off, his thick hair blowing, his hand raised again and again to wave. There was a series of blasts and whistles, the gangplank was pulled up, and then she saw the water widening between ship and pier. Her eyes went hot with tears. Goodbye, my darling Rick, goodbye. I love you so.

Eight

She would have a cable in the morning, telling her it was over. He had cabled from Cherbourg the day he arrived; two more days had passed, and today they were doing the surgery. It was October 1. Paris was five or six hours ahead of New York; she wasn't sure and didn't want to be. It was easier not to visualize, if you weren't able to think, Now, at this very moment. Perhaps it was already done, Jean already in the recovery room. He would wire the moment he could.

She had known there could be no mail for at least two weeks, even though he would mark his letters for one of the fast five-day boats of the Cunard Line or the French Line. She carried his first cable in her purse as if it were the only link between them, the only promise, the only reassurance.

ARRIVED CHERBOURG WROTE DAILY ABOARD
MISS YOU LOVE YOU ALWAYS

She too had written every day; he would find the first two or three letters waiting for him in Paris. She didn't let herself write him during office hours; she saved that up until evenings, so she could have something to look forward to after her solitary dinner was over.

Now she sat at Rick's desk, addressing an envelope for the letter she had just finished. Again she wished there were some other address than Jean's apartment on the Île de la Cité. How babyish that she should wish that. She could hear Rick's dear voice chiding her, "Baby won't do," like that night she wrote the first draft of her letter for Mr. Albright and the Empire State Plate Glass Company: "Cute won't do."

An ache of longing invaded her. It was too bad she had no ads to write—work helped. Marty King, the advertising manager of Lacq, had wanted three more pieces; she had done them all in two evenings and already had her $30 check. Perhaps she ought to use this hiatus, this chasm of time, to get some more free-lancing to do. *Don't stretch it too far*—well, she certainly hadn't. No one on earth could say her work at the office had suffered.

Idly she drew out some of Rick's special yellow paper and wrote her name on it. Joselyn Stone, Joselyn Stone, Joselyn Stone Baird, Joselyn S. Baird, Jossie Baird. By Joselyn Baird.

By Joselyn Baird. That little word, *by*—what that did to you! The day Rick had shown her the copy of *Smart Set* with his first short story in it, the very presence of his name right there in black ink on white paper had sent a thrill along all her nerves. She could see it again as if the opened magazine were in her hands.

The Weary Young
by Cedric U. Baird

She went over to the bookcases on either side of the fireplace and found the issue that contained it. *April 1916,* it said on the cover, that was eight years ago. If only Rick would make himself—he will, she thought, he will. It's the only way he will ever be truly happy, so the time will come when he will. Joseph Conrad didn't begin to write until he was forty-one.

She put the magazine on the bed; she would read his story once more. She stood gazing at the bookshelves. All of Havelock Ellis and Bernard Shaw were there, most of Conrad, many by Arnold Bennett and H. G. Wells and Aldous Huxley. Henry James was there and all the great Russians. Scott Fitzgerald's two famous novels were there, too, and two volumes of his short stories. She had read the earlier one, *Flappers and Philosophers,* but not the other, *Tales of the Jazz Age.* Standing there, she opened it and thumbed through the pages, reading the titles, some of which were already familiar. After a few minutes, she put the book down on the bed. Somehow she resisted Fitzgerald now, especially his endless stream of magazine stories.

Once she had had an idea for a magazine story; it was while she was taking her night course at Columbia's School of Journalism, just about the time she had come up with her silver dollar and the piece of ore. She had thought of a name for it, a phrase she liked. Columbia also had a short story course, given at night, but she had never signed up for it.

She went back to the desk and again drew a sheet of Rick's paper toward her. She wrote the phrase down, printing it, centering it on the page as if it really were the title for a story.

The Flame-colored Evening Dress

She stared at the words, then underlined them, then hesitatingly wrote underneath them.

by Joselyn Stone

> Lila Jordan looked down at the shimmering chiffon and wondered what to call its color. Peach? Orange? It was neither one, rather a wedding of both, and it was beautiful. She had never had an evening dress of her own, until the fluke of winning this lottery, and here it was now, hers, and the glittering headband to go with it.
>
> But I'm the wrong person for it, she thought. Where will I ever wear it? When will I ever need it?

> Lila Jordan was twenty-two, but she had never gone to a dance where people wore evening clothes, never gone to wild parties and raced around in big cars, never been on a yacht and had champagne to drink. She had never danced the Charleston.

Jossie paused. *She had never danced the Charleston.* Maybe that was a better title than the one she had chosen. Scott Fitzgerald would probably call it just that. *She had never danced the Charleston.* It sounded like Fitzgerald.

I've never danced the Charleston either, Jossie thought. When we go dancing, it's in a Greenwich Village restaurant with a dance floor the size of a peanut. If you flung your legs out sideways, that way, you'd knock over somebody's table. I've never done any of the things Scott Fitzgerald is always writing about. It may be the Jazz Age for his gorgeous girls and their rich young men in great ballrooms under crystal chandeliers, but for me and everybody in the whole world I've ever met, it's a million miles from that. Except maybe for a dance or a prom at college, half the time in borrowed clothes.

Mostly we have to work for a living. We have to think about rent and unpaid bills and debts and loans and making it stretch to payday. And it never stretches to evening gowns and drinking champagne and dancing the Charleston.

She glanced at the bed where the book of stories lay. There was something artificial about all those people in all those glittering stories. Maybe that was why she'd been staying away from Scott Fitzgerald, not just Rick. Flappers and Flaming Youth! It even sounded flippant and false.

Once in the office, Red Montana, also a beginner then, had written a funny poem and handed it to her, watching her while she read it. That was at the very start, before she'd had her first date with Rick, before she'd done more than smile at his "Welcome to this idiot place." Fred Montana—Red, for his freckles and hair—was assistant to one of the art directors, and he was one of the first people there to make her feel that Ashley was a pleasant place to work. She had read his poem and laughed.

> Jossie's not a flapper,
> She wants that understood;
> But what a flapper she could be,
> If Jossie only would.
> Her hair is brown, her eyes are huge,
> Her figure makes you swoon,
> If Jossie only had some sense,
> She'd date me pretty soon.

She went back to the yellow page before her. Lila Jordan. Where had that come from? Where did anything come from? The square inch of glass? Any headline she ever wrote? It didn't matter where; it just came when you tried for it and needed it hard enough. With Rick gone, she needed this. Maybe the evenings would be easier if she kept on with it. Evenings were the cruel times. Days you could work and nights you could sleep, but evening was when you knew what it was to be alone.

She began to write again.

> Lila hooked her fingers under the slender straps of the evening dress and held it up before her, moving to the mirror, trying to imagine herself actually wearing it. She would need evening slippers to go with it, silk ones dyed to match, or perhaps sandals of thin gold or silver straps, with high spike heels. She had never owned evening slippers either.
>
> The sensible thing was to go straight back to Macy's, where the dress came from, explain that she had won it as second prize in a lottery, and ask if they would exchange it for something that would fit into the life she actually lived. She had been to Macy's already, to get the dress in her own size, as the Lottery Committee had arranged, but that time she had been too excited to think in such practical terms, and too surprised to see how pretty she could look, her arms and shoulders bare, the lovely color of the dress making her skin look delicate and fresh.
>
> She could see herself going back to the same saleswoman at the store, hear herself explaining, feel the empty drag in her mood as she watched the woman take the box out of her hands, lay back the lid, unfold the tissue paper. The very idea made her draw back. Fluke or no fluke, she would never give up this soft shimmering dress. It was hers and it meant something. It was like an omen of some lovely shining thing ahead in her workaday life.
>
> Lila had worked for a living ever since the day she finished high school. She—

Again Jossie paused. There was a delight in making up this Lila Jordan who had never had an evening dress. It was strange and new and stimulating, creating her, feeling sorry for her, as if she knew her, wondering whether there would be some lovely shining thing ahead for her, wondering how the story would end.

No wonder Rick loved to write. To see something that wasn't there come to *be* there, spinning it out of yourself, reaching inside and somehow pulling out the gossamer thread of invention.

And when it wasn't for some client, when it wasn't about plate glass or nail polish or perfume but about people or emotions or ideas, there was a kind of splendid surprise in it, and a crazy elation. Rick knew all about that; all that vacation week up at the lake, she had seen it in his face.

He had taken his manuscript to Paris, by now a sheaf of about sixty pages, planning to do some work aboard ship, certainly more during the week of Jean's convalescence before he started home. Do it, darling, she thought, really do it, no matter what. Even if you can't see ahead, even if you don't know yet how it will come out. Right now I know exactly what it feels like when you start writing something for your own self.

She wouldn't tell him now about Lila Jordan and the flame-colored evening dress. Now was the wrong time. Certainly she hadn't the faintest idea how it would go. But she could turn to it every night for her own sake while Rick was away; it would be there, waiting for her every evening, promising not a void of time before she could go to bed but a project she cared about, a new kind of solitaire, a riddle and a seduction all in one.

She flipped her two pages together and put them into the desk. She felt happier than she had since the morning the boat sailed.

○ ○ ○

There was still no mail from France. By now his first letters, the ones he had written on the boat and mailed at Cherbourg, should have been here, but the mailbox was empty.

She stood in the small hallway before the shining brass plate that contained the six mailboxes of the house, reopened her morning paper, and turned to the arrivals and departures of all major steamships from France or England. She checked their New York arrival dates and then checked the dateline at the top of the page: Monday, October 6, 1924. She had been sure the first letters would be here by October six.

She could hear herself say it, over and over: "By October sixth I'll have his first letter."

October sixth? Now the two words fell like pebbles, hard on the ground of her disappointment. October sixth. It had some other meaning too. Suddenly she knew.

Then I'm two days late—I should have started Saturday, October fourth. She always knew when it would come next time—exactly twenty-eight days ahead, always twenty-eight. She never thought about it, never made little check marks on her calendar the way Nell did, who was often irregular. She merely ticked off in her mind what the next date would be and it always turned out to be that very day.

October fourth. And this is October sixth—that means I'm overdue, two whole days over. Oh, I can't be, I can't, not now, not while, oh, I just can't.

It's not possible, not while Rick's away, not while I'm here by myself without being able to tell him and ask him what to do. Not at the very same time Jean—

Jean was all right. Rick had cabled fast rate, the moment it was over, just one word, SUCCESSFUL; it had been waiting for her that same afternoon when she got home from the office.

She slapped the brass door of the mailbox shut, and the metallic ting told her she hadn't moved. She began to walk to the office.

She had never lost track before. This time there had just been too many dates to think of, to calculate on: first, September 20 and October 1, then all her private scheduling—he gets there September 28 and his letters start back the next day, September 29; they get to New York five days later, October 4; and I get them a day later, October 5, but October 5 is a Sunday, so it will be October 6.

Never once had she thought in terms of the curse—she hated the schoolgirl word but couldn't break the habit—the only dates in her mind were of the big things that were happening. And now this, the biggest of all.

How could it be? They had been as careful as they had been all along, and for a whole year there had never been a scare. They had come to think of themselves as lucky, almost exempt from any need to worry. But they'd had some frantic nights these last weeks; perhaps just one time they had delayed a moment too long, hating that breaking apart, rushing to the bathroom to douche, wanting only to stay quiet together, waiting through that wonderful ebbing away.

To have it happen now? With Jean lying there, her womb cut away, and me suddenly pregnant—it's horrible. Why did it have to be now?

She stopped at a street corner, out of breath. She had been racing, running from pursuit, by what she did not know. Of all juxtapositions, of all cruel ironies, this was the most insupportable.

Her mind went numb with the enormity of it. She couldn't think; she had to think; it wasn't possible to stay calm enough to do any rational thinking. A roaring of fear went through her.

She would call the office and say she couldn't get in today. She had to see a doctor. There were tests they could make to see if you really were pregnant. She had never been to a gynecologist. The only one she knew of was Nell's; she couldn't ask Nell for his name. She didn't want Nell in on this—sometime she would tell Nell, but not now, when Nell would want to advise her and discuss it with her. Perhaps Edie—no, not Edie either. Mama. "If ever it does happen, I hope you won't try to handle it all by yourself."

There was nobody but Rick who could handle it with her. Only

Rick would believe it at once. Everybody else would say, It's too soon to be sure, wait another week or two, perhaps the strain and worry about Jean's operation and Rick's going—perhaps all that is the real explanation. Emotional problems very often disturb your body chemistry, upset all the normal timetables.

All right, she thought, I'll wait until tomorrow. She clutched her paper and her purse under her arm and began beating her hands together as if they were cold.

She did go to the office. She talked on the telephone, she had a meeting, she wrote some copy, rewrote more, read proof, but all along she felt encased in some stony outer shell, talking or writing as if at a distance, holding on to the thin edge of quiet. Every half hour she went to the ladies' room to see if by some miracle—

She could never force herself to "wait a week or two," never. She might begin to think of it as a pregnancy, instead of a misfortune. This way it was two cells united, but if she waited, she might start thinking of it as a pregnancy. She might *want* that.

o o o

Four letters came in the morning mail, but now the very reading of them was changed. Every word of tenderness, every yielding to his own erotic need, was now fraught with a *double entendre* he had never meant.

> My beloved Jossie,
> I want you near me this very moment; I feel as if I had left the one warm sunny island in my life and gone into storm. I think of your slim lovely body and in that instant I'm hard and hot and desperate for you. But it's more than sex or lust or general depravity; it's your goodness and your mind and your bright ability, and my own sense that with you sharing my life, there are no huge problems, certainly no insoluble ones.

No insoluble ones. What solution could he come up with if she now reversed the cabling and wired him:

> PLEASE COME HOME AM PREGNANT AND FRIGHTENED
> LOVE ALWAYS

She would never do it, could never do it. Not even in a letter, where she might ease the shock for him. To burst in on him with a new crisis while he was sitting for hours at Jean's bedside in the hospital would be a piling up, a compounding, smashing this at him just when he was beginning to come out of the other.

Was it a kind of duty to tell him? Was she honor-bound to let him know? But what could he do, how could he change anything?

She had slept only fitfully the night before, dreaming, tossing, abruptly waking each time and going to the bathroom just in case—

Did it hurt, an abortion? She had never been in a hospital except that one time as a child to have her tonsils out. She could still remember the ether smell right inside the front entrance, remember her hand clutching her mother's, remember the icy block at the pit of her stomach. She probably wasn't very brave.

And how much did an abortion cost? That part of it hadn't occurred to her until this minute. At once she thought, Money, again money. No matter what happens in your life—sickness, crisis, desperation, sorrow, anything—somehow it is tied to money.

Before Rick left he had made over the bill of sale on the car, putting it in her name. "If there's any emergency, darling, sell it and use the money. You'll probably get the same forty it cost us."

"I never have emergencies."

"Then don't sell it. It's like a small insurance policy."

She might do just that. The rest she could manage somehow. If only he were here to tell her how you went about selling a car, about how much you had to hurry, about how safe it was to have an abortion. How to make it safe.

Two or three times she began a letter to him that evening, a letter like any other, a letter of delight that his letters had reached her at last: "Dearest Rick, Four letters came this morning, the first, and they made me so happy—"

Each time she gave up. She couldn't put it in a letter, and she couldn't cable. There was no way to reach him and ask for his help.

I'll wait one more day, she decided at last. Tomorrow I'll call Mama.

o o o

"Oct. 19, '24," she wrote in her journal two Sundays later. "Never will I forget that pain or that night, not if I live to be a hundred. I can't write Rick about it, so I'll put it down here, so I can never even try to forget it.

> There was no anesthesia, and if you could remain alive while you were being disemboweled, that's what it would feel like. My throat nearly split open with the screaming; I couldn't stop. Mama said for all the thick door she could hear me.
>
> Once the doctor shouted at me, "One more yell and you get up and go have that baby," and I hated him as I never knew you could hate anybody on earth.
>
> Mama didn't know he wouldn't use an anesthetic. She was sent to him because he was an expert gynecologist in a real office in his public life, not some filthy midwife who ignored things like sterile instruments. But whoever recommended this Dr. Gordon—that wasn't his real name any more than mine

was Betty Jones—didn't tell her that he never used anesthetics because his license didn't cover anesthesia, and for him to use it by himself increased the risk. He had no nurses except his wife, but she had no license for it either.

The office looked like an ordinary apartment, but the operating room was spotless and scientific, with sterilizers and the rest. When I went in, I asked, "Will it hurt very much?" and he said, "It's over in a few minutes."

"I'm awfully scared, doctor."

"If you want to leave, you may leave right now."

He knew I couldn't leave and it began. Maybe it only took a few minutes—it felt like a forever of agony. They say you forget the pain of childbirth the minute it's over, but that must be because you're so happy. Nobody could forget this kind of pain.

And I'll never forget the way Mama was all through it. When I called her, I said something awful had happened, and she came in that same evening, right to our apartment, which of course she had never seen before. And I told her about Jean's operation and Rick being in Paris, and even before I got to me, she knew why I had asked her to come in.

I didn't tell her until I'd had tests—they take time—but when I did call her and tell her, she just sat there, both her hands on my arm, pressing down, tears running down her face, and the strangest smile too, just sitting there, loving me—I could feel it—and crying at the same time. No talk of disgrace or immorality, no caviling for a minute at the moral or immoral aspect of it in the world's eyes, caring only for me and my fear. She's a beautiful woman. I've got to know it more fully with my fuller maturity since I've had Rick. Her spirit is a shining, stirring thing—fair and understanding and just plain big. I've often felt I ought to be more generous in my love for her—show it more, let her know it every day in ways that touch her, more phone calls, more time with her, and from now on I'm going to try more. I love her, next to Rick—no, not "next to," just in a different solid way.

Well, anyway, she found out whom to go to from our family doctor, saying it was the daughter of her closest friend, he not believing her, but breaking the law himself even to give her the name and address, but doing it because he couldn't turn her away, admiring and respecting her the way he does. She made all the arrangements with Dr. Gordon and Friday night went there with me, and then came here and stayed overnight, sleeping on the sofa, because she didn't want to leave me alone the first night, just in case.

At the doctor's they keep you there for about two hours

afterward, lying on a cot in a sound-proofed cubicle next to the operating room, and Mama was allowed to sit beside me. She hardly spoke, just sat there, her hand on my hair, feeling my forehead every once in a while the way she used to when I was little. But no fever, no hemorrhaging, so then they let you go home, the same night.

And all the time I was on that cot, despite the soundproofing, I could hear periodic screaming, and I knew there were other girls in there going through it, one after another, and I almost couldn't stand that either.

Well, anyway, now Rick's been gone for 3½ weeks and in 10 days he'll be home and I can tell him. Mama never argued with me one way or another, about my telling him or not telling him or when, nor about my saying I had to wait till I could tell him face to face, not in a letter. I'm sure that's right—to write him across an ocean when he can't advise or talk or help would be just inflicting punishment on him, as if our living together were a crime committed by him alone that he had to do penance for.

His letters have sustained me through all these horrible days, each one filled with Rick's own self. Jean's convalescing is going slowly, more so than they'd expected, and he still hasn't had that big serious talk with her about us, though he has told her he would, as soon as she was really strong again, and she's intuitive enough to know it's important and that it's about me.

He says he talks a lot about me, and I'm glad. And he gets a letter from me every day too, and she sees them. When I asked if maybe I ought to address my letters care of Cook's or American Express in Paris, he looked surprised, maybe even shocked. You know the basis of my marriage, he told me, and if anything has changed in it, I'd better know it.

I finally got to the point where I learned how to "write around" the whole pregnant thing and the abortion and could write him normally again, telling him there was something I was saving to tell him when he got home but didn't want to put in a letter and then writing all the other million things I was spilling over with all the time, like the terrific thing about Stuyvesant's on Fifth Avenooooo.

Have to quit now, my fingers are all crampy. I did sell the car for $40. The fee was $50. In cash. No checks.

So, darling Rick, when you talked about a small insurance policy in case of emergency, you were taking care of me, even though we neither of us knew it. Hurry home—I'll die if it's much longer without you.

o o o

Through the windows of Jean's living room, Rick stared out at the lights on the Paris streets. The Île de la Cité was like an offshoot from one of the avenues, like a British mews in London, on the right bank, near the rue de la Paix and the Madeleine, but Jean's apartment was in a run-down old house, given over to small apartments with a monthly rent that one would normally find on the other side of the river.

Something's up, he thought, something's been worrying Jossie and she doesn't want to bother me with it now. Maybe she's more disturbed about my being here with Jean than she expected to be and is holding back. Or disturbed that I haven't talked it all out with Jean by this time. Whatever it is, she doesn't sound like my open-hearted little Jossie, pouring out everything she feels. Not for the last two or three letters.

It will be worse when she knows about the delay. God, the unpredictables in life, the new tide of necessities rolling in on the ebbing of the preceding. She'll take my two tumbles with Lucienne in her stride, or if she doesn't, quite, at first, I'll help her see it for the nothing it was. But she knows I'm not the man to go an entire month with no sex, and that it was as meaningless as going so horny you had to jerk off. After all, it's the basis of our love too, telling instead of concealing—it's been that from the first minute.

But this delay, this need to stay on, the extra cost, the extra Morris Plan payment—maybe two—that I didn't leave her money for—my poor Jossie.

He looked in once more on Jean, sleeping uneasily under the puffy featherbed as if it were winter, then looked in at the children. It was midnight, but he had not even considered sleep. He and Jean had been prepared for the doctor's pronouncement about the wound not healing properly, but having it made today was still a shock. He poured himself another glass of wine.

"It is most distressing, madame," Leclerq had said, "but to ignore this condition longer, in the hope that nature will finally take care of it, would be to run a needless risk that the wound might reopen."

They were in the office, Jean seated and Rick standing beside her. "How could such a thing happen?" Rick had asked.

"As you know, the operating surgeon himself does not do the final closing. In this case, though my young colleague is an excellent man, he apparently made the suturing at too shallow a level. That is why we still have not removed all the stitches."

"And Dr. Marraut agrees with you?"

Leclerq nodded. "We discussed it thoroughly. It is not often that it happens, but when it does, resuturing is the indicated course. This time I will do it myself."

"She would have to be in hospital again for how long?"

"Perhaps only three days. It is minor surgery. We would suggest that Mrs. Baird come in tomorrow."

Tomorrow was the day he was supposed to sail home on the *De Grasse*. It had been apparent for a week that the wound was not healing properly. In the hospital they had removed only every other stitch as a precaution, and she had been permitted to go home that way.

That afternoon he had canceled his passage and booked one for the following week. Ten times during the evening he had tried to figure what this extra week would mean in lost pay, in money needed for the new medical bills, what to do about the November rent and the next Morris Plan payment, not covered by the money he had left with Jossie—possibly the next two payments, before his paychecks began to come in again at the office.

There was no way to handle it; without money set aside there never was any way. He must earn more, would have to earn more and soon. He had talked of leaving Ashley and finding another agency where they would pay him a good deal more, and now he would have to do just that. Circumstance was forcing him to stop thinking and get at it. A spectacular jump in salary was never achieved by the orderly route of waiting for annual raises.

But what to do now? He who never bothered unduly with the bookkeeping of life, who seemed to have it in his blood that there was something picayune in pennies, was now counting pennies. He suddenly remembered his mother's voice so long ago—"If it can't be real silk, then I'll not even try it on"—and all at once felt himself a little boy again, swinging through the flower-laden air of a summer day in the back yard of their house in Richmond. "If it's not the most perfect, then nobody in this family would even consider it."

All day he had known what he would have to do, and he had kept putting it off. The November rent could wait, but not the Morris Plan payments. He didn't know whether a grace period was granted before the co-signers were notified; not once had he entertained the notion that such notification might ever occur.

He had talked to Jean about his loss of another week's salary and asked if she could lend him a couple of hundred dollars from the money she'd had from the Princeton house, but Jean had unhappily said no. What little was left from the Princeton money was in municipal bonds and couldn't be sold for two more years. She had already paid several medical and drug bills out of her own money without even telling him, and she was pretty worried herself about the way money went. He needn't send her the November check—would that help?

"It's all I can do to make out as it is, Rick. Tonette has already said she couldn't manage the food without more money each week." Tonette was the *bonne à tout faire*, without whom Jean could not take her art lessons and do her painting, the good Frenchwoman who cared for the children, stayed with them when Jean had to be out, cleaned, cooked, shopped, sewed, washed, ironed, and mended all their clothes: "All the humdrummery," in Jean's own phrase.

He hadn't wanted to press her while she was ill, though her refusal irked him; it had to mean she was sure he could find a way to manage it himself. It was no time to have a quarrel.

One afternoon when she had returned from the hospital, and before there was any sign of real difficulty with the healing process, he had asked if they might have "one of our good serious old talks."

"You mean about Jossie."

"Yes, about Jossie."

"It's become very important to you—all the letters tell me that it has."

"Very important. It's not just a light affair."

"I ought to say, Let's talk, Rick, but truly I'd rather put it by for now. After all, while I'm here in Paris, I'm not in your way, not challenging anything, and you've been fair about not concealing anything. Just as I've been about François. I'm glad you and he met, I'm glad you got along—he was a little put off at the idea of meeting you, with you knowing. He's not as easy as we are about things like that."

"Deception and intrigue more to his taste?"

"Now, Rick, don't be snide. Or smug. Our way is the exception, after all, and takes practice."

"You're right, darling. I was just making a crack."

"And as for the 'good old serious talk,' you'll be going back to New York next week, so it seems sort of extraneous to have it now."

"But you're not going to stay in Paris forever."

"Of course not." She clasped her arms lightly across her stomach. "Darling, it's not conducive to serious thinking when it hurts so."

"I keep forgetting it still hurts even when they let you leave the hospital. Sorry, Jeanie. You look so well now, you fool me."

She did look well, considering. She had lost weight and the pull of pain still tightened the faint lines in her face, making her look older than her thirty-two. The painkilling medication prescribed for her tended to make her listless and drowsy. If there were no limit to the length of time he would be here with her, he wouldn't have attempted the "good old serious talk" for several more weeks.

Kathy and Kenny had come in from school then and provided a tactful suspension of that attempt, and he wouldn't make another until just before he sailed. Right now it was asking too much.

But about the money problems, there was no way to delay even for a few days. He would have to cable Jossie. His need disgusted him. She would understand, she would want to help, she would shift things around, yes, but it was untenable that he should ask her. Again he felt himself back in the amorphous world of little boyhood. There were things you didn't do; common people might do them, but "our kind of people" never did. Southern ladies and gentlemen—*nobody in this family would even consider it.*

He hated his own memory for taking him back there so accurately to the farce of gentility, his family's refusal to see reality, their insistence on pedigree and status, on an aristocracy whose roots were in decaying family trees.

And yet he could not write the cable. He remembered that afternoon of Jossie and the dispossess notice, saw again her eager face, heard the warmth in her voice. "My college money—that would be a big chunk, a whole third."

Never, not borrowing from my own girl.

Again he tried to print out a cable. To send it as a night letter at reduced rates meant it had to be off before two in the morning, and it would be hard enough to condense it to fifty words. He poured another glass of wine. Then he faced a fresh sheet of paper.

> SORRY TELL YOU FURTHER MINOR SURGERY NEEDED AND HOMECOMING DELAYED WHOLE WEEK STOP CAN POSTPONE NOVEMBER RENT BUT WORRIED NEXT TWO MORRIS PLANS STOP COULD YOU SELL CAR AND COVER BOTH PAYMENTS STOP NOW BOOKED CAPRICE ARRIVING HOME SIXTH THANKS ALL LOVE WILL NEVER LEAVE YOU AGAIN

He finally made a clean copy and went to the nearest cable office. It had been a terrible period anyway, more so for poor Jean but hard for them both. The very notion of sex or making love was banned emotionally. Once the words *cancer* and *hysterectomy* and *surgery* were spoken between them, any train of thought about sexuality was banned, any gesture of stimulation or arousal somehow monstrous.

This must be what being middle-aged is like, he thought once, where you love each other, but where the sexual part of that love is in quiescence, where the clamor and insistence is lessened or perhaps departed.

He thought of Jossie, and a fiery tumescence brought instant guilt, as at a betrayal. He rejected the guilt, denied it, exiled it, but he knew that desire was there and denial useless. Better to accept it, to say *mea culpa* and be shriven by one's own honesty.

It was part of life, the trading of values, the exchange of levels of living: the hot passion of being young for the devotion of time-spawned continuity. His love for Jean was there, deeply there, but illness and financial pressures had, for now, swathed it in so many layers of difficulty that it lay quiet in an insulation that muted its voice.

But it is all there, Rick thought, soundproofed and layered but there, and after this is behind us, Jeanie and I will find our lives on a new level, stronger than before.

But when he slept, he dreamed of Jossie, his ardent loving young Jossie.

Nine

Stuyvesant's on Fifth Avenue was one of the youngest and most talked-about specialty shops in New York. A specialty shop, Jossie quickly learned, was not a smaller department store; it sold no pots and pans, no furniture and bedding, no lamps and curtains and towels. It sold only clothing, and if it was a successful specialty shop like Stuyvesant's, it sold only "high fashion."

Until the day that Marty King, the advertising manager of Lacq, had approved two more nail-polish ads and then asked if she would like to do a little fashion advertising for a friend of his at Stuyvesant's, she had never set foot inside it. It was too expensive. It was the feminine equivalent of all Rick's impeccable stores, of Knox and Brooks Brothers and Dobbs and Sulka and even, in its custom department, a fair contender for the lofty plateau inhabited by Drew, Tailors to Gentlemen.

The chance for a little extra money could scarcely have come at a more opportune time. Rick's cable had left her with no alternatives; the car had gone for something more important than Morris Plans, but those two extra payments stood there like rocks. Suddenly she had remembered the Bursar's office at Cornell and blessed everybody in it. They had forbidden her to do what she'd wanted each week, so by now there was again $66 in her special postal savings account, separated from her checking account and sacrosanct. Without hesitation she had used it. Cornell allowed ten years; maybe they'd have to wait the whole ten.

It was in late October, with her private horror behind her, with Rick's extra week drawing to a close, that she met the head of Stuyvesant's, not the advertising manager but one of the two owners, Jack Weinstein. He was in an obvious state of nerves.

"I heard you were good from Marty King," he greeted her. "I have no time to spare on mistakes. The holiday season is breathing down my neck. The season for evening clothes."

She thought of the flame-colored evening dress. She had worked on it nearly every evening, writing and rewriting, tearing up and starting again. She was at page 14, and by now it was clearly a story, with a middle she liked and an ending she could almost feel sure of.

"Evening clothes," Jack Weinstein repeated. "Gowns, furs, accessories, long gloves, lingerie. The high season."

"The Horse Show next week," Jossie said, nodding. "First nights at the theater, the opera, New Year's Eve."

Mr. Weinstein looked gratified, as if he hadn't been sure she would know what the holiday season meant in the world of fashion.

"And all our advertising for it is down the drain," he said, his right hand making a downward swooshing motion, as if the drain were gaping there at his feet on the thick beige carpet. "I want high fashion, and I get Delancey Street."

"I've never done fashion copy," Jossie said.

"Have you ever been to a real dance? To a first night? To the opera?"

She nodded. She already liked this round red-cheeked little man who was so frank about his eleventh-hour nerves.

"I sit up in the top balcony, but I see all the lovely clothes."

"I don't want only a piece of copy, like you do for Marty King. Nor two pieces of copy. I want an idea to wrap the store around for two entire weeks."

She looked puzzled. "An idea, not copy?"

"Copy comes with the idea, of course, but it's a basic idea for the store I want, smart, not everyday advertising, something extra. Do you think you could? Would you like to try? How much time can you give me? It's breathing down my neck, I tell you."

She held up both palms and her mouth formed the word *Whoa!* She was not nervous; it was the first time she had ever been in somebody's office talking about free-lance copy without being nervous.

"I could give you *all* my spare time for nearly two weeks, except November sixth. You know I have a regular job, at an agency."

"Ashley's, and they'd fire you if they found you working on your own. Marty King told me. They don't tell me their trade secrets; I don't tell them mine."

"They've recently changed their policy about free-lancing. They didn't use to mind."

"They make their own rules, the big agencies. We have a small agency, but we write our stuff here. The agency only does the mechanical work: plates, typesetting, placing it. How much did Marty say he paid you for an ad?"

"This wouldn't be like the ads for Lacq. Especially if I did come up with 'an idea to wrap the whole store around.' That's called promotion, more than advertising."

"So what would you charge?"

"Fifty dollars for each piece." She had had no idea of what she would ask, certainly not five times her usual fee, but as she spoke the words they seemed eminently just. This was not her usual assignment either. A ping of excitement went through her at her daring.

Jack Weinstein merely nodded. "How soon could I see something—a sample, even a rough draft—so I could decide whether your ads would be Delancey Street or Fifth Avenue?"

She laughed a little and again put up her palms. "Could I ask a few questions and see some of the copy you turned down? It would give me a clue about what *not* to think of doing."

He buzzed for his secretary. "Get me all the submissions on evening clothes. And the artwork."

His secretary left, giving Jossie a fleeting look that said, You poor thing.

Mr. Weinstein turned to his desk as if the interview were over. "After you read them, we can decide if you want to try. How long does it take to get an idea and show me some copy?"

"Sometimes a day, sometimes a month. I just can't promise—"

"A month—forget it, goodbye. A month from now is Thanksgiving. We have to start two weeks before Thanksgiving or the season's down the drain." Again his hand made the swooshing motion to the carpet. "Three days, four, is the most, at least to give me an indication. Otherwise I'll have to try somebody else."

For no good reason Jossie changed the subject. "Marty King told me you and Mr. Stuyvesant were co-owners of this marvelous store. Is it true?"

"Fifty-fifty from Day One. We fight, but we succeed together. One without the other's no go."

"I was wondering why it's just called Stuyvesant's."

He turned back from his desk to face her again. What was this girl? Just nosy, or trying to get to know him a little so she could write better for him? His rosy face brightened to a higher shade, as if he were angry. Or delighted.

"I'll tell you," he said, all hurry and tension dissolving, as if he had decided to play along with any whimsy his young visitor might offer. "There are some names go together. Like Bergdorf with Goodman, Lord with Taylor, Abercrombie with Fitch. But Stuyvesant with Weinstein?"

For the third time his hand swept downward and she laughed aloud. "That's funny," she said, meaning it.

"If you were Jewish," he said, "you would know it's not so good for me, but only good for the business."

"I am Jewish. My mother's name is Stein—that's where I got the Stone."

"And your father's name?" Before she could tell him, he said, "Never mind, never mind. Here comes Delancey Street."

His secretary gave a sheaf of papers to Jossie and said, "You can read them in Mr. Stuyvesant's office. He's out today."

"Read them here," Mr. Weinstein said. "You won't bother me."

He immediately ignored her and Jossie began to read. In five minutes she knew what had made him turn all the copy down. It was all gush, typical fashion gush: "the latest Paris fashion," "the newest of haute couture," "the glitter of gold," "dusted with sequins," "the gleam of satin," "the new long waistline," "the newest dip of hemline."

The artwork was all photography. Everybody knew you couldn't get photographs to reproduce well on newspaper stock; *Vanity Fair* and *Vogue* knew it; their fashion pages were printed on heavy paper with a high-gloss finish, from plates that were days in the making, light-years away from the overnight mats for department store advertising in daily newspapers. She had picked up a lot of pointers about engravings and rotogravure and artwork in general from Red Montana, who had been assigned to the Empire State Plate Glass account.

"You've seen enough," Jack Weinstein said, before she had come to the end of the material before her. "You see what I mean?"

"I don't like it much either. I'm not sure why, not yet."

"Because it's all for people who say 'a formal' when they mean an evening dress, and 'a tuxedo' when they mean a dinner jacket."

Again she laughed. "A bit of snob appeal, is that what you're after?"

"What else? Look here, young lady, let me give you a little background. Brick Stuyvesant is from Park Avenue and Yale; me, I'm from Seventh Avenue, and my father before me. But I also had two years at Columbia—I'm not your garment center man. Together Brick and I are from heaven, because we know both sides of this crazy business, and if you should be right for us, it could be heaven for you too."

She set aside the copy and layouts.

"So where do we stand?" he asked. "Where are we? This is Tuesday. Should we say by Friday? Just an indication at least?"

For the first time she did feel nervous. "I ought to see some of the evening dresses you want to advertise, Mr. Weinstein. I've only seen what's in the windows, remember. I'm not exactly a Stuyvesant customer, even though I don't say 'a formal.'"

He started to push the buzzer. "You can make a tour of every department right now."

"No, I can't. My lunch hour is nearly up. I could come back at quarter to six, but the store isn't open then."

"I'll have the doorman wait for you and let you in tonight. One of my best people will wait too, to show you around; Mrs. Pepper, she is. Are we all set?"

"I'd like to try it."

This time he did push the buzzer.

o o o

To wrap the store around. In every odd moment for the rest of the day, Jossie kept thinking, *To wrap the store around.* A theme, a storewide idea, with some unifying thread. Newspaper ads, yes, but that's only part of it. Something to wrap the store around, something extra.

She could think of nothing. Through the evening and all the next day, Wednesday, nothing. By Thursday evening she thought, Two days of cliché, two days of nix, and tomorrow's Friday, my deadline.

Friday was the day Rick was sailing on the *Caprice.* No wonder I can't get an idea, she told herself; all I can think of is Rick being here again. At least Stuyvesant's is keeping me from going mad these last days of waiting for him.

Each lunch hour she'd gone back to Stuyvesant's and sought out Mrs. Pepper. She had tried on evening dresses, imagining herself in them, visualizing herself in the world where they would one night appear, loving their delicacy and color and—admit it—their look of being the most expensive clothes in the world. Like that damn diamond as big as the Ritz, she thought once, and grimaced at herself in the mirror. With due respect, Mr. Fitzgerald, no offense intended.

And then, on her way to the office Friday morning, it came. She recognized it as if it were labeled *This is it, this is right, this will do it.* It was only a phrase, a headline, but a whole concept was locked into it, and unless she was crazy, it was perfect for Stuyvesant's.

Simultaneously she saw the kind of illustration she wanted for it—not photographs at all, but drawings, pen and ink or crayon, something done by a bright illustrator, by somebody who didn't think a girl in an evening dress had to look like a John Held Jr. caricature of a rich flapper.

She went down the aisle to the Art Department the moment she got to the office and stopped at Red Montana's large worktable. "Can you come out in the hall, Red? I want to ask you something." She glanced around the large area, where several other men sat at their tilted drawing tables. In the hall she scarcely waited for his "What's up?" She liked him and he liked her; he was always willing to rough out a first-draft layout for her, and he had talent. He had twice sold illustrations for fiction in women's magazines and she had seen them in print and admired them. "Some day you'll be another James Montgomery Flagg."

Now, as they stood together at one end of the reception room, she said, "Red, how would you like to stay up half the night with me?"

"Your place or mine?" He grinned.

"Yours, where you have sketch pads and pencils and brushes and India ink. Would you think of free-lancing a couple of roughs for me?"

"Would I ever. They can take their new policy and you know what."

"It's a secret, and it might flop. I'd be working right alongside you, giving you headlines, doing some pieces of copy, all short. It's not plate glass, it's fashion. Should I tell you? Cross your heart?" He obligingly made the gesture. "I'll pay for two roughs myself if they don't go for my idea, or the layouts or whatever."

"When do we start?"

They met at seven. She had telephoned Mr. Weinstein and asked for an extension, through the weekend. "I think I've come up with something," she said, "but I'd like to have a layout or two to show at the same time."

"Not the whole weekend. Tomorrow morning, yes."

"All right, Saturdays I get out at one."

"So be here at one-fifteen."

At Red's one-room studio apartment that evening, she laid a single sheet of copy on his oversized worktable, saying, "I wrote it during lunch hour." She laid it face down, while she reported fully on Jack Weinstein's collected stringencies and foibles. Red had never been in Stuyvesant's either, not even to buy a Christmas gift for his best girl, but he was very much the young man on the stag line and knew all about party clothes.

"So everything you do," Jossie ended, "will be a knockout girl in a knockout dress and, just behind her, sort of shadowy, her date, a young man about town in his dinner jacket."

"Just standing there?"

"Maybe a taxi outlined behind them, or a theater marquee."

She turned up her piece of copy.

It's time to dress

Red whistled, "God, what a headline."

"It's going to be part of every ad."

It's time to dress

> The first-night curtain is rising: at Carnegie Hall the Philharmonic is tuning up; at the Met the sopranos and tenors are waiting in the wings; in the ballrooms of famous hotels, the chandeliers are blazing.
>
> The New York season is beginning, and it's time to dress for your part in it.
>
> Whenever you feel that you want a new dress that makes you part of that great New York season, you will want to come to Stuyvesant's. The evening dress shown here is on our third floor today. It is of pale pink chiffon; the appliquéd rose petals are of wine velvet; its line is perhaps daring and its price slightly forbidding.
>
> • STUYVESANT'S INC. •

"It's a million-dollar idea," Red exclaimed.

"Under the dress, in small type, the price: $150. That itself will keep out everybody but the people who can afford Stuyvesant's."

He picked up a crayon and drew his large pad of crackling white transparent paper toward him. Then he read the ad again.

"I want them to have small signs—*It's time to dress*—in all their Fifth Avenue windows," Jossie went on, "and also in every department: furs, accessories, purses, gloves, everything. The whole store wrapped around *It's time to dress* for two whole weeks. That's what he wanted, something that ran right through the whole place."

"You are one smart lady," Red said.

She opened her purse and drew out assorted scraps of paper. "The headline in the second ad might be, 'Opening Night at the Belasco,' but we'd have a diagonal strip across the upper left corner that says, '*It's time to dress.*'"

"Sure, a running device."

She read from another slip. "'Paderewski Plays at Carnegie Hall next Thursday.' But again the diagonal cutting across the corner."

Red whistled. "Jack Weinstein will not only go for it, he'll offer you a job."

"I'd never leave Ashley's."

○ ○ ○

That had been what Rick was to call "Your quantum jump into the big time." When at last he did get home, it had been marvelous for Jossie to have this to tell him about, and an equal marvel for Rick. There was so much for each to tell the other that was dark, somber, distressing, that their first nights were heavy despite the joy of being together again. Even their passion of lovemaking had a new profundity, it seemed to them both, as at a rescue from wracking storm.

When she told him about the abortion, Rick groaned as if he too knew what it was to be disemboweled; for hours he kept returning to it, needing to know every progression of detail, from that morning at the mailbox to her decision not to let him know, to the tests, to her helpless screaming, to her mother's hand on her hair in the soundproof cubicle.

"If only you'd waited for me, my darling. It's so wrong that you had this by yourself."

"Don't you *see?* By then it wouldn't have been just two cells—"

He did see. And she also saw when he told her everything about Jean and the doctors and the stitches left in for safety, and the residue of frustration he tried to ignore. He seemed unwilling to talk even briefly about the new burden of hospital bills and doctors' bills, beyond a disgusted, "Outrageous—about ten times what I'd figured from the curettage last spring. Well, they'll all have to take their turn."

But he did want her to know each sentence, every nuance of his ill-fated talk with Jean. He was scrupulous in his reporting; he made Jean's position totally understandable, free of anything small or mean. He also disclosed his own sense of defeat at the outcome.

"One other thing to tell you, darling," he went on. "One night, after the big operation, with Jean still in hospital and everything going along nicely, as we then thought—one night I stopped at a bistro near the hospital, and there was a girl, a midinette she was at Galeries Lafayette, a place like Macy's, a girl named Lucienne—"

He saw her eyes widen. "And you—oh, Rick, I'd rather not know, really."

"Darling, it was a meaningless—"

"It's the first time it—it—I hate it. Don't make me know."

"Darling, it's part of the foundation we've built on, that we each do know, that we don't keep secrets in some dark place. It was nothing, no more than if I'd had a wet dream or masturbated. She was an ignorant little thing, rather sweet and lonely, not a prostitute, embarrassed when I handed her a few francs."

"Oh, Rick, I know it's nothing, but the very idea that you could—I'd die before I could let anybody."

He hadn't expected her to be so agitated. It irked him, as if she had broken a pledge. He almost said so and was irritated at himself for his impatience. Even so exceptional a girl as Jossie really couldn't see it; perhaps the possessive instinct ran too deep. Well, the one thing he could never put up with was the sense of being possessed in that sense of exclusivity forever, that lack of freedom. But this was no time to have a quarrel with Jossie either.

"Sweetheart, listen. At times a man is just a beast in heat—emotion isn't involved, love isn't, the future isn't, the only thing is to get rid of the big swollen ache in his balls. That's all it was. I must make you see that it didn't count then and doesn't now."

While he was talking she suddenly thought, At least he didn't make love to Jean. Something eased as she thought it.

"I'm glad you told me about it, Rick," she said solemnly. "But I don't want to talk about it any more."

They talked about everything else instead. Like Rick, Jossie needed to know every progression of detail of his month with Jean and kept returning to it, as he had done with her abortion. They both understood the other's need, and slowly, gradually, they fulfilled that need. But each was left with something to absorb, with something that called for strength and wisdom, and each knew that there no longer was for them the light young happiness they had once known.

But everything she told him about Stuyvesant's and Jack Weinstein gave them surcease and laughter.

"You have it," Weinstein had blurted out to Jossie when she saw him that Saturday. "Exactly *it*. We'll run a different one every day for fourteen days. Can you give me fourteen separate ads?" He didn't let her answer. "And your Red Montana for the drawings—can he give me fourteen too? How much will he charge? Never mind that now."

He pressed the buzzer. "Get me Mrs. Pepper," he said to his secretary. "I need some dresses selected. And also Joe Klein from the agency—we'll need some graphics, window streamers, and counter cards. When Brick comes in from lunch, ask him to come in right away."

"I just sat there listening to him," Jossie told Rick, "sort of in a daze, counting on my mental fingers: fourteen times fifty is seven hundred. I can do most of it before Rick gets home, so I'll be free as air."

"The big time," Rick had repeated. "There never was anybody like you."

He had been home for a week when she received her check for $700. She had never seen such a check in her life. At once she decided not to deposit it in her regular checking account, to get all mixed up with her weekly salary and monthly expenses.

"That's called commingling," Rick had told her.

"I want no commingling. It sounds dirty."

The postal savings bank seemed absurd for so vast a sum. She chose a second bank which she immediately dubbed her FLEA account, "free-lance emergency account." Her first check was for $200 for her Cornell loan, $100 for 1923, which she had skipped, and another $100 for 1924. Then she paid, by money order, the delayed November rent, both sides of it, Rick's and her own. And then she called Nell.

"I bet you thought I'd never pay you back," she said when they met for lunch one Saturday. She handed over a check for $100.

"I did know you would. At the time I was so upset at the idea of my kid sister having an abortion, I didn't worry about it anyway."

"I didn't have an abortion that time," Jossie said, with a slight emphasis on the word *that*.

"But you said—"

"I really didn't, Nell. You took it for granted, and I just listened while you told me what I needed the money for. I was too upset myself, about what I did need it for—it was a jam Rick was in. But I was glad you made it so easy for me not to tell you."

Nell looked at the check, folded it, and put it in her purse. "You said you didn't *that* time; does that mean you did some other time?"

"Last month," Jossie said quietly. "Mama got me through it."

"Mama? Why couldn't he?"

"He was in Europe. Otherwise he would have."

Nell's look said, I'll bet, but she kept silent. Jossie relied on her not to get into sisterly warnings and advice, and Nell did not.

"How come you have this extra hundred, anyway?" she asked. "Is it Rick's?"

Jossie told her about Stuyvesant's and her new "flea account," and they ended up laughing.

Rick laughed also. He approved highly of her checks to Cornell and Nell. "And there's no fleas on a four-hundred-dollar balance, my wealthy young friend."

"Three hundred."

"How three, not four?"

"I paid the November rent, to give you a little leeway until your paychecks come in."

Vehemently he said, "Nothing doing!" Before she could speak, he said, "No such thing. You're not paying my rent for me, not now and not ever. No girl's ever going to support me."

"Don't be so damn Southern gentleman," she shot back at him, equally vehement. "It's a loan, not a girl supporting you. I'll get a notebook and keep track of every dime."

She was surprised at her answer, standing up to him instead of folding up like a leaf, as she always had when he disapproved. Apparently he was surprised too.

"Hey, little firebrand," he said in a different tone. "Cool down."

"Oh, darling, if we can be so Havelock Ellis about everything else, why can't we be emancipated and civilized about money?"

"Well, start your damn notebook with the three hundred dispossess money, then forty for the two Morris Plans, and now fifty more."

"Okay, I will. Dates and what-for each time, and you can pay back every last nickel."

She bought a little red notebook the next day, listed the three amounts, and showed it to him. On the first page she had written *Rick Baird—Debtor's Prison.*

He laughed again, and took her to bed, and told her once more that he loved her more than he had ever known he could love anybody. "I never thought at the beginning," he said, "that it would grow into this for me, Jossie. You're part of my life now—I could never go back to a life without you at its core."

For all their renewed closeness, for all the surcease and laughter, it turned into a difficult winter. Rick was often restless and depressed, unable to give a specific reason for it. He fell into silences; his old trick became more frequent, of reaching up to grasp a strand of his hair, twisting it round and round on his index finger. He was drinking more, sometimes red wine, often martinis, even late at night.

Once she did ask if he couldn't give her some general idea by now of what his book was about.

"It's a mixture of fantasy," he explained, "and kind of a running commentary on certain aspects of life that my principal character experiences. Did you ever read *Jurgen?*"

"I kept meaning to."

"Well, mine is sort of opposite to what Cabell did in *Jurgen*."

"Is it a novel? Wasn't *Jurgen* a novel?"

"Yes, but mine isn't a novel. It's something in between." He looked contemplative. "Call it a halfway-house novel."

"It sounds fascinating."

"If it comes off the way I want, it might be."

But he worked less and less happily on it, and his mood seemed to darken every time he did. He admitted that the trip to Paris had somehow dragged down whatever creative impulse he had been building up before.

"Apart from the worry about Jean," he told Jossie one evening, "and the uncertainty and suspense, there was something wounding about being put off from that talk about you and me. I knew why Jean had to do it, but my sutures aren't holding too tightly either."

Jossie felt the wound too. Heaven knew when he would be in Paris again—a year? Two years? And would there then be some other good reason for Jean to say it was the wrong time to talk about it? Like busy ants swarming, doubts again began to leave tiny tracks on the surface of her mind.

I'm still nowhere near thirty, she would think. There's so much time; even if there were no Jean at all, we'd probably want to stay just this way. If only Rick could work the way he did last summer. There must be some way to help him get there again.

And then came an evening when Rick's restlessness was so apparent, from behind the closed door where he was seated at his desk, that a sudden impulse seized Jossie to have him drop it all and go out somewhere.

She could hear him crumpling up paper, hear him opening the drawer for fresh sheets and then slamming it shut, hear him from time to time muttering and swearing under his breath.

At eight-thirty she knocked on the door. His astonishment showed as he opened it. She never interrupted him.

"Darling, let's get out tonight," she said. "I'm all itchy and restless too. Let's call Andy and Edie and maybe go to Gypsy's or somewhere for a drink."

They had both recognized the relief the evening gave them. They began to see more of the Bellocks again, more of other people. Jossie told Rick she thought Red Montana ought to know about their living together; Jack Weinstein had wanted three more ads, aimed at New Year's, and it was too awkward always to specify that they had to work at Red's place. Rick readily agreed, and they had dinner twice with Red and his girl, Suzy Plotnick.

"Almost as improbable," Jossie said, "as Joselyn Yavnowitsky," and they all laughed. "What do you make it at your office?"

"Suzy Platt."

"After all, she's in advertising too," Red said comfortably.

Suzy was with J. Walter Thompson and breezily said she'd had such a fight with her copy chief that afternoon that she wasn't sure her desk would be there in the morning.

"What about?" Rick and Jossie asked together.

"Oh, I was writing about enamel bathroom fixtures—big tubs, ample washbasins, *you* know—and I said, 'and a handsome fixture for the toilet paper.' Well, Miss Mahoney, my copy chief, nearly swooned. 'You can't *say* toilet paper in an ad.'"

Again they laughed. Rick said, "No wonder she swooned. When you think of all the words that are exiled from the vocabulary of all ads, in this the twentieth century—"

"Sweat," Jossie said. "You can't say sweat in an ad."

"Smelly feet," Red said, wagging an admonishing finger.

"Constipation," Suzy said with enthusiasm. "Can you imagine an ad saying, 'Take this pill for constipation'?"

"Kotex," Rick put in. "Or anything about menstrual cramps."

By this time they were vying with one another to think up other unmentionables in their world of taboo-talk, as they called it. Pimples, bad breath, body odor, piles—

"Even if you promoted them and said 'hemorrhoids,'" Rick said. "The nice-Nellies, the sanctimonious bastards."

Later, Jossie said to Rick, "We haven't laughed so much for a long time. It's good to feel just plain silly. Let's see them again soon."

But it was the Bellocks that they called most frequently or who called them. Neither man seemed to remember their fracas last summer over Rick's debt, and not once did Rick consider turning to Andy again for a loan.

"One little nose-bleeder like that," he told Jossie, "and you're fixed for life."

When the bills came in from Leclerq and Marraut and the anesthesiologist and the hospital, Rick stared at them for a moment and then threw them into the bottom drawer of his desk in the bedroom. At times Jossie found herself wishing that these Paris bills, like all his New York bills, were addressed to him at the office, so she would never even have to see them arrive. Once they were in that bottom drawer, he seemed able to forget them, but as if her own eyes had X-ray powers, she felt that she kept on seeing them, day after day, lying in a nasty festering little pile, like a growing tumor.

Twice in the first December nights she awoke with a start, as if the desk and its silent bottom drawer were a living presence in the room with her, angry, explosive, a presence only she could feel.

It's not fair, she thought stormily, the second time. Rick can throw them in there and then sleep like a log all night long, but I just can't. I hate them for being there. Next month another batch will come, marked "second notice," and the little pile will be twice as large.

If only Rick would let me—but he doesn't wake up at night, and he'll never see why I should.

And when her check came from Stuyvesant's for the three New Year's Eve ads, she didn't show it to Rick, as she had her other free-lance checks; she quietly deposited it in her flea account and didn't even tell him she had received it.

Ten

One of those unlikely February thaws came to New York a few weeks later, and the city felt the first promise of spring. Ridges of grimed ice and snow melted at curbs and in the park, the sun shone benevolently from a cloud-tufted sky, and in the streets men walked along with their overcoats draped over their arms.

At dinner with the Bellocks one evening, they talked not only of the weather but about Peekskill and the lake. "This summer," Andy said lazily, "all we'll have of you two up there is the red canoe." They had kept it for them in their boat shed over the winter, blanketed in straw and burlap against the cold.

"Andy knows I have an idea," Edie said slowly. "But it's still up here." She touched her head. "Still wrapped in burlap like the canoe."

Just those words sent a shiver of anticipation through Jossie. In this first unlikely spell of warm weather, she had been thinking of the cabin again, even wishing that some miracle might yet happen before it was sold, to let them make that $1,500 half-payment in cash and buy it themselves.

"My fine wife," Andy put in indulgently, "would never make it as the next Vincent Astor of real estate."

"Andy still wants to sell it," Edie said, addressing herself now to Rick. "But I don't want to at all. We were so sure somebody would snap it up last year, but look what happened."

"You got us—with the help of a Cambridge don," he said, but in his tone there was something that might have been longing.

"I'm sure if we held it for three or four years, we'd get twice as much for it," Edie said, "but of course it's a dead load to carry until then." She looked at Rick, then at Jossie, then picked up her fork and began to etch numbers into the linen tablecloth with one of its tines.

"Land taxes," she said as she outlined a pair of 8's, "are eighty-eight in March and eighty-eight in September." She etched the figure 4. "Water taxes are four dollars every three months." She added two 2's. "And fire insurance is twenty-two a year. It comes to about two hundred ten."

"If we rented it at fifty a month for four months," Andy put in, "we'd have it tax-clear and make a ten-buck profit."

"Oh, Edie, Andy, are you saying—?" Jossie cried.

"Is this a bona fide offer to rent it again this summer?" Rick asked. "For four months this time?"

Andy laughed. "Edie can do a lot of bookkeeping while wrapped in burlap. Sure it is."

"Oh, Rick darling, let's sublet our place for the whole four and be rent-free again."

"Start commuting *May* first? Damned if it doesn't sound good."

"I can't bear it!" Jossie jumped up and went around the table to hug Edie. "I dreamed about the cabin and the lake the other night. I love it so up there."

"And God knows it makes it easier to get some work done," Rick said. He had finally abandoned the halfway-house book and had shifted to the idea of a straight novel. He had written the first chapter.

° ° °

He wrote Jean almost at once about the summer.

> Just this week, we decided to sublet West Tenth and take the cottage we had last summer again, this time for four months. It's not only to live rent-free and pay off some long-overdue bills, but that I work better up there on my book. This is not the old book, on which I blocked up as stiff as a board, but a new idea, one that I have a visceral heat about, that I feel sure will be the dynamo I need all the way to the end.

He glanced over what he had written and saw that he had said *we*. *We* decided. Momentarily he considered starting anew but felt that would be shabby. Jean was well able to stand up to problems again; she was over the operation and convalescence, strong and active once more, and in good spirits about her painting. She had had two pictures shown in a gallery in February, and one had sold for $80.

> You remember the "good old serious talk" we had to put off when we were together, because you were still in such pain? I said then it was no mere affair, between me and Jossie, and you see from this that that is still true. (The *we* still means Jossie and me; no cracks from you about "you and who?")
>
> Jeanie, I know this presents you with interior problems to be handled, perhaps unexpectedly difficult, and I know that the world's cliché has it that you can't love two people at the same time. You and I don't go in for the world's clichés, and we never have.
>
> I see it, as I hope you will, as a coexistence of forces, neither detracting from the other, but united in a kind of fused strength. I'd wanted very much to have this all out while we were together, but you did make me see that not only was my

timing rotten, but that since we were to live apart for the foreseeable future, you in Paris and me here, that it was "sort of extraneous."

From the point of view of *loci* it still is, but I didn't want to move back to the cottage without letting you know where to write or cable me direct.

And I know you'll remember what we've said all along in our marriage and our love, that an occasional heaviness between us never tips the scale of values we live by for more than a little dip, and that we come out on a balance more level than ever.

All love, always,

o o o

They had just signed the sublease with a young couple from Canada when Jack Weinstein summoned Jossie to Stuyvesant's. It was the middle of April, and they had bought another used Ford for Peekskill, again a two-seater runabout, this time for $50. The money came from the flea account.

Her raise at Christmas had more than lived up to Mr. Jerton's promise. Billings on the Empire State Plate Glass account had been larger than expected. She'd been jumped not to $50 but to $60 a week. Her year-end bonus was $150.

Rick had been raised to $6,500 a year, with the more usual bonus of $100. But "unexpecteds" like a car still came from the flea account.

"The bill of sale is made out in your name," Rick said as they closed the deal.

"But I wrote the fifty in the little red notebook already."

"Leave it in the little red notebook. You own the car."

"Oh, Rick, come on."

"Can I ride in it?"

"Now I own a car *and* a canoe. I'm getting to be the Forsyte Saga itself."

That was the day Jack Weinstein called her. As she entered Stuyvesant's, Jossie thought, Wait till he hears I'll be commuting at specified times until fall and can't be available for command performances.

"I hope there's no more changes on the spring ads," she greeted him.

"You call those changes? They were pin adjustments, not more than a tuck and a tightening." He was beaming at her. "You have a knack for fashion writing, Jossie, you must know that."

He had begun to call her Jossie with the spring assignment. It was only seven ads this time, not a storewide promotion. Her opening advertisement, a large one in the better Sunday papers, had again delighted him, and he had told her so.

It's spring
and you're young
(or not so young)

> If you are young you know the longing for one special suit or dress to greet the new season.
>
> And if you are not quite so young, you know the impulse toward renewal, and want at least one important new dress to satisfy it.

It went on, briefly, to describe the dress and state the price, and once again Jack Weinstein had not bothered to conceal his approval. He had invited Brick Stuyvesant into his office to meet Jossie, and Mr. Stuyvesant had been equally open in his praise.

Brick Stuyvesant was a head taller than his partner, and lean to the point of emaciation, particularly next to the rubicund and rotund Jack Weinstein. Jossie got the impression, for all his pleasant words about her work, that he was a little ill at ease talking about promotion and advertising—indeed, about the world of fashion and merchandising itself. She was not sure where the impression came from, though Jack Weinstein had once told her that Brick Stuyvesant had provided most of the original backing for their enterprise when they began five years ago, just after they'd been demobilized together at the end of the war. They had met during the war, had been through some bad times together, and had come out determined to "go out on our own," before they knew in which direction they might go.

This time Jack Weinstein was alone. He didn't rise when she came in; except for the first interview he never did. He waved her to be seated and then lined up eight pencils in a rigid row on his desk. She counted them.

"What do you make over there?" he asked abruptly.

"At Ashley's?"

"Where else? I know what Marty King pays you. He told me."

She hesitated. You weren't supposed to talk about your salary; at the office there was an unwritten rule that you could be reprimanded, even fired, for telling your colleagues exactly what your pay was or how much of a raise you were given.

"I make sixty a week," she said. "Three thousand one twenty a year."

"I'll double it," he said promptly. "A hundred twenty a week. Six thousand two forty a year."

"You *what?*"

"Jossie, don't act surprised. You must have known I'd be offering you a job here, full-time, not this in-and-out, off-again-on-again arrangement."

"But I could never leave Ashley."

"Why couldn't you?"

"I like it there. They trained me. They put a big investment into me, taking me on as a cub copywriter—"

"Ho!" he jeered. "They've sold you *that* bill of goods. They all do it with a talented young kid." He thumped the desk. "Listen, whatever they invested in you, you've repaid plenty by now. How long have you been there?"

"This is the start of my third year."

"And if you hadn't brought them the plate-glass account, you'd be earning thirty-five a week—a fat five-dollar raise each year."

"But I like it at Ashley," she said, a little less firmly. She was thinking, Six thousand a year—that's almost as much as Rick gets. We really could get caught up, once and for all—

"You like it there! I liked it when I worked for my father on Seventh Avenue. It was safe; it was a paycheck every Friday. Should I have stayed there forever? Gone back there after the war when I was getting close to forty?"

Jossie just sat there, looking at his row of pencils. Her neck felt hot; she didn't know how to say what she wanted to say. He rearranged the pencils in another row, this time with the erasers all pointed downward. He waited.

"I'm not sure I would want to work full-time in any store," she said carefully, nervous at her effrontery. "Even so wonderful a store as Stuyvesant's. I mean doing just fashion copy."

"You like plate glass better?"

"I kind of enjoy having different accounts. They use different parts of my brain. I'm not sure just what I mean, but let me think about it for a while."

"Think? You don't need to think. You've already told me: You don't want to limit yourself. Okay." He stared at her and she wondered if she had offended him. Then he leaned forward over her desk. "Then how about free-lancing, half for me, half for all the different clients in the world for the different parts of your brain?"

"Oh, Mr. Weinstein, it's a brand-new idea."

"I'd pay you four thousand for half-time. You probably could make another four thousand the other half." He slid four of the pencils to one side. "Four and four—total eight thousand."

"I can't quite take it in, this idea of half-time—"

"If you didn't make another cent in your own half-time, you'd still be getting more than Ashley's three thousand for full-time."

"I never thought of free-lancing all the time. I wouldn't have any office at all—"

"You could have a little office here."

She grinned impudently at him. "No, you don't, Mr. Weinstein. If I had a little office here, I'd be on hand any minute you needed me—without even getting that six thousand two forty!"

"Smart girl. That's probably right. So who needs an office? Your office is in your head."

She told him about Peekskill and commuting schedules, beginning in two weeks. He shook it off. He dismissed her with a wave at the door and a large grin of his own.

"Go away awhile. Think. You'll decide yes. Because you're too clever not to see it. Look, Jossie, how did you get me for a free-lance client? Marty King told me about you, and you about me. This city is full of companies with small agencies who want big talent. He'll tell you about other people needing ideas, and so will I."

"I know you would."

"Except no fashion ads for anybody anywhere."

"Of course not. Never."

He laughed outright. "I like to see young people make the money they deserve. Go think."

She left the office, not knowing whether to cry or to crow.

○ ○ ○

This time Rick let Jossie read his manuscript from the beginning. She thought it brilliant. It was to be a novel with a theme, and she thought it a powerful searchlight of a theme, like a vast telescope peering into the conscience of the world. There had been some wonderful novels written about the war, and the new hit play, *What Price Glory?*, but Rick's novel, she felt certain, was going to be unlike anything anybody else had ever done. Its opening paragraphs stirred her to the heart.

> "People don't hate war," the young soldier said. "They love it. This country was never so happy as it was during the war."
>
> He saw the look of disbelief and shock on his father's face and expected a tirade, but he didn't care what the old man thought. It was true.
>
> There were never so many jobs, so much money, so much to talk about, so many people starving for news, so many newspaper boys on the street yelling *extra* at all hours.
>
> There was never so much fear, rejoicing, despair, eagerness in people's lives, never a moment that could be called drab. Unless they had a son killed in action, or maimed or missing, their life was at a higher intensity than it had ever been before.
>
> They were happy. If they could admit it, they loved war-

> time and war. They were like men going to brothels. They were supposed to despise what they did, but there was nothing so damned satisfying as a night with a good whore.

As she looked up from the first page, Rick said, "It may shock everybody, but they'll read it. I don't mean the language. I mean the idea."

"You'll be famous, darling. I just know it."

"If only I could stay *with* it, every day, all day. If only I were a Gauguin type and got the hell away to Tahiti or someplace where I wrote only words for my book, not for ads, not for memos, not for letters, not for one damn thing except the next paragraph of a book."

Got the hell away. Trepidation nipped at her. Did he secretly believe that he would be better able to write if he lived alone? She shoved off from the idea, as if she were shoving off from shore in the canoe.

Rick went on. "At least Gauguin worked in a broker's office all day as a clerk, doing numbers and figures and subtraction and addition. If he'd had a job where he was painting all day, but painting shit, then God help his wasted talent."

"You'll have four months in Peekskill-Tahiti," she said, "and I can wear a grass skirt for you." He smiled thinly, and she added, "You'll be famous, darling. It will be a wonderful book."

In her rush of pride, all other considerations clouded over. So he was able to sleep right through second notices, or thirds, or tenths. He was never going to be a good manager, never lay aside money for emergencies, probably never leave Ashley for that bigger job at more pay that he kept talking about.

It didn't mean all that much to him and never would. When she told him about Jack Weinstein's offer of a job at more than six thousand a year, he'd whistled in astonishment and made a gesture of homage. When she told him the alternate offer of four thousand on a free-lance basis, he'd said, "It's a poser, all right."

"What do you think I ought to do, Rick?"

"It's up to you, and only you."

"But what would you think if I did leave Ashley?"

"I'd think you'd make good at anything you tried."

"Oh, Rick, that's not helping me decide."

"I don't want to influence you, Joss. You have to figure it for yourself. What's best for you? What do *you* want to do?"

He expects me to grab at it, she thought. Mr. Weinstein expects me to grab at it too. I'm the only one who doesn't know what to expect. "Well, he said I'm not to go crazy trying to decide in the next five minutes."

"Let him wait. If you only realized it, you've got the upper hand."

"For once in my life?" She wished she could talk about it to somebody who wouldn't be as fair-minded as Rick, who would take sides and be emphatic and tell her she'd be a fool not to grab it. At times she felt Rick was letting her down on this poser. Each time he would agree with her reasoning, when she brought it up again, and then the next time when she offered the opposite side of all her arguments, he would see the justice of those as well. And always that same *I don't want to influence you.*

"You could help me make up my mind," she shouted at him suddenly one night, and burst into a child's frantic tears. He came to her, took her in his arms, comforted her, soothed her until she stopped sobbing. "I know you're right, Rick. I just wish he hadn't ever made such an offer."

One morning she decided to talk to Mr. Jerton about it, to get an executive point of view. Not to Amantha Dunwoodie, although she was also an executive, with just as much capacity as Ben Jerton to think in pure business terms.

But she drew back from the idea of letting Mrs. Dunwoodie know about this. Twice during Rick's absence from the office, last fall, Amantha Dunwoodie had managed to bring his name into the conversation, for no apparent reason, with no apparent train of thought that would justfify it. "I wonder how Rick and his wife are doing in Paris," she said once, as they came to the end of a brief meeting.

"I'm sure everything's going to be all right," she managed to answer, but she felt flustered and wondered if she sounded flustery. Why should Mrs. Dunwoodie assume that she knew anything about how Rick and Jean were doing in Paris?

In the end she spoke to neither of them. If they knew she was even considering leaving Ashley, who could tell what damage it might do her in the office if she decided, after all, to stay? The entire week passed.

Then in the middle of the night a new idea hit her. She thought of the comic strips where a balloon looking like an electric bulb suddenly lights up. Of course! Why hadn't she seen it before? Something had been sticking in her craw all along, and maybe this was it.

She phoned Stuyvesant's the next morning. Mr. Weinstein was tied up for the day but would see her at five-thirty.

"If this were next week, May first," she began as she greeted him, "and you said five-thirty, I'd have to say, 'My train leaves at five-thirty-two. Don't you see, Mr. Weinstein?"

"You want to put it off for the summer."

"It's not just that. It's not just the summer. It's that I can't afford it."

"Can't afford more money?"

"Can't afford to leave Ashley and work for you half-time."

"For God's sake, how do you figure that?"

"The reason I can't afford it is that I'd lose my biggest free-lance client if I did."

"Who's that?"

"You."

"*Lose* me?"

"Do you know how much you've paid me so far?" She put a slip of paper on his desk.

It's time to dress	$700
New Year's ads	150
It's spring	350

Before he could add it, she said, "That's twelve hundred dollars *on top* of my three thousand one twenty at Ashley. It comes to more than four thousand. Don't you see why I can't afford to give up my secure job at Ashley? This way I have Ashley *plus* you."

He slapped the desk with the palms of his hands and pushed himself to a standing position.

"You got me. I never sat down with a pencil. So I'll raise the ante to—"

"I'd die before I'd let you. This is no scheme to get a bigger offer. I just finally decided to say no, wonderful as it seemed. Please don't be angry at me."

"I'm not angry." He sat down, and his face changed. He looked patient, as if he had time for any length of discussion. He gazed at her in a new way, with some private interest, as if he had come to see her not as a clever young kid but as a young woman who lived a life he knew nothing of, and which she would not wish to reveal to him.

"Are you married, Jossie?"

"No." It was the first personal question he had ever put to her.

"Engaged?"

"Not exactly."

"Then you're going with somebody, and he advised you to say no."

"He said I had to decide for myself."

"But there's the explanation. I see now. You have reasons not to risk a change. So okay. No change."

"Are you angry? Are you going to find somebody else for your copy?"

"Am I biting off my nose?"

"Oh, Mr. Weinstein, thank you. I was so worried that you'd—"

"I like kids with spunk. Go catch your train to Peekskill and your young man." As she was going through the door, he called, "Save me some time in August. I don't want the holiday season breathing down my neck again next fall."

° ° °

This time Rick's entire three-week vacation was spent at the lake, while Jossie still had only her single week. During the two weeks when she went to New York alone and came home each evening to find him waiting for her in the car at the station, her first question nearly always was, "Did it go?"

His answer invariably came in terms of pages. "I did three pages." "I only got one page, but it's so right." "I can't believe it, but today I wrote five pages."

She had never seen him so sure of himself, so free of depression or restlessness. Never had he been so free of cynical remarks about Ashley and all its wonders, never so oblivious of the advertising pages in magazines he read. The world of commerce had ceased to exist. In three brief weeks he'd been transformed. He took two hours off each noon for exercise and lunch, but he worked all day.

"Oh, Rick, if only—" she began one night. She had just read four more pages he had let her see.

"If only what?"

"If only you could just keep on with it, straight through to the end. How long do you think it would take?"

"To finish the book? I don't know. You can't ever know."

"Make a guess."

He drew in his underlip, lowered his eyelids, and frowned. His thumb and index finger went up to the crown of his head. But there was nothing moody in his demeanor; he was calculating, making the guess she waited for.

"With any luck, about a year."

"By the next fourth of July?"

"If I wrote two pages a day, average, I'd have a six-hundred-page manuscript by then."

"A whole book! Oh, Rick, if only you could quit Ashley for just one year and *do* it."

"My God, if only."

They left it at that. It was again being a wonderful summer. By now some of last year's newness had given way to the sense of belonging to the lake and the trees and birds and flowering bushes. Familiarity had bred contentment; each evening the cabin was the haven to which they returned from the day's turmoil and challenge. The red canoe at the edge of the water was a happy beacon for Jossie as they drove the last hundred yards of their way home from the station, and tired and hot as they both were from the long day and the steamy train ride, they always began their evening by plunging into the lake the moment they could shed their city clothes. Often they went out once more, before bed, this time naked, their bodies faintly luminous to each other in the still, cool water.

But this evening Jossie could not get that *if only* out of her mind. In her sleep she seemed to be thinking, If only, and once when she changed positions and found Rick's arm across her body, she thought again, If only he could have a year, a free year, a year to write it. If only I could make that year for him, what a happy thing it would be, what a good year for us both.

In her mind's eye she saw a book, a well-bound book, with gold letters on its spine. Cedric U. Baird. There was no title, but there was the name of the author and it was her own beloved's name.

As she was falling asleep, she thought, Rick's pay and mine at Ashley comes to what? Ninety-six hundred a year. If I did a lot of extra free-lancing—

She turned toward him and kissed him in his sleep. He slept on; he always slept as if he were a small baby, protected and loved.

All weekend that *if only* tapped out in her mind, and on Monday she made three calls, one to Mr. Albright, one to Marty King, and one to Jack Weinstein.

"I need one more free-lance account," she said to each. "I wondered if you could recommend me to somebody I might see about doing some copy. Noncompeting with you, of course."

Marty King said he would think about it, but Mr. Albright said he'd get back to her in a day or so, because one of his fraternity brothers was in the dairy business and had just been complaining it was hard for an ad to say anything about your milk versus somebody else's milk.

"Milk doesn't compete with plate glass, anyway," Jossie said. "Please ask him. Something's come up, and I'd be grateful."

As she hung up she thought of a headline for a milk ad, and grinned. "Ask your baby's advice." Somewhere in there was the kernel of a campaign for milk. Except that milk didn't have kernels. Well, then, drops. She grinned again. Mr. Albright had sounded as if it was highly likely. There was something stimulating even in going after more copy. And no more at ten dollars per ad either.

Jack Weinstein she went to see. She knew what his greeting would be, and he didn't disappoint her. "You're not going to get so tied up with this new account you want, that my fall season goes down the drain again!" He robbed it of any question mark.

"You know I never would."

"You told me they changed their policy, your Ashley & Company."

"They don't tell me their business secrets; I don't tell them mine. I never write one free-lance word at the office." She gave up her light tone. "Mr. Weinstein, something's come up, and I really do need one good new account. If you could help me get it, I'd be so grateful."

"Sure I know people who need good copy. Everybody in a business too small to go to the big boys needs better copy than their little two-by-four agencies come up with."

"I've been looking up small agencies in that advertising index or directory. I never knew there were so many."

"The big agencies are no good for retail anyway. Everything takes two months for plates, and retail needs overnight."

"Retail? But no fashion ads for anybody anywhere. Remember?"

"Who says retail fashion? What about food stores, drugstores, flower shops, furniture stores—"

"If you could introduce me to one of those, I'd love it."

He abandoned his matter-of-factness. "Jossie, this something that's come up—are you in some big trouble you need extra money for?"

"It's not trouble. It's something else, and it would be wonderful."

"This 'wonderful' needs you to work you head off?"

"I won't work my head off."

"So how much must you earn every year to be so wonderful?"

"Nine thousand six hundred—but it's not 'every year.' Just this coming year. If you don't mind, I can't explain it better than that."

"It's explained enough. Just keep enough time free for Stuyvesant's, no matter what else you're up to. You promised."

As Red Montana had done that day in the hall, she crossed her heart. He reached for the buzzer.

"Get me Blanchard's Luggage Shop on Park Avenue."

° ° °

They were driving to the station on Monday morning. Next week Rick would be getting on the train with her instead of waving goodbye. His vacation had only a week to go.

"If I hadn't had all that leave-without-pay last summer for Paris," he said, "I'd take an extra month without pay right now and keep on with the book."

"Maybe you'll be able to work on the train, now that you're off to a real start on it."

Irritation flared. "You know I can't work on the damn train. Just because you can work on trains doesn't mean anybody who can't is a lazy bum."

"Darling, don't let's quarrel. I never hold myself up as a model."

"Then lay off trains as a great place to work. If I could work on trains and at nights, I'd be the happiest man on earth."

"If only you had a year free of everything and finished the book, I'd be the happiest girl on earth." He shrugged. "Rick, something might develop—"

"What kind of something?" He looked contrite.

"Well, look at Blanchard's and now the milk people."

"I'm looking. You mean, your flea account might let me take another month's leave without pay? Good Lord, I've just paid off the first Morris Plan—don't get me to start another, even in the little red book."

"You don't need co-signers in the little red book."

"Nothing doing, Joss. It's a great idea, but nothing doing."

But then, the very next day, he drove up alone to Albany, and when he met her at the station in the evening he had a long narrow cardboard box on the seat beside him.

"Don't be sore, now, Joss. You can't sit and write every minute every day. You need time off to regroup your thoughts and work out scenes in your head."

"I know you do. Trollope only wrote for two hours a day, in the morning before going to work, and he wrote—what, twenty novels? Let's see what's in the box."

It was a new fishing rod and reel, and he had paid $60 for it. "Abercrombie and Fitch charge a hundred for the exact same thing." Triumph sounded.

She touched the shining new steel. He would never change. "Gosh," she said. "It's a beauty, all right."

"I can't just sit on the porch and look at the flowers during my noontime break. But when I can drive down to the river and fish for a while, it sets me up again for the whole afternoon."

When the week was over, and commuting and Ashley again filled his days, Rick's writing fell off at once, not merely in the amount of time available for it but in his own fervor about doing it, and in his own confidence that he could do it at all.

"What the devil can a man do in one spurt on Sunday?" he demanded.

"I know. You just lose it in between."

She did know. She still had not finished "The Flame-colored Evening Dress," though she was so close to the end. When she had been so certain that she could see right through to a good ending for it, she had introduced a young man into the story, who was attracted to Lila Jordan and asked her to go to his sister's coming-out party. But when she wrote the actual pages, she crossed them all out, paragraph by paragraph. It was so false, this happy ending; it wouldn't have happened. Lila Jordan didn't meet men with sisters who were having coming-out parties. Lila Jordan had worked as a secretary ever since high school, and her young man undoubtedly had worked as an insurance salesman or haberdashery assistant ever since high school too.

She tore up sheet after sheet and went back to page 14, where she'd been before she began introducing convenient young men with debutante sisters into Lila's world. She would work it all out some day, but heaven knew when.

One evening just before Labor Day, when they were packing for their return to West Tenth Street, Rick stayed silent and remote. He had again been drinking more than was usual for him, not bothering with red wine now, staying with martinis. It was a mean day, drizzling and raw, too cold for the last week of summer, heralding not only fall but winter. Outside, the trees dripped with rain, the canoe was filled, it seemed, if not to the mahogany gunwales, then at least to the cane seats, and the steady *slish* of water on the roof of the cabin was singularly forbidding.

Rick had just put together his manuscript. He wrote longhand still, a large open calligraphy, so there was no crowding of words on the page. Once he had guessed there were no more than 150 words to an average page, and now, gathering them into one sheaf, tapping them into alignment on the oak table where he worked, he said, "Only sixty pages, do you believe that? That's not even ten thousand words."

"But it's such a fine start."

"And I wrote most of it when I was alone all day. Maybe that's what it takes—getting off to an igloo in Alaska and staying alone, seeing nobody, no talk, no friends, no anything."

Gauguin again, she thought, now in an igloo. The hook of fear hit her, as if she were one of the fish he caught with that shining steel hook and rod and reel. Her hands flew up to her throat, cupping her jaws.

I'd die if he ever left me. From the beginning she had said that; she had said it to her mother, she had thought it when he sailed for Paris, she had muttered it half aloud, as she wept into the pillows that first time they'd had an ugly quarrel, over that open desk drawer with its litter of bills. It was ten times truer now.

You could never predict how a love affair would go. You could say you never even thought of marriage, you could say you'd be strong enough to handle it if it had to end. But it had its own life, it made its own decisions, it had its own growth and development. It either thinned down and fell away or it grew richer, stronger, until it was so powerful you were helpless in its grasp.

By now she could not imagine an existence with no Rick in it; she could not be her own ordinary self if she were parted from him. The separation for Paris was bad enough, but always then she had known he would be taking another ship and turning back to her. What if he had gone off announcing that there never would be that returning ship?

She continued with the packing. So much accumulated during four months, not just summer clothes, bathing suits, and sneakers but books, kitchen utensils, letters, proof sheets, carbons of her own work, the recorded stretch of activity for a third of a year. She cooked dinner early; there was no fish from the river to broil; the day-long downpour had stopped even that respite.

It was night before she said, "Rick, could I put an idea to you? A kind of crazy . . . ?"

PART TWO

The Good Provider

Eleven

"Today Rick and I start on a new adventure, me being the good provider, Rick being an artist, with no responsibilities in the world to shackle him. It's marvelous to be doing it—Rick shall have at least one year for his book."

She returned to the top of the page in her journal and wrote, "Sept. 15, 1925."

> It means much work for me, of course, with all our expenses here, and Jean, and R's father in Richmond, and the new Morris Plan in my own name, but all that's perfectly nothing compared to the gorgously strong happiness I feel about being able to help my dearest love to work free of the yoke-y, dismal job of advertising and office hours and money worries and take up a life of writing and freedom and, well, beauty.
>
> I finally persuaded him to take this chance, not worrying about hardship for me or anything else. It took so long to get him to see it, night after night persuading him, and then when he finally agreed, I nearly wrecked the whole thing myself.
>
> I don't know what got into me, but the night Rick left Ashley for good, the night we went out to celebrate, that night after we got home, a night filled with talk about books and authors and writing, I had the impulse to show him the start of "The Flame-colored Evening Dress," only the first few pages.
>
> He sat quietly for many minutes after reading them, and I was thinking he must be looking down on me again for doing it, because it is, in a way, a formula story for some magazine, which is just a cut above writing more ads.
>
> But then he said he couldn't accept a whole year of freedom, that I had something precious and real too, that I needed to begin my own writing, that I ought to have a year's freedom as much as he.
>
> He made me very happy. It was a big thing, to have him say such things about my first writing—that though it was callow perhaps in spots, crude and amateurish in places, the story had emotion, the hardest thing to get into a story—to make somebody reading it get a lump in the throat—that it showed I had real ability for serious writing.
>
> Yet the thought that something we had dreaded through all our discussions night after night, that something might come up to interfere with his breaking away from advertising—that

> that something might be *me*, who loved him so deeply—it was intolerable. I knew I couldn't let him change it around again. I'm five years younger than Rick, and any powers for real work I have can wait. They'll keep. And Rick has waited so long.
>
> Well, I did make him see it at last. When he begins to earn royalties with his fine old book, I'll have my turn. Oh, it will be a glorious year for both of us.

One proviso she had set forth the night she had finally persuaded him was that she was going to clear up all the unpaid bills too. He had resisted that, had argued that there was a kind of anachronism to it, that she should take on debts he had already made before this new venture, but there she had been adamant.

"I just can't stand those damn bills coming in every month, darling. Now they won't be sent to the office, they'll be coming here, and with me handling our finances for this one year, they'd be coming in straight at *me*. I can't just chuck them in the drawer and forget about them and sleep like a log."

"Now you're calling me a no-good and a deadbeat."

"Oh, Rick, don't go oversensitive on me—you'll pay back every dollar when the time comes."

"But it's more than you expect. I've no real idea myself how much they come to."

"I don't care how much. I just can't do *any* of it if I'm not allowed to get rid of those bills."

But when he had made a rough estimate that same evening, not looking anything up, just totting up the major sums he could remember off the top of his head, even she drew back a little. It was nearly $1,500.

"I'll go to the Morris Plan myself, Rick. To consolidate debts is one of their best reasons."

"But it's my turn to be co-signer and they won't take me. They don't regard writers as employed, much less with any good solid earning potential."

"I'll get my mother and Nell. Teachers have regular jobs at regular pay, heaven knows."

She would be bold and borrow a whole $1,000 to wipe out all the major bills. . . . No, they probably wouldn't allow that much of a loan on a $60 salary, and they might not believe her about her free-lancing. Well, $500 then, to start with. The money in the flea account would stay right there, a real emergency fund for something out of the blue.

Just last week Rick had paid his last Morris Plan installment, the fiftieth of the second loan, and he'd vowed, never again. But she didn't let that deter her; she'd never put off the weekly payment to the last minute the way he sometimes did, or have it creep up as a horrid surprise; it would be the first thing off her paycheck, before another dime was spent. There's nothing sure but death and the Morris Plan is what they should have said; taxes you could manage better. This year Rick wouldn't have to shell out $210 for income tax the way he'd had to last year.

Of course this would all have to be a secret; they wouldn't want the Bellocks to know, or Red and Suzy. She supposed Rick would have to tell Jean, and she'd have to tell Mama and Nell about the loan itself, but not all the reasons behind it.

It was almost pleasant asking her mother to be co-signer. This time, since they had the Ford, she'd driven up to New Rochelle instead of asking her mother to come to New York. It was more than a year since she'd been up there; the living room looked smaller than she remembered it, and her father seemed changed. Not much older, though his hair had gone further toward a gray thin sparseness. He was somehow thin and gray in general. He had lost no noticeable weight, yet he seemed diminished. It's because he's so dissatisfied, she thought, he looks empty of juice. Maybe it's mostly that he's so disappointed in the way I've turned out. For an instant she had the impulse to say, I'm sorry, Pa, but she stamped it flat.

For what? she thought. For being me instead of the daughter he planned on? For making money in advertising instead of squeaking along on a teacher's salary? I suppose I'm still the hoor, hooring around in the world of capitalism.

She talked about the election just ahead, volunteering that she was voting for Norman Thomas as Mayor of New York City. The moment they talked of politics, he seemed to deepen in intensity, as if the grayness were taking on more color. Last fall had been the first time she had ever voted for President, and he looked pleased when she said now that she wished Debs had been well enough to have run one more time.

"I'd have liked to vote for him just once," she said.

"So you're a Socialist, despite everything!" Her father sounded as if at last he could approve of her.

"Of course I'm a Socialist."

"I didn't know you cared about such things."

The truth was she didn't care much, or think much, about politics and sometimes wondered why she did not. "It's because your pa always hammered at it," Rick said once. "Like not wanting to know one damn thing about the War Between the States when I was growing up, because my ears were stuffed full of it all the time."

Despite her father's momentary pleasure, Jossie signaled her mother that they go out to the garden in back of the house.

"Mama, could I ask a big favor, without explaining too much?"

"You always can."

"Do you know what a co-signer is?"

"Of course I know."

"I'm making a loan, a big one, and I wondered if you'd be one of my two co-signers. I'm going to ask Nell too."

"Is anything wrong again, Jossie?"

"Anything but wrong. It's happy for me as well as Rick. He'd be the first co-signer, except—it's hard to explain." She hesitated. "Did you read that story in the *World* about a month ago, about the young wife who took a job to put her husband through medical school?"

"Medical school takes four years. Are you going to do this for four years? No, I didn't see the story."

"Only for one year." Again she hesitated, and then it came out with a rush. "Did you ever love Pa enough to want to do something to make *him* happier, to give him a chance to do something he couldn't have done alone?"

Her mother ignored the question, and her voice turned solemn. "As long as you're not buying anything by doing it."

"What could I be buying?

There was a pause. Again her mother let the question slip by unanswered. "How much are you borrowing?"

"Five hundred. I can manage it. I've figured it all out."

"With weekly payments of —?"

"Ten a week. Not so much."

"That doesn't sound like much, but week after week? It's a fat fraction off sixty."

"I'm earning scads on my own, though—six hundred free-lance this one month. Can you imagine?"

"Of course I'll be your co-signer."

"Will you have to tell Pa?"

"I'm not as modern as you are, Jossie. To me it's no crime to keep things to myself."

Nell had showed open skepticism, but in the end she had agreed too. It was she who stipulated that nobody tell her husband and asked Jossie not to make any slips when they were together. "He's a nagger when it comes to big money."

Jossie laughed when she told Rick. "Here I was asking Mama not to tell Pa, and then Nell asked me not to tell her husband. Isn't that just peachy? About who's not to tell what to whom? Thank the Lord, we're not like that."

Rick wasn't really listening. For the first time he was comparing Jean to Jossie, specifically comparing, and it disquieted him that he should be doing it. During all the nights of Jossie's persuasion about this year of freedom, he had found himself wondering how many women in the world would have the impulse to do anything like it, but now, for no logical reason, as he listened to her happy reports about co-signers, his thoughts went beyond the general to the particular.

He remembered Paris and Jean's refusal to make him a loan from her Princeton money; her careful reluctance still rankled whenever he thought of it, but tonight there was a particular bite in the memory. It was one thing for him to say, as he had so often to Jossie, meaning it so urgently each time, "Never, not from my own girl," but it was something else to ask for a loan himself and be refused.

I mustn't do that, he thought in some agitation, mustn't even compare them, mustn't think in terms of contrast. Nobody on earth has Jossie's quick generosity, nobody on earth wants so much to help another human because she loves him. Could *I* do it for her, when the time comes? Am I so sure I would? There never was anybody like this beloved girl. If it takes the rest of my life, I'll find the way to repay her.

° ° °

Jossie set the little red notebook aside and began another record instead. This was a full-size loose-leaf notebook, bound in black leather, the kind she'd used all through college. She titled the front page:

FINANCIAL ENCYCLOPEDIA
of Rick and Jossie Baird
October 1925

Rick protested over the red notebook. "Not until you transfer every item in it to your big new ledger," he insisted. "And every dollar you do pay off on any old bill of mine goes on that list too."

She complied swiftly and showed him the new "Debtor's Prison."

"Now for the bills," she said then. "Every last one. No holdouts, no forgetting, no deciding this one doesn't matter."

He went to his closet and took out his briefcase, in which he had put all his office belongings when he left Ashley. He opened it over the table and dumped the entire contents out before her.

"I'll have to explain some of them."

"Later on, maybe. You needn't ever, though."

It was so characteristic of him, she thought, not even to look through them first. She began to sort them out, store by store and then according to their dates. The oldest ones would come first.

"Don't stand there watching me," she said. "You make me feel funny." He went to the bedroom, and the familiar sound of his pen on the yellow paper came to her.

As she went on with her sorting, she began to see how Rick had found it possible to run debts for so long without being sued or having his salary garnisheed. She had wondered about that from time to time, and now in several separate stacks, she found her answer. It was perfectly proper, certainly perfectly legal. The six or eight Macy bills began with one dated over two years before, when Rick had moved into West Tenth Street, and it was for the bed they slept in, with its stunning headboard of a low brass railing, and its box spring and mattress, all of the highest quality. The original bill was the only one that itemized the merchandise bought, with its total cost: $248.98.

The following statements merely said, "Balance due," but it was easy to follow Rick's management of it. Every three or four months the balance would recede by a payment of $20, a total of $60 in 1924, another $60 in 1925. Probably whenever he received a letter threatening legal action, he sent in a check on account. He still owed Macy's $128.98.

The pattern held true in other groups of bills. Occasionally she came on one that simply repeated, month after month, the same amount, never reduced, never paid in full, and presumably too small for the owner of the store to warrant the expense of a lawsuit, and thus eventually dropped. One of these made her flinch.

It was from Greenwich Florists, and it was for $8. The first one was dated, September 11, 1923, and the item listed was "1 doz. A.B."

The roses, the American Beauty roses. He had sent them to her at the office the morning after they had stayed together that first night. She had never received flowers from a man before, had never dreamed of receiving an entire dozen long-stemmed red American Beauty roses. She had taken them home with her, kept them until they were nothing but rusty crisps. And now she was going to pay for them herself.

She gulped. In a moment she rose from the table and began aimlessly wandering around the room, as if searching. For what? For help? For not caring? She was breathing in short tight little gasps. She made herself stand still and think of nothing.

The next bills were mostly for men's hats, gloves, shoes, shirts, furniture for the apartment, linens, blankets, towels, books, records, picture framing. There were bills for toys sent to Paris for the children, others for gifts sent to Jean. Then she came upon another one that sent her from the table. This was from Lord & Taylor, dated December 22, 1923:

Neg	$28.50
Gown	19.00

The chiffon gown and the silk negligee, her very first. "Now you can junk that old flannel bathrobe from dear old Cornell."

Three more bills from Lord & Taylor: The first read, "Balance $47.20," the next, "Balance $37.50," another, "Balance $27.50." That one was dated June 1925—four months ago.

She had been wearing the nightgown and dressing gown all along, on special occasions, always so happily, loving them, loving the fact that Rick had given them to her. An impulse tore through her now to go and rip them to pieces, never to see them again, certainly never to wear them again. She ground out the impulse the way she'd seen smokers grind out cigarette stubs.

At the office, Rick's resignation and departure had intrigued everybody who knew him, but none more than Amantha Dunwoodie. For several days, it seemed as though she were inventing reasons for asking if Jossie could stop in.

The ostensible reason was always the new account Jossie was writing for, Coal Stove Foods, a major account, but soon she would manage a digression to Rick and his "sabbatical."

"Has Rick all that much money of his own, do you suppose?"

"I'd never thought about it," Jossie murmured.

"Do you really think he's writing a book?"

"Only what he says. He did say so."

"So many men in advertising say they're going to write a book when they're fired—"

"But he wasn't fired, was he?" Jossie sounded gently intrigued.

"Officially, no. But in a big office like this, nobody can keep track of all the underground tremors and *frissons,* so there might have been something sub rosa that isn't public so far."

Jossie thought the foreign tidbits were revolting. She'd have to watch herself more than ever with Amantha Dunwoodie. She was seeing her more than usual, anyway, on Coal Stove Foods, and so much was at stake there, with Mrs. Dunwoodie's backing more essential than ever. "You can stand another client rejection, Jossie," she had stated positively, but stand it or not, she would not welcome any business setback at all right now.

Each day at lunchtime, she met Rick at a Child's restaurant on West Fourteenth Street. He was always there before her, watching for her through the huge window.

"It's the equivalent of driving to the river to fish awhile and clear my head," he told her. "That's another great thing about the new era."

"Thanks for the compliment. Am I the river or the fish?"

But she looked forward to telling him the office news each day, and he said, "Secondhand makes it great." He assured her her new food campaign was "a breakthrough to a modern kind of copy."

"But even Mr. Jerton doesn't go for it—he wants me to turn it around so it's 'positive.'"

"He brought forth the old edict, I bet, about 'no negative headlines.'"

"You can't shake him, Rick. But Dunwoodie wouldn't give an inch. She wants to do a test in the market—pick a couple of small cities. They went at it hip and thigh, like a lover's quarrel."

He laughed. "Ten years out of date, but just like."

"Then I piped up, and I think it annoyed Mr. Jerton. Rick, I *can't* get him sore at me."

"Piped up how?"

"I said, 'What about Lux, and "won't shrink woolens"?' Mrs. Dunwoodie leaped at that. She practically snorted with triumph."

"I might miss the shenanigans, at that," Rick said.

"Read my first piece again, would you, darling? I cut it a bit."

Do you hate to cook?

> It's not a sin; don't be ashamed of it. Some women love to spend hours in the kitchen, but others would give anything to shorten their time there. Now there's a new way to let you do just that.
>
> Coal Stove Foods has gone a step further than other companies who make fine canned foods.
>
> Instead of opening a can that contains just soup, or just string beans, or just corn, you can now buy a can that *combines* wonderful foods that belong together: tiny peas with pearl onions, or baby limas with pecans, or okra with tomatoes, or celery with mushroom caps.
>
> Any two such cans of combined foods and you have all your meal, but for the meat or fish you serve.
>
> And no one will ever guess you secretly hate to cook.
>
> • COAL STOVE FOODS •

She could tell he liked it by the small grin on his face; he read speedily, as he always did, and as he came to the end he blew her an elaborate kiss over the buckwheat cakes and syrup he was having.

"Good cuts, Joss. It's even better this way. What does Jerton want instead?"

"He's written a piece himself. 'Now, a new taste sensation—combined foods from Coal Stove.' Something like that. Del Monte or Van Camp or White Rose—any of them could sign it." She handed over another sheet of copy paper. "Here are a couple of other headlines I did."

Don't feel guilty
because cooking bores you

She saw him nod and handed over another sheet.

**Would you rather read a book
or cook a meal?**

"I'm betting on yours over Jerton's," Rick said.

"But he's even had Stella Beattie write three more pieces of copy using his approach. So it's a competition going—me against their biggest copywriter on food accounts."

He took out half a dollar and slapped it on the table. "Want to bet?"

"You darling." They'd never been so happy, she thought, as she refolded her copy and restored it to her purse. Day after day of this intense closeness, of their delight in Rick's work, in his own sense of accomplishment, slow though it was at times, uneven from day to day, but always there and growing. And in her own sense of being so needed by him, so valuable to him; he found a hundred ways to tell her that he had never guessed before that love could be so enriching, so productive, so giving of life.

"How long will it be before they run the test campaigns?" he asked.

"Weeks. They haven't even decided on the cities to use—maybe Louisville vs. Milwaukee. It'll be like sitting in the dentist's anteroom for two months."

○ ○ ○

Her phone was ringing, one morning a week or two later, when Jossie reached the glassed-in cubicle that still served as her office at Ashley.

"It's me," Rick said. "I won't be at Child's for lunch, if it's okay with you."

"Mary Pickford invited you over."

"Andy Bellock. I said sure. Okay with you?"

"I can go get me that pair of shoes. Sure it's okay."

It was the first time in the new era they would not be meeting for lunch, and privately Jossie had been expecting it; undoubtedly Rick had been too. They had spoken of it weeks before during one of the dozen sessions they had put in, establishing various aspects of the new regimen, and Jossie smiled now as she remembered their talk about money for lunches, cigarettes, magazines, and the like.

"Are you going to hand me an allowance every week?" Rick had asked. "Or do I come and say, 'I need a package of razor blades, can I have a dime?' "

"You can grow a beard."

"Sure, sure. But Joss, there's a small sticking point here, isn't there? If I'm not getting a paycheck of my own every week—?"

"You can't be serious! See those blank spaces on the tentative budget?" She'd shoved over the neat list on the table: Misc. . . . J—$40 and, under that, Misc. . . . . R.—. "I figured my misc. at forty a month, and you were supposed to fill in what your misc. would be." She pronounced it *miss.*

"And when I figure it out, do you hand it over the first of the month? In a check or cash?"

"Come on, Rick, you're joking."

"Joshing Jossie—my favorite sport. Don't be miffed; it suddenly hit me in the shape of a query, and I thought I'd better just ask."

"We're going to have a joint checking account—Mr. and Mrs. Baird—it's perfectly legal to use any name you want on a bank account as long as it's not with criminal intent. I asked."

"You just up and asked?"

"It's like a nom de plume for an author, or a stage name for an actor. So you decide what you draw each month, and we stick to the budget, and it's as simple as that. Did you think I'd be sending monthly checks to Jean and your Dad, signed Joselyn Stone? Dummy!"

He opened his fountain pen and wrote in the blank space, *$50,* saying, "Because you never drift into a speak for a drink and I do. So my *miss* is bigger than your *miss.*"

"And because men don't lunch with their pals at Child's and girls do."

And now he and Andy would be having luncheon at one of their favorite restaurants, and they'd split the check, and that was as it should be. She looked forward to shopping for new shoes; she'd been needing them for a month. She looked into her purse. Twelve dollars—more than enough.

When she got home that evening, wearing her new shoes, Rick wasn't there. He usually heard her key and jumped up from his desk to open the door. There was no note either. A moment later the phone rang. "On my way, sweetie, ten minutes."

He sounded bright, perhaps a little tight. But when he arrived, he wasn't tight at all, just cheerful and high-spirited.

"After lunch I took me to the museum," he greeted her. "Sabbatical for one afternoon."

"The Met?"

"Yes, that Fauvist show. Sometimes you go stir-crazy and have to get away for a couple hours."

"I can imagine."

He worked after dinner that evening, and said at the end, "My four-hour sabbatical pumped up my head again."

But a few nights later when she got home he was not so high-spirited.

"Hi, darling, did it go?"

"Do you have to ask me that every damn day?"

"I'm sorry, I didn't mean—"

"You don't even know you're asking it." His hair was rumpled, one thick spike standing up as if he'd been at it with that twirling motion for hours; his eyes were clouded; he'd been drinking. She could smell it, the metallic smell of gin she had never known him to have before. "It's like a schoolteacher," he went on, "saying 'Did you do your homework?' "

"I won't ask any more," she said quietly, putting her things down. Beside her purse there was a large manila envelope, thick with papers. It's so unfair, she thought; he can be so unfair.

"Are you going to work again tonight?" he asked.

"I have some Blanchard stuff that's due in the morning."

"I wanted to get out tonight—a good movie or something."

She hesitated. They hadn't been out much, it was true. "Then let's do it—I can do the Blanchard when we get home."

"I don't want you killing yourself as a favor to me."

"Killing myself! I never need much sleep—you know I don't. What movie?"

"Or the theater—we haven't been once since we started this."

"I'm dying to see Katharine Cornell in *The Green Hat*—Edie said they loved it."

"Or *The Vortex* by Noel Coward. He's in it himself."

"Come on, Rick, let's see what tickets we can get at McBride's. We can eat someplace uptown near the theater."

They dashed out before ten minutes had elapsed. Rick's taciturnity had fled. It's in the budget anyway, she thought, as they took the trolley. I did put in $8 for the theater once a month and $2 for movies twice, and another $2 for two concerts. Poor old Rick—he probably misses the hullabaloo of the office more than he expected to. Everybody knows writing is a lonely life.

Twelve

December came plunging at them, and the Christmas season with it. Rick had to hurry to get toys off to the children before the third of the month, and the need to do so irritated him as being premature and artificial. He was uncertain and distracted, too, about what to send Jean. They had been writing each other less frequently in recent months, and he felt that he ought to send something special.

They had decided, however, he and Jossie together, to hold Christmas down to $100 all told. That bothered him also. The word *straitjacket* would pop into his mind while he was shopping for cheaper gifts, or *tether,* or even *leash.* He dismissed them all as mindless and childish, but they would arise again to taunt him the next time he had to turn aside from something he wanted to buy because it was too expensive. Christmas was the time to be splashy and extravagant, not to be ruled by budgets and price tags.

It's like being at boarding school again, he thought once, on an allowance, and a resentment at Jossie flared, which his own fairness snickered at immediately. Blaming Jossie indeed, when she'd taken on the burdens of the whole world to free him for writing. Still, Christmas was not a good time for the eternal yardstick of money.

Sending off the few presents, he also sent off the long overdue news to Jean that he had left Ashley. He told her about the sabbatical year that Jossie was making possible. He wrote fully, openly, giving her all the discussions and reasonings behind it.

> It's a maddening way for me to live, except for the writing itself. Budgets and calculations at every other expense are not inherent in my nature, as you very well know, but for the sake of writing my book, I ignore, or try to ignore, every balk in my soul, every resistance.
>
> This of course will not in any way affect the monthly checks for the good old wine and escargots; it's all part of the grand plan, and here's hoping that when the book is finally published, I will speedily repay every dollar the whole sabbatical cost.

It was a long and at times difficult letter, the longest in a year, and it was a relief to mail it and have it off his mind. He took it to the main post office himself, to save a full day in transmission, and then, feeling as if he had earned a reward, he stopped at Scribner's and spent his last $2 on Scott Fitzgerald's new novel, *The Great*

Gatsby. It was not a gift. It was for himself. He wouldn't even open it until his own work was done for the day. As it turned out, he didn't start it until after they had said good night.

"I'll read awhile," he told Jossie.

At two, she awoke to find him still awake, still reading, a high flush in his face, as if he had a fever. He had brought a martini with him when he went to bed, and the glass was still there on the night table, half empty. At first she thought he was so engrossed by his reading that he had forgotten to finish it. Then she saw, beyond it, partially hidden by the tall lamp, the bottle of gin, now also half empty. He had opened it that evening before dinner.

When she stirred and woke, he asked, "Does the light bother you?" and she shook her head, glancing at the book, spread face down on his body, opened in two equal parts.

"Is it any good?" she asked sleepily.

"It's different from anything he's ever done."

"Then I'll read it." She turned over, her back to the light, and fell asleep once more.

In the morning Rick came out in his bathrobe for breakfast. He hadn't showered or shaved; eyestrain made him wince slightly against the morning light, and again a faint odor of juniper or gin came to her when he stooped to kiss her.

"Like a jack, I stayed up till five and finished it," he said. "Nothing, just coffee."

She had started for the kitchenette and its morning aroma of toast and bacon. "You said it was different. Is it good?"

"The best thing he's ever done. It's a thunderclap."

She didn't know what to say in reply: "How wonderful" or "I wish it hadn't come out right at this time" or "How awful for you!" All three phrases came into her mind, detestable, a treachery to Rick by their very presence. Why should she take it for granted that a Fitzgerald success at this time, or any other time, might produce interior problems for him and his own writing? Was he so small a man, so vulnerable? Her spirit sank.

Just last week he had again asked if she'd mind not seeing what he wrote, and she had readily agreed.

"I get self-conscious, Joss, knowing you'll be seeing it that very evening. It's as if I'm writing for your approval, leaving out things you might not like."

"Darling, I can see that. Whenever *you* want somebody's reaction, then let me see it, but not because I'm so eager to see for myself."

Now she thought suddenly, I hope this *Gatsby* book isn't going to sink him in a spell of depression, and she felt a nip of resentment, not at the book but at Rick. She disavowed it, but it laughed at her and stayed solid. It was resentment, nothing less, *a priori*, about what was to come. Writing was hard, but living with a writer could be hard too.

She began to read the new book that evening and saw at once what Rick meant. It was, in one large way, different from everything she had read of Fitzgerald's, and in that one way, ten times truer. There were still the millionaires in their mansions, still the silken yachts on translucent blue water, still strings of pearls worth three hundred thousand dollars, and of course the beautiful young girls in their lovely dresses, and their handsome young men driving huge cars.

But there was also one character who was not born one of the fortunates of the world, this one character looking on, envying, wanting something eternally beyond him, though he too lived in a mansion, though he too managed the lavish parties, the flowing champagne, the great cars, all the splendid outwardness of what the others had by birth.

From the beginning pages, she ached with Jay Gatsby before she knew who he really was, what he did, what he yearned for so desperately. She might never understand why he spent years longing for Daisy, whose voice, he said, was "full of money," Daisy, "in a white palace the King's daughter, the golden girl"—she might never understand that longing, but here at least was one human being who knew what denial was, knew struggle and the misery of rejection, knew the dream foredoomed.

Yes, it was the best thing Scott Fitzgerald had ever written, and she thought, Maybe I've misjudged him all along. Maybe I'll read everything he ever wrote all over again.

But most of this she kept to herself. Only in the most offhand way did Rick ask what she thought of the new book, and equally casually she said she agreed that it was awfully good. Unstated by either of them, there was somehow an understanding that this exchange of opinion would suffice, certainly for the time being. Rick put the book on the shelf alongside the first two novels and the two collections of stories, and there it remained in its silence, its paragraphs and pages caught securely between its closed covers, its subtleties and strengths and originalities withdrawn from anybody's vision. Neither Rick nor Jossie ever mentioned it again.

° ° °

Jossie was still in the dentist's anteroom, though December was a week old. Then came the summons to Amantha Dunwoodie's office that she had been hoping for and dreading in equal proportions. One look at the older woman's face told her the good news.

"Hands down," Mrs. Dunwoodie greeted her, spreading both hands wide, fingers all extended, as if she were signaling something in an athletic contest. "Three to one over Ben Jerton's campaign."

"In sales, does that mean?"

"What else? Our campaign ran exactly the same fourteen days as his did, and Coal Stove sales in Louisville were three hundred percent higher than sales in Milwaukee. It's what you call a landslide."

"I'm so glad." She clutched her shoulders, hugging herself.

"You should be twice as proud as you ever were. It's a real coup."

"Does that mean our campaign is the one they'll use? The only one?"

"Exactly. Not just in local papers but nationally: *Ladies' Home Journal, Good House, McCall's, Delineator, Woman's Home Companion,* and maybe in the *Post* and *Liberty* and *Collier's* too."

"That sounds awfully big."

"About a half million in billings. You've been assigned to it permanently."

Jossie had been standing; now she let herself sprawl into a chair, as if she felt faint. Her eyes shone. "There's no 'negative approach' about the way I feel now."

"That 'negative' talk is so old-fashioned. Our ads actually spoke in the most positive way to every woman who saw them—lots of them *do* hate to cook, but nobody ever let them say so before. We did, so they reacted."

"If you hadn't stuck up for it the way you did, it wouldn't have had a chance. By myself—"

"You're not in anything by yourself, Jossie. Anything you do for Ashley, at least." Her stress on Ashley was unmistakable.

"What does that mean?"

"Why, it means that I phoned Stuyvesant's the other day," Mrs. Dunwoodie answered slowly, thoughtfully, "to find out who was writing their high-fashion copy, because it was so good. They wouldn't tell me, except to say it was being free-lanced."

"You actually phoned them?"

"We're always on the lookout for talent in copy, and when we can get in touch, we often offer a job here. Every agency does it."

"It—I—isn't that called 'raiding' or something?"

Mrs. Dunwoodie laughed. "Precisely what it's called. And it's done all the time. Discreetly, of course."

Jossie remained silent. What had started out as a glorious morning was now hot with confusion and the burn of resentment. She's trying to trap me, she thought. She made a guess and she's fixing it so I'll blurt it all out as if this were a confessional: Amantha, forgive me for I have sinned. Never.

"I like Stuyvesant's copy too," she said, hoping her voice was steady. "I read every one of their ads."

"This new campaign of theirs, 'Are you going?' It's awfully smart, isn't it?"

"Awfully. I wish I could afford to shop at Stuyvesant's." She rose and put on her brightest voice. "Well, thanks for the news about Coal Stove." She started for the door. "Is Mr. Jerton annoyed, do you think?"

Amantha Dunwoodie laughed a little. "He says not."

° ° °

In Paris, Jean received Rick's Christmas letter with its astounding news nearly two weeks before the gifts he had sent. She had barely begun her own preparations for the holiday, for her life had filled with new preoccupations, invisible tendrils of emotion she could swear she had never experienced before.

In the spring, fully recovered at last from her illness and operation, she had gone again to La Baule on the Brittany coast with François Ciardeau, and once again they were part of a congenial group of four. This time the others were not a married couple but two Americans whose letters of credit at Morgan Trust had also brought about their acquaintance with François. The girl, Elizabeth Welling, was a pretty brunette who looked to be in her earliest twenties, and the man was surely twenty years older, tall, a little overweight, more than a little bald, and thoroughly attractive. Even his name attracted her: Jake Mumm.

"Like the champagne?" she asked on being introduced.

"No closer than their bottles." It was obviously a question he had been asked a thousand times, and an answer he had given a thousand times, and suddenly she felt herself as ill at ease as a schoolgirl. "That was inane of me," she said, and again he attracted her by the tact with which he went on to other things. He and Liz Welling, he said, had become "bragging friends" when they were the only two people in the *Île de France* dining room during a killer storm the second night out of New York.

Liz was to be in France only for ten days of vacation before going on to graduate school in London: He, however, was not in France on vacation; he was opening a French agency for his family's business, Browning Tractors, Inc., Deere's largest rival in the field of agricultural implements, and would remain at least a year, establishing and training a French staff.

"Then you must speak French pretty well yourself," Jean said to him in French, and he answered in a French that bore a faint accent she could not quite place, but with such ease and fluency that she envied him immediately. His mother was French-Canadian, becoming an American only when she married his father, so he had grown up in a bilingual household with endless visits to and from all the Quebec relatives.

"When he came to the bank," François put in, "he sounded more of Paris than Quebec."

François's invitation for the weekend had gone only to Liz Welling, it turned out; Jake Mumm's letter of credit was on far too impressive a level for any junior banker to handle by himself. But when Liz asked if she might come with a friend, he was immediately elevated in his own mind on finding that he would be host to such an illustrious guest.

Jean's pleasure in Jake Mumm's presence was antidote enough to that fever of ego, and François saw at once how it was to be. Before the weekend was over, it was apparent to everybody that Jake Mumm was as drawn to Jean as she was to him. Liz Welling obviously didn't mind; she was off in four more days in any case. François minded very much, tried not to show it, and failed so miserably that Jean was conscience-stricken. She had made it clear to him from the beginning that their affair was destined to end; he had even informed her several times since her convalescence that it was already coming to its end, rather boasting that he always was first to sense any diminishing in a love affair, whether that diminishing was within him or, alas, about him.

Apart from the flickering disquiet of her conscience, Jean knew an elation and self-assurance she had missed for a long time. She had recently taken to having her blond hair treated with an ash-blond rinse; it was even lighter, if possible, and more becoming and, against her early spring tan, striking and dramatic. She was thirty-three, yes, but she knew she had never been as good-looking. In France, anyway, there was none of this American fetishism about extreme youth.

Driving back from La Baule on Sunday, it was nearly midnight when they reached Paris. They had all four traveled in Jake Mumm's roomy car, for François's small Citroen held only two, and it was nearly one in the morning before Jake had dropped Liz Welling off at her small hotel and then François off at his apartment.

François's good night was painful to Jean; it said farewell rather than a simple *au revoir,* and she knew it. When Jake at last pulled up in the Île de la Cité, he looked at her and she nodded. They went upstairs together.

Now, five months later, what had begun as an infatuation had, for Jean, shifted into something filled with newness and expectation. Jake Mumm was unlike Rick and unlike Arthur before Rick. He was fifty, not the forty she had taken him to be, and a widower with two grown sons. One of the two was married and had recently had a baby; Jake was dumbfounded at finding himself a grandfather and delighted to be one. He loved children; Kathy and Kenny became pets of his from the start. They were instructed to call him Jake. No more "Uncle" business, she thought.

Jean had never been close to a man of fifty; it made her feel younger than she had in years, free of the awareness that she was three years older than Rick. And she found herself exhilarated by the sense of power in Jake Mumm, a practical, even materialistic strength that went hand-in-hand with his being rich but also superseded it. He was a total change from the assistant professor who had once been her husband and from the would-be writer who was her husband now.

Jake knew little about art and rarely read books or went to concerts; he was industrialist pure and simple, and his reading was of industry and finance. He called her paintings "pretty" or "interesting," or even "puzzling," and bought two of them—she would accept only her current price of $80 each—for the large apartment he had taken off the Étoile.

He had grown up in Michigan, went to M.I.T., where he easily took his degree in civil engineering, and then promptly joined the staff of his father's headquarters in Detroit. The Mumms held 49 percent of Browning Tractor's stock and were powers throughout the world of industry. Industry fascinated Jake from the start; he had no understanding of any businessman who decried or belittled the work he did.

He would have been downright uncomfortable, Jean once thought, spending an evening with Rick or even with poor Arthur at Princeton. He had barely heard of Havelock Ellis and was half amused when she tried to condense for him the philosophy of honesty-in-marriage that she and Rick had always lived by.

"Don't tell me anything much about this husband of yours," he had said, only partly joking. "If you were my wife and elected to live a whole ocean away from me for a couple of years, I'd raise one hell of a row, and I'll never understand why he didn't. Why he doesn't."

It was easy to follow his admonition not to talk much about Rick, and it was also easy to remain vague about Jake Mumm when she did write to Rick. She had fallen out of the habit of writing frequently; the past six months or so had seemed to usher in a new phase of silence for Rick as well.

When was it that she had begun to wonder whether she was outgrowing Rick's basic beliefs about marriage, which he had successfully inculcated in her in their first year or two? Back there when he had first cabled her about the cottage in Peekskill—that's when her nebulous wonders had crystalized into real doubt; she remembered thinking rather sharply, then, that though he still maintained that honesty was everything, she had begun to think longingly of such old-fashioned matters as tact and privacy.

By now she was convinced that she was reverting, or had already reverted, to a more conventional view of marriage than any Rick had ever held. She didn't let herself think very often of what he might be up to in this, the start of the third year of their separation; she didn't let herself wonder whether he was still enamored of that girl, Jossie.

Now, with Christmas so close, thoughts of family and absence were supposed to seize one, but she was reluctant to fall into old sentimentalities. Soon there would be Rick's gifts for the children and for her, and thank-you letters to write, and this year she rather dreaded the whole rigmarole. The children had all but forgotten Uncle Rick; she had let it happen. She had already sent Rick a splendid lizard belt, but she was spending ten times as much thought on what to give Jake. It would be her first present to him, and there was an agitated excitement about making the right choice that also made her feel like a girl again.

And then, on the tenth of December, Rick's letter arrived, speedy in transit despite the Christmas crush in transatlantic mails. She opened it, and as she read, her peaceful new detachment shattered.

It was impossible. Rick had gone mad, to think that such bizarre arrangements could be part of her life. She thought of Jake knowing about them and drew back as she imagined his disbelief. Her anger grew at this fantasized embarrassment. She would be seeing Jake this evening, less than two hours from now. Of course she would say not one word about this preposterous idea.

What had happened to Rick anyway? How could he possibly think she would fall in with such a scheme? She read his letter through once more and then marched to her dressing table where she kept her stationery. She wrote in a kind of spluttering haste, then checked the fast mail boats to New York, addressed the envelope, and went down to leave it with the concierge in his small wooden mailbox marked POSTE ÉTRANGÈRE.

o o o

Rick and Jossie had bought a small tree and had set it up between the windows of the living room. It was the week before Christmas and, $100 limit or no, they were both caught up in the holiday mood. The bell from the front hall gave its staccato little rings that announced the afternoon mail.

"You stay up there with that star," Jossie said. "I'll get it." She came back with the blue envelope, thinking, It's a big thick one, I hope nothing's wrong. She watched Rick open it and saw his face darken with the first lines.

"I'll be back in a minute," he said and then went to the bedroom, closing the door behind him. He was not back in a minute; he stayed on and on, the tree forgotten, the wine he had opened left behind.

Damn it anyway, Jossie thought, turning off the Victrola that had been filling the room with *Good King Wenceslas*. What a time to pick for trouble. Christmas was always a hard time for people with problems; she had read that somewhere and had known it herself, as a little girl who felt left out of nearly everything at Christmas. Her parents did make something of Christmas—a kind of "folk festival," they nicknamed it—as if they were heads of a progressive Montessori school, thinking only of keeping the children calm and pleasant. But there was no fervor in it for either Nell or herself, no real belief and excitement the way other kids felt at Christmas.

At his desk, Rick read the letter for the third time. There were first a few perfunctory lines thanking him for the gifts that had not yet arrived, the toys for Kathy and Kenny, the scarf for her, and then the words, *But I am humiliated—*

Those four words jumped out of the first paragraph at him; even they infuriated him.

> But I am humiliated at the very notion that my monthly check should be coming from the girl you're living with. This hundred a month that is supposed to supply the "wine and escargots"—once I knew it was being handed over to you by your girl and then relayed on to me—I'd choke before I'd take one swallow of anything bought with it.
>
> That hundred doesn't go for wine and escargots; it goes toward our food and rent and shoes and Tonette's pay and all the rest of everything I don't take care of myself. But if I never touch a paintbrush again and have to find some sort of job as saleswoman or clerk, I'll never accept any of her money. I could never respect myself if I did.
>
> You say you have promised to return a "free year" to her, as well as repaying every last dime and every dollar she pays on your old bills, and I know you mean every word of it. But you said the same thing to me about the times you borrowed a hundred or so from me—it came to about $500, I think. I never kept exact track, and I'd never have brought it up except for this extraordinary development.
>
> You've never had any real responsibility about money, but this goes further than anything yet. I should be saying Merry Christmas and a Happy New Year, but I'm too outraged to be able to say either. I will just wish you well with your book, since that seems more important to you by now than most of the considerations that other people rule their lives by.

It was signed, *Always, Jean.*

Always for women's rights, he thought bitterly, always for equality, until the man steps out of his preordained role as wage earner. Always the emancipated woman, unless it's the man who needs his turn at a little emancipation too.

He would not answer that letter for a good while—he didn't trust his temper or his own outrage. Jean's painting was one of the considerations *she* lived by, major enough to take her away from Princeton, take her away from their life together, off to Paris. Her work was the dynamo that provided the great running current of her creative life: fine, good. But his writing?

Nonsense, my good man, you're supposed to earn the family's living and the hell with any talent you may have, with any inner need that drives you. You are now a parasite, living off a woman, and I'll touch nothing you get from her.

He could not show Jean's letter to Jossie just yet; try as he might to contain himself, he would explode into a violation of his code, that you don't complain in public about your wife, not even to anybody as close as Jossie, that you maintain a certain decorum during quarrels or antagonisms, behind whatever screen you have to erect.

But he seethed each time he thought of the letter. What was he to do at the start of January? Send no check at all? Send it as usual and have it thrown back in his teeth? For the first time since his marriage to Jean, he wished he were free of it and of the maddening bondage of all marriage.

o o o

With New Year's Eve only three days off, Stuyvesant's campaign for the holiday season had just about run its course, and once more Jack Weinstein was congratulating himself on his perspicacity. He had found this Joselyn Stone, had accepted her offbeat approach in her first ads, had given her her head in later ads, and was gladly accepting his just deserts, not only in increased sales of evening clothes but in the widening prestige attaching itself to Stuyvesant's in general. This time he'd run some of the ads in the new magazine *The New Yorker,* not that it was so much as far as circulation went, but that it was so right for the people drawn to Stuyvesant's.

"No matter what I come up with this time," Jossie had told him in late summer, when he commissioned another series from her, "no matter how good it is, you'll never like it as much as 'It's time to dress.' "

"You're probably right," he'd told her. "So try to beat me down. This time I might want sixteen or even eighteen pieces."

He had been pessimistic himself, had even considered Brick's idea of running last year's storewide promotion again, except for the merchandise shown in each ad. But he had kept his doubts to himself, as any businessman would do.

And then, a month later, the girl had walked in with a few sheets of copy and a rolled-up sheaf of crackling white drawing paper with layouts and rough sketches by that Red Montana, and once again he was pleased, not only with her but with himself for recognizing what she had that other copywriters so sadly did not.

Now he idly opened the large proof book at the side of his desk, turning the pages backward to the first ad of the new campaingn.

Are you going?
The opera season opens monday night

> Will you be there? If not, you have some other marvel of an evening ahead and you've been told "Black tie."
>
> For you that may mean white satin, like the new shorter dress now on our third floor . . .

She has the touch, he thought. Whatever she writes, you have to read it. He turned the page.

Are you going?
Another Lunt and Fontanne first night

> Are you going? There will be a smart party that same night—are you going there instead?
>
> Whatever your plans in the big holiday season, this pale blue velvet evening dress . . .

Headline after headline came up at him as he turned the pages, and each gave him the sense he wanted, that by a kind of natural selection it was choosing, from all the hundreds of thousands of people out there, the ones who would find Stuyvesant's the perfect place for the things they understood and valued and were prepared to pay well for.

She hadn't even asked for a raise, this Jossie who was so smart, so clever. If she demanded $70 for each piece, or even $80, he would pay it rather than let her go and try to find somebody else. Try, and then try some more—and be handed Delancey Street all over again, with "haute couture" and "latest from Paris" and all those *words*. Jossie didn't use words. She used something else, he didn't know exactly what. But he recognized it every time he saw it.

He'd given her a Christmas bonus, a big one, $150. But he should have talked out frankly to her before this about higher fees. One of these days she would wake up, and then God knows what she'd take it into her head to demand. A momentary anger at her cupidity assailed him, but in an instant he thought, Hey, hold it.

He telephoned her, though it was nearly seven. She had recently installed a special phone at home, "for my free-lance life," she had explained, wanting to be called less at the office, and she was reachable nearly every evening. What kind of life was that for a pretty young girl? This not-exactly-engaged friend of hers who gave her advice must be an invalid; they were always there.

"Happy New Year almost," he began when she answered.

"Mr. Weinstein! Hello. Is—"

"No changes, nothing. Just Happy New Year and I'm giving you a raise when you start the spring series."

"A raise?"

"To sixty an ad instead of fifty."

"How wonderful! You're just so great to work for."

"So anyway, Happy New Year."

"It *is* happy. And to you too. Thank you, thanks a million."

○ ○ ○

But New Year's Eve was not particularly happy. They had invited the Bellocks and Red and Suzy over for part of the evening, and Rick went out in the afternoon to get an extra bottle of gin and another of Scotch from the man he knew at Gypsy's.

When he came home, he had not a package but a carton, heavy enough so that he bent slightly sideways, to accommodate one edge of it on his right hip.

"You'll never guess the bargain, darling," he said sunnily. "Real imported champagne from France."

He ripped open the top of the carton. There, beside the two bottles of gin and Scotch, were six bottles of champagne, their long slender necks wrapped in silver paper.

"Champagne? French champagne *now?* But what did—how much did it cost?"

"It's New Year's Eve, Happy Nineteen Twenty-six, and he let me have it for—you can't believe it—six a bottle."

"But that comes to—oh, Rick, you didn't!"

"It can all come off my *miss* for January."

She stared at the silver-topped bottles, looked at him, and then did the one thing she hated most: Her face crumpled like a child's, and she burst into angry tears. It was wrong, it was horrible of him to put her into the position of spoilsport, the stingy shrew. Was she the only one who could see ahead to the moment in January when his remaining few dollars would be gone and he would have to dig into his February money? Had he no control, the sort adults ought to have?

This time, Rick did not come to soothe or comfort her. He shoved the carton halfway off the table. "Can't you spare me the tears? Just once?" he demanded.

"Can't you ever say, just once, 'No, we can't afford it'?"

"You mean, *I* can't afford it, me, I, the man without a job. I'm the one can't afford it."

"I never meant that."

"Well, you looked it." He went to the bedroom and slammed the door.

The diffusing hurt was like the slow seeping of blood through bandages. Three months of the new adventure and *this?* This enraged Rick, furious, lashing out? In a moment he might leave the house, the way he'd done that first time they'd had a fight about money. Suppose he was still out when Edie and Andy arrived, or Red and Suzy?

She should have said nothing, not tonight. It was New Year's Eve, after all; he did have the instincts of any good host, to offer the best to his guests. She wiped her eyes, but they kept refilling. *You look like a gargoyle when you cry.* She went to the kitchen sink and sloshed cold water on her face. It was being a cold winter; the water was icy; she gasped at the sting, but it felt good. She went on sloshing until the skin on her cheekbones began to burn.

Come out of there, Rick, she thought, and let's make up. I'm sorry I said anything to rile you, I hate it when you get angry at me, I feel so separate—like a mummy in a locked glass case.

He didn't come out. She stopped crying at last and began laying out the party food they would have later: tiny sandwiches, narrow strips of ham and cheese, fat black olives.

She glanced at her watch; it was nearly six. It's time to dress, she thought, and began to cry again, softly now, her face calm, the tears sliding easily down her cheeks.

He was going to stay there until she had to go in, until she had to make the first move. This was a new Rick and it was awful. He wanted her to say not a word about money, no matter what wild thing he did, and he wanted her to say not one word about his book or how it was going or could she see any more of it.

The book, she thought, his writing. That was it. It wasn't the money today—back of everything was his book. It wasn't going well any more, it hadn't been going well for quite a time. That was why he never talked of it and wanted her not to see any of it or even ask about it. If it were going well, if he still felt sure of it, the whole world could tell it.

He came to the door then, looking past her to the table. The carton was still there. "Good Lord, they should have been on ice this whole time." He took the champagne, three bottles at a time, and put them into the refrigerator.

He didn't look at her and said nothing to erase their quarrel. A new year was beginning, but somewhere, Jossie felt, a notch of change had been cut.

○ ○ ○

My God, I'm hung over, Rick thought the next day at noon. "Buried under" would be more like it; this mountain pressing down on him was too crushing for the concept of anything hanging or floating. Apart from the headache and the furry throat, foul-tasting, it was as if he were pinned flat by a savage weight. He thought of Jean's letter but knew it was compounded of far more than that.

He remembered last night and then moved further back to yesterday afternoon. It was a bad thing, hard to recall, harder to justify. He hated to see her so wounded, so surprised into pain, but he had done it, he and nobody else. God damn that champagne.

They had made up, after a fashion, before the others got there, and by the time they'd all gone through the first three bottles of the stuff, there could have been no more lighthearted group in the world. But he knew his Jossie. Under the bright jokes and ready laughter, she'd been a poor hurt thing, bewildered by his ferocity, trying to get over it, succeeding none too well.

Women, girls, people in love—how vulnerable they all were, how easy for a man to fall into the trap of that vulnerability and send whistling at it the arrows that would pierce through it. Why hadn't he been able to admit to her, as he arrived with the carton of wine, I've been feeling so *down*, I had to do something big and splashy to make myself feel like a big man again? A big successful writer, or on my way to being one.

He hadn't seen it himself for hours, and then hadn't been able to put it into words, because putting it into words was to make it real, and he would not, could not, let it be real. It was a passing attack of nerves, a tearing down of confidence, a momentary phase that would pass, as other phases like it had passed. Now, twenty hours later, in this heavy clarity of remorse, now he could face up to it, and see that for days he had been obsessed with the damn manuscript's not going the way it was going during the summer, and the sudden notion of the great bargain in champagne had appeared like a momentary cure-all.

During the evening he had come close to blurting out the truth, that he'd been drying up on his book for weeks, that he had no more sap rising in him when he faced the desk.

"Only resolution for me," he'd said, during the hubbub of their jokes about New Year's resolutions, "is 'back to one page a day at least.' "

"My only resolution," Red had said, "is back to one screw a night."

They had all shrieked at that, though he doubted now that they actually had been that drunk. Certainly not Jossie. She never was much of a drinker, and last night she had barely tasted the champagne, as if it offended her. He had never seen her look the way she had last night, suddenly less of a college girl and more of a stunning young woman. She had acquired her very first dress from Stuyvesant's, on sale after the big season, perhaps especially reduced by that Mrs. Pepper just for her, and made even more possible by the additional 20 percent discount permitted employees. "You're an 'honorable' employee," Mrs. Pepper had said, and Jossie had gone to her flea account.

It was not an evening dress, since he had long since abandoned his Princeton dinner jacket; it was a party dress, though, some fluttering thin silk in two colors he never would have thought could go together, pale yellow and deep orange. She looked like a tulip in it, or some other slender bending flower.

She certainly had heard his "back to one page a day." She had looked at him, about to say something, but had not spoken. After all, he'd made it all too clear that he didn't want her saying anything about the book or asking anything either. It probably hurt her, to be so shut out, but he couldn't help it. Still, it was pretty poor payment for everything she was doing.

My God, this head, he thought again. He got up and showered, calling out to her. She'd been up for some time—through his tattered sleep toward the end, he'd heard the crackle of layout paper—she'd been working.

Yes, she'd been up since nine, she said, and would make fresh coffee in a jiffy. She cleared the table of all her working paraphernalia, not only layouts but sheets of copy, proofs of earlier ads for her milk account, pencils, rubber cement, long shears which she used to cut out a new paragraph and paste it up over some unsatisfactory one.

There was no sign of rebuke in her, and he was grateful. Long-drawn-out examinations of a dead quarrel were hateful to him, and she knew that. Her own instincts were to talk things out thoroughly, even in retrospect, to "try to understand what made it go wrong." But his instincts were to let it lie there, dead and buried and forgotten.

"I'm not doing too well with the book," he said without preamble, as she brought in his orange juice. "Could we talk it out a bit some time?"

"Any time."

He reached across the table and laid his hand over hers. "I've been secretive and rotten about it, because it's not been moving the way I thought it would."

She turned her hand up so that her palm lay open to his. "I thought maybe."

"The trouble is, I keep writing about the real war, instead of staying with what I'm supposed to be writing about, the war back here, among people who think they hate war but really love it."

"Writing about the trenches? Soldiers wounded and dying, no-man's-land? Is that what you mean?"

"That and air fights—as if I ever got that far in a plane." He glanced at the one framed picture of himself that he permitted her to keep on the mantel over the fireplace. It was of him in uniform, with his new lieutenant's bars, standing beside his plane, the old one-engined Jenny biplane they used for training in the air corps. Then, on impulse, he jumped up from the table, went to his desk, and returned with his manuscript. "How far was I this summer?" he demanded. "When we were leaving the lake to come home?"

"Sixty pages, you said."

"That's right. So look at it now." He offered the sheaf of pages, and she turned to the last one. The number at the top was 101. "Forty-one pages in three months!" Disgust sounded. "If I'd really been able to do two pages a day, it would be at about two fifty by now."

"But it's always hard to adjust to a new situation."

"Darling, don't make alibis for me. It's bad enough when I do it." She was leafing through the manuscript, looking only at the page numbers at the top, and he saw the surprise in her face and the dismay. "Of course that's not counting the hundreds of pages I tear up and throw out," he went on.

"I know—I can hear you in there, crumpling up paper and firing it at the wastebasket." She was indeed surprised; she'd had no idea of his progress in terms of pages, only in terms of his moods. He never left the manuscript lying open on top of the desk. Each time he left it for the day, he turned it face down inside the deep bottom drawer and put the unused stack of paper on top of it. Once or twice she had been tempted to look and see what lay under those empty yellow sheets on top, but it would have been like reading somebody else's mail.

"It's not just an alibi, Rick," she went on. "It *is* a new life for you, not going to an office every morning, being alone all day, no meetings, no people, just here alone writing—"

"There's something else too." He waved at the layouts, proofs, pencils, copy paper she had just cleared from the table. "I'm losing my girl. You're forever working."

"You're not losing me, ever."

"You've no idea how your free-lance stuff has changed our time together. Evenings, weekends, even today, New Year's Day—"

"But I have to."

"Sure, but it takes you a million miles off."

"Only for those particular minutes when I'm writing copy."

"Particular minutes? Hours at a time. Our whole life's changed. We can't go out without reckoning first on those deadlines. We can't play records, we can't read together. We can't even make love unless you've finished your work."

"That's not fair. It's not true."

"It's true enough. Jossie, maybe this great idea of a free year for me is turning out to be a mistake."

"Don't, Rick. That's discouragement talking, because your book is going badly at the moment—but you've got yourself out of bad periods before. It's not a mistake. I never dreamed you felt this way," she ended slowly.

"I never put it into words."

"I'm glad you did. If we really have changed because of all the deadlines, we'll just have to fix it so we can change back."

She thought, It means leaving Ashley.

B&T THE BAKER & TAYLOR COMPANY

GLADIOLA AVENUE, MOMENCE, ILLINOIS 60954

SALE BOOK	A.V.	MISCELLANEOUS

Customer's Order No.	Date 19
Sold to Milly Basso	
Address	

Sold by	Cash	C.O.D.	Charge	On Acct	Mdse. Ret.	Paid Out	Ordered by

Quantity	Description	Price	Amount	
			2	00
		Tax		
Thank You Present this bill with claims or returned mdse.		Total		

No. 14135

Uarco Business Forms

Rec'd by

RS 510-2

Thirteen

I won't even ask him what he thinks, she decided. He'd only say he doesn't want to influence me.

But if I did, I'd never have to work at home at all, not one evening, not one Saturday or Sunday. If I had all eight hours to free-lance in, instead of just the chinks and crevices of time I've been having, I could earn everything we need and never give him that feeling he's losing his girl to deadlines.

She had been raised to $80 a week at Christmas, and that came to $4,160 a year. With a $20 raise each December, it still would take six more years to reach that fabled $10,000 a year; 1926 plus six would be 1932. And she would be past thirty.

That little spasm of arithmetic had taken her mind the day Mr. Jerton had told her she was again getting twice the usual raise for young copywriters; he had also said, with what he thought was lightness, "We ought to let you do more free-lancing—you might bring in another good account."

But now the little spasm came back with more of a jolt—what would happen if she tried this crazy life with Rick for six more years? The red thread of apprehension stitched itself along her nerves.

She wished it were January 2 right this minute, with offices open again. She would have to give Ashley two weeks' notice, maybe more, and she would have to write a lot of copy in advance for Empire State and Coal Stove and her other office assignments. Perhaps she ought to see Jack Weinstein before she said a word at the office; he would have to be her Number One client on some sort of binding promise, or she couldn't risk it at all.

It would be a big step, leaving Ashley, and in a way it hurt to do it. After all, she thought, I've been there nearly three years, and there aren't so many periods that long that I can remember—four years at high, four at college, now three at Ashley. So it *is* one of the large areas of my life that's coming to an end. If it weren't for Rick, it would be sort of scary.

She'd have to get a little place she could make her office. My studio, she thought. If she stayed at home with Rick all day, that would never work. It never did; she'd read that somewhere, or seen it in a play, that husbands and wives seeing each other all day every day was never a good idea.

She remembered the studio apartment on West Fifty-third Street for $25 a month. Was it only two years ago? She could find a one-room studio in the neighborhood; any small place would do since she wouldn't have to sleep or cook there. She turned to the Rooms for Rent columns in the *World.* It felt surreptitious, but when she told Rick why she needed it, the separate room for her would only excite him. The very first day she was installed, she knew exactly what he would come over and do. "To christen the place," he would say. A wavy stir of arousal unfurled like a flag on a lazy breezy day in summer, and she smiled. Everything would be marvelous again.

○ ○ ○

I can't help it, she had thought, way back there in September when the Morris Plan $460 had finally come through. She had mailed the three checks before she even began deciding what precedence and what amounts to assign to all the others.

The first check she wrote was for Macy's, $128.98, and she'd thought, Now I can sleep in our bed without thinking it's not all paid for. The second, for $27.50, went to Lord & Taylor for her chiffon nightgown and robe, and she could wear them again. The third, $8 to Greenwich Florists, seemed larger than all the others.

Only when she had actually stamped and mailed the three had she begun on the puzzle of what to allocate each of the other twenty-five bills. At last she decided to distribute the remaining $296 indiscriminately, $12 on each unpaid amount. Across the face of each bill she wrote, "On account—further payment next month." This legend she had ringed in heavy blue crayon.

Now, in this first week of the new year, she glanced back through the four monthly pages of the "financial encyclopedia," and a small grim satisfaction coursed through her. The $1,500 debt had become $1,040 in October, then $840 in November, and $640 in December. January should make it $440. She was really doing it. The Morris Plan itself was down to a bearable $380.

But Rick would have to put up with her working at night and weekends for a few weeks more, until leaving Ashley and setting up her own studio were facts instead of plans.

"Guess what," she greeted him as she came home the day the office opened again.

"Okay, what?"

"I resigned."

"You what?"

"Resigned from the famous firm of Ashley & Company. I am now Madam Free Lance."

He seized her and swung her round and round the room. "As of when?"

"Three weeks from today. I have to write a lot of copy in advance—practically a year's worth—and break in the new writers on Empire State and Coal Stove."

"Are you glad? How does it feel? Whom did you talk to, Amantha or Ben Jerton?"

"Hold it, you sound like Jack Weinstein, one question after another and no time to answer any of them."

"Hurray for Jack Weinstein. He's become your patron saint."

"—have to break in the new writers and keep going on all my free-lance stuff besides. It's going to be pure murder—don't expect much free time by tomorrow night."

The step seemed to stimulate him; his own work went better once more. They went room-hunting together and found a small square one-room apartment on Bleecker Street, only a few minutes' walk away. *Hot plate allowed; no gas range,* a sign said. But it was furnished in not too bad a manner, rather like a dormitory room at college, with a chastely narrow single bed and good direct light from the street. Its main charm for Jossie was an elongated oak table, about seven feet long, which would serve as a capacious working area, even strewn with unwieldy layouts. The rent was $30 a month.

"And I'll have to buy a typewriter," she said. "No more office pool of typists to make clean copy for the client. I'll have to be my own office pool. What they call a 'renewed' Corona costs thirty-six dollars, or two bucks down and three a month. But you know me with monthly payments."

"That's a coincidence. I've been wondering whether working on a typewriter would make things go faster for me."

"Now, Rick—"

"Just jealousy. Don't let it hit a nerve."

Night after night she brought work home, as she had predicted she'd have to do. He didn't complain, didn't seem to resent it. He tried to do his own work, he read, he played music softly. But then came the evening when he said, "Let's knock it off just once and take in a movie."

This time she couldn't fall in with his mood. "Darling, I just can't." She waved at the cram of papers before her.

"Then I think I'll take a breather for a while."

He left and she worked on until she finished. At ten he was still out. By eleven she undressed and got ready for bed. She began to read. By midnight he had still not come back, and she began to worry. But soon she fell into the sleep of eyestrain and fatigue.

In the morning he was sleeping heavily. Vaguely she had known when he came in; it seemed to her now that it was very late, perhaps near morning. She leaned down over him and drew back. That odor of gin—it really had become offensive to her.

He was still asleep when she left for the office. At noon he telephoned an apology. "Yes, I'm all right. I'll tell you when you get home."

The red stitch of apprehension once more. All day she was uneasy; at times she wished she need not go to West Tenth Street at all for a while.

And then there it was. We don't lie to each other; concealment and evasion are not for us. These things meant nothing.

"Oh, Rick, what—"

"Yes, Joss, I'm just arranging my thoughts." He had first gone to Gypsy's but only grew depressed at being alone there, talking to the bartender. He got thinking of his book, had thought of how slow and difficult it had become, with just a fine spurt here and there. There was also a letter from Jean that kept rankling everything in him. He'd grown pretty despondent in general.

At last he called a girl he knew, hoping she wouldn't answer the phone, a girl who was never too busy to go out in the evening. She had answered and they had gone to another speakeasy. Then he'd taken her home and they'd spent the night together.

Through it all Jossie held herself in, rigid, as if she were chaining herself upright to an iron stanchion. At last she said, "That was snide, about a girl who's never too busy to go out in the evening. Who was she?"

"That doesn't matter."

"Last time you told me."

"Jossie, leave it."

"What sort of girl?"

"A decent enough girl. These things have no real meaning."

"Was it anyone we know?"

"You don't need to ask that."

"Was it? You said her name right out, Lucienne, that girl in Paris, the midinette at the Galeries Lafayette. Is this girl a midinette at Macy's?"

"No, she isn't."

"Then what is she? Why can't you say this one's name?"

"Because there's no point in specifics."

"Isn't it specific enough? Is she anyone we know?"

"Jossie, don't make an issue of 'who is she?' "

"You tell *me* not to make issues? It *was* somebody we know. Who?"

"Suzy."

"Suzy? Red's Suzy? Suzy Platt?"

"She broke with Red right after New Year's. She's not Red's Suzy any more."

"Is she yours?" She covered her face with her hands, fingers sliding upward to the roots of her hair, the outer edges of her palms tight together, making a solid screen across her mouth, jaws, eyes. She hated him for this, hated him for telling her, hated him for doing it but most of all for telling her. She hated Suzy—she could never talk to her again. And she hated Havelock Ellis, for all that preaching about total honesty—and total cruelty—between husband and wife, between lover and beloved.

o o o

"I haven't written for ages," she wrote in her journal several weeks later. "The unhappiest time I've ever lived through was that about Suzy. I can't make myself write it down even now, in words that will jump up at me one day and kill me all over again. I can never forget what it was, so writing it out would be a sort of self-torture. Without any anesthetic."

> For the first nights afterward I couldn't let him touch me or kiss me, and as for making love—I couldn't stop thinking of him with her—I don't even want to write it. I keep saying that and then write it anyhow.
>
> Of course it's getting easier. Of course Rick was brimming with all kinds of remorse; at times he suffered more than I. But after the first few days, he seemed all done with it, as if he had handed it over to me, into my safekeeping, so that it was now mine, not his any longer, but my sole possession. Sometimes I wonder if the net result of all this honesty isn't that you can present your guilt, like a neat little package, to somebody else and just leave it there, no longer yours. Oh, Mr. Ellis!
>
> But I don't want to philosophize about that now, because that's also putting it down in words—All right, *enough!*
>
> Anyway, somehow or other I did manage to get through all the pileup at Ashley and take my departure once and for all. Red Montana threw me a farewell party in the Art Dep't.—lots of people came, even Amantha Dunwoodie. She got in her usual little dig when we had a moment alone: "So you're leaving us too. Not to write a book, I hope."
>
> "Definitely no book."
>
> "How is Rick Baird's book going?"
>
> "I often wonder that myself."
>
> "Come on, Jossie, everybody knows you two are—are great friends."
>
> I ducked that with some goo about this or that and was left with the good old Dunwoodie barb in my brain. Not that it matters any more whether she suspects, actually knows, or has seen us in bed together—now that I'm out of Ashley, I'm through with Dunwoodian barbs forever.
>
> Other things:
>
> Yesterday something funny happened to me. I'd just read

May Sinclair's "A Cure for Souls," and it left me in a mood I haven't known for a long time, reminding me of the way I felt when Rick was in Paris and I began "The Flame-colored Evening Dress," reminding me how wonderful you can feel when you're writing—not advertising, not selling things of trade and business, but something that comes out of *you* instead of a product.

I don't mean write a book. I could never do that, but something that comes out of thinking and feeling, trying to do what May Sinclair did to me with this novel. What is it? This simple story of a selfish man—not beauty in itself, but something that moves me and reaches into me.

Maybe it's my long-ago dream of writing for a newspaper, writing about people and what happens to them, instead of about things and how to sell them. Anyway, right then, quite unexpected, this gale of desire swept through me, to be done forever with just earning money and more money, and paying bills and more bills, and making budgets and thinking of how to allocate which amounts to what stores.

Right then, a sudden feeling came at me that this thing for Rick is not just some sweet little thing I'm doing because I'm in love, but something big and terribly hard at times. Why be afraid to think of it that way, Jossie, you child? Don't be afraid to think into your own self because you always keep away from self-sacrifice bunk.

But I did keep thinking of how people do run away from what they really feel, or even what they're really doing, hide emotion in their hearts under oh-it's-nothing or clever talk and sophisticated remarks. Sentiment is bourgeois, tears are loutish, grief or joy is unaristocratic.

Then just today in the trolley coming home from uptown, I was thinking of the play we'd seen by Lonsdale, the scintillating British playwright, and I remembered Cyrano and Roxanne, and compared the beauty and tragedy of their play to this brassy British comedy. And suddenly I was crying, right there in the trolley.

I thought of our writers today and the magazines and papers, the smart Menckens and Nathans scorning everybody, and F.P.A. and Heywood Broun and Alexander Woollcott—everywhere I find this cleverness, this surface glitter, even about the most lovely things life has, music, poetry, art, love, kindness. Emotion is taboo. It's so rarely that anything written today really touches my heart, with that sharply indrawn breath and the rush of tears at a lovely phrase.

Anyway, in this mood I'm in tonight, it seems to me that

we're all afraid of being stirred, that we've all gone away from the shabby sunburned Walt Whitmans and the poverty-stricken Curies and just the lovely shape of words—"Good night, sweet Prince," or "Great God, I'd rather be a pagan, suckled in a creed outworn."

I'd better quit and go back to the words I do have to live with, to earn the money we must have, back to the sophisticated phrase, the happy turn of a cheap sentence. I don't know why I'm so dispirited tonight. Next time I write, I'll be chipper as a chipmunk.

° ° °

"Rick, can we have lunch? The most spectacular, weird, wonderful thing—"

"Tell me right now."

"Oh, I can't. I'd split the phone wires. Come on over—I can make toasted cheese sandwiches on the hot plate, and I'll have coffee."

"Right away?"

"This minute. I'll bust if you don't."

"Ten minutes. Don't explode."

He put on a tie and reached for his overcoat and hat. No need—another one of those premature spring days. Not so premature; it was early March.

She was doing well, as he'd known she would. Jack Weinstein had readily accepted her proposition, that Stuyvesant be her Number One client, with first call on about half her time, to write not only special ads for holiday seasons but all their ads all year, "even for lace brassieres."

"So you've come to your senses," Weinstein had told her, and scarcely paused when she said that for "first call on my head" she would want an annual fee not of the $4,000 he had once offered, but $5,000.

She had found work easily with several small agencies for various products, some of which he knew, like Daggett & Ramsdell's Cold Cream and Frostilla Lotion, and others he knew nothing about, all of satisfactory importance and solvency. She was averaging $800 a month, very near that $10,000 a year that had for so long held some mythic meaning for her.

And she was as good as her word about not working at home in the evenings any more, or over weekends. Since she'd begun full-time free-lancing at the studio, she had locked the door on the business part of her life each day at five or six. And she was happy.

God, to be happy with what you were doing. To be sure of yourself. He used to be sure of himself all the time.

She was waiting for him on the sidewalk in front of the place on

Bleecker Street. Her face looked the way her voice had sounded when she called him, excited, aglow, larky.

"Darling," she greeted him, kissing him in full disregard of any passersby. "Wait till you hear!"

Upstairs she had a small pitcher of martinis waiting and went to it. "Never mind that," he said. "Out with it or you're nothing but a little tease."

"This morning, the minute I got here, Ben Jerton called me. They have this telephone number. They think I live here."

"Ben Jerton called you—"

"And said, Would I come to the office?

" 'Over to Ashley?' I said.

" 'Yes, to my office. Can you make it?'

" 'When?'

" 'Right now, by cab if you can.'

"So I dropped whatever and dashed over. There he was waiting for me, and with him, of all the angel people in this world, was Grover Cleveland Albright of the Empire State Plate Glass Company."

"Didn't Albright know you'd left Ashley?"

"I'd told him myself, and told him I'd be breaking in the next copywriter and everything." She burst into a brief squealing laugh, like a teenager. "He'd seen the first copy from the new writer and hated it. Turned it down flat. And Rick, he wants Ashley to let me keep writing all Empire State copy *free-lance.* "

"They'd never agree—"

"They never have used anybody outside the office, not once in all their illustrious years, but Mr. Albright sort of reminded Mr. Jerton why he had come to Ashley in the first place—"

"Well, I'll be damned, Joss. No major agency ever uses free-lancers for copy. Never. Not one of them, not ever."

"Ben Jerton told him all that, and the twice-blessed Mr. Albright wouldn't budge. He even hinted that they'd better make an exception, or else. Finally Mr. Jerton gave in and phoned me."

"With Albright staying right there, to be sure he put it to you fair and square. It's the damndest thing."

"And to hear what Ashley would pay me. They both looked a bit stunned when I said a hundred for each ad."

"Even for trade papers?"

"That's just what Mr. Jerton asked. 'That boring old ad in *Glass World,*' I told him, 'is what started me on free-lancing.' "

"Did he say touché?"

"He didn't have time. Mr. Albright was saying that the trades were as vital to them as anything else. And I said that a sliding scale was too messy any time anybody tried it."

"You great little kid, Jossie. I salute you."

"Rick, they run twenty ads a year."

"Two thousand dollars and a sure thing. Would Andrew Carnegie approve?" He put his arms around her, kissed her, held her, and kissed her again. "There never was anybody like you, Jossie, not in my whole life."

Then, to her astonishment, his look of pleasure vanished, driven from his eyes by a somber reflectiveness. Her mood changed correspondingly; something was going to be said, something was going to happen. She knew him too intimately to misread any shift in his emotional climate. She was immediately braced, as if for a storm. Perhaps for tornado, hurricane, typhoon. She thought of Suzy and begged the heavens that this be no return to that catastrophe.

"What is it, Rick?" she prompted at last.

"I've been thinking about this for some time now," he said quietly. "And now, right here, with you and your great news, I know it's right."

Trepidation left her. It was not going to be any return to catastrophe of the Suzy kind. He was struggling for the words he needed, and a sweep of compassion cleansed her mind of all the debris of resentment and anger of the past weeks.

"It's a sort of last-ditch maneuver about my writing," he said. "It might work, but if it hurt you, it wouldn't be worth it."

"What sort of maneuver?"

"I got wondering why my book went best up there at the lake during that three weeks, remember?"

"I sometimes wonder about that too."

"It had something to do with being so apart, apart from phones, apart from everybody, alone at noon to do a little fishing; it was as if I could get into a mood that was never dissipated by the small contacts of talk and being together."

"Gauguin," she said, trying to make it light. "Off somewhere."

"Not off somewhere, never. But I did wonder what it might do to the writing if I were totally alone for a stretch at a time."

"How much stretch?"

"Through the week, say, and then having our weekend together with no thought of work, no guilt about not working, no excuses necessary." He gazed around the studio, looked at the single bed, at the hot plate in the screened-off kitchenette.

"To live apart all week?" she asked. Cold metal began piling up within her, steel bolts in winter, one on top of another.

"Think of what Friday night would be like," he said, "with the two of us together again; think of knowing all week that Friday was getting closer every minute, like me on the ship sailing home from Paris, every minute getting nearer—" He put his arms around her.

"It would be like coming home to each other after a week of real work, don't you see?"

"Like coming back together." Her eyes filled; she did not turn from him. There was no hiding this forlorn new knowledge that he could choose to be away from her.

"If the damn book started going faster, if it felt the way it did during vacation—remember how happy we *both* were?"

"I do remember. Oh, Rick, I'd give anything to see you that way again, so sure of it, so absorbed in it." I would, she thought. "Just anything," she repeated. Then, without transition, she added, "I wish I hadn't asked you to come over here so I could brag about my free-lancing at Ashley for Mr. Albright."

"That had nothing to do with it. I've been thinking about it since you got the studio."

"But I got the studio—" She dried her eyes with her fingers and from behind her raised hands asked, "When would we start?"

"We won't start at all if you're this unhappy about it. I love you too much to bull it through, no matter—"

"I'll be all right. It just takes time to get used to the idea."

"Then let's forget it for a while."

"Oh, I couldn't. Not once you brought it up, not if it might help you work better and feel happier."

"Happier about the writing, that's all, darling. It's not going to be happy for me without you, either. But then there'll be those Fridays to look forward to, and the Saturdays and the Sundays."

It *would* be fiercely exciting, she thought, like those nights of waiting for him to get back from Europe, when she would almost reach orgasm just thinking ahead to what it would be.

"If we're to try it, Rick," she said carefully, "then the only thing is to start right now, not 'forget it for a while.' "

"Right now? When?"

"Tonight," she said with difficulty. "I'll just sleep here."

"Are you sure?"

"I couldn't stand a week or two of getting ready for it." She turned away from him. "Please go now, darling. See you Friday."

Fourteen

See you Friday. Over and over the phrase echoed; it seemed to take shape, a curved swinging phrase, like a loop of syllables in the silent room. She tried to think and could not. She tried to work and turned from the long table. Of everything that had gone wrong between them, this was the most frightening, this the one that hurt most. He could say that a Lucienne or a Suzy meant nothing, but this—he must know that this did mean something. He needed to be away from her.

If he thought it might help his writing, they would have to try it. She could not stand up to him and say, "No, I won't even give this a chance." She could not say, "It won't change one thing about your writing or not writing." She might think it, but to say it would be impossible. Anyway, how could she be so sure? It was true that nobody knew why a creative mood was sustained or why it drooped, not even the writer. It was true that writing was the backbone of Rick's life—he had made that clear from their first day together. If this truly was a last-ditch maneuver, there was nothing for it but to try it.

She shouldn't have called him in the middle of the day and asked him to drop everything and come right over, just because she was so full of herself about Jerton's news. It was her own conceit that did it, not thinking of Rick at his desk, perhaps in the middle of a scene, but her own need to tell him what wonderful thing had happened to her.

At the beginning she had tended to keep silent with him about her copywriting, and whatever little triumphs she had, just as she did with her father, forgetting that Rick too looked down on the world of advertising and everything in it. Then she'd begun to feel that she was an exception, that *her* copy and her success stood in a special niche for him. But even if it did, his writing still came first.

She lay down on the narrow bed, trying not to think, but at once she was remembering the morning they had rented the studio, hearing him say, "No bed is too narrow," making love to her without waiting for her to get fully undressed. She flung away from the memory, burying her face in her arms, tasting the salt on her wet skin. Her eyelids stung with heat; she fell asleep.

It was midafternoon when she awoke. *See you Friday*. It came at her like a javelin hurled. She ought to go out and get some food in for supper; she had a second hot plate and could manage soup and a chop. She ought to go home and get some of her clothes, and her night things, and a toothbrush. But she could not go there and explain to Rick why she had to show up, in violation of the new pact, on the very first day.

She thought of calling Edie and asking if she might drop by for a bit that evening, making some excuse about Rick off on a business dinner. She did not go near the phone. She thought of Nell, who had quit teaching to have a baby, but that meant seeing her husband, Eddy Resnick. She tried to fall asleep again, but sleep was now beyond her.

At five she called her mother. "Are you doing anything special tonight, Mama?"

"No, dear. Anything wrong?"

"Nothing like that other time—it's just I have to be alone tonight, and I'm pretty low, and I got wondering if I might go for a drive in the car—"

"Can you get here for dinner?"

"Is Pa there?"

"Of course he is, but do come on up. He's not as insensitive as you think he is. I'll tell him we want to talk, and that will be that."

"Oh, Mama, I think I will drive up at that. Is dinner still at seven?"

If I'd never rented the studio, she thought, as she began to drive north through the city traffic of late afternoon, Rick would never have thought of this. But the only reason I did rent it was because he didn't want me to work at home every night, and all my work in the first place was to free him so he could write.

It's so unfair. Something about this is so unfair.

This was worse than hearing about Suzy. That had happened one terrible night, and you could try to forget it, after a few days, and even start to get over it. But this living apart would happen again tomorrow and the day after and then again until Friday. Rick had never mentioned Suzy again, and hadn't gone out alone again, but now, alone every night for four nights in a row, would he make love to her again?

Would she, Jossie, know or never know? After seeing how outraged and wounded she was that time he told her, would he decide she wasn't up to the Havelock Ellis standard of honesty-in-love? Would it be worse if he never told her one way or the other? Keep her guessing from now on, or keep on telling her?

I'll go mad with all of this, she thought. She had left the city limits and was nearly at New Rochelle. I mustn't tell Mama any of this part at all. I mustn't tell her too much anyway. Rick always says it's not good taste to complain about your wife or your husband, not even to your most intimate friend. Look at that bad letter he got from Jean around Christmas; he told me it was bad and upsetting and even insulting, and then said he would tell me all about it later, when he was sure he wouldn't burst out at Jean. All he did was say that he wouldn't be sending her the $100 a month for a while, that he'd put it aside in a special account somewhere, so as to have it intact when he did decide to send it again. Then he took that photograph of her from the top of his desk and put it away in a drawer.

God, how many special accounts we have: my Cornell account, and the flea account, and our joint Baird account, and now this new Jean account. But even when he was telling me this much about Jean's letter, he did manage to hold back whatever anger he was bursting with.

Tonight I'll have to hold back any outbursts at him, no awful weeping, no accusations. It's just that I can't be alone, not this first night. Mama never makes me explain when I show I don't want to.

Dinner with her parents was quiet, almost formal. She talked only a little about her work; her mother helped her by steering the conversation to her own problems of teaching English Lit to high-schoolers, and her father joined in with a general disquisition on what was unsatisfactory in the public school system. They all talked about Nell's new baby, now six months old.

But later, as they began to clear the table, she saw her mother signal her father and was grateful that he went to his own room. They finished the dishes in silence.

"Your eyes look red, maybe a bit swollen," her mother said as she put away the dish towel and closed the cupboard doors. "What is it, Jossie, why are you so unhappy?"

"Oh, Mama." And then, despite all the rules of decorum she had absorbed from Rick, despite her vow not to complain, not to reveal, not even to weep, she went all the way back to the day Rick had first told her about the story he had sold Mencken's *Smart Set* while he was at college, to her understanding of his desperate longing for the life of an artist, the brilliant opening of his novel attacking the hypocrisy of the home front during the war; she talked of Jean and Havelock Ellis; she talked of unpaid bills strewn in the top drawer of Rick's desk, and the way she would wake up at night planning how to pay them, what percentages, what priorities; she came at last to her own dream of giving him a year of total freedom, her joy at helping him become the man he wanted to be. And she ended with his suggestion that very morning that they live apart except for weekends.

"This is Monday," she ended. "I won't see him until Friday."

It was like the night of the abortion, she thought once, while the words and sentences came pouring out, her mother just sitting there, her hand sometimes reaching out to squeeze hers, her own eyes filling while she listened. She kept expecting her mother to denounce

Rick, excoriate him, show she abhorred him. But nothing of the sort happened.

"You're so young, Jossie, to carry such burdens," she said at last. "All the burdens of a family—not only Rick, but Jean and Rick's father, and the rent and food and doctors' bills and debts. It's so much, Jossie, so much."

"It's not too much. I can do it. I am doing it. Part of it is even fun—and so wonderful to know I can help him."

"Just the same, to be sleepless over bills, to have to borrow five hundred dollars to get a start on those debts, to have to split up sums into fractions for a dozen stores, to deny yourself a new dress or hat or books you might want, and jolly silly extravagances once in a while just for yourself—"

"Mama, none of that compares to being in love the way Rick and I are in love."

"A couple of years ago," her mother went on, "you were a carefree college girl, bright and free, facing the whole world to make it into *your* world." Her voice broke and her throat thickened, so her last words came out in what Jossie thought of as little chunks with furry edges. "Now you're head of a family, plunged into responsibilities a mile deep, thinking only of making the world that Rick wants."

"I'll have my turn—he's promised me. I never even knew what I *did* want until I met Rick. I'd die if—I just couldn't live if I didn't have Rick."

Her mother nodded and then nodded once more. They were still in the kitchen. Her mother wiped her eyes and Jossie's breathing became less labored, like a child's when it stops sobbing. Her mother said, "Would you like to stay over tonight? Your bed's always made."

"No, thanks, really not. It would be like running home to Mama."

"What's so wrong with running home to Mama when you're miserable?"

"It's exactly what I did do, isn't it?" She went to the icebox and poured herself a glass of water. Before she drank it she held the icy glass to her forehead and then her cheeks. "No, I'd better get through this first night right there in my happy little studio, on my own, and see what it's like."

"Don't be too brave, Jossie."

"I'm not being brave at all. Look at me."

"I never give you motherly advice, do I, but might I make an exception this once?"

"This is exceptional, for sure."

"Ask yourself once in a while whether you still are really happy, or whether it's partly that you're afraid of being *un*happy."

Jossie shook her head wildly. "I just know I'd die without Rick."

o o o

She drove back to the city, surprised at an odd sense of comfort. Something had eased a bit. Maybe the new business of going to a psychoanalyst and blatting it all out—maybe there was something valid to it after all. Probably you'd get just as much release talking to your priest or your rabbi—well, she had no priest or rabbi, but her mother was no slouch when things were at their rottenest. Even as they were parting, she hadn't attacked Rick or called him self-centered or worse. She seemed to understand in her own way, seemed to know what drove a writer on. Most of all, she seemed to know what it meant to love somebody the way she loved Rick.

Again and again her eyes filled with tears as she drove; twice she drew the car to the side of the road because she couldn't see the macadam pavement clearly enough. They ought to invent windshield wipers for the eyes of people who can't stop crying, she thought, and the vision of two tiny wipers going right-left-right-left across her lids made her smile faintly as she dabbed at her eyes with her scarf. Her handkerchief was a sopping ball in her purse. She should have asked her mother for a sleeping pill; she had never taken one in her life, but this was the night for it. She could never sleep with this pain exploding over and over again, every time she thought, Alone.

At home she fell asleep at once, wearing only her brief silk teddy. She had stopped at a drugstore, bought toothpaste and a brush, had parked in front of a delicatessen, but the thought of food had repelled her and she drove on. She'd have toast and coffee in the morning; there was that much of a larder in the studio already.

In the morning the telephone rang her awake, and she raced toward it. Let it be Rick, she thought, please let it be Rick. To her astonishment it was Mary Watts.

"Hi, cookie," she began, "don't fall over. It's me, Mary W."

"Don't tell me Mr. Jerton wants me to grab a cab again."

"No, this is me. I was wondering if we could have lunch one day."

"Sure, I'd love to. Say when."

"Tomorrow? Next day?"

"Either."

"Thanks, cookie. Let's make it tomorrow."

They had fixed on a small restaurant near the office, and Jossie's curiosity grew as she waited for Mary to join her there. She had been Ben Jerton's secretary for the entire time he had been at Ashley; surely this luncheon would not be because she was fired or leaving and looking for another job. She liked Mary Watts; ever since the day she'd repaid that $50 loan and Mary had said, "Any time, cookie, you're a fast payer," she'd had the sense that Mary approved of her in some way that had nothing to do with writing copy. Occasionally when the weather was too inclement for Mary at noon, she would order in a sandwich and invite Jossie to join her with her own lunch in a little brown paper bag, brought all the way from New Rochelle. That was in the $25-a-week days.

Now, after they had ordered, after the preliminary talk was over, Mary said, "I'm not sure I ought to tell you this."

"You are sure, or we wouldn't be here."

"You're right. I've been through all the yes-I-will, no-I-won't, and here I am."

"Is it about Mr. Jerton?"

"Not primarily. It's about Mr. Jerton *and* Mrs. Dunwoodie."

"Oh, I'd heard that long ago they—"

"This isn't about that old gossip. I wouldn't be passing it on, if it were. I didn't when it was happening."

"I don't know why I said that—I'm sure you never would."

"It's mostly about Amantha Dunwoodie and you."

"And me? How on earth?"

"She tried to stop Mr. Jerton from agreeing to Mr. Albright's idea about your free-lancing Empire State."

"She didn't!"

"I heard her in there, the day before he called you to come over. The door was open and she got sore and her voice goes way up when she gets sore. Anyway, I stopped typing just to listen."

"I know how her voice goes up."

"Well, first she argued that it would set up a dangerous precedent, to let a client *choose* who should write his copy—that then other clients would take it into their heads to pick and choose which writer was the only one they'd have on their accounts."

"How could it become a precedent? Nobody would know about it outside."

"That's just what he said, but she said you'd be just conceited enough to blab it around and every agency in town would get to hear about it."

"What a dirty thing to say." She put down her sandwich.

"She said you know Red Montana's girl, Suzy Something, at J. Walter, and they're our biggest rivals."

"I don't ever see her any more."

"Then, when all that precedent stuff got nowhere, Dunwoodie said, 'Anyway, she's not exactly the Ashley type and that has already set a different kind of precedent—we're getting more and more applicants of the wrong kind.' Mr. Jerton didn't like that. I've worked for him for twelve years, and I know what every change in his voice means. He said, 'You mean about her religion, I suppose.' "

Jossie waited in silence. Her heart was beating faster.

"Then Dunwoodie went on about Stone not being your real name, that your mother's name was Stein and nobody could even pronounce your father's name." Unexpectedly, Mary Watts grinned widely. "That's when he pushed the buzzer for me. 'She's Jewish,' he said to Dunwoodie, as I came in. 'She told me so the day I hired her. Also her father's name. I can't pronounce it either.' "

"Oh, Mary."

"Dunwoodie had her back to the door; she didn't see me. So then she got in her last dig. 'And she has the morals of a tomcat—she's been having an affair with Rick Baird for a couple of years, a married man.' Mr. Jerton looked up at me, and then she saw me, too, and got up. Mr. Jerton said, 'I think you have your gender wrong about cats, Amantha.' "

"Oh, Mary, *why?* I always thought she liked me. She got my Coal Stove copy through for me, running those market tests."

"It was herself she was getting it through for. Coal Stove's one of her major accounts."

Jossie was shaking her head in disbelief. "But why would she try to kill my Albright deal? It doesn't hurt her any."

"It doesn't help her any either. Empire State is Mr. Jerton's account, and it's growing. She'll try to shoot down every ad you write. That's why I thought I ought to warn you."

"My God, and I thought—she'd hint things, and keep me guessing, but all along I did think she liked me."

"You were awfully young when you came to Ashley, Jossie. I used to think, How wonderful to be so young."

"I'm not so young any more."

They stared at each other and resumed eating their luncheon.

At last Jossie said quietly, "You don't like Amantha Dunwoodie very much, do you?"

"No. Not since she tried every trick in the book to get Mr. Jerton to marry her."

"That was a long time ago."

"And some things don't wear off even after a long time."

Suddenly Jossie saw it. Mary Watts was still in love with her boss, one of the saddest situations a working woman could find herself in. Still in love—oh, God, she thought, what would it be like if I ever were still in love, and Rick— She could not finish.

"Well, thanks, Mary. I'll watch out. As I said, I'm not so young any more. This kind of nasty makes me feel fifty."

o o o

Yesterday Rick and today Dunwoodie, she thought as she started back to her studio. What next? What's suddenly gone wrong?

She thought of the evening ahead, alone, and felt she could never stand it, at least not yet, maybe later on, but not so soon, not tonight. Again she thought of Edie and Andy and again shied from the idea; they were Rick's best friends and if she broke down—impossible. At home she went straight to work; the copy went well for two paragraphs and then halted.

At last she called her sister and asked if she might drop by in the evening after dinner. "I'm sort of blue."

"Why not *for* dinner. It'll cheer you up."

"You know the way Ed and I are—he'll get going on Russia and the N.E.P. or something and we'll start screaming at each other."

"He's forgotten all about the New Economic Policy and Russia and everything else. He just bought a new Buick roadster—he won't talk about anything but that."

"A roadster?"

"What else? He's got four brothers and eight cousins and doesn't want them tagging along."

"Will he mind if I come over?"

"He'll probably take you for a drive before you can eat. One look at the baby and then down to his beloved automobile."

Nell was right. From the moment Jossie entered their apartment uptown, a block east of Central Park, the talk was of the new maroon Buick. Jossie had already seen it. It was parked in front of the five-story brownstone, where they had a full floor, and as Jossie came north on the Madison Avenue trolley toward Sixty-eighth Street she saw it at the curb.

Half a dozen people were gathered around the great heavy machine on its newfangled fat balloon tires, looking at its gleaming surface, its sleek lines, its top down to expose the wide red leather seat behind the steering wheel. The rumble seat behind was closed, and a small boy was running his fingernails under the locked lid, trying to open it.

She was cheered; the car would help keep her from any repeat performance of the night before with her mother. Ed did suggest a drive, and she didn't have to feign her admiration for the car. He drove north the entire length of Riverside Drive and then all the way down to the Battery. There he had to stop for gasoline, which cost him $3.00. The Ford could be filled for $1.20; that in itself showed the magnitude and power of this marvelous machine.

On the Drive, the sight of the river in the early evening brought to her vividly her old love for it. She and Rick never saw the Hudson downtown; it actually was only a few blocks farther west from the apartment or the studio, but it never occurred to them to walk through the warehouses and piers to get close to it. We'll walk over, she thought and quickly added, When we see each other.

It was after dinner when they were alone in the baby's nursery that Nell suddenly said, "What's up, anyway? You look sunk."

"Nothing much. Working hard."

"You don't get the blues from work. It's Rick, isn't it?" She didn't wait for a reply. "How long is it, by now?"

"Is what? Rick and me?"

"I know how long that is. How long has that wife of his been living in Paris? Wasn't it supposed to be for 'a year or two'?"

Jean had moved to Paris in the spring of 1923. "Well, she's been doing so well with her painting under that art teacher—one gallery sells some of her canvases—she's staying awhile longer."

"Come off it, Jossie. She went before you started with Rick. Doesn't all this delay mean something? Those two don't make sense. Why doesn't he get a divorce? Why doesn't she?"

Jossie said nothing. Whenever Rick did talk about Jean's decision to stay on a bit more, he always added that the schedule was up to Jean, and Jossie ignored whatever implications there might be.

Nell put the baby back into his crib. "Don't you ever want a child?" Nell demanded into her silence. "I never thought I did either, until I had Jimmy, but it's the most wonderful thing that can ever happen to you."

"I never even think of having a baby," Jossie answered in a flare of irritation. "Or of getting married either—not until I'm about thirty. I'm not even twenty-six."

"Don't get riled at *me*."

"I'm not. Oh, Nell—" Her voice quavered and she rose abruptly. "I'd better get going. I'm way behind schedule on everything this week. But thanks for having me over, sweetie, it was lovely. And the car, and especially the baby."

"Ed thinks it's the other way around."

They laughed, and Nell let her go. She's sunk, she thought, as the door closed. I wish that damn Rick would—I wish she would— She could finish neither sentence.

The moment she got home, Jossie went to the long oak table and picked up the copy she had been trying to do that afternoon. This time it worked. For nearly two hours she could concentrate on it.

Well, that's two days got through, she thought, and went to bed.

○ ○ ○

It was Thursday evening, and at last Rick was answering Jean's infuriating letter. Since he'd left Jossie, he had seen no one; all day every day, with time out for brisk walks, he had worked, in kind of a dream state of power; everything he set down seemed to be sound and good. There was the usual tearing up and the usual rewriting, but Tuesday, Wednesday, and all day today he'd known this new experiment was working. Painful as it was to see Jossie's face when they parted, often as he turned to the phone to call her, hateful as sleep was without her there, the new lines and paragraphs and pages rolling out from under his pen were making it all worthwhile.

In time Jossie would see it as he did. If his book were to be the success she was so sure it would be—"you'll be famous, darling"—then she would share in every part of that success.

But writing this letter to Jean was as forbidding a task as he'd ever faced. More than three months had passed; taking a few weeks to get hold of himself was fair enough, but by now he had to get down to it. Tomorrow evening he would be with Jossie again. This seemed somehow the final opportunity.

> It's taken me all this time, Jean, to cool down enough to write a civil answer to your blast, and what I have to say may surprise you.
>
> Your scorn and vitriol at my accepting help, financial help, for a free year of writing, would never have erupted if that financial help had come from my father—as yours came from your father.
>
> Yes, your father. If he hadn't worked all his life to make that Princeton house mortgage-free so you could sell it for $10,000, you would never have had the money to move to Paris to study art. God knows I couldn't have paid for a two-family, two-country existence.
>
> But when that help comes not from a father or a husband but from a woman, all your modern ideas of equality fall apart into a rubbish heap, and you revert to the stereotypic lady who looks only to a husband, a father, or possibly a male lover for support.
>
> Some emancipated woman! I remember when I urged you to stop signing your paintings Kimble, and you thought I meant you should sign them Baird. "I can't start all over again," you said, missing the point. I remember your surprise when I said you should have signed them Ganther, your own name, because at the easel you were not a Kimble, not a Baird, but *you*, a Ganther.
>
> If you can't see the connection between this old mumbo-jumbo that you're a man's daughter or a husband's wife but never you in your own selfhood—the connection between that crap and your horror that I should be willing to accept help from a woman—then you've gone back into the dark ages where votes for women was still a fighting issue. Thank God I have not.
>
> And if a woman is my equal and I hers, then I have no

> shame in letting her help me, as she would have no shame at letting me help her.
>
> And this woman, this Jossie, is indeed my equal, anybody's equal. Since you think that help from her is tainted, I have put the January, February, and March checks into a kind of unofficial escrow account; you can send for them any time you wish. Nor will I be sending any further monthly checks to you until they are purified by being earned by a male.

He signed it, *Always, Rick,* and thought, Tomorrow is Friday and I see my Jossie again.

Fifteen

Friday was breathless. It was barely eight in the morning when Rick phoned her. "My darling, I feel as if we'd just met—I can't sleep for wanting you."

"Oh, Rick, me too."

"Shall we say five?"

"Five. It *is* like our first week."

"Will you come here? But let's not cook. We'll go out."

"I'll be there."

"And Joss—"

"What, darling?"

"I've done fourteen pages. I think they're good, and I love you more than you'll ever believe."

"And I you." They had spoken only once all week. It was Rick who had made the call, to ask about her clothes, and she had suggested that she go over during the hour he went for his daily walk. His alacrity in accepting made her wonder whether he too was afraid of breaking down if they were together too soon.

On Thursday afternoon, she'd gone to a beauty parlor and had her hair washed and cut in the new style, "windblown." It was not the old shingle; it was shaped to her head with little points of hair coming forward over her cheekbones and down toward her eyebrows in uneven little spikes across her forehead. Her eyes looked bigger than ever.

She had also yielded to impulse and bought a new spring dress; it was a silk print in light blue, with sprays of white twigs strewn over it. I don't care if it costs $20, she thought, it's spring and you're young.

And now it was Friday, and at five he had the door open before she could use her key. "You beautiful thing," he said. "My God, you're more beautiful than ever."

° ° °

The telephone was ringing as they got back from dinner. They had made love before they went out, and it was nearly eleven. Before Rick lifted the receiver, he asked, "Do we want to go anywhere this weekend, or see anyone?"

"Nobody."

It was Andy Bellock. "I've been trying you all night," he started. "We've got news. I'll put Edie on and let her tell you."

"I don't know if this will be such great news for you to hear," she began, "but I was right on holding out on the cabin."

"You sold it."

"Just today. For six thousand—double what we'd asked for at the beginning. So I'm not such a bad Vincent Astor after all."

"Whew!" He turned to Jossie. "They sold the cabin for six thousand." He saw her face fall and turned back to the phone. "I guess congratulations are in order."

"They're taking possession April first. Only two free weekends left. Would you want—?"

"Would we ever!" He turned to Jossie. "Edie's inviting us up there one more time. Here, you talk to her."

Jossie took the phone. She hadn't yet thought ahead to summer and Peekskill. Now the cabin was gone except for one last weekend. Another separation. A summer in steaming New York.

"So what's to become of my canoe?" she greeted Edie, as if chiding her. "Congratulations on getting all that dough."

They agreed on the weekend after next. "The last of the Mohegans," Edie punned.

"Tell Lisa she can make believe the canoe is all hers, till we decide what to do with it." She turned ruefully back to Rick. "Well, we can have a couple of weekends at Coney Island or Asbury Park—we still have the Ford."

On the second Friday of the new regimen, he went over to her studio, early by a full hour, and again they were like new lovers. Maybe separation created more than it deleted, Jossie thought, new beginnings on and on. Rick had again written well during the entire week—only ten pages this time, but ten pages that gave him "a kind of high."

"I never have it when I'm faltering around," he said. "It's as if I have a built-in critic inside, who says 'Okay, buddy' or else 'Try again, buddy, it stinks.' "

"Can you imagine what it will be like when the critics on the *Times* and the *World* and the *Sun* all say 'Okay, buddy'?" She clasped her hands together. "Oh, Rick, this new scheme *is* working out for you."

"What about you?"

"At first it was so awful, so scary—"

"I know, sweetheart."

"But by now, in a funny way, it just seems to add, to deepen—"

The telephone rang. She glanced at her watch; it was already after five. None of her clients would call her after five on a Friday afternoon. None except Jack Weinstein.

"What do you know about Boston, Jossie?" he greeted her when she answered. His voice boomed over the phone. Rick could hear him from three feet away.

"Nothing. Hello, Mr. Weinstein."

"Have you ever lived there?"

"Never."

"Visited there?"

"No, never."

"Have you any friends from there? At Cornell wasn't there one single girl from Boston? It's impossible. On the law of averages."

"Nobody I knew, why?" She grinned at Rick. Was she supposed to feel apologetic for not being up on Boston?

"Because we're opening our first branch store in Boston," he said. "That's why."

"How wonderful. When?"

"Maybe October. We're rebuilding two stores into one, renovating throughout, decorating, the most modern store old Boston has ever seen. If not October, then November for sure."

"Stuyvesant of Boston. It sounds so elegant. And you want me to think of an announcement ad *now?* In March?"

"I want you to think about going up there on a business trip and living at the Copley Plaza a whole week before you write one word."

She gasped. Rick stepped nearer the phone, also astonished.

"A business trip? I've never gone on a business trip."

"So it's time you did. All expenses paid, of course."

"Away for a whole week? But my other clients—"

"You can arrange with your other clients. Maybe not a whole week; three–four days would be enough."

"To do what?"

"Study the city, look at the stores, read all their ads, see Jordan Marsh and Filene's, find any specialty shops with customers like ours. You'll need some Stuyvesant clothes—Mrs. Pepper will outfit you with a couple of things. On the house too, naturally."

"I can't take this all in."

"You'll have time for taking it in. You won't be going until June first, when you can see what a branch store should look like." His laugh sounded strong and authoritative. "Brick and I just finished talking it all out, so I called you."

"Oh, Mr. Weinstein, I'm just flabbergasted."

"I told you it could be heaven for you too, didn't I?"

As she put up the receiver, Jossie whirled toward Rick. "Let's both go. We aren't having any vacation this summer—let's go together."

° ° °

For once their weekend with the Bellocks, despite some high moments, was very nearly a failure. Driving up on the last Friday in March, in unseasonably warm weather, they talked again about their lack of a real vacation this year, even of a commuting change of scene, and Rick said, "It almost makes me appreciate the old three-weeks-with-pay I used to kick about."

"We'll have the four days in Boston."

"I'm not so sure."

"Darling, don't get going on that again." Several times he had said she ought to go alone.

"I tell you, you're not facing the sheer mechanics of it." He was suddenly impatient. "If I went, I'd show up on your hotel bills: room for two, meals for two. Or are you good at swindle sheets?"

"I don't know what a swindle sheet is."

"But you're planning to learn. Come on, Joss, it's not in you. Damn this budget life we lead. Of course I'd go, if I had my own salary every week."

"We'd have separate rooms anyway; we can't sign in as Mr. and Mrs. Baird. I have to be Miss Stone up there. We'd have separate hotel bills—Jack Weinstein would never get to see yours. We'd pay cash for meals too. There'd be no swindle sheet about it."

"In any case, I can't see myself in a great hotel, scrimping on every tip I gave a bellboy."

It's not the bellboy, she thought, it's not Boston at all; it's the book again. This week it couldn't have gone well—he hasn't said one solitary word about it. The new momentum that had surged so brilliantly for a week or two is already pausing for breath. It's remarkable how transparent he is about his work—a baby could interpret his moods.

And when they reached Peekskill, there was a melancholy about the cabin and the lake, a sense of finality and farewell. The next time they were up here they would no longer have their own cabin, their own porch, the canoe at the end of the walkway; they would be houseguests of the Bellocks, arrival and departure set in advance.

"How's it going with the book?" Andy asked as they were having drinks on their arrival.

"Up and down," Rick said. "On the whole, I'd say okay."

"We met Bill Abbott one night. He's an editor at D & P."

"Dawes & Powers?"

"That's right." D & P was a publishing house, a younger firm than Scribner's and Macmillan and Little, Brown, but already nearly as well known.

"You never said you knew any editors," Rick said.

"I didn't, but he was at the Jenkses where we were, and we got talking about new books and writers and publishing in general. He says it's in a bad way. With books at two and three dollars a copy, people resent the prices. Unless you have a top best-seller, forget it."

"I've heard that before," Rick said.

"Well, I got talking about you and your novel. I told him you were only about halfway through, but that its basic idea was good and strong and original."

"Did you now!" Rick glanced at Jossie, who was listening as intently as he. Andy had never read one word of the manuscript.

"I didn't say what the idea was, of course, just that it was a humdinger. So then Abbott asked who your publisher was. I said Mencken had published some of your stories, but I didn't think you had a regular publisher."

"Oh, Andy," Jossie said.

"He asked if I'd read the manuscript and I said I had and that it was great."

"That was decent, you old liar," Rick said.

"He went on to say he'd like to see what you have, if you'd want him to."

"It's not 'halfway through,' " it's about a hundred and fifty pages, about a third through." A jerk of pleasure tugged at his nerves, at the idea that a professional eye might soon read his work.

"They don't usually read 'work in progress' from strangers, he said, but if it came through a friend, they might."

"Don't publishers give authors advances," Edie asked, "even while they're still writing a book?"

"They do?" Jossie asked.

"But I'd never even thought of an editor seeing it," Rick said, "until it was finished, corrected, final draft. If it ever gets that far." He sounded eager and dubious simultaneously.

"It might give you a terrific boost," Andy said. "I can't even get through a piece of copy unless somebody tells me I'm on the right track."

"Me too," said Jossie. "And if they like it, I can finish it in a whirl."

Between the dubious and the eager, the several strands of Rick's emotions tightened into a rope of tension long before the evening was over. The moment they were alone again in their cabin, he asked Jossie what she thought of this unheard-of idea.

"Andy said it might give you a terrific boost for writing the rest of it."

"What if Abbott didn't like it?"

"Oh, darling, why look at that side of it? That's not like you."

"Well, he might not."

Again and again he came back to Bill Abbott and D & P. He had never got as far as imagining an editor reading his novel; he hadn't even begun to think of submitting it to a publishing house. If he had, he probably would have thought of Scribner's; why, he didn't know. Of course I know, he thought, and don't be such a damn jackass. Scribner's published Scott Fitzgerald.

"What are you grinning at?" Jossie asked.

"Myself for being such an ass." He told her about Scribner's, ready to have her laugh at him and finding a small expiation when she did.

He slept badly, tossing and restless the night through. In the morning he said, "I wish you'd open up and tell me what you really think."

"Rick, you have to decide."

"You've been awfully judicious so far." He sounded testy. "As if you don't want to stick your neck out."

"Remember when you wouldn't help me decide about Jack Weinstein's first proposition to leave Ashley?" He began to pace the room. He went to the window and looked out; it was a cheerless day, gray and rainy. To his back Jossie continued, "You said you didn't want to influence me. I got so I wanted to scream, but you were right. It has to be your decision, nobody else's."

This exchange was repeated a dozen times during what seemed to be a long weekend. It was far too early for tennis or swimming; both canoes and the sailboat were still in drydock, and the brief warmth that had started them from New York had jelled into a half-solid sleety mist over the roads, so they didn't enjoy walking. Even Jossie began to wish they were back in town, though Sunday night meant parting again.

"I'd have to get it all typed," Rick said suddenly as they were driving home. "You can't submit anything to an editor in handwriting."

"Mary Watts knows a girl who types manuscripts for authors."

"At ten cents a page, and a cent extra for each carbon, or so I've heard. That would come to over fifteen dollars."

"Oh, Rick, what a time to think of money."

○ ○ ○

The waiting was unbearable. He had sent the manuscript by messenger on the eighth of April, and here it was the first of May with no word from Abbott. A hundred times he read the brief note he had included, clipped to the top page, which was headed.

Untitled Novel
by Cedric U. Baird

Dear Mr. Abbott,

It gave me a good deal of pleasure to hear from Andrew Bellock that you might take time to read an unfinished novel, and a good deal of trepidation at the idea that the "work in progress" might be my own.

> Here are my first 150 pages, which I would think make a third of my book. I thank you for the time you may spend on the ms. and for any comment you may wish to make.

Rereading his note kept him aware that he actually had submitted a manuscript to a publisher, but when he tried to go on writing, he could not set down ten words. He could not read more than a few pages of the manuscript when he tried to "prime the pump" by doing so. He had gone through it the day the typist returned it, proofreading it himself, in a compulsive need, though she had assured him it was thoroughly proofed already.

He was fascinated to see how different his words looked in the clean straight lines of typing, unsullied by any words or phrases or paragraphs crossed out, unmarred by splotches of ink, with no variance in the clarity of his writing, as his hand, cramped and tired, began to crowd characters together or let lines straggle downward.

Without visible signs of hesitation and struggle, he could forget where his uncertainties and problems had occurred. There was an authority to this clean crisp manuscript that was like the print of an actual book. He could see it as it would be, page after page of print, with his name on the title page and the Dawes & Powers imprint to add prestige. He would be an author at last, not somebody writing a book but a published author.

But as the days passed, then the weeks, he could not look at it. Whenever he sat down at his desk, thinking he would write, whenever he opened the drawer where his handwritten pages and the carbon copy lay, he would draw back as if from an attacking animal. If it were any good, he'd have heard from them by now.

"It's wonderful," Jossie had said when he let her read it in entirety, from first page to last. "Just wonderful."

But that was Jossie. Could she ever have said it wasn't good, it's a disappointment? What counted now was an editor's opinion, not Jossie's, not his own.

Morning after morning he went out to the mailbox in his bathrobe to get the mail; every afternoon, when the second post was due, he was out on the street waiting for the mailman. He kept trying to work, but he would sit there, pen in hand, wondering what he would do if they rejected it.

He knew how crowded Abbott's days must be, but editors read manuscripts all the time; they must take a fast look at the first pages at least, and if they were good, they'd always go through the rest of it.

But his opening pages *were* good. Whatever trouble he'd had had come much later, but nobody could read that opening chapter and not be taken with it. Abbott *must* have gone on with it.

As May began he ended all his dogged attempts to keep on writing. "It's like force-feeding," he told Jossie one Friday night, in open desperation. "Every word I think of just backs up, as if I'd vomit on it."

"How can they be so heartless?"

"He'll have some great reason—he wants to see more of it before deciding, or their schedule seems to be overloaded with novels about the war. You'll see."

"Oh, darling, I hate it." They were at the studio. The long table had been tidied up, but there was plenty of evidence that she was working well. Copy and layouts were turned face down; she had set small paperweights on the corners of the layouts so they wouldn't blow beneath the opened window.

"Tell me what you're working at," he said.

"Not now, Rick, it's not the time to talk about ads."

"I saw the one in the paper this morning—it was one of the best ever."

The new spring series for Stuyvesant, running to ten advertisements this year, was about halfway through. Now Jossie was spending time in the fitting rooms there, having her first suit made to order for the trip to Boston. She had heard of slubbed silk, but this was slubbed linen, a crisp nubbly fabric she had never even seen before, and it was in a color she would never have dreamed of choosing, lavender.

"Lavender's for old ladies," she had protested to Mrs. Pepper, before she had seen it, only to be told, "Not this lavender." And Mrs. Pepper was right, as usual; this was lavender with flecks of pink and green and white through its whole uneven weave, and it was strange and stunning.

"You never saw anything like this in a department store," Mrs. Pepper told her, with her customary air of a duchess speaking. "You'd have to go straight to Chanel."

Much to her surprise, Jossie was also being provided with an evening dress. "We have tickets for you for the Boston Symphony," Jack Weinstein had explained. "And for an opening night at the theater—Boston is where they try out half the plays we get on Broadway. I don't know what show yet, but we're getting you tickets."

"Tickets? Plural?"

"You think I don't know you'll have some boyfriend up there? But he pays his own expenses out of his own pocket on everything else."

"You just slay me, Mr. Weinstein, you always do."

"You better come back with some good copy ideas, especially the announcement ad."

But she had already written the first draft of what might be the big opening announcement. She was not sure of it, had shown it to nobody, certainly not to Rick, who was strung so high in the tightening noose of tension.

And then at last came the reply from Abbott. Another ten days had passed; it was more than a month since Rick had so joyously sent over his manuscript.

> My dear Mr. Baird,
>
> My delay must have irked you, but it was caused by my desire to have your book read by two other editors here.
>
> Unhappily enough, they agree with me that though your idea is excellent, of a novel depicting the self-delusions of people safely at home during wartime, there is not a strong enough narrative thread to make an absorbing story.
>
> Perhaps you would consider trying this as nonfiction instead, a journalistic rendering, on a nationwide scale, of the same elements you seek to cover.
>
> If that should prove to be the case, I trust you would wish to submit your manuscript to us once more.
>
> With best wishes,

As he read, his heart turned to rock. His whole body seemed filled with it, as if the rock were made of some expanding lava that had not yet congealed to its stoniest expanse. He clenched both fists over the manila envelope that had brought back his manuscript and flung it down on his desk with such force that the table lamp tottered.

Journalistic rendering! Not a novel at all, just another book full of facts and statistics. A year of research is what that would take, maybe two, traveling the country, visiting factory workers whose pay had shot sky-high in munitions, turning himself into some sort of reporter. Never.

There were other publishers. Scores of manuscripts had been turned down by publishers, by a succession of publishers, and then found one house with the vision to see merit where nobody else had, with the courage to go ahead and publish, only to find a huge success on their hands, to the chagrin of all the nay-sayers who had preceded them. Like *David Harum*. When he was a little boy, he suddenly remembered, his mother and father and the whole world seemed to be reading it, a novel that six or eight publishers had flatly rejected.

He would ask around and send the manuscript out again right away. It was like a bad landing in a training plane in the air corps; you had to get right back in that cockpit and take off until you came in on a perfect three-pointer.

He went to the telephone to call Jossie but hung up before she could answer. She would say Abbott must have liked it in some ways or he wouldn't have asked two other editors for their opinion. He couldn't take any attempts at silver linings; he couldn't talk about this at all yet.

He went to the tray that served as a bar and stared at the bottles there; he had forgotten that it was still morning, and when he remembered, he turned away. He went to his desk. The thing was to go ahead, no matter what Abbott thought. Perhaps in another fifty pages, the goddam narrative thread would be stronger.

Christ, who could sit there hour after hour and write?

° ° °

For the first time Rick thought of postponing Friday evening and the weekend. He had told Jossie by telephone and that had been painful enough. Her disbelief touched him, yet everything she said in praise to reassure him might have been said in praise of a series of essays—with no narrative thread at all. He turned away thinking, I'm just a goddam essayist, not a novelist. There's some trick to this narrative thread. What the hell is it?

But when he did go to pick her up at the studio, she was tact itself. "You decide whether to talk about it or not, Rick."

"Let's not. Let's talk about you. My God, you're a stunner in that."

She was wearing her new lavender suit, delivered that very day. Boston was only twelve days off. Mrs. Pepper had ordered a special blouse for it, row on row of minature tucks, and the millinery department had made a straw cloche that capped her head. She was wearing that too.

"Your opening ad for Boston could be," Rick went on, "how they fell over when you walked into the Copley dining room."

"I've already got a first draft of the opening ad."

"Let's have a look at it."

"It's just a first draft. Anyway, let's not talk copy now. I've got a good dry martini ready."

But he was already moving toward the long table. "I don't have to be pampered or protected because your work goes well. Where is it?"

"Well, all right." She drew out a piece of copy from a sheaf of paper. "It's going to be mostly white space," she said. "About a quarter page, with just one block of small but nice open type in the center, and way down below a thumbnail sketch of one dress, no more than an inch high." She gave it to him.

Many fine New York shops
have opened branches
in Palm Beach and Miami
but
Stuyvesant of New York
chooses Boston

Stuyvesant of Fifth Avenue has never had a branch store. Tomorrow we open our first, across from the Copley Plaza. It is planned for those people in Boston who want a subtle excellence in their clothes and who are willing to pay for that subtlety.

• STUYVESANT, INC. •
NEW YORK BOSTON

Below the inch-high sketch in the right-hand corner was one line: "Cocoa chiffon, discreetly beaded, $210."

"It couldn't be better, Joss. And Jack Weinstein has the taste to see it." Before she could reply, he said, "My God, it's wonderful to be doing something you know you're good at. I've been thinking a lot about that recently. I used to be tops as a copy chief. I want to be tops once again."

"You will be. You just wait until another publisher—"

"I don't mean about the book. I'm one hell of a copywriter and one hell of a copy chief, and I want to be one hell of a something again. I'm going back."

"Writing copy? Being a copy chief? Oh, Rick, you hated it. Don't let that letter from Abbott—"

"It's not just Abbott. It's all this fumbling about, one good week, two good weeks, then the slide down again—reaching for something a hundred miles beyond my grasp. Look at the way you feel when *you* work."

"But that's only advertising."

"It's knowing you're tops. I think I've known for a good long time that I've got to get back to something I'm expert at."

"And give up your book? Oh, darling, no."

He began to speak more slowly, his tone reflective. "It's been nine months, Jossie, three quarters of a year, since you presented me with this great chance, and I'll always love you for it. But every copywriter on Madison Avenue thinks he could write a book if he didn't have to write ads, and every layout man and illustrator is sure he could paint like Matisse or Picasso if he could get his nose off the grindstone. I was one of those 'thinkers' too. Now I'm going back, but not to that same old delusion."

"I can't bear it, for you to give up your book."

"Say I'm just putting it in a cool, dark place for a while, like wine. Maybe it'll mature. If not—" He shrugged and crossed the small room to the pitcher of martinis. In silence she watched him. He poured one but held it in his hand, swirling it gently but not drinking it. His reflective look had deepened. Somehow he looked peaceful.

"Yes, Joss, it's been a great experiment, and now it's over. I want to be one hell of a something again."

Sixteen

And I want to earn money again. That's what I should have said, Rick thought later. To earn my own money again, and use it for whatever I need or want, pay what I have to pay, and not have to explain a single bill, paid or unpaid, not to Jossie or to anybody else.

What's more, I want my own checking account again, not a joint account, not commingled funds, just what any man needs, to be his own boss about his own money.

Earning your own money was one of the necessities of mature life; only a child could feel right about having everything provided for him by some other being. It had been an entirely rational experiment, this free year for writing, but perhaps the very free-ness of it had turned into a hurdle nobody had foreseen, a hurdle high enough to turn back every free emotion, every free idea. One had to earn freedom, not take it as a gift.

He hadn't seen that, nor had Jossie.

Well, now he had. He went to the telephone. Ashley was not the only big agency that had automotive accounts and tire accounts; he had friends in half a dozen places who knew he'd left Ashley last year. He might have to take a little ribbing from them about the book he didn't finish, but he could stand all they could dish out. Of course it took time to get interviews set up at the sort of agency he wanted, time and lunches at the right places with the right people, people who were connected with firms like J. Walter Thompson, George Batten Company, and Gaylord, Bryant, Inc.

He'd have to schedule the interviews so as not to collide with the Boston trip. Once the process of job-hunting started, it was awkward, even damaging, to stop it by being out of town or unreachable. He could have preliminary lunches, though, with people he knew at various agencies and set up the official interviews only after June fourth, when they'd be back home.

And he needed time to get a suit made. It was over two years since he'd had a new suit; to go for interviews on a big job, you needed total confidence, and in some odd way, no doubt vain, a new suit made expressly for you added to that confidence.

Not since the dispossess notice, in fact, had he had anything new: no shirts, no ties, not even new shoes. Not since the dispossess notice—that meant, not since Jossie. A prick of resentment nicked him at all her budgeting; he banished it as unjust, but there it stayed. She had implanted in him a guilt quotient he had never before had about unpaid bills, an awareness of cost and price he could scarcely stomach any longer. Such self-control was inherent in her nature, and therefore she assumed it could be nurtured in his.

There was that one failing in Jossie; he had only recently begun to see it for what it was. She loved him so much that she put a burden on him to be the ideal man she thought he was, the good manager, the persistent writer, the talented creative man.

What he was now was a man looking for a big job, and any man alive knew what appearance meant in business. He telephoned Drew, Tailors to Gentlemen, and made an appointment for the morning. They normally wanted three weeks to do a suit, but he could persuade them to speed this up in time for Boston.

"We thought you had left us for good," said Ian McNichol, head of the New York branch, welcoming Rick as a long-lost treasure, happily reclaimed.

"I've been abroad part of the time." As always Rick was amused by McNichols and his perfect British accent. He was born a Scot and had been persistent in elocution lessons when he began with Drew in London.

"We had wondered if you had selected another tailor." McNichol sounded relieved. He raised a beckoning index finger toward a half-open door. "Are you still with Ashley & Company, Mr. Baird?"

"No, I'm making a new connection. It's still confidential."

As always, the master tailor, one John Webley, came forward to greet him, followed by a youthful assistant bearing several bolts of woolens. One immediately caught Rick's eye, an iron-gray sharkskin. There was a herringbone behind it and a good plaid behind that.

"I'll want the sharkskin," he said at once. "Though that plaid is very nice."

"Perhaps both?" Ian McNichol asked gently.

One was all he could manage, Rick was about to say, but he had always ordered two together, and for the moment he let the matter go. Why had McNichols asked about Ashley? Was there going to be trouble about his charge account?

The youthful assistant had barely begun unrolling lengths of the fabrics when McNichol was drawn aside by another employee. The newcomer bore an old-fashioned ledger and was on his way with it to Mr. McNichol's office at the far corner of the showroom. "Sir," he half whispered as he passed them, addressing himself to Mr. McNichol. "Might I trouble you?" In some surprise at being disturbed while with a client, McNichol excused himself, murmuring something Rick barely heard. Later he realized the murmur must have been, "Our bookkeeper."

Several minutes later, McNichol reappeared, to ask Rick if he would come into his office for a moment. "Please wait, Webley," he said, indicating the bolts of cloth too. He returned to his desk, ushering Rick to a leather wing chair at its side.

On the desk, the ledger was lying open, tilted so as to be legible even with a sideways glance. The upper half of the page looked like an ordinary ledger page, but just below the last regular entry there was something else, a series of short lines. He could make them out easily from where he sat.

9/25 $12
10/25 $12
11/25 $12
12/25 $12
1/26 $12
2/26 $12
3/26 $12
4/26 $12
5/26 $12

He flushed. He was more embarrassed than he had been in years. It was one thing to have an unpaid balance of $162; you had neglected it, overlooked it, let it slide. One check for $162 would clear it all up when you got around to it.

But regular payments of this picayune $12 meant penury. It meant you couldn't write a check for $162. It meant you were broke.

A sweep of anger took him. Jossie had never told him what she was doing with the unpaid bills, merely that she had brought the total down from $1,500 to $1,040, then $840, then $640, and the like. For the past three months she had managed only a $100 reduction each time, but even that had pleased her. By now there was only about $140 to go, she'd boasted just the other day, and something less than $200 on her Morris Plan.

But not once had he visualized so mortifying a moment as this in the presence of Ian McNichol. There was no comment forthcoming from McNichol now, only a pause. The bookkeeper had departed.

Rick reached out and pulled the ledger toward him, to end any pretense that he misunderstood its presence. There was still an unpaid balance of $54; for two years he had paid in nothing, and then those obnoxious $12s had begun.

To say, "I've changed my mind," and leave now, muttering apologies? To go past Webley and his gawky adolescent holding the partially unrolled bolts of cloth? To say "Would you like a deposit?" All this was beneath consideration. He wished he had never come in this morning.

Then an idea struck him. He slid the ledger back toward McNichol, smiling as he did so.

"Does Mrs. McNichol have a passion for budgets?" he asked, his tone indulgent. He drew out a checkbook and began to write a check. "Let me clear this balance and pay you in advance for the suits," he said. "What would that come to?"

"Two suits would be three hundred, Mr. Baird. Everything has been going up of late, labor, fabrics, simply impossible."

Rick wrote a check for $354, signed it, and handed it over. It was on the bank that carried the special "Jean account" of accumulating funds. In June they had decided to stop the deposits, but there was $500 in it. He would make it up as soon as he had his new job.

o o o

The moment he came in, wearing his new suit, Jossie knew where it had come from. He had said he'd be "needing a new suit and some things" for his return to business life, and she'd assumed that also meant a couple of new shirts and ties. Nor did she think he would be going to any ordinary store for men's clothing; of course it would have to be Brooks Brothers.

But now he appeared in a gray suit that he called sharkskin, and she knew at once it was not a Brooks suit but a custom-made suit from Drew. Never before Rick had she known how marked a difference there was between a man's suit bought ready-made and one made-to-measure, but all his old suits had taught her that difference, just as Stuyvesant had taught her the difference in custom-made clothes for women. It was a wonderful suit; she told him so.

"Is your charge account at Drew still open after all this time?" she asked. "And an unpaid balance still on it?"

"I didn't charge it."

"Then how—?"

"I paid in advance. For this and one other suit."

"But we don't have that much in the bank."

"Your damn monthly payments of twelve and twelve and twelve and twelve," he said acidly. "They showed me the ledger. I thought I'd go through the floor."

"You're not saying *how*."

He told her.

"But that wasn't your money to spend." Her voice rose. "Even though it's in your name."

"You're reminding me it's *your* money—that it should be in your name."

"I didn't say a word about my money. It's Jean's money and it should have been in her name, so you couldn't draw on it."

"You make me sick when you get going on money. I told you I'll put it back."

"What you've done makes *me* sick,"she cried out. "It's the worst thing you've ever done. It's disgusting, it's perfectly horrible." The last words were screamed at him. She ran out of the room and closed the door in his face.

It was the night before they were to leave for Boston. They had given up their split-week plan of living as soon as Rick had given up his book, and returning to their life together in the apartment seemed wonderful. Now she lay on their bed, engulfed by disgust. It was contemptible, what he had done, weak and miserable and not to be borne. When it came to money he was . . . he was—she had never named it before, but he was a weakling.

"Damn it," he said, opening the door and standing in the doorway. "The whole three fifty-four will be repaid out of my first few salary checks." His voice was rough. "You have no right to make me out some sort of heel."

"It's just what a heel would do," she shouted back. "That money wasn't yours, not to borrow from, not to use, not to touch."

"Don't you tell me what I'm not to touch, not to use. Have you become my boss, for God's sake?"

"I'm not your boss, I'm not your *anything*." She jumped up and ran past him, out to the front door. "I'm going back to the studio. I'll stay there overnight."

"We're leaving for Boston at nine in the morning."

"I'll go by myself."

She slammed out and half raced along the streets that led to the studio. If she stayed there with him, they'd only keep on with this terrible fight. It was not just the check to Drew; she had kept her mouth shut as the boxes with their famous labels had begun arriving, and kept it shut as he opened them and revealed their contents. Not just "a couple of things" but six shirts from Dobbs, four new ties from Sulka, new Brooks brogues with the perforated tips he liked, and the snap-brim felt hat from Knox that was so becoming to him.

Most of those accounts had been paid off completely, and he had charged everything. She had expected that he would—he did need to be ready for appointments and interviews, and of course he'd never do anything in a small way. But now he'd committed his next four or five salaries to repaying Jean's $354; now she could see the bills that would be coming in on the first of the month and remain unpaid. She could see the "second notice" bills the month after, and the month after that.

He had begun again. The whole thing was starting all over again.

○ ○ ○

They did go to Boston together. Three hours after she'd left him, Rick appeared at the studio and they made up. Made up, she thought; what a phrase. Kids can make up after a spat, but when people in love are so furious, so far apart, making up is just cosmetic, a bitter play on words, nothing deeper. She finally went back to the apartment with him, but they did not reach for each other in bed, and all through the night an ashy residue was left for her.

Next morning in their facing parlor chairs on the Pullman, she could barely look directly at him in his handsome new clothes, and their talk was stilted. She kept gazing upward at the luggage rack, where the porter had put their bags, hers a new one in dark leather, from Blanchard's, her first fine suitcase ever. In some absurd transference, she suddenly disliked her own new things, the lavender suit, the hand-tucked blouse, the tight little cloche, feeling them somehow implicated in the whole compulsion to look prosperous and smart, smarter than anybody else and more prosperous.

Suddenly she remembered herself back at Cornell, feeling as well dressed as anybody on campus in a new sweater and pleated plaid skirt. Did values always have to change? Did people always change as time went on, or did they remain the same, while one's perceptions of them changed? How had she changed in Rick's eyes? Oh, God, she thought, he thinks I'm a shrew and a Puritan. Or worse. And every single time we fight, money's right in there, making us. She thought of Suzy. Well, nearly every single time.

When they were established in their separate rooms at the Copley Plaza, she told Rick she felt rather carsick and wanted only to take a nap. They met for dinner, and again constraint lay between them, like a palpable substance.

Apparently Rick had no remorse. If anything he retained his wrath over those $12 payments that had so mortified him. They ordered, they had a good wine—chosen by Rick and expensive—but more than half the time they remained silent. She found herself thinking back to things she had thought were long forgotten: the six bottles of champagne, and then the red canoe, and his new fishing rod and reel—"it's a bargain; Abercrombie and Fitch charge a hundred"—and each unwanted memory stirred the ashy residue, sending a flurry flying, like the gray puffball of a dandelion in midsummer.

He would never change, but she would have to. She would never say one word again about what he bought and what he spent. She would never take on his debts again. She would have to say it at last, in a sort of pact with herself, say it and say it again, and then she would have to say it to him. "I will never take on your debts again."

She recoiled from the idea. There would be another dreadful fight, words he might forget but that she would remember. They might as well be fighting now, at this lovely table, in this elegant dining room.

They might as well be fighting now, in this cool silence of theirs. She glanced at the couples around them, many of whom were dining in the same awful silence, their jaws working on their food, their gullets moving as they drank their wine. We're like an old married couple, she thought, stiff with age and boredom. We used to laugh so much and never stop talking.

"Let's go to a movie," she said when dinner was ending. "The new Charlie Chaplin is playing up here, *The Gold Rush.*"

"Let's."

Later Jossie made no excuses about being carsick. "I'm still upset, Rick," she told him. "We'd better sleep in our separate rooms."

The first two days were comfortable for Jossie only when she was alone on her official duties. She visited the stores, large and small, made notes of the advertisements in the papers, snapped mental pictures of what well-dressed people were wearing: in restaurants, at the concert, at the theater.

She jotted down a dozen phrases for future ads for the Boston branch; she kept meticulous notes on the clothes she tried on in the better shops, noting their prices and the chatter of the salesgirls attending her, about her own clothes, as she was changing in the fitting rooms.

But the moment she was through with her official tasks, she ached with the dismal knowledge that there was no real joy or pleasure for either Rick or herself on this Boston trip they had looked forward to with such anticipation. They went sightseeing to Beacon Hill, Harvard, and M.I.T., they walked along the Thames and went out to Brookline, but there was for her a clothy feeling all the time, and Rick remained subdued.

This must be, she thought morosely, what it feels like when you're getting ready for a "civilized divorce." At the end of the second day, in a cab returning to the hotel, she said, "Boston is a disappointing place, isn't it?"

"It's not, really. It's because you're still sore at me." His tone asked for reconciliation.

"Oh, Rick, I can't help it."

"Are *you* perfect all the time? Can't you accept people the way they are?"

"Mostly I do, you know I do."

"Then accept me again. I love you, Jossie. I'll have a new job soon and square things away on Jean's account, and we can forget all about it and be happy again."

For the first time on the trip her eyes filled. It would be so wonderful to be happy again.

He saw her tears and took her hands in his. He meant every word of it. He would be a successful man again, instead of a penurious would-be author. He had two interviews set up for the following week, with highly placed people at first-rank agencies. During the preliminary lunches he'd had setting up those interviews, he'd casually managed to slip in the salary he wanted, and in no case did the figure act as a brake. He never said his Ashley salary had been

$6,500; that wasn't done in the cheery commerce of preliminary lunches. He did say that he understood $7,500 was "the going salary" for top copywriters and copy chiefs, and his luncheon companions never denied it.

He had begun to think of himself as "a $7,500-a-year man."

o o o

It took a good deal longer to get a good job than Rick had anticipated. It was the beginning of summer, and several times he was told that the man he wanted to meet was off on vacation or about to leave for Europe, or he was given some other irritating reason for delay. June ran into July, and still nothing definite had developed.

Twice he had felt certain he was close; his big leather proof book had made good impressions at J. Walter Thompson and at Gaylord, Bryant, Inc., and there had been a pleasing ease in the interview at each agency that sent him off convinced that an offer would be forthcoming or that he'd be summoned back to meet other executives for further discussion. Nothing further had happened at either place.

During all the preliminary lunches, the sum for his miscellaneous expenses had doubled to $100 a month, even more. Jossie had understood completely. "Of course you can't stick to the old *miss* of fifty," she said, "and invite somebody to lunch and sit back when the check comes."

"They'd think I was a deadbeat if I let them pick up the tab."

"What a time to think of money."

That's what she'd said in the car that night when he'd talked about having the manuscript typed. The memory was like a quick turn of a wrench.

And this waiting for a call from an agency reminded him of that other waiting about the book. By God, he was not going to become a victim of that damn failure and start expecting everything else to end in failure too. That kind of self-pity was disgusting.

Disgusting. He wished Jossie hadn't said disgusting. It was hard to forgive her for that attack; she really could let fly when she wanted to. She had been such a delight to live with at the start; now she often posed problems she didn't even know she was posing. Not problems about his being married, not about Lucienne or even Suzy, except for the conventional flare-ups, but nearly always about money. What had once seemed so generous and loving, had metamorphosed into some virus, latent much of the time but ready to blow into a full-scale disease. He no longer could live in dread of that dormant infection; it simply was not his style to be eternally guarded about what he spent. Once he was back at an agency, doing a bang-up job, he would be the old Rick Baird again.

Nobody earning $7,500 a year could be expected to live on a

pinchpenny scale, and nobody could ever again transform him into a meek little fellow who did.

° ° °

It was the middle of August, and the middle of a heat wave that had held New York gasping for days. Rick sat in an office on the fourteenth floor of a new building on Madison Avenue, twenty blocks north of Ashley & Company. The window was opened as far as it would go and a powerful floor fan blew air across his ankles, but his shirt clung to his back and his pencil was slippery in his fingers. He didn't mind. After three interviews with various members of the copy department and executive offices, he had been taken on by James Bryant himself, the president of Gaylord, Bryant, Inc.

The final interview had been brief and delightful. Bryant was a man in his early forties, with an easy speech and an easy smile. Rick's proof book lay on his desk, closed, and as Rick was introduced, Bryant nodded at the book and said, "I'd read most of the ads in the magazines or papers as they appeared."

Rick felt sudden pride in the work he had once regarded with such high-minded scorn, and in ten minutes he knew he would work well with this James Bryant. They could even be friends.

"It looks as if we should give it a try," Bryant said then. "What were you thinking of in the way of salary?"

"I thought eight," Rick said with no hesitation.

"How soon could you start? McCrae's walkout has put us in a bind." McCrae had written their main automotive account for six years, on the Watch roadster and the Watch sedan, closest rivals to General Motors' various Buicks. Watch Motors had originally been Wacht Motors, founded by an engineering genius who had been connected with Mercedes in Germany, and the name had been Anglicized to Watch during the war.

As Rick sat at his desk two weeks later, he stared at the first check from Gaylord, Bryant, Inc. It was for $333.33; they paid twice a month. Twice would come to $666.66. Eight thousand a year. He had never earned as much.

As he endorsed the check, he ran up a Jossie-like budget in his mind. Of this first check, $50 would go for his half of the rent again, $100 to his father, $100 to Jean—

He paused. He ought also restore $100 a month to Jean's special account, as he'd said he would; that meant for more than three months his salary would be only $566.66. And he also ought to start reducing the amount in "Debtor's Prison"—by now he owed Jossie over $2,000, starting with the $300 dispossess money and then the $1,500 debts and God knows what else.

The check seemed to change in value as he stared at it. It was peanuts, it was picayune. Even at $8,000 a year, he would never get out of the hole he was in.

The $100 to Jean stuck in his craw. She had never answered his letter. Was he just to throw the $100 for September into an envelope and send it with a two-line note? "This is a pure and holy check, earned by a male. I have a new job."

All these months since her attack—"I could never respect myself if I did"—all these eight months, a new stiffening resistance had been coming to the surface about Jean. How long did she plan to stay over there in Paris? The time they had envisioned was long since past; never had she said a word about coming back.

In some strange way, not sending the $100 each month had reinforced the sense of separation. It was as if he had no wife in Paris, as if they had decided to part permanently. That was her doing to start with, of course, but had he not been unconsciously more and more acquiescent? The ritual of the $100 check each month had been visible proof of connection, the outward manifestation of a continuing entity, their marriage. And finally she had torn it across like a thin ribbon, a frayed tape. Was their marriage also torn in two?

Something prodded him to find out. Pride, perhaps, masculine ego, wounded feeling, but something needed to know whether she still felt their marriage was intact. Did he himself?

What if he wrote more than a two-line letter when he resumed the monthly checks? What if he asked when she planned to come back to New York? What if he said it was high time she did come back?

The moment he thought of it, he knew he would have to do it. Face it, one way or the other. Make Jean face it. Perhaps the eight months without the symbol of that check each month had enhanced her own sense of separation. Perhaps she wanted to stay separated for good. It was time to know.

Was she still having an affair with that François Ciardeau of the Morgan Bank? He had rather liked him when they'd met during Jean's convalescence, though he always felt alienated from anybody who planned a life in the banking fraternity. And once there'd been a casual mention of another man, come to think of it, an older man, in some letter of hers that was mainly "humdrummery," her old word. He'd always liked that word, and a nostalgia for it arose briefly. Once they had been so close, he and Jean.

Mumm's the word, he thought suddenly, remembering the name of the man she'd mentioned. Jacob Mumm, fifty years old, big shot in tractors and farm machinery. She had never mentioned him again, and he'd paid little attention. Jean with a man of fifty? She'd been distressed about the age of her professor husband, who was forty-four.

It didn't matter, in any case. They really were oceans apart now, figuratively as well as literally. Neither of them really wanted to face that question, Is our marriage still intact?

How could it be intact, he thought? Do I feel toward her as I did when she announced she was going to France? Do I feel the way I did when I had to go to Paris for the operation?

When it comes down to it, did he feel the way he used to feel about anything? He was thirty-one, back in harness in the world of business. All those assumptions one made in one's earliest youth, all those possibilities lying out there ahead, of being an author, of being well known—"you'll be famous, darling"—all the boundless aspirations had already receded into a gray half-life, with the slow grudging pulse of inertia and regret.

He telephoned Jossie. "I got my first check from G.B.I. Let's go out for dinner, somewhere with a decent band."

"The Trocadero, with Paul Whiteman."

° ° °

"Snowstorm," Jossie wrote in her journal, "catching the world off guard so early in November. The square of it that I can see through the window is a furious thing, in full gusty fury the moment it was unleashed."

> The bushes and trees in our back yard and neighboring yards are whipping around—the snow itself has a curious rhythm, swirling in great circular motions for a few moments, then a strange catch for a second, then once again the swirling in another direction and on another plane. Large, flat, cottony flakes, millions of them, darting, floating, swept along on the wind. It is a lovely, active sight—but I want calm sweet spring.
>
> So much has been happening so quickly, I don't know how long since I've written. (Last entry not dated—it was after Suzy.) Anyway, we've been in a whirl, mostly good, some awful. After Rick got going at Gaylord, Bryant, he wrote Jean a kind of blunt letter, with a resumption of the monthly checks.
>
> Was she planning to stay on indefinitely, he wanted to know? She didn't answer for a good long while, and then she sounded sort of blunt too. She most surely was making no change right at the moment; she had sold four more canvases, at $110 per, and to pull up stakes now and return was out of the question. Return to what? She'd stopped being so malleable about Rick's youthful theories about marriage and honesty and infidelity and wondered what sort of married existence he was now proposing if she did come back.
>
> Rick never shows me her letters, nor his to Jean, but he didn't sound too surprised when he told me all this. Nor too upset either. Quite the opposite.

And at one point, he did look at me in that funny gentle way that used to be so much a part of him. "If I ever were divorced, would you honor me by becoming my wife? Not just on the mailbox, darling, not on our joint bank account, but Mrs. Cedric U. Baird for real?"

I must admit my heart blew up like a crazy balloon. It's been true that I've never really thought about being married, it's not been an act put on to cover secret yearnings. But somehow, in the last few months, I have begun to wonder what it would be like to have children. Maybe Nell's little Jimmy has done that to me—waked up some latent instinct or something. It sounds awfully mushy, but can you imagine what a two-year-old Rick would look like? Or a tiny girl with his wonderful looks? I sort of go limp when I do think of it.

But that's only *en passant*, as Pa says when he plays chess. Anyway, once, a long time ago, Rick did say that even if we did ever have a child and he had to go away one week after it was born, on some business trip, he wouldn't want to feel *bound* not to go, just because there was a new baby. In theory, I suppose, it's intolerable for a man like Rick to feel *bound* to do this or that, but I've sort of begun to wonder whether there isn't some justification for the abstraction we call Duty or Responsibility or just plain Rightness.

Which brings me to the awful part, and I don't want to make too much of it, bad as it is. *It's my money*, Rick now says if we have a fight about money, and of course it is. With his first check from G.B.I., he opened a separate account for himself again and our joint account was no more—he closed it officially. The perfectly legal *nom de plume* account of Mr. and Mrs. Baird was a memory.

If only he'd told me first, I could understand it better. He said he saw me look away fast from the new bills from Knox and Dobbs and the rest and decided then, the minute he had a job and a check to deposit, to reopen his old bank account. He said it was not just for his own sake, to feel independent again, but for my sake mostly, to ease my mind forever about things like bills.

But it reminded me of that time he said we should live apart until Fridays, a kind of awful symbol of something marked *finis*. And when he says now *It's my money*, he's shutting me off from any right to have an opinion. He can't see that a sudden wild thing like $50 a month for ten months to buy an Electrola—what's wrong about it, how it might affect other aspects of our life.

"But you love music as much as I do," he said when he told me he'd bought this new $500 machine the Victrola people have put out. It does give glorious music, God knows. It comes in a huge cabinet, mahogany, standing chest high and about 2½ feet square, connected like a lamp to an electric socket, and with a tone that's like all the vault of heaven singing.

The worst thing is, he bought it to please me, to celebrate the success of his first big campaign at G.B.I. for Watch Motors. Mr. Bryant okayed it without a change and the clients did too. I was all caught up in it too, wanting so desperately for him to have a smash hit, to start him off with over there, that my stomach was wound up like a ball of hard yarn. They'd loaned him a Watch roadster for three days, so he could get the feel of it for himself, and it's so marvelous, we spent three nights riding in it. No wonder—a $1,650 car!

As for me and good old free-lancing—all's well with Stuyvesant, Boston & N.Y. both, with Daggett, Frostilla, Houbigant, Lacq, Blanchard, and even my headache, Green Meadows Milk. Oops, a slip of the pen that had me screaming-laughing in their faces. They had wanted a new name for their milk and cream, and I thought Green Meadows Milk had a lovely country sound, but Mr. Gordon, the Pres., said everybody would think the milk was *green,* the color green. That's why it's still called Gordon's, still rhyming with Borden's, which is why they wanted a new name to start with. But I still think of it as Green Meadows Milk or Green Meadows Cream, out of spite probably.

Enough for now. I'll write about Ashley and plate glass and especially dear transparent Amantha D. next time.

She began to put the narrow notebook away but turned back to the table and opened her pen once more.

P.S. I forgot to say one glorious thing: I don't owe one dollar to one store or one landlord or one florist or one phone company in all New York City, New York State, the U.S.A., the earth, the planet, the universe, as we used to write in our textbooks in grade school.

In Sept. I paid the last damn $10 to the M. Plan, and I'd finished off the last of the $1,500 debts in July.

God, what a feeling. Free! Caught up! Nothing to allocate, no excuses to make, no "further payment next month" to write on the bill and ring it in a big crayon ellipse they can't miss.

I didn't realize until then how sick I'd grown of debts and budgets and balances and please remits, at times literally sick, queasy stomach, restless sleep, nightmare columns of figures in dreams, piled up like great unwavering stone posts. Thank God it's over!

Seventeen

Just before Thanksgiving, Jim Bryant asked Rick if he'd like to spend the holiday weekend in Cold Spring Harbor with the Bryant family. "Since your wife's in Paris," he'd said, "you fit into our scheme for waifs and strays."

"I'm spending it with another waif and stray," Rick promptly answered. "She'd be alone if I accepted. Sorry."

"Why not ask her as your date?"

"Thanks, I will."

Bryant had a large family, he knew, a large house, and a stableful of horses on Long Island, not far from Oyster Bay. This they kept open for weekends through the winter, his wife and three children all being riding enthusiasts. Though he'd been in the office for less than four months, he'd heard from two or three other writers that the boss was a convivial soul about weekends, and especially about holiday weekends. His two older children brought a raft of friends home from their schools, and often there were sixteen people sitting down to meals.

When Rick told Jossie about the invitation, she said, "Does Jim Bryant know about us?"

"Unless he and Amantha are pals, of course not."

"I wouldn't be too upset, by now, if he did know. Or anybody else."

"You sound a bit defiant. Why, all of a sudden?"

"I meant, know we were having an affair. I'd hate it if anybody knew we called ourselves Mr. and Mrs. Baird."

"But nobody does, except the old handful. Why bring that up after all this time?"

"Maybe it's having my own name on the mailbox at the studio, and listed in the phone book, and having Mary Watts come right there—it's so comfortable."

This wasn't like Jossie, he felt. Perhaps telling her of that new exchange of letters with Jean had disturbed her. Perhaps he should never have talked about a possible divorce. He could be an insensitive lout at times.

"Look at this," he said, glad to change the subject. "It's a road map about driving to the Bryants' place, how to get from Oyster Bay to their place in Cold Spring Harbor."

"It's printed. They must have guests all the time."

"I wish I'd said we'd be going by train."

"Why would you say that?"

"That Ford of ours is pretty beat up by now. A man writing their biggest automotive account—"

"Now, Rick—" She could see him at the wheel of his own Watch roadster.

"Jossie, listen to me. Making a prosperous impression is one of the techniques of business. Like overhead, like promotion and public relations and advertising. How prosperous can you look, driving up their curving cinder driveway in a battered four-year-old Model T with skinny tires?"

To his astonishment she began to laugh. "'Only fifty a month,'" she mocked him. "For a million months. Oh, Rick, you're impossible—wild, crazy impossible."

He laughed with her, a little awkwardly. "You're ahead of me. You've been expecting me to suggest a new car all along."

"Ever since those three nights riding around in the Watch."

"The down payment is five hundred fifty, with ninety a month and eighteen months to pay. The interest is one and a half percent a month, and that's all figured in. So is a year's insurance."

"How do you know all that?"

"When I returned the dealer's car, I asked them."

"And you made the down payment then and there!"

He seized her with an air of victory over a battle already won. "Not till Jim Bryant invited us. I wanted to be sure we'd have delivery before Thanksgiving."

o o o

In Paris, dinner was ending in Jake Mumm's dining room, a handsome room in a handsome apartment. He and Jean were alone. Though he entertained often, with Jean always there acting as his hostess, he enjoyed having dinner with her as his only guest and arranged it two or three times a week.

Now he was saying, in what Jean called his "executive voice," that the notion of going back to New York was not one that called for a speedy decision. "You want Paris, you prefer Paris, or you would not have stayed on so long."

"But now Rick's making an issue of it."

"Which does not obligate you to make an issue of it too."

"When I wrote him that I had no plans of going back any time soon, I did tell him I'd outgrown those ideas of his and asked what sort of married life he was now proposing. It was all left hanging." Across the months she had told Jake a good deal more about Rick than she had originally intended to.

"Suppose he now promises a pure and holy Victorian family life, would you believe him?"

She shook her head. "He'd mean every word, and he'd live up to it for about six weeks, and then he'd be the same old Rick." Before he could speak, she added, "I haven't led such a pure and holy Victorian family life either, Jake."

"You're very good with Kathy and Kenny, you're very good and persistent with your painting, nothing of the dilettante about it, you're not restless and silly. You must know that if you had a firm, sound marriage, you would be only too happy to be Victorian and holy forever after."

"Don't, Jake. I'm confused enough as it is."

"I don't want to add confusions. Maybe you ought to go to New York for a short visit, perhaps for Christmas, and have a few conferences with him."

She was startled. "I couldn't leave the children at Christmas."

"Take them with you then."

"Oh, no. They've almost forgotten Uncle Rick—it would get them all confused and agitated."

"Dear girl, you're agitated yourself. It was just an idea, a memo dropped in the Suggestion Box."

She *was* agitated. She supposed she could afford the trip—her municipals were now in stocks and rising every day—she could even take the kids. But to go there, see Rick? If it developed into a confrontation, it would be too hateful to endure. If it went pleasantly, if a few days together should reawaken their old feelings, even as a swift mirage—did she really want that to be the outcome? Maybe she had become one of the Parisian expatriates everybody was writing about, an expatriate who had never met Gertrude Stein. That would be a new twist!

"Or the kids could be my houseguests while you were abroad," Jake said. "Tonette could take care of them here as well as there, and you'd not risk any upheaval for them."

"That's sweet, Jake, thanks for saying it."

They had become deeply attached to each other. His new agency for Browning Tractors was doing well but was not yet ready for a change in command; he was staying on into the indefinite future, surely for another year. He was not restless either, she knew by now; he had told her once that in the twenty-four years of his marriage, until his wife's death, he had "been with other women" only four times, always when he'd been away from home for more than a month.

Locutions like this one about "being with other women" appealed to some atavism in her. Rick would have used short strong verbs, and so would François. Everybody and everything was so postwar modern and uninhibited that old-fashioned restraint seemed charming. She was no Puritan little homebody; being in Paris alone as a painter proved that. But there was a strictness in Jake she responded to more and more.

"Jake, why did you say that about a firm sound marriage?"

"Because I've been thinking for myself how good it would be to have a firm sound marriage again." He sounded almost as if he were in an important business meeting, judicious, sure, reasonable. "You know, Jean, when I came here to open the agency, I had some idea that I might sooner or later meet an attractive Frenchwoman and ask her to marry me."

"A Frenchwoman? Specifically?"

"The language was important, for living here, entertaining here; yes, specifically somebody French."

"So then you met me, from Princeton, New Jersey."

"Then I met you, and the first thing you said to me was said in perfect French, with that delightful accent."

"And it put marriage right out of your mind."

"Yes."

It was an uncomfortable moment. The *yes* was so precise, so final. Why hadn't she let the conversation drop when he'd made his offer about having the kids as houseguests? It had been a gaffe to go on; she'd made too much of a casual phrase.

"Then," he went on, "when it came back into my mind, I knew I had to wait until you resolved your situation with Rick."

He was still attending a business meeting; he hadn't moved toward her; his pleasant friendly mien hadn't altered. Now her own agitation was again rising; she concentrated on it, controlling it.

"It really was a good marriage for a long while," she said. "Even when I came here to study and paint, it remained good—"

"If I had a wife who studied and painted, Jean, she would do all that in Paris as long as I lived in Paris. Then when I went back to the U.S.A., she would still study and paint, but it would be right there in the U.S.A. There are great art teachers and painters in the U.S.A. They're not all in Paris on the Left Bank. I would want my wife to *want* to be with me, as soon as she put down her brushes for the day."

His voice had changed at last. Now he was persuasive, eager. He was leaning toward her. It was for him a wordy speech, and as he went on with it, he had warmed to it.

"You mean I speak French well enough?" Jean asked.

This he ignored. "My dear girl, when will you realize that your marriage to Rick ended a long time ago?"

"I don't know when." She closed her eyes as if to shut out his uncomfortable directness.

"When you do know, then we'll talk about us." He took her hands in his, without pressure, without ardor. "My best idea for the Suggestion Box is that you go to New York not for a conference, but when your lawyer summons you to appear there in court for the divorce proceeding."

o o o

Those barbaric office parties at Christmas, Jossie thought. Rick had come home after seven, quite drunk from his first big party at G.B.I., too drunk for dinner, and had gone to bed. Now it was nearly midnight but he was still sleeping; she had kept dinner as long as it was feasible, and then had eaten by herself. It's not right, on Christmas Eve, she thought.

He had been drinking more and more of late, not like an alcoholic, never with that imbecilic lack of control, but like a man who was a good heavy social drinker just the same. When he slept while he was drunk, he had begun to snore; it had become a nerve-wracking attack on her as she lay awake beside him. Several times recently she had got up from bed and gone into the living room, weeping and forlorn without knowing why. Tonight she remained in the living room, not wanting to go in to him at all.

He was doing well at the agency, and yet he was falling back into his old habit of denigrating his own work. He had just read a new book that everybody was talking about, *The Sun Also Rises,* by Ernest Hemingway, and for a time it had shattered his new composure about his shelved manuscript.

How dreadful to go into a depression each time you read a good book by a new author, she thought, especially about a new author who was a young man. He was never upset when he read a new book by a woman, old or young, an established name or a new one. But to feel destroyed because somebody else was doing something you wanted to do—that went beyond good normal human jealousy, didn't it? I don't sink to the lower depths whenever I read some well-written story in a newspaper; it doesn't set me back six years to college days when my one dream was to work for a newspaper. Poor Rick, he makes everything into a personal challenge, as if each new book thumbed its nose at him and said, "Y-a-a-h, you can't do it, but I can."

Once or twice, in the middle of a Sunday afternoon, he had asked if she'd mind if he went off for a while in the car by himself, "to get over this rotten mood," and then had driven off in his beloved Watch roadster, one time for an hour, another time for three. Of course she minded; life with a failed writer could be hard too. A suspended writer, rather; she would not admit that he had failed forever.

There were so many things she would not admit. Her curiosity about that down payment he'd made on the new car—she didn't let herself own up to it by asking him. He couldn't have put by enough for it from his salary; he must have borrowed it, but from whom? Already borrowing from new friends at Gaylord, Bryant? Going back to John Slade and Andy Bellock?

She sat forward. The Morris Plan, of course, the damn Morris Plan again. For that he could have gone to new friends at G.B.I., asking them to be co-signers.

He'd had the grace not to ask John Slade again, and he'd had plenty of reason by now not to ask her. Not to say one word about it to her. She'd tried to avoid the whole matter of that down payment ever since Thanksgiving.

I wish I hadn't faced up to it tonight, she thought, as she sat on by herself. It's being a new kind of Christmas Eve anyway. The tree was already decorated; on the Electrola a record was playing, not jolly old Wenceslas but a Mozart piano concerto of a piercing sweetness, and she had lighted the two hickory logs in the fireplace.

All the proper Christmas atmosphere, she thought, but Rick's in there and I'm in here. The other end-of-the-year excitements were lopsided too this time. It was too early for Rick to have a Christmas raise or bonus at his new job, and when she'd told him of her $300 bonus from Jack Weinstein, he'd said, "That's great," as if it didn't much interest him. And the big news about the Empire State Plate Glass schedule for 1927 had left him cold.

"Mr. Albright's scheduling thirty ads next year instead of twenty," she'd just told him yesterday.

"That means Ashley will have to fork over three thousand to you instead of two."

"It puts me past ten thousand a year."

"Congratulations."

But there had been a lukewarmness in it, a kind of pushed-into-it congratulations. She remembered the time he had seized her and whirled her round and round the room when she'd told him she'd resigned from Ashley.

Did he mind her earning $10,000 a year when he was making $8,000?

In a way there was lukewarmness in her own reaction to the news. Once $10,000 a year had seemed like untold millions, unheard-of wealth that could take care of every need, fulfill every wish, guarantee every human happiness.

Now here it was. It was indeed a lot of money for a girl of twenty-six, with no bills, no debts. She had bought another suit on her own, and two pairs of shoes at once, the first time in her life she'd ever done so, and her first real cashmere sweater, in a natural beige color and costing $20. She had bought a monster teddy bear for young Jimmy and given Nell and her mother sweaters of real cashmere too, an impossible gift at any time prior to this. Her big Christmas present to Rick was a stunning gold wristwatch from Tiffany; he hadn't had a new one for years, and this was as thin as a wafer, oblong, on a dark-brown alligator strap. It was the most beautiful wristwatch for a man that she'd ever seen. It was the smallest package under the tree right now.

It was $95, and she had paid for it by check. She paid for everything by check. She had no charge accounts and felt a superstitious fear of starting one in any store in the city.

She had even given herself a psychological present and paid off the rest of her Student Loan at Cornell. "Enclosed find" not the dinky $2 checks she had naively tried out so long ago, not the major checks she had managed to send in each year, but one last splendid check to clear the books forever. Let Professor Smithson and Andrew Carnegie between them extoll the uses of credit, let the Student Loan Fund say it grew by stretching out interest for ten years, it still remained true that for this one borrowing student, Joselyn S. Yavnowitsky, five years of collegiate indebtedness were enough. "Enclosed please find my check for $400 which, apart from interest due, clears up the remainder of my student loan. With renewed gratitude, yours."

Yes, $10,000 a year let you do things you'd never dared dream of. She would love to go abroad for the first time, and when Rick began to get paid vacations from G.B.I. she would suggest it. She had closed her flea account—there was no need for desperate planning for emergencies; there was always enough balance in her own checking account to cover any that might arise.

It was all wonderful, to be so solvent, so comfortable about money. Yet there was something wrong. The magic that used to hover over the very idea of $10,000 a year had disappeared.

The Mozart was ending. She turned off the Electrola and idly went over to the Christmas tree, bending to switch it on. The sudden brightness, the pendant glass ornaments gleaming in the lights strung through the branches, the smell of pine in the warm room, combined into a dream-tumble of moments long gone, when purest joy had filled her before just such a tree, in the warmth of just such a fire.

The first Christmas they had spent together, she in her chiffon nightgown and silken robe, Rick so elated at having her there with him, so fervent in his love, so demanding in his lovemaking. . . .

She gulped. She'd been making $30 a week then, and she'd just devised the escape for him from the horror of that dispossess notice, in a joy of helping him. Only $30 a week, but that's where the unheard-of wealth had been.

o o o

Jean had let an entire month go by before thanking Rick for the toys he'd sent Kathy and Kenny and the gift he'd sent her. When her letter came on the first of February, Rick abandoned all his rules of decorum and let go to Jossie about the few lines it contained, ending, *And thanks for my gift too. I didn't send you one because it seemed hypocritical now when we're so up in the air.*

"It *is* hypocritical," he stormed. "I was a damn fool to feel I couldn't be rude enough to send her nothing."

"You weren't being hypocritical. Whatever's up in the air, you couldn't go in for a cheap slap in the face." Even this much criticism of Jean went against her own rules of decorum, but it felt right to say it. How much old Southern gallantry had she unconsciously absorbed, about what you could say about the wife of the man you loved? It was so artificial not ever to say a derogatory word about Jean, about their marriage, their behavior.

"God damn it," Rick said. "It's degrading, letting things hang fire any longer. I ought to go over there and make her face it."

He poured gin into a wineglass and drank it off in angry gulps. He had been drinking ever since he'd come home, protesting that he shouldn't have another drop because of the work he'd brought with him to do that evening. He'd fallen behind and tomorrow was deadline, with the client due in at the office at ten. The layouts were excellent, the artwork already in, but he'd been dissatisfied with his copy and unwilling to show it to Bryant even today.

"Here, see for yourself," he told Jossie, handing her two typed sheets. They were both for Watch Motors. "It's pedestrian, the usual guff about smooth performance, power, and every other bromide in the book."

"You'll get it, darling. After dinner, when you're relaxed."

But after dinner he was not relaxed. He was jumpy and irritable. "I'll take a nap," he said. "Call me if I'm not awake by ten. It's got to be ready by morning."

But when she called him at ten, he said, "Five more minutes," and turned over. Let him sleep, poor man, she thought. I could wring Jean's neck for keeping him in this state.

She waked him again at eleven. "I've got a clanking headache," he muttered. He looked it. His skin was pale and hot; the smell of gin and cigarettes was strong. "I'll get up early and do it then."

"Should I try a headline or two, darling?" she asked as he fell back again. "A springboard for you?"

"Would you, Joss?" He was once again asleep. She put her hand on his forehead. Was this more than alcohol? He soon would have to get hold of this matter of drinking, even though he handled it so well in public.

At the Bryants' over Thanksgiving there were two other waif-and-stray guests, both rather quickly achieving the slurred speech and fumbling movements of anybody tight, and yet Rick had had drink for drink with them without showing the slighest effect, except to be wittier and more amusing. Especially with the woman guest, a good-looking woman recently divorced, probably in her late thirties, named Gloriana Carlton, who lived in Boston.

"As in Ritz?" Rick asked when they were introduced.

"Just as in. But don't call me by my absurd first name," Mrs. Carlton said. "Everybody calls me Glory."

To Jossie, Rick said, "At last you know a real live Bostonian. Jack Weinstein will be so happy."

The other "real live" was a newspaper man, who was at her left at the table. She had liked this Ted Bonning even before she learned that he was an assistant managing editor at the *World*, her favorite paper, and the fact that she had never met a real newspaper writer before made him doubly interesting. He was divorced too, middle-aged, overweight, a chain smoker and a chain drinker, but full of newspaper stories, and she thought not of how drunk he was but how fascinating.

She wasn't the person, anyway, to make judgments about how much drinking was too much drinking. One cocktail before dinner, one sip of wine to be polite, and she'd had it for the evening. A second drink made her not drunk but sleepy and vaguely uncomfortable.

"You're the cheapest lush in town, darling," Rick had once teased her, and people like the Bellocks, both rather immoderate about the number of times they had their glasses refilled with wine, would urge her on. "Oh, come on, Jossie, the wine's not as bad as all that." Once she'd heard herself getting testy, saying, "If I don't make remarks about how much you *do* drink, why should you make them about how much I *don't*?"

At the Thanksgiving dinner, the newspaper editor, Ted Bonning, had turned to her as soon as he could. "And are you one of Bryant's high-priced stars, Miss Stone?"

"No, I free-lance." She was still a little nervous, being a guest in such a huge house, dining in such surroundings.

"For what firms?"

She told him, leaving out most of them.

"Stuyvesant," he said. "They run their ads in my paper. I never read ads, but I do read those. So you're the one who writes them." He stuck out his hand in congratulation and tipped over the glass of water next to his wine. Jossie shook his hand with her left one, her right hand busily sopping up the spill with her napkin.

"Knocked me over, as you can see," he said, grinning. "Every one of those about the missing person."

Remembering Ted Bonning now cheered her. She'd liked writing the Christmas campaign too. Again Jack Weinstein had called it an idea "to wrap the store around," and again it became what was technically known as a storewide promotion. This series was not about dresses but about accessories: purses, costume jewelry, gloves, silk stockings, sweaters, scarves, headbands, hats. She could remember every word of the opening ad of the series.

Give yourself a gift

> There's somebody missing on your Christmas list.
>
> You.
>
> Your own importance in your world is immeasurable—play up to it with at least one special gift.
>
> It can be anything simple, some small nonsense you've always wanted. Or it might be something outstanding.
>
> At Stuyvesant's we deal in women's accessories that *are* outstanding. Remember that missing person. Merry Christmas.

Some of the other headlines flashed by in her memory. "Who's missing on your Christmas list? You." And another she liked. "You forgot a major name on your Christmas list—yours." Jack Weinstein had dubbed them "the you campaign" and okayed them all.

Enough reminiscing, she thought now. She opened the door to the bedroom and got the two typed sheets Rick had discarded. He was right; they were pedestrian. Change the logo to Buick or Ford or Oldsmobile, and his copy would fit. She took the sheets with her into the living room, and the layouts as well. Each showed a huge picture of a car: one a roadster, another a sedan, the third a coupé.

She studied the pictures and thought of Rick's own Watch roadster on the street downstairs, where he always parked it for the night. She could see herself sitting beside him, driving, could hear his words of praise for it. He never talked of performance and power; he talked about it as if it were a person he was crazy about and proud of. "You can rely on this baby," he'd suddenly say. Or, "Remember how the old Ford would spit and cough and stutter when we cranked it? Not this little smoothie."

She glanced at her wrist. It was past midnight already. She picked up a pencil and began to sketch tiny pictures of roadsters. She couldn't draw a box in perspective, but the doodles she was making, oblongs with four wheels and a windshield, were all Watch Motors. Then she wrote four words.

The Watch ticks over

She leaned forward. There was something here that was on the right track. Something that was different.

The Watch keeps running

A small excitement took her. With that huge picture of the car right above there, in the headline, nobody on earth could think it meant a wristwatch or any other kind of timepiece. The name had always been a difficulty for copywriters—you could never write phrases like, "Get in your Watch," or "Drive your Watch." But turned around this way, the single name could evolve, no longer a handicap but a trademark advantage. She took a fresh sheet of paper.

The Watch ticks over

> On and on, mile after mile, month after month, this precision instrument, the Watch roadster, gives the unfailing performance that every motorist wants from his car.

She went on, lifting technical phrases from Rick's copy for the rest of it, about cylinders and brakes and miles per hour and engines, and then wrote the copy under the other headline. She then made clear copies of both pieces and spread them out on the breakfast table, in case Rick should wake up before she did. She slipped into bed beside him, her body achy with fatigue. It was three o'clock in the morning.

Three o'clock in the morning, she hummed in her mind, *we've danced the whole night through.*

In his sleep, feeling her slide next to him, Rick turned toward her for a moment, then collapsed once more on his back, the position that always made him snore. She listened; she had to listen.

It's three o'clock in the morning, her secret humming went on, *and I'm in love with you.* It had such a melancholy sound, this song; she'd never heard that in it before. She fell into the sleep of sheer weariness.

"They're terrific, Joss," Rick was shouting as she sprang awake. It was early morning; it was barely gray outside the open window, and winter-cold. The smell of new snow was in the air. He was in his pajamas, reading the two pieces of copy once more. She ran in to him, ignoring dressing gown and slippers despite the freezing room.

"I'm so glad," she cried. "Can you use them?"

"Damn it to hell, you're better at this than I am."

He wasn't joking; he said it with vigor and said it in anger. It was so unexpected that she stepped back, away from him and the two sheets of copy he held.

"Just because for once, Rick—"

"Not just 'for once,' it's always. You make me feel like a yokel." He set the copy down on the table and in a more moderate tone said, "They really are good, but they won't accept them."

"Because of that old company rule?"

"Standing operating procedure since 1914, when they changed the name. Always must say Watch Motors or Watch sedan or Watch roadster, never just Watch."

"But nobody could think the ad was about anything but a car.

Can't you try to wean them of that old stuffy nonsense?"

"They're unweanable."

"When you say a Ford, not a Ford roadster or a Ford sedan, just a Ford, nobody thinks you mean a river crossing."

"You tell them that!"

"You could be a hero, if you got them to shift."

"Some hero. My girl has to write my copy."

"I can just hear Jim Bryant saying to them, 'Our Mr. Baird has come up with a more modern slant.' Oh, Rick, at least show it to Bryant."

"I suppose I might give it a shot."

o o o

It was the first week in March when Jean's one-page letter arrived. Rick read it swiftly and handed it to Jossie.

> Dear Rick,
>
> It's too bad, but there seems no better solution to our problems than to end them now by separating, officially as well as the unofficial way we've done ever since I came to Paris.
>
> I mean a divorce. I've already engaged attorneys in New York, Keech, Smith and Keech, recommended highly by a man I wrote you about, Jake Mumm. I will pay whatever fees there will be, and court costs too. I will not ask for any alimony or support.
>
> As you know, there's just the one ground for divorce in N.Y. State, and my attorneys have already obtained the legal proof necessary, but I've instructed them to name nobody by name. Your superintendent has confirmed the fact that you and she have lived there for over 3 yrs. as man and wife.
>
> I am sorry, but this seems best all around.
>
> Yours, Jean

"The one ground," Jossie said, "being adultery. It sounds so evil when you say it out loud, or see it in writing. I'm sure Jean doesn't feel evil, yet the same ugly word could apply to her if you were the one instituting the divorce."

"Except that I'd never use it. I've lived thirty-one years without thinking in terms like 'adultery' or 'sin' or 'evil,' and I'm not going to start now. I've loved you and always will love you. That's what the attorneys should offer in legal phraseology." He took back the letter. In sudden warmth he said, "It's only a word, darling."

"So is 'unfair' and 'one-sided' and 'awful.' " She tried to smile. "How do you feel about it, the divorce itself?"

"Relieved, more than anything. I've felt it coming a long while."

"I have too." She studied his face. He seemed more like the old loving Rick than he had for some time. "What are you going to do about it?"

"Go along with it. No recriminations, no name-calling. Jean knows I'd never contest it."

"When will it happen?"

"She'll probably have to come over here, maybe in May or June, I'm not sure when, for the legal day in court, but if I don't fight it, it should all be brief, routine, and private."

"Oh, darling, I'm glad you don't mind too much."

"I do mind," he said slowly. "You have to mind when you fail at something you once cared about completely."

"She probably minds too."

"She's failed as much as I. Maybe neither of us was ever meant for a tight little marriage, in a tight little house, with the usual tight little bonds, fidelity, the usual restrictions."

He refilled his coffee cup, and they sat on in silence. Then he began to write across the back of the letter, printing several words. He turned the sheet so Jossie could read them.

WON'T CONTEST ACTION. WAS WONDERFUL
WHILE IT WAS WONDERFUL. SORRY TOO.

"I'll send it fast rate," he said, and rose. He went around the table to Jossie and kissed her. She reached up into his arms.

"It's a nice cable, Rick." Her voice was unsteady. "But it's so sad."

"It will never happen to us, sweetheart, never."

Eighteen

Waiting to be sued for divorce, Rick thought wryly, can get a man nervous. The objective calmness he'd felt for the first days after Jean's announcement gave way to a thready irritability, which he tried to analyze without much success. It's because she initiated it, he decided, not me. If I'd asked for it, I'd have been a villain, but in the active mode instead of the passive. A man always feels like a punk when women do the deciding.

He had already told the Bellocks and Jim Bryant and several of his other friends, even a few people at the office. He had written to his father, and there he'd had an inspiration he was glad of. *And since I won't be sending monthly checks to Paris any more, Dad, I'll be making yours $125 instead of $100. I know the old one meant a little pinching, so go have a few drinks on me.*

He had even taken time to comfort poor Joe Marvin, their superintendent, who had been struck with horror when he learned what he had accomplished by so politely answering all the questions put to him by that young man a few weeks back, who wanted to know about Mr. and Mrs. Baird and how long they had lived there.

"I didn't even catch on when he showed me that snapshot," he told Rick, "of you and a lady that wasn't Mrs. Baird at all. 'It's Mister, all right,' I told him, 'but not Missus.' "

"That's okay, Joe, forget it."

From time to time he had to comfort Jossie. "If I hadn't ever been in your life," she would say, "maybe it never would have happened."

"Don't blame yourself, don't blame anybody, not even Jean or me. If you have to blame somebody, blame nature. Trees grow leaves and then they lose them, plants bloom and then they die, even people—they get tired and bored, they get older, they change."

And as the waiting continued through March and into April and almost to May with no further word about when it would be heard in court and get itself done with, he needed to comfort himself too. He'd been having big dental trouble to contend with for the first time—an abscessed incisor that had to come out and root-canal work in the first molar next to it. The gap was right at the corner of his mouth, showing as he talked, and a costly chaise bridge was the one decent way to cope with it, though it meant about ten visits. Dentists were avaricious brutes; it had come to nearly $200. The minute they heard you were with a big agency, they kited their bills to the skies.

He still had a good deal of pain to cope with, and it added to the general malaise. He had sworn off drinking once or twice, but he needed to cheer up at lunch with office people or clients and it did set him up to go to the best restaurants in town and often pick up the entire bill. After office hours, too, he'd fallen into the habit of stopping in at a speakeasy near the office, known simply as Nineteen East, though everybody knew it was 19 East 47th Street.

He'd treated himself to things he'd always wanted and could now afford, with his $8,000 a year: decent wines and books as often as he chose, and thick albums of records for the Electrola. He'd bought new tennis rackets for himself and Jossie, and special accessories for the car. Even in winter they liked to ride with the top down, and he'd bought two fur lap robes, one up front and one for the rumble.

Jossie no longer said anything about what he bought. After he'd started at G.B.I., after he'd closed their joint account, he'd made rather a point of reminding her that *It's my money*, and though it hurt her feelings, she finally said she was never going to say a word about what he did with it. And she didn't, though at times he could tell she was bursting with questions. That knock-down-drag-out fight before Boston must have warned her she could go too far.

They went out often at night, and not to the little places in the Village, with two-by-four dance floors, but uptown to the famous big bands. He never let her go Dutch on the check—those days were over.

He was doing well at Gaylord, Bryant, and knew it. The new Watch campaign was now running in all major magazines; Jim Bryant and he had finally persuaded old man Watch, and the younger people at Watch Motors, to give up feeling spooked by their name and make a feature of it, a big plus. His follow-up copy had gone over big, like the first couple of pieces.

Watch gets you there on time

> No delays, no breakdowns, no motor troubles when you drive your Watch car. . . .

No, that was one more of Jossie's headlines and leads—she'd left it among her scratch papers that night and he'd spotted it and remembered it. She really was a marvel when it came to headlines and opening copy, but all the others were his all the way. And the tire account, and the shaving cream, and the others—all being okayed. He was copy chief on two of them already; that took time at a big agency. You couldn't yank a writer off an account just because a new man arrived on the scene.

So everything was going great guns, and he should feel swell all the time. Well, not everything. All the innuendo in Jean's letters about total honesty may have had some effect on him—he was certainly being a bit more cagey about what he told Jossie. Not ever an outright lie, just avoiding things bound to upset her, like the damn bills again piling up in his desk and the whole business of the down payment on the car.

From the moment they first fell in love, he'd told her that his problems about bills and debts were *his* problems and not hers, and now that the great sabbatical experiment was over, that's the way it had to be once more.

He didn't even tell her much about problems like what he'd do if Jean wanted to meet face to face when she finally got here, nor his problem of lining up an attorney of his own. He'd never needed an attorney; he'd had lunch with Andy and asked for the name of theirs.

"So it's here at last," Andy said dryly. "How long did you think this bohemian arrangement with Jean could go on?"

"It wasn't bohemian to start with," he'd answered with some asperity. "It wasn't bohemian for the first six months after she got to Paris, was it? For the first year? There aren't ready-made handy labels for things that go sour. They have to grow into their own labels."

"Take it easy."

It had offended him. He and Andy were drifting apart, for a fact. Funny, how your business life tended to dictate your social life, tended to shape it for you, how you found yourself lunching with people you worked with, being asked to their house for dinner, asking them back. Of course asking them back for him always meant inviting them to go to some decent restaurant, where he could have Jossie as his girl. That would end soon, God be praised. They could afford to move to a larger apartment, with a dining room, hire a maid, ask people home for dinner.

God, he thought, just listen to that—me describing the tight little marriage in the tight little house with the tight little social life!

The telephone on his desk rang. "It's Miss Lyon at Reception?" a voice said, as if she were asking a question. "There's a gentleman here to see you, a Mr. Haight. He says should he send in his card." This time it was a declarative sentence.

"A Mr. who? Has he an appointment?"

"Mr. Thomas Haight, of the Murray Hill Finance Company. He has no appointment."

He sat suddenly straighter. He'd had a reminding letter a week ago, maybe two weeks ago, about the installment he'd skipped. The installments. They were the company that had arranged the time payments on his car.

"I'll talk to him out there in the reception room," he said. "Ask him if he'd just wait a few minutes." He drew out the special file in the bottom right-hand drawer of his desk. It was not just an open folder like everything else in his file drawer; this was of a mottled dark red paper, heavier than usual, a kind of accordion-pleated expander, with a string around it. He didn't think Lydia looked through it—Lydia was the secretary he shared with another copywriter—but if she did, it didn't matter. Everybody in God's green world had bills overdue, and everybody except Jossie knew it and accepted it as part of daily life.

He found the letter they'd sent a while ago. It wasn't for just one skipped installment, it was for two, with a third coming due in May. When he bought the car, they'd proudly told him of the generous grace period they allowed, and he had of course taken it for granted that he'd never exceed it. Those unexpected dental bills had thrown everything askew.

Rapidly he searched through the assortment of bills in the dark red accordion. Knox, Dobbs, Sulka, Bailey's Phonograph, Abercrombie for the fur lap robes—at last he found the various vouchers for payments made to Murray Hill Finance.

It's impossible, he thought. Not since February? He'd bought the Watch last Thanksgiving, and paid promptly in December and January and February. And then nothing for March, nothing for April? He just didn't believe it; they must have made a mistake. He couldn't have used up the whole grace period. It would take $180 to catch up, with his next pay not due for ten days. He opened his checkbook. The balance was $86.20.

He went out to the reception room. Mr. Thomas Haight rose as Miss Lyon indicated Rick with her head and murmured, "Mr. Baird, Mr. Haight." They shook hands and Rick led his visitor to the far corner of the room, out of earshot of people waiting for appointments and especially out of earshot of Miss Lyon.

"We always see our clients in person," Mr. Haight said in a low voice, after handing Rick his card and letting him read it. "Before we make any move to repossess."

"Repossess? I did overlook—what's this grace period your man told me about when I made the deal last November?"

"That runs for forty days. Regular banks only allow twenty to thirty days, but as of today you are thirty-eight days in arrears."

"Forty days' grace from when?"

"On March twenty-first you were one day delinquent, Mr. Baird," his caller said patiently. "On April twenty-first you were thirty-one days delinquent. This is April twenty-eighth and in two days we will have no recourse but to repossess."

"There must be some mistake."

Mr. Haight produced records and sat patiently while Rick glanced at them. They were accurate, hatefully accurate. Hate, he thought, the man's name is Haight. He managed to grin. "I guess this calls for a calling-down for my new secretary," he said. "My checkbook's at home. You'll have both payments Monday."

Mr. Haight, clearly unimpressed, rose and extended his hand. He was still speaking in confidential tones. "Repossessing isn't even a profitable part of our business," he said mournfully, and went to the elevators. Rick could have murdered him.

○ ○ ○

There's no other way, Rick kept thinking all through the rest of the day. Jossie had been as good as her word about what he did with his money, even that day the lap robes had arrived in their two gigantic boxes. "Real fur?" Her voice had risen almost to a squeal, like an astonished child's.

"Lapin is just rabbit, probably the cheapest fur there is. They breed themselves right out of the high-price range, the dumb bunnies."

She managed a smile at that, but not one word about what they had cost, and he'd let it go. He had to get back into practice himself, about not talking about prices; he never used to mention cost or price. He'd been trained in childhood not to; it showed bad breeding, and it was time now to retreat to that old reticence.

It wasn't always easy; half a dozen times in the car, he could tell she was dying to ask about how he'd managed the down payment, but she'd stuck to her pledge, as he'd counted on her to do. He had never volunteered, nary one word, God, what a howling quarrel there would be if he ever did.

But here was this ghastly threat about repossessing the car. Why was his bank balance so low anyway? He had repaid $50 three times to Debtor's Prison and had deposited $50 in the special Jean account, but after the divorce cable, he and Jossie had agreed there was no point in going on with it. "Forget the rest of what you borrowed from it, Rick, and let's just close it."

"But the three hundred four I still owe it—that has to go down in Debtor's Prison," he insisted. "I said I'd pay back all of it and I will."

She had jotted it down without comment. Fair enough, but now, even if he dared turn again to the Jean account, there was no such thing any more.

He would lose the car. It was excruciating just to think it. They had sold the old Ford, but even if they still had it, he could never again appear in such an old crate. Everybody who expected to do well in business understood these things. Everybody but Jossie.

Would the Morris Plan increase his loan? Not likely. Some other company for a second loan? He couldn't go through that again, about two co-signers; it had been tough enough getting them for the down payment, and going back as a repeater would worry the devil out of both of them.

No, it had to be Jossie. There was no other way. He'd come to dread their quarrels, and he'd better leave the office early and get this one done with. He couldn't do any decent work any more anyway, with this hanging over him. How did they repossess a car? Come with a tow truck and haul it off the street when you weren't looking? He gritted his teeth. The whole chaise bridge hurt.

He did leave early, but he went first to Nineteen East and ordered a double Scotch, and then another. Jossie could be the most beloved creature in the world, but she could also be the most difficult. She still expected too much of him. What man wanted to be on a pedestal, like a vestal virgin, masculine gender? He began to get angry at her.

As so often, she astonished him.

"I'm in a jam," he said when he got home. "About the car."

"What sort of jam?"

"The goddam dentist fees knocked everything into a loop, and I've fallen behind on it."

"How far behind?"

"Two installments. I just can't believe it."

"A hundred eighty, that comes to."

"They sent a so-called representative to the office, really a bill collector in advance, to warn me they would repossess if I overstepped the forty-day grace period."

"Repossess it? You've had it since last fall."

"Repossess it."

"But haven't you paid in more than half of it by now?"

"That doesn't matter. They can repossess it on Monday and they will."

She simply left him standing there and went into their bedroom where she kept her three-to-a-page checkbook. She wrote out a check for $180 and returned with it, together with a 2¢ stamped envelope and handed them both to Rick.

"You can endorse it over to them and mail it tonight," she said in her ordinary voice. "They'll have it first mail Monday."

He took the check, staring at it. "Thanks, Joss," he said. Automatically he reached for his fountain pen and did endorse it. There's something behind this, he thought, addressing the envelope to the Murray Hill Finance Company. Something pretty unnatural.

"Aren't you going to say anything?" he demanded.

"I told you I wouldn't, not any more."

"You're acting so holier-than-thou, I'd rather have it the other way."

"I'm not acting anything—oh, Rick, isn't there *anything* I can do right when it comes to money?"

"You can quit being so damn noble, for one thing. It gets me sick."

"Stop it, don't start attacking me about holier-than-thou and I make you sick." She burst into angry tears.

"There we go again," he exploded. "Heartbroken tears, make me feel like a rotter and a cad. Why don't you come out with it and say I'm a heel and a disgusting weakling?"

"Stop that, I say. That's so unfair, you turning on *me*."

"Fair, unfair! I'd rather have you yelling at me about money than have this martyr act."

"It's not just money," she stormed. "It's character, that's what it really is. It *is* being weak, it's like a child screaming for a toy—got to have it, must have it—"

She went back to the bedroom, this time slamming the door in his face. She heard him go out, closing the front door softly. To show me up, she thought furiously, his good manners versus my screaming ones. He's gone to mail the letter and then go driving at breakneck speed for hours.

He came back within ten minutes. His face was drawn, his voice tight. It was only the end of April, but pinpoints of sweat dotted his forehead. He came straight in to her as she stood by the opened windows overlooking the garden with its early buds and leaves of spring.

"We're fighting so much," he said. "We were happier with our Fridays. I think we'd better go back to that."

○ ○ ○

See you Friday. But this *is* Friday, she thought, as she reached for her suitcase on the top shelf of the closet. Rick had gone out right after he had said it, not waiting for her to answer, just turned again and left. To his retreating back she had flung the words, "We can start tonight." It was ludicrous, the way it sounded, fury wrapped in a sob, but nothing could have made her stay there with that door closing so softly once more behind him.

This time it's forever, she thought. He'll probably get that divorce and feel free as air and become the footloose young bachelor. The notion tore her through. Like the abortion, she thought once more, without any anesthetic.

She flung the suitcase open on the bed and began to pack her clothes in it, all her clothes, cashmere sweater, lavender suit, everything, as if for a long stay. Just before she closed it, she put her journal into it too.

"Your Blanchard bag carries more than your clothes," her first headline had run, so long ago when she'd first gone after new accounts, to help Rick write. "Your Blanchard bag carries your whole image too. Whether you're struggling or successful—your luggage tells that to the world. Whether you're a newcomer to business or one of the substantial people already at the top—your suitcase tells that too."

Something like that. They'd approved it all, with minor changes. They didn't like the word *suitcase;* there was some distinction for them in their special words; *luggage, bags, attaché case,* and *briefcase* were all right but *suitcase* was n.g., the way yachtsmen felt it awful to say *ship* instead of *boat,* or vice versa, she never could remember which. She could do Blanchard's copy in about half an hour a week; they ran nothing but small ads in the "quality magazines" like *Atlantic Monthly* and *Harper's* and *Vanity Fair;* they didn't bother with newspapers, except for the financial pages of the *Times* and the *Wall Street Journal.* They thought her "a find" and said so, not only to Jack Weinstein, who'd sent her there, but right to her face.

I'm a find, all right, she thought now. Why am I remembering Blanchard's anyway? This suitcase carries *my* image too, a great big success except where I want it most. Maybe if I'd never made a cent, Rick and I would be as wonderful as ever; maybe if I earned only half what he earns, we'd never have these terrible fights.

There I go again, blaming everything on me. But oh, God, what I said was true. It *is* character as much as money. It's character about debts, it's character about the book. He could have been so happy if he'd stuck it out. The words *Mrs. Trollope* sounded in her mind, but they slipped by without registering. And if he had stuck it out and one day got it published, then this awful hurt would never have happened.

Oh, Rick, I can't bear it.

This time she called nobody. It was already evening when she reached the studio; she unpacked the things that needed hangers and went out. She could not eat; she'd do that later. She began to walk around Washington Square, and on up Sixth Avenue under its screeching el, and then back again down to the Square.

At the corner of Twelfth and Sixth was the French restaurant Henri's, where they'd gone once or twice to celebrate something; it was too expensive for them to go to often. Passing it now, she could see through the plate-glass windows the very table where Rick had taken her the night they'd begun to sleep together, and she turned from it as if it were there just to taunt her: it's over, it really is over. People do get over fights and keep on loving each other, but not fights like these.

All her great resolve about Rick and money! She'd stuck to it, and the fight was worse than ever. Could she have refused to help with that beloved car? Could she have stood there and said, "Well let them repossess your damn car; you never should have bought it in the first place?" She couldn't, not in a million years.

Did that make her a sap, a weak fool, just to write out the check and hand it over?

She had called him weak, a weakling—was she a weakling too?

She had never thought of that before. She stood still on the sidewalk. He *was* weak, but maybe the weak only preyed on other weaklings; maybe strong people resisted and finally got to the point where they stopped saying that eternal yes and began to say no.

Come on, Rick, you're going too far. Should she not have found the strength somewhere to say that by now? Wasn't it your own responsibility to set decent limits to human arrangements, no matter how much you loved somebody?

Suddenly she heard her own voice asking her mother, a long time back, out there in the garden behind their house in New Rochelle, "Did you ever love Pa enough to want to help him do something he couldn't do by himself?"

And her mother's voice, so quiet, answering, "So long as you aren't buying something by doing it."

Was this what her mother had meant? She'd hardly paid attention then, but was this what she'd meant? That you were unconsciously buying gratitude and love? That you were buying insurance, to keep Rick in love with you?

That would be so awful, so cheapening, sort of the bribery of love. I'll pay you to like me, I'll pay you to love me, like a child racing home with a good report card from school to hear her father say, "You're a good little girl."

At the thought of her father she suddenly began to cry. Why, for God's sake, she thought, *why?* I've never given a damn about what he thinks, about college, about not teaching, about being a hoor to go into advertising! What am I crying about? I'm not a little girl any longer.

Half blindly she walked on, turning left at West Tenth, not realizing she had done it until she passed the houses near Fifth Avenue, in one of which Amantha Dunwoodie still lived. I'm alone now, she thought, all by myself. Why don't you look out of your window and see me without Rick, without anybody?

She again turned at the corner and walked down Fifth Avenue toward Washington Square once more. From here the great arch stood tall and serene, gleaming in the moonlight and the illumination of the park's own lamps. The park itself was crowded, in the sweet mildness of April; a few children were still at play, but mostly there were couples, a man and a woman, paired, walking arm in arm, talking, laughing.

Envy welled high; that was the way it was meant to be. Just then a man alone walked under the arch, going into the park, his back to her. He was too far away for her to see him distinctly, but he was not very tall and he was wearing a snap-brim hat. . . .

He's come to find me, she thought, and started forward. In the next instant she saw that it wasn't Rick at all; the man didn't even look like Rick.

At last she turned west and went back to the studio. Maybe Rick would be there, waiting for her. Maybe they could make this up, like all the other times.

° ° °

He was not there. The weekend passed, and he did not come. He did not telephone. Two or three times she opened her journal, but immediately put it away. She could not set any of this down. You could never write what you felt in white-hot pain like this; you had to wait for time, like cooling water, to flow over it so you could touch it.

Early Sunday evening she drew out the sheaf of pages, "The Flame-colored Evening Dress." It was still at page 14, back where she had put it after ripping out the artificial phony ending she had once set down.

From time to time she had thought of Lila Jordan, always with a secret affection for her and sympathy for her plight. One day she would find a believable ending for Lila's story about the evening dress she had never had a chance to wear, and mail it off to some magazine. But it wouldn't have that trashy contrived turn in the plot where some man with a debutante sister invites her to a coming-out ball at a grand hotel.

She began to read the opening pages, remembering Rick when he had read it, remembering what he had said, how happy his words had made her. Now, suddenly, she knew how to end it. She would have Lila invited out to a dance, not by the rich young man with the debutante sister but by a boy she'd gone to high school with. He also would be twenty-two now, and he also would have held mediocre jobs ever since he was graduated. The moment he invited her, she would think, At last, at last I can wear it.

But a moment later he'd say, "It's at the old gym, so don't be fancy."

"Of course not."

It would be closing time at her office, and she would race to the subway and then home, as if the dance were that very night. It would be a wintry night, and when she entered the small frame house in the Bronx where she'd been born, it would be warm and for the moment comforting. She would go straight to her closet, and open the long clothes bag that held her summer dresses and her one beloved evening gown, still wrapped in tissue, even though it was protected by the outer bag. She wouldn't even undo the tissue, wouldn't even look under it. She would go straight downstairs to the cellar, to the furnace.

She would open the door and then stand there, uncertain. For a few seconds, perhaps a full minute, she'd do nothing but stare into the blaze inside the open door. Then at last she would lift one layer of the tissue paper and reveal the gleam of the lovely flame-colored chiffon. The matching headband, pinned to the shoulder, where pin marks wouldn't show when she wore it, would be hanging straight down at one side of the dress, and she'd think of it as an arrow pointing down to sorrow.

For another half minute she would stand there, the heat from the fire burning her face. Then she would thrust the dress into the flames and run upstairs.

Jossie began to write in a kind of frenzy, first draft, not pausing, not reading back, not judging. She wrote eight more pages before she stopped.

Again it was three o'clock in the morning. I'll edit and rewrite for the next couple of days and then type it double-spaced and send it off. Maybe to *McCall*'s or the *Ladies' Home Journal*. They'll never take it, but I'll send it anyway.

But things do end in ashes. They ought to see that. Lovely shimmery things do end in ashes.

Nineteen

It was the middle of May when Amantha Dunwoodie greeted her in the long inner corridor that separated the outside offices of the major people at Ashley from the glassed-in cubbyholes of the lesser lights. She was standing idly, doing nothing, and Jossie got the impression she was on the lookout for her arrival, for she waved a greeting while Jossie was fifty feet away.

Except for special meetings, with the client present, the scheduled time for her appearance on the Empire State Plate Glass account was every other Monday at ten, and never before had Mrs. Dunwoodie even looked up as she passed her office. Now she called out, "Come on in for a minute. Coffee."

Jossie hesitated. Was she up to some new attempt to put the kibosh on her free-lancing at Ashley's? She was in no mood for combat; she was a few minutes ahead of time and would dearly love some strong black coffee, but it would only stir up her buried resentments about this woman, feelings she had so far managed to keep in check whenever she was at Ashley.

The second weekend had just passed with Rick, and it had only a thin resemblance to the breathless Fridays when they had first started their split-week existence. Both times there seemed to be a glaze of restraint and memories of the hideous night of the $180 check. Neither of them mentioned it, and after an hour or two they had managed to get out from under the glaze and be what might be called happy again. They'd made love and gone out, once to the theater, once dancing, the great emancipator for people caught up in difficulties too sensitive to talk about. But when they parted, each Sunday night, she for one felt a kind of sad relief. Probably he did too.

Now, she looked at her watch as she went in with Mrs. Dunwoodie. "My meeting's in ten minutes," she said. "Might we have the coffee after it's over?"

"I'll be tied up then." She was already reaching for the Thermos and the china-mug. "We've hardly had a minute recently."

"Everybody's always so busy." She accepted the coffee, again trying to assay this convivial mood.

"I've been hearing great things about Rick Baird at Gaylord, Bryant," Mrs. Dunwoodie said. "You're still friends, aren't you?"

Jossie nodded. "People love compliments—why not call him there and tell him?"

"I might at that. I nearly told him in person a few nights ago at Henri's."

"Henri's at Sixth and Twelfth?"

"Yes, he was there with a—with some people, and I didn't want to break in." She laughed reminiscently. "Remember when I told you I wasn't much of a walker, always grabbed a cab?"

"I do remember."

"But Henri's is only one block over and two up, so I can manage that much of a walk if I have to."

"Of course you can."

"And my cook's been ill, so I've been going there a lot, rather than cook. I hate to cook." Again she laughed. "'Do you hate to cook? It's not a sin.' Remember that campaign, Jossie? It was such fun, putting it through, wasn't it?"

"Yes, it was fun. I still read Coal Stove ads—whoever's writing them is just great." It was harder to breathe. Amantha Dunwoodie was steering her to Henri's because Rick—

"Anyway, the compliment about Rick is that Watch Motors is up for the annual Three A award this year. Maybe you'd like to tell him yourself."

"How wonderful! Where'd you hear that?"

"Private sources, and I promised not to tell who. It's one of the three top contenders. It's exciting, isn't it? Both times I saw him, I nearly went over and spilled the beans—I would have, if he had been alone."

Her secretary appeared at the door. "Mr. Jerton's ready, Jossie. Mary Watts just phoned."

She jumped up. "Thanks for the coffee." She set the china mug down on the desk; it was virtually full and it sloshed over. "I'm so sorry."

"Nothing, nothing," Mrs. Dunwoodie said. She sounded pleased.

At one point in the meeting with Mr. Jerton, he said, "Don't you like your own copy, Jossie?"

"Of course I do. Why?"

"You seem a mile away, as if it bored you."

"It's just—" She was going to plead a headache, but instead she said, "I've got a lot on my mind, sorry."

But the moment the session was over, she found she could think of nothing except calling Rick. It would delight him, lift him for a while out of those divorce nerves. In two weeks Jean was sailing on the *Aquitania;* the court proceedings were scheduled for the day after she arrived, the first week in June. There was no plan for them to meet, but at the last minute she could change her mind and he could hardly refuse. No wonder he was in a state.

She called him from a phone booth in the Ashley lobby. "Are you sitting down?" she began. "I just heard something terrific about you."

"From whom?"

"Never mind who. Your Watch campaign is up for the annual award of the Advertising Association of America."

"It *what*?"

"It's one of three contenders. I'm so proud of you I could—"

"My God, Joss, where'd you hear that?"

"From an admirer." She laughed. "Amantha. I was just over there with Jerton."

"The Three A award! I'll be damned. Hey, thanks for calling me."

"I'd choke if I didn't."

"Let's have lunch—hell, no, I'm lunching with Old Razorblades. Is this supposed to be confidential?"

"I don't know. I forgot to ask. She wouldn't say who told her."

"I'd better clam up, in case it falls through. My God, the Three A award! Thanks again, Joss."

She could hear the elation. She was elated herself; telling good news was like doing a favor—you felt good doing it. She hadn't told him the news about finishing her story and mailing it off; even talking about writing might be salt in that old wound. If they ever accepted it and published it—well, better not think of that bridge for a while.

As for now, what was all that talk of Dunwoodie's about Henri's? That was rather elaborate, wasn't it? All that explaining how she happened to go to a restaurant, her cook being ill, the short distance to walk for her who detested walking and always took cabs?

"He was there with a—with some people." That's what she had said. With a—with some people. And then something about both times she'd seen him, again making the point that he was not alone. Her heart thudded. Here it was, the real reason for all the jolly camaraderie this morning. Amantha Dunwoodie *was* steering her to Henri's—the big news about Rick's campaign had sidetracked her, but she'd caught it on the fly when the woman had first slipped it in.

Foreboding filled her. Don't be silly, she told herself; Rick doesn't much like to cook either—he must go out to dinner a couple of nights a week and he's not great about dining alone, with a book propped up against the sugar bowl. He's made new friends at Gaylord, Bryant, he even mentioned a couple of girls writing copy, one named Margie Something and the other Liz Haynes. Probably he was having dinner with one of the G.B.I. people, maybe even with Liz or Margie. He was no hermit.

Still, Henri's was not just your little neighborhood restaurant. It was rather regal, a place for entertaining. After all, it was the place Rick had taken her to, their very first night together. She had never before even been in such a place. Dining at Henri's was usually an event. And Amantha Dunwoodie knew it and was implying that there was something special about Rick's being there with a—with some people.

And she, Jossie, couldn't even find out if it meant anything or not. The last place on earth that she'd go to herself, now, would be Henri's. It would be like spying, slinking around on the lookout. Never.

That evening she went uptown, clear out of the neighborhood, to a movie. She could never go to the theater alone; it would be too embarrassing to meet somebody she knew and have them know she had nobody to take her to the theater. But movies had no intermission, no lobbies where people came out between the acts and stood in clusters, smoking, talking, looking around. It was a show they'd missed when it came out, *The Hunchback of Notre Dame*, but it proved to be the wrong choice, for she pitied the gypsy dancer, Esmeralda, all the way through to her execution and came out wishing Rick were there to talk to about it.

Suppose you always had to do things alone? Suppose you never had anyone to talk to when you wanted to talk over a party or a book or a play? Suppose you went to Carnegie by yourself, with no one at your side, feeling the sweep of the music as you felt it? The word *alone* had become one of the underlined words to her, not just an ordinary word like *milk* or *bread* or *rain* or *snow*, but a special word that carried its own stress inside it, as if its very letters were in italics. Alone. Lonely.

The next evening she went out for a walk and retraced the route she had taken on her last solitary excursion, down to Washington Square, and up Sixth. . . .

As she neared Twelfth, she thought of crossing the avenue, so she couldn't possibly glance through the windows. But the idea seemed so craven, so puny, she banished it and walked on. She could just walk right past Henri's, eyes straight ahead. And she did, past it, up to Thirteenth, to Fourteenth. Then she turned and started back.

This time, somehow, she couldn't help it. As she came abreast of the large expanse of windows, it was as if a force made her head swivel, and she gazed inside. At once she saw them.

Not Rick and some people. Not Rick and some girl from the agency, no Margie, no Liz.

It was Rick and Suzy.

Rick and Suzy laughing, leaning toward each other, their dinner ignored, Rick talking with his old animation. And one of his hands comfortably closed over one of Suzy's on the table.

Jealousy tore at her, clawing, giant talons in a craze of power. This was what Amantha Dunwoodie had seen, not once but twice, Rick and a girl, an attractive girl, a girl whose name she didn't even know, except that it wasn't Jossie.

She stood locked in place. There was a wine cooler beside their table, a silver neck rising from its icy hold. Champagne, the wine of celebration, the wine of lovemaking. A waiter approached their table, asking something. Rick nodded but never looked up, never took his eyes from Suzy's face. Suzy's shoulders jumped at the pop of the cork, and Rick laughed with his old delight.

○ ○ ○

There was no sleeping for Jossie until exhaustion released her at dawn. Nothing she could do eased it, nothing she could plan suited her needs. To call him and say the weekend was off, without explanation, had a falsity she couldn't contemplate; to see him on Friday and pretend everything was as usual was beyond her; she never was any good at subterfuge. That word *civilized* meant many things for her, but they did not include the mien of an indifferent princess when you felt like a screaming heartbroken peasant.

She slept until ten. She woke with a thump of recognition—she could see them at their table as if she were gazing through that wide window still. She started coffee and remembered she was due at Stuyvesant's at that very moment. She telephoned and told Jack Weinstein's secretary, Elsie, she'd been badly delayed and would make it by eleven, if he were free then to see her. She had never failed to be on time for a meeting with Jack Weinstein.

"You sound shook up," Elsie said. "Were you in some sort of accident?"

"In a way. No bones broken. Is he tied up at eleven?"

"Hold on a sec."

She literally held on to the bar of the telephone as if it might support her. Even by eleven she'd be in no state to see him, to sound ordinary, to smile and discuss copy.

Elsie came back to the phone. "He says could you make it at three. He's snowed under around eleven."

"Thanks. Three." Three would give her time to get hold of herself. Pull herself together. Shattered and scattered—and all the king's horses and all the king's men . . . I'll put you together again, my lovely bright girl. . . .

What hurt most was not the terrible things but the sudden remembering of happy ones. Then came that stiletto of longing for the past, that piercing yearning for beginnings, when everything was young and unstained and filled with new love, when you never even considered pain as one of the possibilities ahead of you.

I can't even phone Rick to tell him this weekend is off. My voice would crack, the way it does.

She drew out a sheet of notepaper, the same long white vellum she had bought for her first letter to Grover Cleveland Albright that day she'd read *Glass World.*

Dear Rick,

I saw you and Suzy at Henri's last night, and I truly think we'd better not be together this weekend.

You'll say these things mean nothing, but just looking at you with her, I could tell that they do.

We both hate quarrels, and I don't think this could end in anything happier. Let's just skip until the week after.

Always, J.

She hadn't written him a letter since he was in Paris. On the envelope she wrote only *Rick,* and took it over to the apartment. The red-brick house on West Tenth Street—how she loved it, how much she had discovered here, of joy and love and music and poetry and books. She went up the three low marble steps to the little vestibule and slipped her letter into the mailbox. The sliver of card still read *Mr. and Mrs. C. U. Baird.*

She had a busy day ahead: Blanchard's before eleven, and then Lacq and Gordon's. She telephoned everywhere, changing her times of arrival, and by the time she reached Stuyvesant's she was harried and worn out. She'd forgotten to renew her makeup, even her lipstick.

"You look good and frazzled," Jack Weinstein greeted her. "What's up?"

"Nothing." She sank down on the small sofa, laying her envelope of copy down beside her as if it were too heavy to hold.

"Jossie, that fancy 'nothing' doesn't go with me, you should know that by now. What's wrong?"

"Please, let's leave it. I've had some rotten news, that's all." She looked past him to the open window behind him.

"This young man of yours, is it still the same one?" She didn't answer. "The one you needed nine thousand six hundred for, but for one year only?"

She still didn't answer.

His memory was as good as hers.

"You said it wasn't trouble," he persisted, "just 'wonderful.' So what happened to the 'wonderful'?"

"Oh, Mr. Weinstein, *leave* it!" Her voice did break and her eyes did fill. She slid her hands up in the old familiar gesture, making a screen across her face. She heard his chair shove back against the carpet. He was coming around his desk. He laid a hand on her shoulder.

"I'm sorry I kept pressing," he said in a low voice she had never heard from him before. She glanced up from behind her hands; his rubicund face was pinker than ever; he had gained weight; he stood there like a benevolent and miserable Kewpie.

"It's all right," she whispered.

"It's just that you're too classy for the usual."

"Nobody is."

"You're good goods, Jossie. Don't let yourself in for the usual *dreck*. Do you know what *dreck* means?"

"Yes."

"I thought you said you don't speak Jewish."

"I just know some words. Mostly dirty ones." To her surprise, she laughed a little.

"So let yourself think them about what makes you cry. They mean more in Jewish."

"I only know a few: schlemiel, nebbish, no-goodnik—"

"That's Broadway, not Jewish."

He was still standing there; he had removed his hand, but he showed no sign of returning to his desk. She had wiped her eyes and could look at him. He really likes me, she thought, it's not just my copy.

"I suppose I should tell you, take a trip," he said. "Take a few days off, go away awhile. But trips and go-aways never work. You know we're opening our new fur department."

"Now? At the start of summer?"

"When better? To make a mink coat to order takes time."

"You mean that I should start working on fur ads?"

"Would you rather just cry?"

She began to scribble on the envelope beside her and then handed it over.

Think of mink
quick as a wink
even though
our prices stink

"Something like that," he said solemnly. "Good goods, Jossie. Don't you ever forget it." He went back to his desk.

○ ○ ○

Good and frazzled is right, Jossie thought, as the long day at last came to its end. I'm going to go straight to bed. For once she took a taxi instead of a trolley, leaning back into it and closing her eyes. When she opened them, the cab was speeding down lower Fifth Avenue, toward the Arch. They were just passing West Tenth. Rick would be getting home soon—he'd find her letter.

I've got to get out of this neighborhood for good, she thought in a sudden frenzy, not just that one night at the movies. Down here everything is always going to mean Rick; I can't just wallow around and cry all the time.

The idea didn't shake loose a few moments later, the way ideas often did. She kept thinking of it after she got home. A better studio, she thought, a little larger, with some of my own things, with a gas range instead of these two hot plates, a little nicer place, where I could have somebody over, or even meet a client. Some place farther uptown, near Central Park maybe, like Nell.

Rick could get there in five minutes in the car, and we could still have our weekends. Change is good for people.

What I really ought to change, she thought a moment later, is just about everything I do. It's crazy to keep on with all my accounts now, the way I did when it was for Rick to write. I could give up a couple of them anyway—Lacq, maybe, and Gordon's, even Houbigant.

It was exciting to contemplate. She didn't have to have their fees any more, not the way she once did. She never would have taken on so many just for the joy of earning more and more. With the main motive gone, the main dynamo was gone too. Mr. Weinstein was right, of course—work was the only way to bear things—but even cutting down like that, she wouldn't be exactly idle.

And maybe giving up some of her accounts wasn't going far enough. She had been swept with a gale of desire to quit earning money and more money, to pay off bills and more bills, right after that first discovery about Suzy, thinking how marvelous it would be to write not of products and how to sell them but about people and what happened to them. That didn't mean a book, not even a short story, it meant the old longing for a job on a newspaper.

Every time some dreadful thing happened, she seemed to go back to that long-ago dream at Cornell, when she was writing her tidbits for *Women's Wear* about what coeds were wearing to football games and regattas, when she was sending in little news items to the *Evening Mail* about student elections and college theatricals, racing down the hill at night to the railroad station, to hand over her two envelopes to the train porter so he might mail them in New York.

Maybe the time had come to go all the way back to the kind of work she had always wanted to do but never could start while that Student Loan stood mocking her. First that, and then loving Rick so much that the only dynamo charging her was the need to make enough money to help him—

"When he begins to earn royalties with his fine old book, then I'll have my turn."

Fully formed, the sentence seemed to speak aloud to her, a remembered quotation, insistent, vital. Where had it come from? To whom had she said it? Her mother? Nell? Suddenly she remembered. She had written it in her journal after she had finally persuaded him to try a free year for writing—*Today Rick and I started on a new adventure, me being the good provider, Rick being an artist.*

Well, that was ended now, had been ended for months, and yet she had gone right on free-lancing, in a sort of momentum she had never yet questioned.

This was the time to question it. This, now, not tomorrow, not sometime, but now.

There was the ting of the bell and Rick's key in the door. He came in, saying, "But it *doesn't* mean anything—when will you accept that?"

"It means something to me."

"If you were a man, you'd understand—"

"I'm not a man."

"Did you think I'd never see another soul during the time we're apart?"

"She's not just 'another soul.'"

"Another girl then, another woman."

"I thought you'd never see Suzy Platt. You know how I felt about you and Suzy—I thought you never saw her again after that one horrible time."

"And I didn't, until—"

"You could at least have picked somebody else."

"I did stop seeing Suzy. I didn't see her for months. If it weren't for the damn mess about the co-signer—" He stopped short.

"The co-signer?"

"The Morris Plan, for the down payment."

"Suzy! You went to Suzy?"

"I tried everybody else. John Slade said sure, he'd have another go-around, but there wasn't another soul to ask. I was too new at the office, I couldn't go to Andy Bellock, and God knows I couldn't ask you. There'd be hell to pay if I did."

"So you looked up Suzy. And she said she'd love to help you. And you said how generous and sweet and you took her to Henri's out of gratitude and then you went home and slept with her all night."

Suddenly he was shouting. "That's just what I did, and she never once said one word about debts or bills or what I could afford, or me being weak, not one goddam word about character—"

She stood before this onslaught, leaning forward slightly as if she were heading into a gale. Suzy was his co-signer. He had asked Suzy for help and she'd given that help and then he had made love to her and begun seeing her and dining with her and making love again and again.

"I hate it," she cried. "I hate everything about it."

"You hate me."

"It wouldn't be so horrible if it *did* mean something, if you were in love with her—"

"I'm not in love with her. I told you that."

"Then you took help about money from a girl you don't even love. That's a cheapskate trick—it's common as dirt."

"Don't you lecture me on common or well-bred!"

"And it's the ultimate insult to *me*." She was shouting now, her voice high and raucous. "It makes all my help about money just a—a—just a convenience, not part of being in love."

"For Christ's sake, stop twisting everything around."

"It *is* twisted, it's a snake pit full of money—co-signers and money, bills and money, down payments and money, making love and money. Everything that's ever happened to us is mixed up with money, everything that's happening now—"

"It's happening, all right." He had her letter in his hand now, motioning with it toward the door. "So you exile me for the weekend. Your Majesty banishes me. Okay, I'll spend the weekend by myself."

"With Suzy."

"Not with Suzy." He was no longer shouting. His voice was suddenly colorless, as if a voice could turn white. "I had been invited up to Boston and I'd declined. But now I'll phone and say I can go after all."

"To Boston? Who do we know lives in Boston?"

"Glory Carlton lives in Boston."

"That Mrs. Carlton at Thanksgiving?"

"She's having a birthday party this weekend, and now I think I'll go."

He left her. She stayed where she was, looking at the blank face of the door. This was the second weekend out of four that they were to be apart. It no longer was *See you Friday*. Now it was *See you sometime*.

Twenty

See you sometime. For days the phrase sounded, as if he had actually spoken it; for nights she lay crushed under the crossed and flashing swords of what he'd said and what she'd said. The weekend was a time of paralysis; she couldn't even take her familiar walks around the Square and past Henri's. She opened books and read nothing; she went to movies and saw nothing; she went to Carnegie Hall and heard nothing, watching the baton as if it were some object swung by a hypnotist to quiet her into sleep.

See you sometime. She not only had to move out of the neighborhood, she had to find new friends, new interests, maybe even new work.

New work. How often had she thought about it, without ever doing anything to test it! Just the other day she had decided that this was at last the time to take definite steps, and then again had done nothing. Was it to remain a perpetual daydream, to come forth when she was miserable, only to recede into the realm of fantasy when her spirits lifted?

She'd had no choice when she got out of school; Andrew Carnegie had robbed her of any free will about what she wanted to do as the young college graduate facing the big wide world. And then the years with Rick—

But now? Wasn't this the perfect time, the ordained time, to try a new core of living? No big permanent farewells in it, but perhaps a few new conduits toward new seas?

What if she were to telephone that Ted Bonning on the *World* and ask if she might see him? For an instant a meteor streaked through her mind, its tail ablaze.

"How many girls get jobs on newspapers?" her father had mocked when she first announced what she wanted to do after school. She heard the jeering words again, and then her mother answering, "Jossie will be the one who does."

She looked at the telephone. She picked up the phone book. But she just couldn't. It would be the old question, "What experience have you had?" and the old shy agony of saying, "None, but—" and then that bored look on the other face, and her own abashed attempt to ask how you could have experience unless you found a job to get experience. And this time, no lucky piece, no silver dollar and the piece of ore.

Come off it! she thought. That's pure malarkey. She picked up the phone.

In a moment she was saying, "Mr. Bonning, please, the assistant managing editor."

"His line is busy now."

"I'll wait."

What would she say, how would she put it? If it were about a new free-lance account she wanted, she'd begin in the usual way—"I've been writing Stuyvesant's copy and"—but who on the staff of the *New York World* thought in terms of fashion ads or nail polish or plate glass or fine luggage?

"You can have Mr. Bonning now."

"Oh, Mr. Bonning, this is Joselyn Stone. I—"

"Who?"

"Out at Cold Spring Harbor at the Bryants', on Thanksgiving, Joselyn Stone, I—"

"Those 'missing person' Christmas ads for Stuyvesant's," he said with sudden energy. "You're the girl who made me knock over my glass of wine."

"It was only water. I'm so glad you remember meeting me."

"The only ads in my paper I bother to read. Of course I remember. What can I do for you?"

"I wondered—" She couldn't say it. She had expected him to have a secretary who would answer the phone, and to whom she could give some small hint about her reason for calling. But maybe newspaper editors didn't have secretaries.

"You wondered what?"

"If I might ask you to see me for a few minutes." The words hurtled out. "About a job as a reporter."

"A job as a reporter? You said you free-lanced ad copy."

"I was—I mean, I do. But if I could just see you for a few minutes when you're not too busy—"

"'When I'm not too busy.' There's no such animal on a paper. But sure, if you want to see me, come on."

"Oh, gosh, thanks." She could have shot herself, it sounded so girlish. "When would be a good time?"

"Say tomorrow at four."

"Four in the afternoon?"

"The *World*'s a morning paper, remember? I don't get here till four."

She felt like a fool. "I'll be there at four."

"Ask for the city room."

She felt like shouting with excitement. Rick would—she'd forgotten. She wouldn't be telling things to Rick now, not for a while. Maybe never.

She called her mother, telling her what she had done. It was possible to talk about it without putting in one word about *that*; it astonished her that it was so. "I'm so glad, dear," her mother said. "Whatever happens, I'm so glad you called him. Let me hear tomorrow, the minute you've seen him."

I can't wait till four tomorrow, she thought; I'll never sleep. I never can sleep any more anyway, but at least this is exciting insomnia instead of the other kind. But the other kind swarmed all over her the moment her eyes closed: Rick asking Suzy to be his co-signer, Rick and Suzy at Henri's, Rick and his trip to Glory Carlton's birthday party in Boston. . . .

Don't think about Rick, she commanded herself. You better think what you'd do if this Ted Bonning says yes.

She'd already thought of giving up some of her accounts, Lacq, and Blanchard's Luggage, and Gordon's, but what if a miracle happened tomorrow and Ted Bonning did say yes? Would that mean giving up all her accounts? Every single one? She could just see herself walking into Mr. Weinstein's office to tell him she was leaving—

This time she did have a sleeping pill, borrowed once from Nell. She got out of bed and gulped it down. She had never had one. Suppose this little blue capsule knocked her out so she missed her four-o'clock appointment? She fell asleep.

The morning mail brought a large manila envelope, her manuscript, but instead of the printed rejection slip she had heard so much about, there was a letter addressed to her.

> Dear Miss Stone,
>
> It is with great reluctance that I return "The Flame-colored Evening Dress." You have a real flair for fiction.
>
> Your story opens compellingly, but the second half is so negative and sad that we cannot accept it for publication.
>
> We find that many young writers who are going through a difficult time in their private lives unknowingly transmit their own moods to their fiction.
>
> But with a young writer who reveals as much talent as you do, we can only hope that as time passes, his or her work will shift to happier thematic substance.
>
> Most sincerely,

Under the signature were the typed words, Fiction Editor. Jossie read the letter twice. "'Happier thematic substance,'" she muttered, half aloud. "Why can't she say 'happy ending'?"

In the same instant she thought, What luck I'm seeing Ted Bonning this afternoon—otherwise I'd feel awful. She did feel awful, but it was an easier awful than half the awfuls she'd been having in the last few months. This awful didn't crush you inside, didn't tear through, didn't threaten your whole life. It just sat there, a turndown, like the time Starlight Cream had rejected her idea about I'm 35 but everybody thinks I'm 25. Mrs. Dunwoodie had comforted her that time, had told her everybody goes through rejections by clients—imagine Amantha Dunwoodie trying to help you through anything.

She started for Park Row twenty minutes too early. Again she was wearing her lavender suit; just about a year had passed since she'd first worn it. It was a kind of talisman—it had meant her first business trip, a milestone. Maybe it would mean a new milestone today. She was nervous about this meeting; she never felt nervous any more about interviews for ads and free-lancing, but this wasn't just ads and free-lancing.

It was a muggy day, and as she entered the World building there was immediately the smell of hot metal, even of hot paper, of ink and dust and people. Her eagerness rose—how different this was from the smart remote offices of Ashley and all advertising agencies.

The big city room was full of desks and typewriters and ringing phones, and down at the far end sat Ted Bonning, in his shirt sleeves, collar opened, tie half looped off. He waved when he saw her coming toward him, left his desk, and came forward to meet her.

"We'll get away from this racket," he said by way of greeting. "Here, in there." He piloted her by the elbow into an empty office. "We can talk in here. It's the boss's office. He keeps human hours."

"Thanks for seeing me, Mr. Bonning."

"Ted. Mister doesn't go around here."

"Ted." She felt shy saying it. In all the years she'd worked for Stuyvesant's, she'd never called Mr. Weinstein anything but Mr. Weinstein.

"What's on your mind, Jossie?" he asked, sitting down at the desk and motioning her to a chair. He offered her a cigarette and she said, "Not now, thanks."

"Okay, let's have it. A job as a reporter is what you said. Have you ever been a reporter?"

"In a crazy small way, at college." She told him about her items for *Women's Wear* and the *Mail*. "And all through college, my one dream was to be a cub reporter, for a real newspaper, but I had a Student Loan to pay off first and I just had to start writing ads."

"Do you know what we pay a cub reporter? Twenty-five a week." He put out his cigarette. "And we're crawling with reporters."

He was going to stand up and send her away with some kind words. Her heart plummeted. This was ten times worse than the rejection letter from the fiction editor this morning, a thousand times worse than the turndown from Starlight Cream. She was suddenly frantic with desire to work for him, to change herself from being just a copywriter into something she had always wanted to be.

"Mr. Bonning—Ted—would any newspaper try somebody for a week, say, just to see if a person could write for a paper?"

He lighted another cigarette. "Jossie, you could write for anybody—I've seen the way you write. But you're forgetting twenty-five a week." He suddenly looked angry. "Damn all your free-lance bosses and ad agencies—they price everybody else right out of the competition for young kids who can write." He started to get up. Jossie didn't say a polite thanks and rise with him; she didn't budge.

"Not *everybody* else," she said, "not if—Ted, would any newspaper even hire a cub reporter and let him do some other work on the side?"

"No. It's a full-time job, reporting. Six days a week."

"If somebody *had* to give over his day off," she persisted, "wanted to, to do something else he was committed to—?"

"What are you driving at?"

"I was just wondering." Her face felt hot. She ran her fingers over her forehead; they came away moist. "If I could be allowed to keep on writing ads for Mr. Weinstein—he's Stuyvesant's—the major campaigns only, not the daily stuff, and if I gave up all my other accounts?" He was staring at her as if she was suddenly talking gibberish. "I mean, could I try out as a reporter if I dropped everything except Stuyvesant's and did that on my day off?"

"Give up all your other free-lancing for a job here as a cub reporter? Is that what you're asking?"

"I'd give anything to try it. Would my day off have to be Sunday? Stuyvesant's is closed Sundays."

"You'd be lucky if you saw a free Sunday in five years. Any day except Sunday is the way it works for beginners." He lighted another cigarette and walked around the room before he spoke to her again. "How much do you make free-lancing?"

"It doesn't matter. I don't have a family. I'm alone."

"Six–eight thousand a year, Jossie. You must make at least that."

She nodded. He'd turn her out of the building if he knew it was over eleven.

"And if I said, Sure, keep on with Stuyvesant's, you'd start here at twenty-five a week?"

"I'd give anything if you'd let me try."

"Well, I'll be damned." He stomped out his cigarette and immediately reached for another one. "This wouldn't be romantic, you know, no working all night till the dawn came up like thunder, nothing like that."

"I'm not thinking about being romantic."

"You'd be on the day side, to start with, anyway, and it's damned hard work."

"Oh, Mr. Bonning, Ted, I just know I could do it, if you'd only give me a chance."

"You're a crazy kid, all right, Jossie." He put out his hand as if in congratulation. "Can you start Monday?"

"Oh, God, no. I have to give everybody notice—I have eight clients—I'd have to help break in new people—oh, please give me time."

"Okay, a month from Monday." He glanced at the calendar on the desk. "Last Monday in June. I'll wangle thirty a week for you. You better be good."

° ° °

As she left the World building, she saw a man half a block away, sauntering along the way Rick often did in warm weather, a trait acquired during a boyhood in the South. The man wasn't very tall and he wore a snap-brim hat—

It can't be, she thought angrily, you know it's not; what would he be doing down on Park Row? Are you going to spend the rest of your life seeing Rick every time you walk down a street?

Five minutes ago she was on the wings of excitement and hope; now she was sucked down into the primeval muck of misery over a dying love. You'd think the two lobes of my brain were clutching each other in there, interlocked, refusing to let go, one lobe light and happy, the other heavy and stiff with wounds.

She walked all the way home. If she was to move, this was the time to do it, before she started her new life and while she could afford it.

Why had she said Stuyvesant's instead of Empire State? Mr. Albright was the very first person who showed any faith in her, the very first who took a chance. Why hadn't she said that the one account she would have to keep was Empire State? It just was the inevitable choice. Maybe, she thought a moment later, it's because Mr. Albright thinks of me as a copywriter and Mr. Weinstein thinks of me as a human being. I just can't help it.

People do change jobs without being disloyal. All the other clients will know that, so why should I worry about Mr. Albright? I'll take special trouble breaking in any copywriter they assign at Ashley—and then I'll never have to go there again and never have to lay eyes on Amantha Dunwoodie for the rest of my days.

She stopped at a telephone booth. Rick had called her when he got home from Boston, just to let her know he was back. He had even troubled to indicate it wasn't any great success, but he had said nothing about the coming weekend. Neither had she. But not to tell him this piece of news? She wouldn't make too much of it, just tell him. No matter what lay ahead, no wall of steel would be coming down between them. They weren't that type, either of them.

The phone booth was occupied. She remembered that time she'd gone into one of the booths in Ashley's lobby, with the news about Rick's possible award from the Three A's. And had come out and suddenly faced the real meaning of Amantha's big hints about Henri's.

The inhabitant of the booth came out and she went inside. She had a nickel ready, but her hand stopped at the coin slot. She leaned slightly against the metal of the instrument, as if she were very tired.

Not now, she thought. He'd want to celebrate or something, he'd come over, he'd take me out to dinner, and then he'd want to make love.

She left the booth and resumed her walk. When she reached for her key, she found that the nickel was still tight in her palm.

° ° °

At least she had no time to think. With all those clients to visit personally, with all the new writers to break in, with a new apartment to find and move into, the last Monday in June would be coming up like thunder even if Ted Bonning's dawn was not.

She had luck with the apartment, finding one the second time she went out, on the third floor of a brownstone on East Fifty-eighth Street. It was only two blocks from the lower edge of Central Park and only one from the subway. With a change to the express at Forty-second street, she could be at the paper in less than twenty minutes.

The rent was more than she had expected to pay, $90 a month, but your rent was supposed to be all right if it didn't exceed a quarter of your salary, and unless something went wild with Mr. Weinstein when she told him what she was doing, he certainly wouldn't cut her below $4,000 or $3,500 a year; with her $1,500 from the *World*, she'd be making about five thousand and certainly could afford this attractive new place.

It was still occupied, but would be vacant two weeks before she reported for her new job. There was a lease to sign, one year minimum, with no permission to sublet. There was a finality to it; she could not change her mind. She signed and left the first month's rent.

It was the first lease she had ever signed in her life. There had been no lease for the studio down on Bleecker; that was just a rooms-to-let affair. But this was a real apartment, a living room, bedroom, tiny kitchen with a four-burner range, and bath.

The woman who owned the house had taste; it was a pretty place, and the living room had a fireplace. It would not be just a makeshift like the studio, but a place she could be happy in.

Happy! What a word.

Marty King at Lacq was the first of her clients to whom she gave notice of her departure. Her promise to break in whatever new writer he hired scarcely brought a thank-you. He didn't try to disguise his annoyance at the bother of having to find somebody else.

To lesser degrees, it amounted to the same thing at Blanchard's and Gordon's and the others. They extended rather formal good wishes for her new job but were clearly irked that she should have any plans at variance with their own needs.

Irk or no irk, she thought once, it *is* a free country even in advertising, and as long as I'm giving them plenty of notice and help for the changeover, they could quit making me feel like Benedict Arnold. Business is business and all that—they'd tell me so like a shot if it was vice versa about who leaves who.

Grover C. Albright, however, surprised her. "Well, Jossie, I'll miss working with you, but I'm in your debt anyway, so here's the best of luck in your new work."

"In my debt?"

"You taught me so much about what to expect for that fifteen-percent commission."

"What a nice thing to say."

"And Jerton knows I know what to expect, so he'll see they assign somebody good." He rose and shook hands. "If it doesn't work out at the *World,* you know where to come."

"And that's a nice thing to say too."

She had left Jack Weinstein for last. If for some unimagined reason he were to turn down the idea of a new arrangement on a reduced one-day-a-week level, what would she do? She should have seen him first, before burning all the other bridges, but some instinct, God knows what one, had made her wager everything on him.

"Can you save me some real time?" she had asked on the phone. "It's sort of big, the thing I want to talk about, and I can wait until you have an easy half hour."

"Who has easy half hours? Come over now. If you're getting married you can still—"

"Nothing like that, Mr. Weinstein, just nothing."

As she had not dreamed of doing with the others, she told him all of it, her schoolgirl longings to work on a paper, her asking Ted Bonning to see her, the interview, the $30 pay she would get, the decision to quit nearly all her free-lancing.

"But I told him the one client I *couldn't* leave was you, that I wanted him to know it straight out, that I'd have to drop the whole idea if they wouldn't let me use my day off for Stuyvesant's."

Jack Weinstein was leaning back in his chair, listening as a child listens to a favorite story. He's beaming, Jossie thought, like the proverbial Cheshire whoosis. He's going to say yes.

"Just major campaigns," she explained. "The way we started—the fall holiday season breathing down your neck, then spring fashions, special things like announcing a new branch. You could go back to paying me so much per ad again."

"You're a great financier," he jeered. "By now, if I paid so much per ad, you'd price me right off Fifth Avenue, like two hundred per."

"I would not! It's true my fees have been going up—"

"Piecework I don't like. Round numbers save time. How much are you making from us now?"

"Six thousand."

"I'll have to hire somebody for the lace brassieres and silk stockings and lingerie—even twenty-five a week comes to thirteen hundred a year."

"I know you'll have to cut back on my pay to cover another salary."

"How about five per annum?"

"Five thousand! That's more than piecework would come to."

"So buy a few extra copies of the *World* if they ever print anything you write."

Suddenly he looked solemn, almost somber. "This one time, Jossie, what you call 'wonderful' is the kind of wonderful that *is* wonderful, not somebody else's wonderful but your own future wonderful. You take chances while you're young, you grow."

Still solemn, with no trace of a smile, he stood up and snapped her a salute as if he were still in the army.

"Oh, Mr. Weinstein, *don't.*" But she loved him because he had.

o o o

"So now I'm no longer a married man," Rick said to Jossie.

"No." The first week of June was ending, and the divorce proceedings were over. Jean had made no move to see him during the two days she was in New York; she hadn't even let him know at which hotel she was staying.

There had been no snags or delays in the process itself. Joe Marvin, the superintendent, had been summoned, whether by subpoena, cajolery, or irresistible tip they never knew, and had duly testified on behalf of the plaintiff.

Rick's attorney had uttered no word of dissent, no name was entered in any document beyond "the so-called Mrs. Baird" as the cohabitant with Mr. Baird for the specified term of years at West Tenth Street, and in less than thirty minutes, a marriage that had begun nine years before was formally ended.

Rick and Jossie had again spent two weekends together, but again both weekends had had what she had come to call "the glaze." He said nothing about his trip to Boston and little about Gaylord, Bryant; she told him about her new job, which had astonished him to the point of saying, "I don't believe it, I can't believe it," but not to the point of asking how she would adjust to earning so much less.

"And I'm moving to a larger place than the studio," she had said. "A real apartment, with a kitchen, where I can do a bit more gourmet cooking than the hot-plate kind."

"Good luck with apartment-hunting."

"Oh, I've already—" She broke off. Something held her back from telling him that he had misunderstood, that she had already found an apartment, that she had signed a lease for it. If he were to talk about "christening it," it would have hurt too much.

Both weekends they had tried to crack the glaze, and to an extent they had succeeded. Again they had gone to the theater, again they had gone dancing. They had even gone to bed.

One thing only had suddenly broken through the glaze. The day after Jean sailed for Paris, a messenger had brought Rick a tubular package, about twenty-four inches long. Telling Jossie about it had come hard; she could see it in his averted eyes, hear it in his thickened voice. It was one of Jean's paintings, a gouache on canvas, which she had brought with her as a goodbye present. It was a street scene of Paris, painted from her window in the Île de la Cité, where he had last seen her during the operation and convalescence. On the back of it, with a fine-tipped brush and blue paint, she had put down the date and painted, *Wonderful while it was wonderful. Jean.*

"It got to me in a big way," Rick had said. "It put a kind of finality on everything, more than the divorce itself."

Now he repeated to Jossie, "Well, it's all over and I'm no longer a married man. Do you remember what we used to say, about after the divorce came through?"

She nodded. Was he going to talk about marriage? Mr. and Mrs. Baird for real, not just on the mailbox with the shiny brass plate in the hall? Was it the old Southern gallantry again, a debt of honor that must be paid?

"It's not been much good for me the last few months," he went on. "I don't think for you either."

She shook her head slightly.

"I'm in too much of a hole right now to ask you," he said. "But the minute I'm in the clear—I'll always love you, Joss."

"Are you in debt again, Rick?"

"Way in. But I'm working at getting it down, and as soon as I do—"

"Let's not talk about it." She was still shaking her head in negation, a tiny swing, no more than an inch in either direction, like somebody very old with a palsy.

As if in some need to flagellate himself, he persisted. "I don't know how it ever gets piled up like that, but it's way up again."

"Up to fifteen hundred?"

"More. There's a big dinner at the Waldorf next month—Gaylord, Bryant's tenth anniversary—and I had to go to Drew for a decent dinner jacket."

Now she nodded in agreement.

He blurted out his next words as if to rid himself of their weight. "That put it up to two thousand."

"Poor Rick."

Twenty-one

One more weekend to get through alone, Jossie thought, and then I'll never have another to get through by myself. It was the Friday before the last Monday in June. Thank God for the country's greatest newspaper that never gives cub reporters Sundays off.

Again she had hardly slept. Strange new bed, she thought wryly, strange new narrow bed for one. She was installed in her new apartment and enjoying its light colors and pretty curtains, floor-length crewel curtains with the embroidered "Tree of Life" pattern in bright reds and blues and greens. It was too late in June for the fireplace, but on her first night there, she had lighted three sticks of kindling and one small log, just to have a fire in her own fireplace.

Fridays had stopped meaning a possibility of Rick; they had not even talked since the day she called her "nonproposal day." She had written him a note with her new address and phone number, even the number of the *World*, but he had neither answered it nor phoned. Each time the phone did ring she jumped for it.

I'm like one of Pavlov's damn dogs, she thought stormily one night when she leaped from her chair at the first ring. It's not going to be Rick, not for a while, maybe never.

But on this last pre-newspaper Friday, when it rang one noon, she again sprang up and tore the receiver from its cradle.

"Jossie? It's Edie."

"Edie! Hello! Are you calling from Peekskill?"

"No, I had to be in town today. I wanted to ask you something about your canoe, and I got your new number from Information."

"My red canoe?" It was still up there at the lake, of course, still in its burlap. Those two marvelous summers wrapped up inside that burlap.

"To ask if you'd sell it. Our old green one has gotten all mush-keeled and leaky, and the kids aren't allowed to use it. It's breaking Lisa's heart."

"I couldn't sell it, Edie. It was a present." That summer day flashed through her mind. *It's a surprise, darling, Happy Birthday.* "But Edie, I'll make another present of it. To Lisa, with my love."

"I can't let you do that."

"I'll bet Lisa could."

"She'll go mad with it; she's always raved about the beautiful red one, and she's really been bereaved without any."

They laughed and Edie suddenly said, "Why don't you come up for a weekend some time, Jossie?"

There was a silence. Peekskill without Rick? To see the lake again without him, to see the cabin again? Or did Edie mean why didn't she and Rick come up?

"I know about you and Rick," Edie said then. "I meant why don't you come up by yourself? We'd love to see you again."

"Oh, Edie." She hadn't seen them since—since—certainly not since *that* at Henri's. She'd assumed they were still seeing Rick; after all, they'd been his friends long before she'd come along, and they'd stay friends with him.

"Come on, Jossie, take the plunge. Let's pick a weekend right this minute."

"I'll be working weekends from now till God-knows-when," she said more brightly. "You don't know about my new job as Nelly Bly, lady reporter, on the *New York World*."

"How great! When—how did you ever—?"

"Edie, why don't you come over here for lunch, since you're in town. I'd love you to see my new apartment, and I'm dying to tell you about my job. Come *on*."

They talked for an hour about everything. Lisa was now nine, Tony a gangly eleven, and the baby three and a total nuisance because he liked the water far more than sundecks or dry land. They had seen Rick once during the summer; it hadn't gone any too well.

"How do you mean, 'not too well'?" It sounded so artificial. Would she ever be able to be natural when she spoke of Rick?

"Jossie, look. I don't know whether you'd rather shut up about things or talk about them."

"We don't have to shut up about Rick. I'm getting past that point. Mostly."

Edie looked dubious but also relieved. "Did you know he's writing a book again?"

"Oh, no! The same book? No, I didn't know."

"I think it's a different one. Yes, it must be. He said, 'This one has a narrative thread a mile wide.'"

"Then it is another book. The old one didn't have enough narrative—"

She broke off. Rick writing a book. Rick again facing that smooth yellow paper, setting down wonderful phrases and sentences, his pen making that silky sound as it traveled from left to right, phrases and sentences she would never see. Recollection, memory, longing engulfed her.

"It must be a new book," she said slowly. "I'm glad he's trying again."

Edie was deciding something; she could tell. Edie was still the person who never dealt in hints and implications and undertones you had to interpret or decipher.

"I'll bet that woman he's seeing," Edie went on, "persuaded him to try it again. She just loves books and authors."

"Suzy?"

"Heavens, no." She looked embarrassed for a moment. "Don't you know about his friend who lives at the Ritz-Carlton?"

"Lives there? She must be rich as Croesus."

"I don't know why I thought you—yes, Rick did say you'd met once. We met her that time with Rick and didn't take to her much."

"Somebody I know lives at the Ritz?"

"She doesn't live there all the time, she really lives in Boston, but she's rented a place for when she's in New York, and she's in New York an awful lot."

"Mrs. Carlton, as in Ritz." She could hear Rick saying it when they were introduced at the Bryants', and suddenly she burst out laughing, hilarious laughing, not just a little laugh, no titter, no polite small laugh, but a wild grunting guffaw.

"What's so funny?" Edie asked.

Gloriana Carlton, Jossie thought, call me Glory, rich Glory Carlton who loves books and authors, and after a while she'll find out he can't write because he's so swamped with debts and bills, and facing garnishees and repossesses, and she'll take care of everything so he can keep on writing, and he'll tell her he'll pay back every dime and every dollar—

"Oh, God, I hope he writes it," she cried out when she could talk again. "Writes it all, all the way to the end, all the way to the last chapter, no matter what, like Mrs. Trollope."

Edie rushed over and shook her by the shoulders. "Stop laughing like that! What's wrong? Did you say Mrs. *Trollope?*"

"Oh, Edie." Abruptly she left the room, washed her face, took a glass of water. "Some day," she said when she rejoined Edie, "I'll tell you what set me off like a lunatic, but I can't now. Is that okay?"

"Of course it's okay. But Jossie, you *are* coming up to the lake sometime soon? Remember, we kind of like you."

° ° °

"Sept. 10, 1927," Jossie wrote in her journal. "Look at that date—Sept. 10, '27. It would have been the fourth anniversary of Rick and me, but now it's only some numbers on a piece of paper, numbers that make me cry when I write them down."

> Not cry the way I used to cry, not with that twisting, disemboweled feeling. Something does get easier as time goes on, if you can only live through it enough to get there.
>
> Maybe it's wrong to keep a journal; I've certainly found, in

the last year or two, that I only wrote in it after some frightful thing had happened, and then only long afterward, when the first hot hurt had cooled down. At the beginning, when I first began to keep this journal, every time I wrote, it was about something happy, something to feel joy about, and love and being loved. Do other people go through this turning around too?

Anyway, I do have something happy to write about, not the old kind of happy but something exciting just the same. Something to brag about, then, to write down for my own dear little ego, that's been plenty knocked about recently. It's late, and the sensible thing would be to get some sleep for another killing day as a cub reporter, but I've never been famous for having sense.

And look at this page! Not written by hand like the rest of my journal, but taken off the three rings in my loose-leaf and rolled into my Corona.

It's lucky I've become good and fast on the typewriter. If there's one thing you learn in 2½ months on a newspaper, it's to write right on the machine, no first draft in pencil and then copy it, but type it fast and never look back, because on any story for the next edition, a copy boy comes at you after each paragraph—they call it "a take"—and pulls it right out from the roller the minute you've put your last period down, and then he shoots it over to the city desk.

Ted Bonning isn't the one who gets it—he's not even there most of the day shift and hasn't anything to do with regular daily editing. I wish he did—he'd be easier on me. The city editor is Bob Smith, known by one and all, of course, as "B.S.," and he can be rough. Once he just drew a big full-size X through a whole page of my copy and wrote "Try again" and sent it back by the copy boy, without a word of explanation. A full-size X measures 8½ by 11 inches, so that's quite an X. But you learn to take it and try again—they're X-ing out your copy, not X-ing out you.

That word "copy"—once it meant plate glass and nail polish and foods and luggage and milk and face cream and roadsters and razors, and now, except for dear old Stuyvesant's on Fifth Avenoooo, as I once called it to Rick—now copy means people on strike, a symposium of world-famous scientists, or 30 workmen drowned in an exploded barge in the Hudson River—the first really gruesome assignment I ever was sent out on. That's what that little word "copy" means now. It's kind of wonderful, the difference.

These first ten weeks on the paper have been like an entire

new world opening for me (not a pun). My very first assignment was about a bundled-up baby in a carton left in the subway at Fourteenth St. and taken to the police station. I raced over and saw it; it couldn't have been two weeks old and the only thing printed on the note pinned to its shirt was the word "catholic," with a lower-case c. I knew everybody expected me to write sob-sister goo, so I wrote a tight hard who-what-when-where, about three sticks of type, no more. B.S. okayed it, yelled "Boy," and just said, "There's a fire in Hearn's basement on Fourteenth. Get up there and have a look."

It went that way for July and most of August, and then one day I had my first hideous story to do. It came as a fluke—that explosion of a workmen's barge up around 168th on the Hudson, and everybody on the staff was out on assignment except me. "Have you ever seen a corpse?" B.S. asked, half scornful. "A real live corpse? Or are you going to be sick and throw up so you can't phone it in?"

I did just about collapse for the first few minutes. There were already 18 bodies out of the boat by the time I got there by subway, some of them horribly burned as well as drowned, piled four in a row, four bodies high. The boat looked like some ramshackle old tub that ought never to have had its license renewed for the last ten years.

I did make my phone in to the rewrite desk, all facts and numbers and good practical voice. But then I got thinking of all the wives and kids of all those men, and that none of them knew yet what I already knew, that pretty soon there'd be a knock on the door and some cop from the nearest precinct would be saying, You'll never see your husband again, or your father. His cheap rotten workmen's barge exploded and he's piled up with a bunch of other drowned men on the shore of the beautiful Hudson River.

But that's not what I have to brag about, though when I got back to the paper, B.S. did give me a sort of nod and said, "Getting to be a pro, aren't you?"

The brag happened just before Labor Day. Labor Day used to mean we were leaving the lake and the cabin and the summer and starting another year in the city, and I'd been dreading this first Labor Day alone. I suppose I'll dread Thanksgiving too, and Christmas—

Well, anyway, the week before Labor Day, B.S. said to me, "You're going out of town on assignment next Wednesday, for three days." I tried not to look knocked over and he told me it was an international symposium of leading medical research scientists, Nobel winners and everything, from France, England, Canada, and the U.S., gathering at Johns Hopkins in Baltimore.

He wrote out some vouchers for expense money and railroad fares. "Don't try to be a medical reporter," he told me. "We'll get all that in the flimsies. I want *people*—a lot of famous characters are going to be there, the insulin man, that cardiologist from Boston, researchers on polio—try to talk to them about what's ahead, about what cures may be coming, and life in general."

Well, it's all in my *World* folder, the longest piece I had ever written up to that time, and if I reread it, which I did no more than six times the day it came out, I sort of can see why they gave me my first byline on it, "by Joselyn Stone" in real print, not just in daydreams. Because those brilliant busy scientists and doctors did talk to me, maybe because a girl reporter is still sort of a surprise, and they did answer some of my questions about what hope might be ahead for kids with polio, people with polio, rather, since we talked about Franklin D. Roosevelt, and people with TB and diabetes and cancer and heart attacks and everything.

Apparently I asked questions they didn't expect, like how they felt if years of experiment ended in failure, and what kept them doing battle in their various wars against disease, if some other great scientist said in public that it was a lost cause, that it had already been proved wrong.

It ran over four full columns and B.S. cut only a few paras. Apart from the byline, I won the $5 prize for "best-written story of the week" and my head just about shot off my shoulders. Gil Blose, a crabby character across the aisle from me, made some crack about beginner's luck and lady reporters, but most of the men were very big with slaps on the back.

My first byline! And this payday, I found $35 in my pay envelope instead of $30.

Ted Bonning came over to me the afternoon I got it, and what he said was like another $5 raise.

"Maybe you weren't such a crazy kid, Jossie. You must have known ahead of time that you'd make it."

○ ○ ○

Sept. 11, 1927. Same night, but one calendar day after that would-have-been fourth anniversary. I lay down there for a minute because my back was cracking in half, and apparently I fell asleep as if I'd blacked out, because now it's 4 A.M. "Four o'clock in the morning—we've danced the whole night through." At least it's not sad old three o'clock in the morning—I'm making progress!

Maybe one reason I conked out so hard was that I wanted to avoid writing this next part about seeing Rick again. It's crazy to write at 4 A.M., but I feel sort of obsessed, now that I've opened my journal again, to catch up with everything, get this hard part down, so I can put it behind me. Otherwise I'd feel as if I'd said To Be Continued in the Next Issue, and I'd have to face it some other time.

It happened just last week. We hadn't seen each other all summer, not since that day I used to call my non-proposal day, except that it sounded bitter in my own mind and I finally thought, What good is it, remembering it and going all acid inside?

He hadn't even phoned to tell me he'd won second prize in the Three A Awards for his Watch campaign—I had to read it in the tradepapers, and for one mean-spirited moment I thought, He's probably even forgotten he had any help writing it.

But then he phoned me at the paper to ask could he come over after the office for a drink, to tell me some good news about him. I said, "If it's just for a drink," and he knew what I meant and came over that same day.

I might as well confess that while I was waiting all day for time to pass so I could get home, I kept wondering if it wasn't going to turn out to be about his $2,000 mountain of debts.

For once I did remember what I'd finally worked out for myself, that people exploit you only if you practically ask to be exploited, especially if you're so much in love you'd do *anything* to keep that love. Women are forever saying they are victims, and I've begun to wonder if you don't *help* people victimize you. I mean in private life, between lovers or spouses.

I don't mean you can't offer help openly and purely to your husband, or he to his wife, but when it goes on beyond a specific situation or crisis and becomes sort of habitual, a taking-for-granted, then that lovely sweet word "help" becomes a different word, something like "use me."

But it wasn't about debts after all. The moment I opened the door and saw him standing there was like a violent gasp through my whole body, not just my lungs but the whole of me.

It must have been something special for him too, because he just stood there for a moment, in the doorway, looking at me, not even saying hello, and then he said, "My God, Jossie, you get more beautiful all the time."

The news was that he'd been given a big new toothpaste account and a raise to $8,500 and just had to let me know, "the way we used to tell each other everything and celebrate," he ended.

We fixed drinks and talked a lot about his news, and about me and the paper, and everything except his new book. I said not one word about it and neither did he. Nor of course about Glory Carlton as in Ritz.

He did talk about Jean. After the divorce decree becomes final, she's going to marry her Mr. Mumm and go live in his gorgeous big apartment, with two servants and a chef, besides Tonette for the kids. She's still painting away—you have to hand it to her—still selling her canvases, now for as much as $150 each.

By this time, Rick went and fixed another pitcher of martinis, and he kept staying on another few minutes, and then another few, and the thing I'm trying not to say is that of course, after about another hour, it happened.

And it was the first time I ever felt ashamed. I who never felt shame about making love, even as a child being "naughty"—I remember that time when I was only about eight, and just discovering in a sort of accidental way what being naughty was and how wonderful it was, and then feeling ashamed, and then a little while later figuring out for myself, "Well, I'm a good little girl, so it must mean that good little girls *do* do that."

Remembering that child that I was, writing it down, makes my eyes fill with tears, I don't know why. I've never told it to one soul, and now, remembering it and remembering my awful feeling of deep shame after Rick that evening—

It's all mixed up, guilt is, isn't it? But that time with Rick I did feel afterward that I'd just melted like a candle, unable to stop the melt, as if I were some kind of soft blobby wax. It took me days to get it right again and think, Well, I'm a good little girl, so it must mean—

I didn't intend to write any of this when I started writing in my journal tonight, and maybe I ought to rip this page off the roller of my typewriter, like the copy boy, and throw it out and never slip it over the three rings, so I'll never have to come across it again.

But I don't know. Why be ashamed again? This journal's mine, and it's supposed to be me, with no city editor to put a great big 8½-by-11 X through any of it.

So stet and good night. Good morning, rather. It's getting light.

° ° °

Everybody on the paper seemed to have a car, for assignments up in the Bronx or out in Brooklyn or on the Island, and the day she won her second $5 prize for the best-written story of the week, she decided to treat herself to the biggest present ever and buy a brand-new car.

The new Fords were coming out, the 1928 Fords, and it took her no more than ten minutes at a Ford showroom to say, "How much is it?"

"We can arrange easy terms--"

"I hate easy terms," she said. "I've been saving up." She took out her checkbook and wrote a check for $325. "When can I have delivery?"

"As soon as your check clears, miss." He read the check as if he had never seen one before. No easy terms?

"Could it be Tuesday? My day off is Tuesday."

And today was Tuesday. She drove straight to her sister's and took Nell and Jimmy out for a ride, up and down Fifth Avenue. Jimmy, now nearly two, went crazy about Aunt Jossie's new car, blasting at the horn until his mother, holding him in her lap, had to pinion his arms.

"Wouldn't you know it?" Nell said. "He likes it better than his Daddy's big maroon Buick."

"So do I." Maybe even better, she thought, than a big beautiful Watch roadster.

Late in the afternoon—public high schools had opened again—she drove off to New Rochelle.

Her mother was expecting her. She knew that it was over with Rick; all through the summer, in various phone calls, Jossie had kept her fairly informed, but each call, except for news of the paper, had remained vague, rather disjointed, and her mother had never pressed for detail or greater clarity.

Every time I do call her, Jossie thought, as she was driving up in her grand new two-seater, it goes sort of piecemeal, the way you talk when you're afraid to sound as if you were drowning in self-pity.

Not today. The time I wrote in my journal that I was going to show her lots more about how much I really love her, call her more often, go see her more often—have I really done any of that? Well, maybe by phone.

"It's a lovely car," her mother greeted her from the porch as she pulled up in front of the house.

"You look like one of their billboards," her father said. He had changed toward her, her mother had reported, since she began working for the *World.* All his acrimony about the business world, about advertising, about hooring to earn money—nearly all of it had vanished, giving way to a sudden sparkling pride in "my newspaper daughter."

Just the same, Jossie was impatient to have dinner over and have him perform his customary vanishing act.

"Are you keeping to yourself too much?" her mother asked then. "Do you see other people—?"

"Sure I see other people. There are a million newspaper people on every story you're sent out on."

"I didn't mean on the paper. Do you go out dancing, see people just for fun?"

"Of course I do. Red Montana takes me out to dinner every once in a while, and then I met a man named Alex Abbott—no relation to that Bill Abbott who turned down Rick's book, but this Abbott is a publisher too, with a firm I never heard of."

"A book publisher sounds interesting."

"Now, Mama. He's only thirty and he's been married twice and divorced twice."

She laughed a little but there wasn't much merriment in it, and they fell into one of their silences. After a while her mother said, "If you want to tell me, Jossie," but never finished her sentence.

"Without too much spillage," Jossie said, reminding her mother of that summertime luncheon they had had long ago.

She started back with Rick's decision to abandon his book and go back to advertising, and told her everything that had happened since, told it in sequence as much as she could manage to, told it as fully as she could, leaving it to her mother's insight to fill in whatever was too private to put into words.

"The real break," she ended, "might have come that time I made the ghastly mistake of wanting so much to avoid a big fight about that repossess warning that I just wrote a check for a hundred eighty and handed it over without saying a word."

"Nobody ever knows when the real break comes, Jossie. Something that seems insignificant may turn out later to be one of the most massive of all. Maybe it came long before his warning about the car being repossessed."

"Dispossess, repossess," Jossie said thoughtfully. "There's a kind of format to it, Mama, like the two arcs of a parenthesis, one at the start and one at the end, enclosing all the good and all the awful of nearly four years."

"It's a good way of putting it."

"It's a matter of getting old enough to stand it."

"It's not just a matter of standing it," her mother said. "It's maturing, growth, it's being not a girl but a woman. A mature woman. If you'll let me be sentimental, I'd say a pretty splendid woman." Over the last words, her voice broke, her eyes filled, and she put her hand on Jossie's arm and squeezed it.

With the gesture, Jossie was suddenly back in the soundproof cubicle when she could hear the other girls screaming. Only this time, though the tears were sliding quietly down her mother's face, she also seemed, in a way, to be smiling.

It was ten before she drove off again in her dazzling new possession. It had turned cool and blowy, an October night, full of stars, though October was half a month in the future. Again she felt an ease, a release she could not name. She thought of that other night, when she wished there were tiny windshield wipers for weeping eyes, so you could see the road well enough to drive.

She still cried too much when she thought of Rick, when she remembered what it meant to be in love and happy, still felt she would never get used to life without him. But tonight she felt, too, that somewhere another notch of change had been cut.

Maturity, she thought. It had a kind of splendid sound, at that. It took a long time to get it, if you ever did. Money and success couldn't buy it, nobody could give it to you. You had to work for it, try for it, reach for it, and then, if you could stand enough and absorb enough, maybe at last you'd have it.

And if you did have it, it would be worth anything. Untold millions, and forever.